Caterina

Caterina

Jane Aiken Hodge

ST. MARTIN'S PRESS ⚅ NEW YORK

c. 1

ISBN 0-312-20507-4

First published in Great Britain by Robert Hale Limited

First U.S. Edition: August 1999

10 9 8 7 6 5 4 3 2 1

Historical Note

When Napoleon's army invaded Portugal in 1807, the royal family fled to Brazil and could not be persuaded to come back until 1821. King John then left his eldest son, Pedro, behind as regent, while the younger son, dissolute Miguel, his mother's favourite, returned to Lisbon with his parents, who hated each other. There were liberal stirrings both in Portugal (particularly Oporto) and in Brazil, where Pedro, liberal himself, soon found it necessary to defy his father and declare himself emperor. In 1825, Sir Charles Stuart helped negotiate an agreement between father and son, under which the two thrones were to remain separate.

King John died the following year and Pedro granted Portugal a constitution before abdicating in favour of his baby daughter, Maria da Gloria, on the understanding that she would ultimately marry her uncle, his brother Miguel. In the meanwhile, her aunt, Pedro's sister, would act as regent. But Miguel had become the focus of fierce conservative opposition to Pedro's constitutional reform. He ousted the regent in 1828 and established a regime of bloody absolutism, backed by church and aristocracy. It lasted until Pedro was forced to abdicate in Brazil in favour of his own son thus finding himself free to champion his now teenage daughter's cause.

In March 1832, Pedro reached Terceira in the Azores where a group of liberals had managed to hold out against Miguel. In July, he landed and took Oporto unopposed. But there was no general rising in his support; he missed the moment when a quick march might have taken Lisbon, and sat out a grim winter of siege in Oporto. Foreign intervention by England, Spain and France bedevilled the situation throughout. Pedro had been prevented from employing the liberal hero, Saldanha, as commander in chief and the deadlock continued until Saldanha and one of the formidable Napier brothers, a turbulent young admiral, came to his help in the spring of 1833. Charles Napier took over Pedro's little fleet, adding some vital new steamships, defeated the Miguelites at St Vincent and landed a liberal army under Saldanha at Faro. Saldanha took Lisbon unopposed and Maria da Gloria was declared of age and became queen at fifteen. But the absolutist threat continued as a running sore in Portugal until Miguel died in 1866.

Chapter 1

'Greville! Thank God you have come. What is going on?' Caterina Fonsa had jumped up from the breakfast-table to greet her caller. 'The drums kept me awake all night. Have some coffee. Is there any more news of Dom Pedro?'

'Nothing since his emissary was turned away from Vila do Conde with a flea in his ear.' Greville Faulkes accepted a steaming cup and sat down across the broad mahogany table from his employer. 'But he and his little fleet must be still lying off at sea somewhere or Santa Marta's drums would not have beaten the alarm all night. Porto's in turmoil this morning. I came to warn you that anything may happen. Don't think of going out today, and be ready to close the palace gates and stand siege if necessary.'

'As bad as that?'

'Quite as bad. The town is awash with rumours; each one more alarming than the last. Santa Marta has been in council all night. Tell your servants you are at home to no one. God knows what extreme measures the absolutists might not take against known liberals like you, if they are in the panic people say.'

'Which must mean that the threat – the promise of Dom Pedro is real. That there is hope at last of an end to Miguelite tyranny?'

He looked quickly to the closed doors of the room. 'Be careful what you say, Caterina. Even here. The usurper has spies in every house.'

'Not in mine.' She had been mistress of the Sanchez Palace for years.

'Take nothing for granted. I'm more glad than I can say that you insisted on that pseudonym for your cartoons. I heard from Mrs Wallis, the agent in London, by the way. She is delighted with the ones I sent her. She is getting them reproduced right away and says she will be glad to act for you.'

'Now that is good news.' Her eyes shone and she looked suddenly the eager girl he remembered from their first meeting all those years ago. His friend, Jeremy Craddock, had got him the job as her agent and he had brought her two-year-old son from England with him. After the hideous journey with the spoiled brat from the orphanage, he had almost meant to hand in his notice at once. His first sight of Caterina Fonsa had changed all that. But she was in deep mourning for her husband then, and preoccupied with her problem son. And he himself was a ruined man, disinherited, penniless, her dependent. The years had changed her only for the better, but now she was racked with new anxiety for her son. Would it never be the time to speak? But she was in danger now.

'Caterina—' he began.

'Yes?' But she was already turning away. 'Harriet.' She greeted her old friend Harriet Ware. 'What brings you here so early?'

'Frank said I should come. For the safety of your strong walls. Hetta's coming too. But I can see you have not heard. We thought you might not have.'

'Heard what?'

'We saw it from our windows. Mayhem on the bridge of boats, a headlong flight south for Lisbon. Santa Marta is running for it, and the absolutist rats with him. Frank said he would feel much happier if Hetta and I were here with you until things settle. He has gone to the office to try and keep Josiah Bankes steady. I hope he can.' Frank was her twenty-year-old son whose father had died in Santa Marta's stinking prison a few years before. 'You know what Bankes is like.' She held out a friendly hand to Greville.

'I am afraid I do,' he said. 'It will be a good day when Frank comes of age and takes over at Ware and Company. But this is wonderful news, Mrs Ware. I do wonder just what precipitated this flight. Ah—' He turned as Caterina's major domo, Tomas, appeared.

'News at last, *minha senhora!* Dom Pedro has landed at Mindello, the Miguelite trash are running for their lives.'

'He has landed unopposed?' asked Greville, amazed.

'That's what they say, *senhor*. A great day for Portugal!'

'Yes, but I will be glad when it is well over,' said Greville. 'It's not much more than six miles to Mindello but I doubt the Duke of Braganza will get his forces landed and into town today. Everything I said still holds, Caterina. I must go, like young Frank, and make sure all's well at Gomez and Daughter. Lock your gates behind me; let no one in but Hetta. I am glad you two are coming to keep Caterina company, Mrs Ware. It's lonely for her in this great palace.'

Left alone, the two old friends kissed each other warmly, then moved by common consent out into hot July sun on the terrace. Peering down over the balustrade, they could not see upriver to the bridge of boats that linked Oporto with Villa Nova da Gaia on the south bank, but the lower stretch of the Douro that they could see was alive with traffic.

'All going south,' said Caterina.

'Yes. I wish Hetta would get here. I'm sorry I left her now, but Frank wanted me to come ahead and warn you. No day to be going out, he says.'

'No. Not till Dom Pedro gets here and takes charge.'

'We must learn to call him the Duke of Braganza now that he has abdicated both as King of Portugal and Emperor of Brazil.'

'And to think of his daughter as Queen Maria da Gloria of Portugal.'

'When it is all over. Please God it happens fast. Without time for reprisals. Is there any news of Lewis, Cat?' Caterina's son, Lewis, had been first jailed and then exiled as a schoolboy, caught throwing stones at the usurping governor. Worse still, Harriet's husband, another Frank, had tried to intercede for him, been jailed for it, and had died of his mistreatment there.

'Not a word. Nothing since those two dreadful letters when they expelled him from Stonyhurst. Where did I go wrong with him, Harry?'

'Stop blaming yourself, love. It's not just you. Think of the way he grew up, poor boy, torn to bits between those two domineering old people, Madame Fonsa here and your father across the valley in the Gomez house. And he always had a short fuse, our Lewis.' They were both silent for a moment, thinking of Harriet's daughter Hetta, scarred for life after a childhood tantrum of her dear friend Lewis. 'I wish Hetta would come,' said her mother again.

'Hetta's a girl who can take care of herself,' said Caterina. 'I have always admired her for it.'

'It's true. I cannot begin to tell you what a comfort she is to me now Bess is married and gone. We have such plans for what she calls "our old age". But I keep hoping—'

'Of course we do.' They were both picturing the beautiful face, irredeemably scarred down one cheek. 'Lewis was terribly sorry—'

'Still is, I am sure. He's my boy, too, remember.' Harriet had suckled little Lewis when Caterina could not.

'I love you for loving him. But it wasn't ideal was it? Two mothers and no father.'

'And those overpowering grandparents. Maybe he just stuck at going to old Lady Trellgarten because of that.'

'I never thought of that.' Lady Trellgarten was her own grandmother, whom she had never met, an almost mythical figure living in Wales. 'If only the old fathers at Stonyhurst had said why they were expelling him.' She always came back to this. 'There must have been more to it than being absent without leave. Specially when that was to see our old friend, Saldanha, the great liberal hope of Portugal.'

'I don't suppose Portuguese affairs seem so important to the Englishmen who run Stonyhurst,' said Harriet. 'And we don't know what had gone before, do we? No one could call Lewis a good letter writer.'

'I did try,' said Caterina. 'I wrote to him every day, that time I went to Bordeaux.'

'I remember,' said Harriet. She also remembered that it had been impossible to explain to Lewis why his mother was away during his summer holidays. Still less could she get him to answer the letters. 'I wish Saldanha was with Dom Pedro now.' She changed the subject.

'Oh, so do I! Everyone loves him here in Porto, since he was governor, and Dom Pedro hasn't been here since he was a small boy, before the royal family fled to Brazil. It's too hot out here, Harry, let's go in. I wish the river was not so crowded with boats.'

'The laden galleys of the nobility. It's not exactly a vote of confidence in Dom Pedro, is it? But here is Carlotta, full of news.'

A thin, wiry, ageless woman, Carlotta had lived at the Sanchez Palace all her life. 'Tonio is just back from town,' she told them breathlessly. 'It's murder there, he says. They've opened up the gaols and killed the gaoler. And there's a message from your daughter, *senhora*,' she said to Harriet. 'She sent a man to say she's not coming, she thinks she should stay in the Rua Nova in case she's needed there.'

'She's absolutely right,' said Harriet. 'If the gaols are open, some of the liberal prisoners who knew my Frank may come to us for shelter. I must be there to receive them. Will you come too, Cat? I don't like to leave you here alone.'

'I don't like to let you go. But my place is here. Think, Harry, Dom Pedro is bound to come this way if he marches in from Mindello in the morning. I must be here to greet him. He'll stay in the Carrancas Palace up the road, of course, Portuguese royalty always do. I'll be his nearest neighbour; he must dine with me. I know! A celebration. A banquet. You saw how many of the nobility's boats were crossing the river, running for it. Someone must make the Liberator welcome. Carlotta, tell the chef to start preparing a feast, and have the state rooms opened up. And I'll need Tonio to take a note to the Carrancas Palace for me. Do stay, Harry, and help me prepare.'

'I mustn't. But, Cat—' Carlotta had left them. 'Are you serious about inviting Dom Pedro? You know his reputation?'

'All those mistresses? I have no doubt he has brought the current one with him from the Azores along with the rest of his baggage, since his wife and the little queen are safe in Paris. But what's to stop a respectable old widow like me giving him a dinner, representing my son, who, after all, is in exile for backing his cause?'

'Only the fact that you don't look like a respectable old widow,' said her friend. 'Or dress like one. Lord, I remember how cross the Portuguese tabbies were when you came out of your blacks.'

'They were cross enough when I went into them,' said Caterina cheerfully. 'How strange it was, mourning that invented English husband. I can't even remember the name the lawyers picked for him, since old Madame Fonsa insisted on adopting me as well as Lewis and we've both been Fonsas ever since.'

'They did a good job, those lawyers.'

'Yes, they made Fonsas of us, but they couldn't persuade the Portuguese ladies to accept me. If it hadn't been for you, Harry, I'd have had a sad enough time of it all these years.'

'And your work.'

'And they don't approve of that either, though they are not above letting me paint their children's portraits, so long as I keep my tongue in my cheek. What a thing it would be if Dom Pedro would let me paint him. Or the young queen.'

'He'll be marching on Lisbon if he has any sense, and she is safe in Paris with her stepmother,' said Harriet. 'I wish you had someone more formidable than Carlotta as a companion.' Carlotta had been old Madame Fonsa's personal maid and had turned housekeeper and chaperon to Caterina after the old lady's death.

'She suits me very well, and when I dine with the emperor you shall come too, to add a note of British respectability, and bring the children to be presented, if you think dear Hetta will be safe with him.'

'I am afraid she will,' said Hetta's mother. 'But of course we'll come. I know Frank will be mad to meet the Liberator. Will you invite the rest of the English colony?'

'I shall invite everyone.'

'But will they come?'

'What a spoilsport you are, Harry! Only promise me one thing.'
'Yes?'

'Don't wear black. Not for this celebration. It's almost four years, Harriet. Life has to go on.'

'You say that to me? But you're right, Cat, the children have been grumbling about my blacks. We had good years, Frank and I, but life does go on. And that goes for you too. We may be widows but we're not old ladies yet.'

'I'm not even really a widow. And we neither of us look a day over thirty. Wear that becoming grey I designed for you and I'll wear my red and we'll do our best to dazzle the Liberator.' They took hands and kissed, the big glass at the end of the room witnessing the contrast between Caterina's dark, formidable good looks and Harriet's gentler blonde ones. Harriet was right; though well into their thirties, they had both kept their figures, and time had merely added character to Caterina who hardly needed it, and to Harriet, whose mild appearance had always been deceptive.

Frank Ware got home that night in a quiet rage. 'Thank goodness you're back, Mama.' He greeted her warmly. 'I need someone to grumble to. Old Bankes is in a panic, his wife is busy packing their things, he talks of going on board one of the British ships for safety.'

'I believe many of the English are doing so,' said his mother.

'But we're not going to,' said Hetta.

'I thought you were up at Aunt Caterina's.'

'I changed my mind.' He knew that determined tone of his sister's too well to argue. 'Mother says Aunt Caterina has invited Dom Pedro to dine,' she went on. 'We're all to go, if he accepts.'

'He'd be better occupied marching straight on Lisbon,' said Frank. 'The feeling in town is very strange today. Oh, the mob are dancing in the streets, and weaving garlands to welcome the Liberator, but there's not much rejoicing among the nobility, and the priests have all run for it.'

'I like it much better without them,' said his sister. 'Is Dom Pedro really expected tomorrow?'

'Yes, there's to be a reception in the Praça Nova. But I think we should be up at the Sanchez Palace with Aunt Caterina, don't you, Mama? She ought not to be there all alone to greet him.'

'If only Lewis was here,' said Hetta. 'I don't suppose there has been any word from him, Mama?'

'Nothing. I can hardly bear to ask Caterina.'

'Lewis never did think of anyone but himself,' said Frank, with a sideways look at his sister's scarred face.

When Hetta blushed, the scar showed light against the rest of her flushed face. 'Lewis had a lot to put up with,' she said. 'Those two old tyrants quarrelling over him as if he was their chattel, and Carlotta loving him to death—' She paused: this was dangerous ground.

The youngest of the little group of children who had grown up together, she had noticed as no one else had the slight effort Caterina had had to make to be a mother to Lewis. She had been a tigress in his defence when she found the old grandparents interfering in his education; she had been enormously, visibly proud of him, but had she been too busy with her own work quite to love him? Hetta had never been sure.

'I've got all the girls at work sewing blue and white flags,' she went on. 'And some for Caterina, too. She'll probably be hard at work in her studio and never think of it.'

'I wish I knew what we should do for the best.' Frank suddenly felt his responsibility as head of the family heavy upon him. 'I wonder if you should not take the next Falmouth packet, Hetta, and go and stay with Bess. You know she would love to have you, with the baby coming.'

'Not on your life,' said Hetta.

Caterina's servants had been sewing flags too, and weaving long garlands of jasmine and myrtle, and they formed a cheerful little group next morning under the huge ilex tree that stood outside the gates of the Sanchez Palace.

'Thank God for a quiet night.' Harriet kissed Caterina. 'But it's not quite the turnout I'd expected. Frank says many of the English merchants are waiting to see which way the cat will jump. And not a sign of life outside the big Portuguese houses we passed on the way up. No ceremonial hangings. Nothing.'

'I'm so glad you came,' said Caterina. 'We must just put on the best show we can.'

'But where is Greville Faulkes? I was sure he would be here at your side.'

'And so was I. But he sent word that he has been asked to join in the ceremonial welcome in the Praça Nova, and of course he had to agree.'

'That's a great compliment.'

'It's a great nuisance. Yes, Hetta?' Hetta and her brother had just joined them.

'I was wondering if you had had any news from the liberating army, Aunt Caterina.'

'News? But why should I?'

'I just wondered—' Hetta's blush showed up the mark on her cheek. 'Listen, they're coming!' In the little silence, they could all hear the sound of military music, the thud of marching feet and a roar from the crowd up the hill near the Carrancas Palace.

'What's that they are singing?' asked Caterina.

'It will be the liberation song,' Frank told her. 'Dom Pedro wrote it himself, would you believe it? He does sound the most amazing man. Constitutions and song-writing! Are you really going to ask him to dinner, Aunt Caterina?'

'I already have. There's a note waiting for him at the Carrancas Palace, asking him to name his day. And I think it is time you two stopped calling me "aunt". It makes me feel a million years old.' And then, laughing, 'Do you realize, Harry, that you and I are actually older than the Duke of Braganza, as we must remember to call him!'

'Yes,' said Harriet. 'It's a very diminishing thought. Imagine having given away two kingdoms before one was thirty-five.'

'I wonder if his daughter is grateful,' said Frank. 'Or if she would really not prefer to stay snug in Paris. Here they come! Up with your flags, girls,' he called in Portuguese to the servants. 'And a strong huzza for the Liberator and his army.'

'Lord, they do look hot, poor things,' said Hetta, as the first marchers came into sight at the top of the sloping avenue that led down from the Carrancas Palace. 'What are they?'

'Regulars,' her brother told her. 'Portuguese Light Infantry, you can tell them by those elegant grey uniforms.'

'Elegant once,' said Hetta as they came nearer. 'They look shabby enough now, Lord knows.' And then, conscience-stricken, raised a shout of, ' "*Viva o exercito libertador*".'

'That's the dandy,' Frank approved as the maids joined in. 'And here come the *caçadores*. They say they are Dom Pedro's favourite troops.'

'I suppose that is why they have such splendid brown uniforms,' said Caterina. 'I'd like to paint them, with their black shakos.'

'I hope they won't be in town long enough to have their pictures painted, Aunt Caterina. Sorry,' correcting himself, 'Caterina. And, thank you.' But Caterina had turned away to speak to Harriet.

'What is it, Hetta?' His sister was pulling his arm.

'Look! In that next group, with the beards. The one in the dashing hat. It's Lewis, I swear it is!' But the crowd surged forward as she spoke, obscuring her view. 'It was him, I'm sure of it,' she repeated, as the group of randomly dressed, bearded young men marched away.

'It could be, I suppose.' Frank was straining his eyes to follow the group. 'They're the Academic Battalion, exiled students from Coimbra University. I saw Almeida Garrett among them. Do you remember him? A great liberal. We used to play with him when we were children.'

But Hetta was not interested in Almeida Garrett. 'Should I tell Aunt Caterina?' she asked.

'Better not, don't you think? In case it turns out that you were wrong. One bearded man is very like another after all.'

'Not if he's Lewis,' said Hetta. 'But you're right, just the same.' Every instinct warned her not to tell Caterina that she had recognized her son when she, his mother, had failed to do so.

'Here come the foreigners,' said Frank. 'Odd to see French and English marching side by side. It's not twenty years since Waterloo, after all. I do wonder how they get on.' The cheering was getting louder now, with shouts of '*Viva il Liberator*' and '*Viva Maria Secunda*'.

'Here he comes,' exclaimed Frank, and then: 'What a miserable horse!'

'Why, he's quite stout,' said Hetta. 'And not a bit handsome.'

'Hush.' Frank drowned her comment with a loud '*Viva*' as the ex-emperor rode by, the only mounted man in the procession and therefore clearly visible to the crowds as he took off his cocked hat and bowed to right and left. Petitioners were swarming round him and he leaned down courteously to listen to them, but seemed to be giving them all the same short answer.

'What's he telling them?' asked Hetta. 'Did you hear?' Frank laughed. 'To join his army, and then he'll listen to their grievances. Some of them seem to like it better than others. Look, here come the bigwigs, his government in exile. How odd to see them on foot, in all their decorations!'

'It makes them seem more human,' said his sister. 'Walking like that. Dom Miguel's henchmen would never have trusted themselves on foot among the crowd.'

'No, but I doubt it will impress the peasants,' said Frank. 'Specially after the campaign of vilification the priests have been mounting against Dom Pedro since he signed that order confiscating their property and abolishing the tithe. They hate that even more than the constitution he granted. They know they have everything to lose if he wins.'

'We aren't going to follow the procession, are we?' said Hetta as the last stragglers drew away and the sounds of cheering and military music grew fainter.

'No. Not at all the thing for you ladies,' said Frank regretfully. 'Though I'd dearly like to be among the crowd further into town, getting a feel of how they are taking it all. You could hardly call it a tremendous show of strength, could you?'

'No, but then, think, Frank. Two days ago Dom Pedro had no strength in Portugal at all and now he is taking control of Oporto.'

'I can't think why General Santa Marta took to his heels like that,' said Frank. 'But it most certainly was a great stroke of luck for the liberals. What is it, Het?' He was belatedly aware of his sister's simmering tension.

'Please, Frank, go after them. You can! Find out if it's Lewis! He never looked this way.'

'Of course not. Under discipline,' said her brother. 'He'll come here soon enough when they dismiss. If it's he. And till then, not a word.' The little party began to move through the great gates into the courtyard of the Sanchez Palace. 'You weren't tempted to step forward and invite Dom Pedro in person?' he asked Caterina.

'Yes, but I resisted it. I'm a scandalous figure enough without calling that kind of attention to myself. But he'll find my invitation when he gets back to the palace.'

Frank had been thinking about this. 'I have to say that I hope he refuses,' he told her. 'I am sure the best thing he can do is make a dash for it on Lisbon, while the Miguelites are in such a state of confusion and surprise.'

'Even though there hasn't been a mass rising in his support?'

'Just because of that.' They moved out on to the terrace, where Caterina had ordered a cold luncheon under the shade of an awning. 'The river is quiet enough now.' Looking down from the marble balustrade. 'The rats are all fled.' Frank accepted a glass of wine from a hovering servant. 'Here's to the Liberator.'

As they drank the toast, solemnly standing, sporadic firing broke out from below on the waterfront. 'Not quite all fled.' Hetta was shivering as if with cold, and they were all silent for a moment.

'Mother!' Frank broke the silence. 'I've been thinking. Would you write me a note to Bankes authorizing me to collect some friends and take the company boats across to fetch all the wine we can move from our cellars across the river at Vila Nova da Gaia? We might get away with it today, but we most certainly won't if Miguel's men should establish themselves on the south bank. There's no time to be lost; Bankes must see that if you put it to him.'

'I don't like to interfere.' But she was obviously hesitating.

'I think Frank's right,' Caterina intervened. 'Come indoors with me, love, and I'll find you pen and paper. If it's to be done, it must be done quickly. And will you take a note for me to Greville Faulkes at Gomez and Daughter, Frank? I'll ask him to join you and do the same for us. Could you perhaps join forces? We have that huge warehouse downriver on this side. I am sure you could fit both your wine and ours there, if you stowed it well. Moving won't do it any good, of course, but better that than losing it.'

'Exactly,' he agreed. 'And thanks: a splendid idea. I'd been wondering what to do with it if we did manage to get it clear. I'll be happy to work with Faulkes, he's a good fellow.'

'Yes, it was a lucky day for me when my friend Jeremy Craddock persuaded him to come and manage things for me. He's a tower of strength in his quiet way.' She was writing as she spoke. 'There you are, Frank, give him that with my regards. And, good luck. Be careful.'

'Believe me, I will. No need to look anxious, Mama, we're neutral, we British, remember. The last thing either side wants to do is involve us.'

'It's an odd kind of neutrality,' said Caterina when Frank had left and the women had moved back on to the terrace to peer anxiously down towards the river. 'I wish we could see your house from here, Harry. It sounds as if some of the firing might be from that direction. I sent a man with Frank, just in case. And told him to come back here for the night. He agreed that you would all be better here until things settle down a bit in town. You know what a fortress this house is, when it needs to be, and I've an army of idle menservants to protect us if necessary, the result of combining two households. Do stay.' She saw that Harriet was hesitating and was pleased and surprised when Hetta spoke up.

'Yes, do let's stay, Mama. I quite long to know whether Dom Pedro will come to dinner.' She saw her mother's look of surprise and hurried on, 'He wasn't at all what I expected. I imagined a Byronic figure, all dark good looks and romantic air, and in fact he's going bald and growing his hair to hide it. But he looks formidable just the same. I wonder when he will dismiss his men and get back to the palace. He'll have to find them quarters, I suppose.'

'I offered him my father's house when I wrote,' Caterina told her. 'It would be good for it to be used after standing empty all these years, with only a housekeeper and a handful of maids.'

'That house always frightened me,' said Hetta. 'I didn't like it when we all went to play there. And nor did Lewis.'

'I'm not surprised,' said Caterina. 'His grandfather wasn't an easy man. I didn't like it either, Hetta, to tell you the truth. I meant to live there part of the time, but the way my father treated little Lewis made it impossible.'

'Spoiled half the time and bullied the rest,' said Hetta. 'At least here with old Madame Fonsa it was all spoiling. And Carlotta too, come to that.'

'I didn't spoil him,' Caterina was surprised into saying.

'Oh no,' said Hetta.

Chapter 2

'Heigh ho, who would be a woman,' sighed Hetta at the end of a long afternoon of no news. Pretending to sew under the awning on the terrace, they had thought they could make out Ware and Gomez boats on the river, and no sign of trouble on the other side where the wine lodges were, but there had been sporadic bursts of gunfire from below them and Tomas had pointed out lugubriously that the river was less than a musket shot wide.

'Santa Marta and his men will be able to sit over there on the south bank and take pot shots at us if they are so minded,' he told them with a kind of horrid satisfaction.

'What's the matter with the girl?' asked Caterina, when Hetta went indoors on yet another pretext. 'She's like a cat on hot bricks today.'

'Well, aren't we all?' said Harriet. 'She's just younger and less skilled at hiding it.'

'She usually seems to have her world so well in hand. I do agree with you, Harry, she's a splendid girl, full of go. If only some man will have the good sense to see the person behind the scar.'

'Let's not talk about it,' said Harriet.

Caterina kept Portuguese hours, with early breakfast and dinner, and a light supper at night, and it was almost time for this when a messenger finally brought a note from Frank. 'He begs to be excused.' His mother read it rapidly. 'They are doing well, he says, and will work until the last of the daylight tonight and start again first thing. There has been no trouble so far, and we are not to worry about him. He will spend the night at home in the Rua Nova dos Inglesas, so as to lose no time in the morning. Greville Faulkes

21

is to stay with him, since he lives out of town too, on the south bank, come to think of it. We are to take no notice of the sounds of shooting, Frank says; it's nothing to signify.'

'I do wonder just what he means by that,' said Caterina. 'Does he say how Mr Bankes took the idea?'

'He doesn't mention him. He wrote in a great hurry, one can see. I do hope it is all for the best. Goodness, what in the world is going on—' They could hear shouts from the courtyard at the front of the house.

'It's cheering.' Hetta had just rejoined them. 'It has to be—' She broke off as a tall, black-bearded figure emerged from the house and crossed the terrace with long strides to envelop Caterina in a bear hug.

'Mother,' he said. 'I came as soon as I could. Did you spot me in the procession? I hoped you would.'

'Lewis!' She pulled away to look up at him. 'In the procession?'

'Of course. You've not had my letter from Terceira?'

'Nothing. Not a word since those dreadful ones about your expulsion. Oh, my dearest boy, you are here, you are safe! I've been so worried.' And then, smiling up at him. 'Wasted worry, I can see. You're taller than ever, and you look so well, Lewis. But how did you get here? What are you doing?'

'Serving the Liberator, of course, the Duke of Braganza. Fighting for the freedom of Portugal. Vengeance for your husband, Aunt Harriet.' With a smile for her. 'And tonight, bringing you a message, Mother. Dom Pedro gave me leave of absence for the evening. He accepts the offer of the Gomez House with many thanks, and he would dearly like to dine with you tomorrow unless he and his advisers decide we should march at once on Lisbon.'

'That's what Frank says they should do.' Hetta's intervention brought his eyes round to her.

'Hetta! I didn't recognize you.' He hugged her then drew away. 'But I should not. Nobody told me you had grown up, Het.'

'Well,' she smiled. 'What did you expect? Did you think we would stay snoring here like the sleeping beauty's family till you chose to come back? Anyway, just look at you! All that beard! No wonder we didn't know you. And Bess is married, Lewis. That's grown up, if you like.' Something odd in her tone?

'Bess, married! Just fancy that, though I suppose one should have expected it. She was always a goer, was Bess. How about you, Het, are you spoken for?' And then, aware of an odd quality in the little silence, 'But you speak of Frank. Where is he? How is he? Running the firm, I suppose.'

'Not yet,' said Caterina. 'But he's busy right now getting Ware and Company's wine, and mine, across river from Vila Nova de Gaia.'

'And a very sound move too,' Lewis approved. 'Lord, Mother, there's so much to tell you, so much to learn, but would you ladies be shocked if I told you I was starving? When old Carlotta stopped screaming and hugging me I asked her to hurry up supper and she said she would. I hope you don't mind.' With a look for all three ladies that took assent for granted.

'I was beginning to wonder where she was,' said Caterina. 'This will be a red-letter day in her calendar, as it is in mine. But here she is to summon us. You shall tell us your whole story while we eat.'

'Or as much of it as is fit for ladies' ears,' said Hetta. 'I long to know how you found your way to Dom Pedro on Terceira.'

'I was there first.' He smiled at her. 'When those old curmudgeons at Stonyhurst threw me out – but that is another story—' He broke off as they entered the dining-room to find an unusually formal array of servants. He paused for a moment, his mother's arm in his, looking at the big carved chair where she had always sat at the head of the table, and Carlotta standing behind it. 'Mother.' It was not quite a question.

She looked up at him. 'I never thought! But it's quite true: you are lord and master here now, Lewis. Welcome to your home.'

'Thank you, Mother.' There was a little stir of approval from the servants as he seated Caterina on his right, with a quick apologetic aside to Harriet, put Hetta beside her and Harriet on his left. He turned back to his mother and went on, 'I went straight to old Lady Trellgarten in Wales, as you had told me to do, Mother. But you never told me what a tartar she was.'

'I never met her. But the word in the family always was that she was maddish.'

'Mad, bad and dangerous to know,' said Lewis cheerfully. 'But mainly dangerous. An old woman who has had her own way ever since her husband died, about sixty years ago. Lives in a great barbarous Welsh castle with a pack of servants trained to obey her slightest whim. Not much room there for a great-grandson with a hearty appetite, I can tell you. She was still in blackest mourning when I got there, for the death of an old friend called Eleanor Butler. All her thoughts were bent on persuading the lady's friend, Sarah Ponsonby, to come and live with her. The last thing she wanted was a great hulk of a man about the place.'

'You mean the Ladies of Llangollen?' asked Hetta awestruck. 'But they are practically a national monument! Did you meet Miss Ponsonby?'

'No. It's sad, really, when you think about it. The two old ladies live two valleys apart, but Welsh roads are almost as bad as ours and both of the old ladies were past travelling anyway. Grandmother Trellgarten was crying for the moon when she hoped to get Miss Ponsonby to live with her, but she was never one to listen to reason. Anyway, she got it into her head that it was my presence in the house that stopped her friend coming, so she was glad enough to bribe me to leave.'

'Bribe you?' asked Caterina, shocked.

'Don't look so scandalized, Mother dear. When I read in the paper that the Marquis of Palmela and Count Villa Flor had raised the liberal standard in the Azores and Dom Pedro had recognized Palmela as regent – well, I told Great Grandma about it – she hated it when I called her that – and she said, quick as a flash – she's not mad, Mother, far from it – "And you long to go there, my boy, do you not?" And I said, meek as a mouse, "Yes, ma'am, but I have no money". And that was that. I will say for the old dame, she coughed up handsomely in the end. I'm only beginning to run short now.' Another of his quick glances for his mother. 'So you see.'

He turned back to Hetta. 'I was on Terceira before Dom Pedro had even abdicated from the throne of Brazil. I was one of the happy few who welcomed him when he landed to take up his daughter's cause. And what a day that was! What a man! I long for you to meet him, Mother.'

'Yes,' said Caterina. 'I'm sure he is a great man, but, Lewis, do you mean to tell me that you have been on Terceira for a year, and not a word to me?'

'Not a bit of it. I wrote you, with my direction, as soon as I had one. When I got no answer, I wrote again, of course, but not exactly at once. We were quite busy there you know, with money to get, supplies, everything; not to mention the drilling. It wasn't exactly a bed of roses, life on Terceira, and when Dom Pedro did get there: mayhem! Wonderful mayhem. And I wrote a third time, just before we sailed, gave it to Villa Flor's wife to post in Paris when she got there to join the young queen. We've made better time than the letter, that's all. And you have to remember, Mother, that communication between rebel Terceira and Miguelite Portugal was bound to be a trifle uncertain. I didn't worry too much when I had no answer from you, felt sure of seeing you soon enough. And here I am.'

'A soldier,' said Caterina. 'Oh, Lewis, I thought you would be at the university by now.'

'University? What university? You're not thinking, Mother! That's just why we all had to hang around at Stonyhurst in that limbo of a top form they called the Philosophers, because Oxford and Cambridge are closed to us Roman Catholics. No need to look so downcast, there will be time enough for the university when the war is won. If I decide to go. We've got Almeida Garrett in the Academic Battalion, I'll have you know, and what he says about Coimbra makes me think that might be the place for me. You'll meet him tomorrow, I hope, unless we do march for Lisbon. I rather think he is a great man, Almeida. In a very different line from Dom Pedro. He had no education at all, you know, the Liberator, or nothing to signify. He can read and write, mind you, which some say is more than his brother Miguel can, if the usurper is more than Dom Pedro's half-brother, which I myself very much doubt.'

'Lewis!' Caterina glanced quickly round, but the servants had put the dessert on the table and left the room.

'Don't pretend you haven't heard the stories about Carlota Joaquina, the wicked queen. She and her husband lived apart, publicly hating each other in Brazil. Dom Miguel lived with her, Dom Pedro with his father, who seems to have brought him up better, though he was as amazed as everyone else when Dom Pedro came out as a liberal. They are going to be golden days for Portugal, when he takes charge.'

'For his daughter,' put in Hetta.

'Quite right, Het, for his daughter. And Maria da Gloria is being educated in Louis Philippe's liberal Paris, since Wellington was so ungracious to her in England. If the duke was still in office, we wouldn't be here, I can tell you. It's the new Whig government, turning a blindish eye, has made it possible, but I'm afraid the unfriendly treatment he and his daughter received from Wellington's Tories has left the Liberator well and truly prejudiced against the British. Well, you have to say their soldiers are a rough enough lot, though Colonel Hodges has done a great deal to whip them into shape.'

'It was odd to see them marching side by side with the French,' said Hetta.

'I should just about say so! There have been some incidents, of course. There are officers both in our army and in the Miguelites who served on opposite sides in the Peninsular War. It's a horrible business, civil war.' He looked at the clock. 'Good God, I must be off. We're quartered at the Franciscans'. I wasn't just sure it was wise of Dom Pedro to act so swiftly against the tyranny of the religious orders, but it has certainly meant that we have found their buildings empty, all ready for use as barracks. I only hope we aren't here too long, good though it is to see you all.' He rose to his feet. 'Oh, one other thing, the duke's a wonderful man, and a brilliant leader, but don't ever be alone in a room with him, any of you.' He kissed his mother, bowed with a surprising, formal grace to Harriet and Hetta and left.

Frank arrived next morning looking exhausted and angry. 'Just as well we lost no time,' he told them. 'We found Miguelite guards on the wine lodges this morning, and short of violence there was no way of shifting them. But we got the best stuff out yesterday, which is more than anyone else did. You never saw such confusion and indecision as there is among the merchants. And by what I hear the Duke of Braganza and his advisers are no better. All talk, no action. But it's wonderful news about Lewis, I long to see him and hear what he has to tell of life on Terceira. You were right after all, Hetta.' Turning to his sister.

'Right?' asked Caterina.

'I did just fancy I saw Lewis in the procession.' Hetta made light of it. 'But Frank thought I was crazy and I didn't want to raise false hopes. But, Frank,' changing the subject, 'what is old Bankes doing all this time?'

'Hiding under his bed, for all I know. There's not been a sign of him at the office. He lives out of town, upriver, remember? Maybe he thought it best to stay out of harm's way.'

'You mean you didn't have his consent for what you did yesterday?' asked his mother.

'Of course not. He'd never have given it. It was a crowning mercy he stayed away.'

'He'll be furious when he finds out,' said Hetta.

'Not if he has any sense. Ours will be the only houses in town with supplies, so far as I know.' He was justifiably pleased with himself. 'It's all safely stowed in that old warehouse of yours downriver from the Franciscans', Aunt Caterina, with a guard on it. And talking of guards, may I ask your hospitality for my mother and sister for a few more days until things settle down one way or another? I don't altogether like the feel of things in town this morning. There's all kinds of wild talk. Anything could happen.'

'Yes, of course,' said Caterina. 'I'd meant you all to stay. You will too, I hope, Frank.'

'It's good of you, but I think I should get back and keep an eye on things. I'd as soon be there when old Bankes does choose to turn up. And I count on your support, Mama.'

'Of course. You will be careful, Frank.' She reached up to kiss him. 'He's grown up,' she said to Caterina when he had left. 'A man of action. Just like his father.'

Caterina was surprised to find herself catching Hetta's eye as they remembered the older Frank Ware who had been brought up by a domineering mother and passed from her tutelage to his wife's more loving control. His finest moment had been when he came out in public defence of young Lewis, and he had paid for that brave act with his life.

'He was a fine man,' said Caterina, remembering all this. 'Don't cry, Harry. Come and help me plan for this dinner I may or may not be giving.'

'Gladly,' said Harriet, 'but it smells to me as if things are well in hand already.' Powerful odours of stew, salt cod, tomato and garlic were coming from the kitchen and girls were busy polishing furniture in the state rooms.

'If they don't come, we shall have a clean house and enough food for several regiments of the Liberator's troops,' said Caterina.

'If they don't come it will mean that the troops have marched south,' Hetta pointed out. 'It's hard to know just what to wish for.'

But after a long day of agitated discussion, Dom Pedro ignored the advice of Palmella and Villa Flor, who wanted an immediate march on Lisbon, while the enemy was still disorganized, and followed the more cautious councils of his elderly, ailing Minister for War, Agostinho Freire.

'In a way it's just as well the notice is so short,' said Caterina when the message of acceptance came. 'It will make it less obvious that so many people, British as well as Portuguese, have decided that they had as soon not commit themselves to the liberal cause.'

'Not until it seems a great deal better established than it is now,' agreed Hetta. 'But the Procters are coming, I know, and their friend Cuthbert Armstrong, who brought the first news of the landing, and Greville Faulkes, of course, and I believe Mr Bankes has come out from under his bed, forgiven Frank for saving the firm's wine and decided to join us. Not that he will add much to the brilliance of the occasion, still less his wife.'

'If she comes,' said Caterina. 'Mrs Bankes does not approve of me. We are going to be short of ladies, I am afraid, as usual here in Portugal, where they keep their women cooped up at home. And, as usual, I don't know what I would do without you, Harriet – and Hetta too,' she added. 'But . . . I have been wondering . . . I know all the other English families have packed their traps, ready to go on board the English ships in the river if necessary. Should you not be doing so?'

'No,' said Harriet. 'We talked it over with Frank. He did suggest it, bless his heart, but we aren't going, Hetta and I. Not unless things get so bad that you decide to come too.'

'I'll never do that. This is my home.'

'I thought you'd say that. Let the rats run, if they must. We'll stay.'

'I'm glad.' She turned to take a note from Tomas. 'Well, my goodness!' She handed it to Harriet. 'Here are two more ladies for our party.'

'Rachel Emerson! But she was a French spy, Cat.'

'That was twenty years ago,' Caterina reminded her. 'And in the meantime the French have become our friends and she seems to have lost her husband and gained a daughter, whom she longs to introduce to me. "My little Ruth".' Her tone was scathing. 'How I disliked that woman. And rightly as it turned out.'

'Her husband was worse,' said Harriet fairly.

'Not saying much, love. At least he is dead. Don't you think the easiest answer to this is to invite them to join the party tomorrow and get it over with?'

'Well, it's undoubtedly what she wants,' said Harriet. 'But I do wonder what brings her here, now of all times.'

'No good, you can count on that,' Caterina told her. 'I wonder how old the daughter is.'

'I hope you realize what a lucky fellow you are, Frank.' Greville Faulkes turned to his younger friend after finishing the last bite of a luxurious English breakfast. 'With a mother and sister like yours. Two remarkable women. And what a household they run. I don't get service like this, I can tell you. Hard-boiled eggs and stewed green tea are my lot.'

'You need a wife, Greville.'

'Yes, I do, don't I? But where am I to find one? Maybe now Lewis is home I'll ask leave of absence and go to England on a bride-hunt.' A plain, dark, strongly built man in his mid-thirties, he did not sound in the least serious.

'But Lewis is in the army.' Frank had been thinking about this. 'He won't be able to take charge yet.'

'No, but when it is over he will. I wonder what he is like now. You've not met him yet?'

'No. He always had a will of his own.' Frank smiled to himself, remembering childhood days when Lewis, a few years older than himself, had been the leader in all their games, and often a tyrannical one.

'I sometimes thought he bullied you and the girls a bit.' Greville might have read his mind. 'But you had good times together. I did wonder, though, how it felt for him to find himself an insignificant new boy at Stonyhurst, after ruling the roost here the way he did.'

'Terrible,' said Frank. 'He told me. I wasn't a bit surprised when they expelled him. Really, it was a miracle he stuck it out so long. And they endured him. And an even greater one that he has found something so worthwhile to do.'

'Yes, I think the army will suit him better than the university, specially with such a cause.'

'So long as the liberals win,' said Frank soberly. 'Do you realise that if Braganza fails, Lewis will be an exile for life?'

'And very likely his mother with him,' said Greville.

'I wish they had marched on Lisbon today.'

'So do I. I don't at all like the feeling of divided councils around Dom Pedro. Did you hear the shouts for Saldanha when they marched into town yesterday? He is going to be sadly missed, I am afraid. Now there was a man who made up his mind and stuck to it. I suppose you hardly remember back to when he was governor here in Porto, Frank? I cannot understand why he is not at the Liberator's side. He's badly needed there. Oh well, time to get to work.' He put his starched damask napkin on the table and rose. 'I'll see you at Caterina's dinner, Frank.'

'I look forward to it. Yes, Rosa?' A trim maid had entered the room and bobbed a curtsey; and he switched to Portuguese for the question.

'A gentleman to see you, sir. A stranger.'

'Not really a stranger.' The tall man who had followed her into the room smiled at them both. 'Here's luck: both of you together!

But where are your mother and sister, Frank? Safe and well, I hope? And Caterina?' Jeremy Craddock turned from shaking Frank's hand to take Greville's. 'It's too long since I've seen you both. May I beg a cup of coffee, Frank? I'm just off the packet and the devil of a crossing we had of it. And landed at Foz too, since Captain Bradford didn't fancy risking his precious ship in these dangerous waters. But tell me all the news. That's what I am here for.' He was seated now, eagerly drinking coffee. 'To report on the liberals' chances.'

'For Palmerston?' It was hardly a question from Greville Faulkes.

'Yes. I just hope I can make a good case for instant British aid.'

'The liberals are certainly going to need it, by the look of things,' Greville told him. 'Frank and I were just saying that Saldanha is sadly missed. Dom Pedro's new ministers are at loggerheads already, by all reports. But you couldn't have timed your arrival better. Caterina Fonsa dines the duke and his people today. You'll come, of course.'

'I most certainly will. And Lewis? I heard he was on Terceira.'

'He's here, with the Academic Brigade. Almeida Garrett too.'

'No lack of top brass. But what of the foot soldiers?'

'Not enough of them,' said Greville.

'And half trained,' put in Frank. 'I watched them disperse on the Praça Nova yesterday, and it was chaos. International chaos, too.' Ruefully. 'British infantrymen swearing at French, French swearing at Portuguese, and officers cursing the lot of them in various languages.'

'I'm told things are just as bad among the Miguelites,' said Greville. 'If not worse. This may be going to be a war won by whomever makes the fewest mistakes.'

'But I'm afraid it is going to be a very unpleasant business,' said Jeremy Craddock. 'I think your mother and sister, Frank, and Caterina too, should pack their bags and be on the packet when she sails for England tomorrow.'

'I never heard such nonsense,' said Greville.

The Sanchez Palace glittered with polished furniture and sparkling chandeliers and smelled of beeswax and good food. Caterina looked up from the place cards she was arranging on the vast, loaded table to greet an early guest. 'Greville!' Pleased and surprised. 'I did not expect you so soon.'

'No, forgive me. I'll only take a minute of your time. I know how busy you are. But there are two things I must say to you. Before the party.'

'Yes?' She took his arm and led him out to the shade of the terrace. 'They can finish in there. You know I am always glad to see you.'

'Thank you. Has anyone told you that Jeremy Craddock is here?' It had been Jeremy, then her suitor, who had got him his job with Caterina.

'Jeremy Craddock! Here? No, they most certainly have not. What is he doing here after all these years?' She had refused Jeremy twice, once in person, once by post. Had she regretted it?

'Came on the packet,' Greville told her. 'A mission from the British Government, reporting to Palmerston, the Foreign Secretary. I thought young Frank might not have let you know.'

'And thought I'd be glad to be warned. Thank you, Greville, you were quite right. It is a surprise.' She smiled. 'And I will have a surprise for him, too. Do you remember my speaking of the Emersons?'

'French spies. Of course I do. What of them?'

'He is dead, and she is here, with a daughter. I cannot begin to imagine why. But she is coming to my dinner. And Jeremy was spell-bound by her for a while.'

'Was he so? I didn't know that. I shall look forward to seeing them meet.'

'So shall I. And the other thing you wanted to say to me?'

'I hear that Lewis is back. When he wants to take over, you shall have my resignation, dear Caterina, in any form it needs to take.'

'Thank you. But I doubt it will come to that. For the moment, he is totally committed to Dom Pedro and the army. Anyway,' smiling ruefully, 'you're forgetting: it's to him you would have to hand in your resignation, not to me. He is absolute master here; has been ever since he was twenty-one. Do you know, I had quite forgotten it myself; wrote Dom Pedro offering him the Gomez estate as if it was mine to offer. It was only when I saw that the servants expected Lewis to sit at the head of the table that I recollected myself.'

'Those two monstrous wills,' Greville said angrily. 'Both of them to leave him everything, your father and old Madame Fonsa.'

'They doted on him, remember? And he's a man. The heir they both longed for. Why should they think of me? No need to look so cross. Lewis will never let me starve. And besides, I have my work.' Her tone changed totally. 'There's just time. I want to show you something. In the studio. Quickly.'

'It's formidable.' Up in the studio, Greville had stood for a long moment gazing at the bold charcoal sketch of a bearded man on a pony, long legs almost brushing the ground. A few confident strokes suggested a crowd of supplicants around him. Was there just a hint of a halo? 'Dom Pedro as Christ?' She nodded. 'It's the best thing you've done, Caterina. That time you spent studying with Goya in Bordeaux was not wasted. Lord, what a lot of lies I had to tell.'

'And how grateful I was. I've pushed my luck far enough with my portraits. They are just respectable for a lady, but not this. It has to be kept secret.'

'Yes.' He was still looking with something like awe at the picture. 'It most certainly does. Will you tell Lewis?' He went straight to the heart of the matter.

'Not yet anyway. We have to get to know each other again first. Four years is a long time. He's out of leading strings now.'

'He was never in them much, that I remember. So – a secret still, and you'll let me deal with Mrs Wallis for you?'

'And be grateful. Lord, there's someone arriving already.' She locked the studio door behind them and he watched her change, as they walked down the last ceremonial flight of stairs side by side, from the eager creator, proud of her work, to a demure hostess, expecting exalted company. But when they saw the two women who were standing, a little forlornly, in the great empty, shining saloon, he felt her stiffen beside him.

'Mrs Emerson.' She went forward, hand outstretched, voice cool as winter. 'Welcome back to Porto. And this is your daughter ... Ruth?'

Rachel Emerson had preserved her blonde handsomeness with an effort that was a little too visible, but her daughter was a dark miracle. Everything about her was exactly right, the white dress, the simple hairstyle, the quick blush and the look almost of apology with which her amazing black eyes met Caterina's.

'My fatherless child.' Rachel Emerson put a lace-trimmed handkerchief to her eyes, but they swivelled at once to take in Greville Faulkes, and Caterina duly introduced him to them both and was grateful to him when he moved away with them as a stream of other guests began to arrive. She had only time as she curtsied and smiled and shook hands to think that Rachel Emerson's 'little Ruth' was older than she had expected, despite the ingenuous air. But here was Jeremy Craddock. He was elegant as he had always been in best broadcloth and a miraculous cravat, but her artist's analytic eye found something not quite satisfactory about his good looks. He had not aged, but he had most certainly changed, and she felt a pang of gratitude to Greville Faulkes for sparing her the surprise this might have been.

'Jeremy,' smiling at him warmly. 'It's good to see you. But what a surprise! You are come, I understand, to report on our liberal doings to your authorities.'

'You are well informed.' He did not altogether like it. 'But surely your authorities, too?'

'Oh, no. I am quite a Portuguese rebel now, Mr Craddock.'

'You called me Jeremy just now.' Reproachfully.

'A slip of the tongue. We are all grown up now, the older generation. Have you met my Lewis yet?'

'No, I look forward to it. He is in the rebel army, I understand.'

'Not rebel, liberating.' She was glad to see Harriet and Hetta approaching. 'Here are some old friends for you.' As they greeted each other she looked about the now crowded room for Greville and the Emersons, but a stir outside in the courtyard warned her that her guest of honour must be arriving and she hurried to greet Dom Pedro at the head of the steps, and wonder as she did so if she should not have arranged for Lewis to be here in her place.

But he was at the Duke of Braganza's side and instead of greeting the Liberator she found herself being made known to him and fell into her deepest curtsey, scarlet taffeta rustling around her. He did not look well, she thought, rising, and he looked as if he had a bad temper. But today he was all smiles, praising her looks, her house, her son until she felt quite exhausted with grateful responses. And found herself just for an instant, remembering with something almost like regret that Christ figure in her studio that Greville would send to England for her. But done was done. She smiled at the Liberator and took his arm for a ceremonial parade of her guests, too few of them, she now realized, quite important enough.

If the duke was aware of this too, he concealed it admirably, bowing graciously this way and that, pausing for a friendly word here and there, saying everything that was proper about Oporto as a great liberal centre. 'I have not been here since I was a child,' he told Mrs Procter who probably did not understand him. 'It is twenty-five years since I saw my native shores.'

'You must see some changes,' Caterina came to Dorothy Procter's rescue, wishing as she did so that the wives of British merchants who lived in Oporto would take the trouble to learn the language.

'I most certainly do. For the better, of course. But who is the charming young lady?' His expert eye had picked out Ruth Emerson from the crowd. 'Pray present me, ma'am?' to Caterina.

'She is American, Your Excellency.' Was this the right way to address him? She should have asked Greville. 'Will speak not a word of Portuguese, I am afraid.'

'Then your son, who is my right hand, will have to interpret for me,' he said, as they approached the corner of the room where the Emerson ladies were holding court in a crowd of eager young men, Frank Ware among them.

Introduced to royalty, Ruth Emerson behaved perfectly, blushing, smiling and actually managing two stammered words of a Portuguese greeting.

As Lewis began to translate the duke's reply, Caterina became aware that she had been dismissed, quietly, civilly, but definitely, by royalty, and found herself, for a strange moment, stranded, visibly alone, at her own party.

It was only a moment, then Greville Faulkes was at her side. 'Palmela and Villa Flor are over there,' he told her. 'Do you think you should greet them?'

After that, she was back in charge of her entertainment, and thought it went well enough, considering the odd mix of people. She had, in fact, to be grateful for the Emersons' unexpected arrival. Ruth Emerson's beautiful, unexpected presence was a guarantee of success for any party.

'What a stunner.' Frank Ware paused for a moment beside her. 'Where in the world did you find her, Aunt Caterina?'

'She's the daughter of an old friend,' she said, and then, 'That's not true, Frank, she is the daughter of an old enemy. Ask your mother about them before you enrol yourself among her conquests.' She was looking as she spoke to the corner of the room where Ruth Emerson still held sway. The duke had returned to his duties as principal guest but Lewis was still beside her. 'I think it is time we dined,' she said abruptly. 'Will you do me a kindness, Frank, and tell Carlotta?'

Inevitably, she sat next to the duke at dinner and observed that he was a frugal eater and hardly drank at all. It was just as well, she thought, trying not to look at the way his immense beard swept the table. Lewis had told her that he had sworn not to touch it with a razor until his brother Miguel was defeated and his daughter Maria established in his place. It must be a terrible nuisance to him, she thought, rescuing a wine glass as he turned away to talk to his other neighbour. She was able to look for a moment unobserved at the pale, fleshy face behind the beard, and the balding head of the hero who was here to place his daughter on a throne. What were his chances of success, she wondered, and what disasters would he plunge them all into as he fought for it? Her eyes moved to where Lewis had found himself a place beside Ruth Emerson: *what is going to happen to us all?*

At the other end of the table Jeremy Craddock was wondering the same thing. Nothing had worked out as he had expected. Agreeing to come to Oporto on Palmerston's fact-finding mission, he had expected to find his old love Caterina settled down, a respectable matron whom he half consciously meant to turn into a mother figure to replace the one he had never had. He had taken it for granted that he would stay with her, as he had years ago with his cousin, her father. The Sanchez Palace would make an admirable observation post. One look at Caterina had made him very glad indeed that he had played safe by going first to the Wares' house. She was not at all what he had meant her to be. He had developed an eye for women's clothes over the years and her scarlet taffeta struck him as something quite out of the ordinary. But then, so was the whole of her appearance. Where other women sported regimented rows of curls, she had made a kind of coronet of her long dark hair and looked, he thought, a queen. This was no mother figure, this was a woman in her prime. Absorbing this, trying to decide what it meant to him, he had missed the moment when the duke spotted the Emersons and it was not until just before dinner that he had another shock, and a most unpleasant one, when a soft hand fell on his arm, and a roguish voice reproached him.

'Mr Craddock,' said Rachel Emerson, 'how could you cut an old friend so?'

Unlike Caterina, she had aged and he had not recognized her, but now he did so with a sinking heart.

'Mrs Emerson, forgive me. My thoughts were miles away. But what in the world brings you here, to this distressed city?'

'I've timed it badly, have I not, but I always meant to come back to see my old friends here. And it is a happy chance to find you. We have a great deal to talk about, you and I. But I am neglecting my duties as a chaperon. Come with me, Mr Craddock, and let me make you known to my daughter, my little Ruth.'

Something in her tone alarmed him, and he went reluctantly across the room with her to be made known as, 'My old friend, Mr Craddock', to the paragon who was holding court there. Ruth Emerson was a beauty to put all others in the shade, but of whom did she remind him?

He was relieved to be interrupted before they had finished with the first few polite nothings, by a move towards the dining-room, but it was disconcerting to see Lewis abandon his duties as host and swoop down on Ruth Emerson. He turned instinctively to escape from her mother and felt a hand on his arm.

'Mr Craddock, you don't remember me—'

But it was impossible to forget that scarred face. 'Of course I do – as a madcap in petticoats – but I must call you Miss Ware now. What can I do for you, Miss Ware?'

'Help me sort out the chaos into which Lewis has thrown Aunt Caterina's arrangements. She's fully occupied with the great duke and I can't see Greville Faulkes anywhere.'

'He meant to be here.'

'He was for a while,' she said impatiently. 'But now we need him he has vanished.'

Chapter 3

Caterina's party ended with dancing, since Dom Pedro was known to love it. Taking the floor with her guest of honour she was sorry to see Lewis leading out Ruth Emerson, but there was no time to fret about them. The duke proved a formidable waltzer, she had to keep her wits about her to follow him, but enjoyed it. How long was it since she had danced? When the music stopped, she found that either by accident or the duke's design they were standing close to Lewis and his partner and the next minute she was dancing with her son while Dom Pedro swept Ruth Emerson off across the floor. Since she had taught Lewis herself their steps matched well and she was able to relax and look about her. Jeremy Craddock was dancing with Hetta and she blessed him in her heart. But where was Greville? Harriet and Rachel Emerson were standing together among the chaperons and she blamed him for not coming to Harriet's rescue. She looked up at her silent son, whose eyes, like hers, were scanning the dancers. She had warned Frank Ware about the Emersons; did she dare warn Lewis?

She had still not decided when the music came to a sudden stop. The duke was crossing the floor to her, Ruth Emerson radiant on his arm.

'*Senhora*, a thousand pardons, but duty calls, an urgent message from Admiral Sartorius. I must call my council together.' He looked about the room collecting the eyes of his ministers, thanked her profusely, and left, Lewis following him with one backward glance, for her, or for Ruth Emerson?

Now she missed Greville Faulkes badly. He would have helped

her get the party going again, but, after one more rather lethargic dance the other guests also began to take their leave.

'May I congratulate you on a most successful party?' Jeremy Craddock came up to her with Frank Ware. 'And may I call tomorrow to hear all your news? I do not need to ask how you are.' With an admiring glance. 'And Lewis seems in good heart too, does he not?'

'I shall be delighted to see you. It has been a long time. Mr Craddock is staying with you?' She turned to Frank, relieved to have realized this. There had been an awkward moment when she wondered if Craddock expected her to invite him to her house. No longer her house. How strange.

'He'll be company while my mother and sister stay safe with you, Caterina. I'm afraid it may have to be a little longer than I had thought. Things are a bit warm in our part of town just now. It's lucky our houses are granite built.'

'You mean you really are in rifle shot of the enemy? Tomas said something about it.'

'I'm afraid so. But our houses are stout; it's just a question of looking sharp in the cross streets. So long as they don't get cannon into position, but I am sure the Liberator will have them out of there in no time.'

'The trouble is,' said Caterina thoughtfully, 'Dom Pedro seems to think that the whole countryside is going to rise spontaneously for his cause. He doesn't want actually to come to blows with his brother's troops if he can help it. Once blood is shed, he says, everything will be different.'

'Well, of course, it will,' said Jeremy Craddock. 'You can't have a war without the shedding of blood.'

'He hopes not to have a war.'

'And so do we all,' said Frank. 'I just hope Dom Pedro proves right, but the dispossessed priests have been busy telling the peasants the most horrendous tales about him, making him out practically the Antichrist himself. I cannot honestly say that I am very hopeful. So, please, Caterina, keep my mother and sister here.'

'Of course I will. You know how I enjoy having them.' She looked beyond him and could not help a slight grimace.

'Caterina.' Rachel Emerson swooped to clasp her in a strongly scented embrace. 'What a wonderful party! And what looks you are in! And how wonderful to see you and all our old friends – and new ones.' With her best smile for Frank. 'Now I have a great favour to ask you. I had no idea that your party would go on so long, and the town in such a ferment too, with everything at sixes and sevens. My little Ruth and I are staying in my old apartments below the cathedral. Our carriage awaits us; it's nothing of a drive in the usual way of things, but with strange servants and the light going, and the city in turmoil, I wondered if I might make bold to ask the loan of a really reliable man to see us home. Unless these gentlemen—' With an appealing glance for the two men.

'I'll gladly send Tomas with you, Mrs Emerson.' She did not at all wish this woman to call her by her christian name. But at least they were not asking to stay.

But Frank intervened. 'No, no, of course we will see you ladies home, won't we, Mr Craddock? We're on foot anyway and it's nothing to drop down from the cathedral to my house afterwards. You don't mind, do you, sir?' to Jeremy.

Caterina rather thought Jeremy did, but there was not much, as Frank's guest, that he could do about it, and she was glad to see them go, almost the last to leave.

Servants were beginning to snuff candles and tidy the rooms, Carlotta in charge. After a quick word of thanks to them all, Caterina turned to Harriet and Hetta. 'Are you as hot as I am? Let's go out on the terrace, it will be fresher there.'

'Yes,' said Harriet. 'And the light not exactly going either. It's only indoors it seems dark.'

'Yes. She's shameless. Should I have prevented your Frank going?'

'I don't see how you could have. I didn't think Jeremy Craddock looked best pleased either. What a surprise that was.' With a quick look for her friend.

'Yes.' Smiling. 'I can't begin to tell you how grateful I am to Frank for inviting him to stay. I hope you won't find him a nuisance. When you can move back home, that is. Frank says you two must stay with me until the enemy are cleared from the south

bank, and, of course, I am delighted to have you.' She turned to
Hetta, who had stood silently listening. 'Did you enjoy the party,
Hetta?'

'I found it enormously interesting,' said the girl.

'How strange it is to wake to all this military noise,' said Caterina
over coffee and rolls next morning.

'More today surely?' said Hetta. 'I do hope it means the march
on Lisbon has begun. I'm sorry, Aunt Caterina,' turning impulsively to her hostess. 'I know it means we lose Lewis again, so soon
after his return, but the sooner he leaves the sooner he will be back.'

'I'm sure you are right,' agreed Caterina. 'Carlotta said something last night about confusion in the Miguelite forces. I suspect
there is more coming and going across the river than the authorities know about. She dried up when I questioned her further and I
didn't like to press her. But this must be the right moment for Dom
Pedro to move.' And besides she would much rather see Lewis
march on Lisbon than watch him dangle after Ruth Emerson. She
finished her coffee and rose. 'Will you excuse me? I asked Greville
to come this morning to discuss the arrangements for handing over
to Lewis.'

'And explain where he vanished to yesterday?' asked Harriet.

'That too,' smiling. 'We did miss him, did we not?'

Alone with her mother, Hetta asked a question that had been at
the front of her mind since the night of Lewis's return. 'Tell me
about the Fonsa and Gomez estates, Mama? Surely those selfish old
things left something to Caterina?'

'Not a penny,' said her mother. 'I couldn't believe it at the time;
I still can't. She had looked after them both devotedly for years as
they got older and more demanding. Worst of all, she had had to
stand by and watch them spoil Lewis, which they did, you know.'

'Oh yes, I do know.' Hetta had been there to see.

'I can understand her father's cutting her out,' Harriet went on.
'She did defy him, refusing to marry Jeremy Craddock. It would
have tidied things up,' she said now. 'If she had. Simplified them. I
have often wondered – too late now. As to the old lady, she was a
tyrant if ever I met one. Things were never easy in that household;

Caterina had too much character, that was the trouble. They both liked their own way, those two. And I'm afraid the fact is that when it came down to cases old Madame Fonsa was just as bad as any other Portuguese in thinking a woman's place was in the boudoir and on the balcony. Except her own, of course. That was different. She was in the driving seat, and it was her money, Fonsa not Sanchez. Her son-in-law had squandered the Sanchez estate. And then she never quite forgave Caterina for even considering going to live with her father in the Gomez house.'

'But Caterina never did. It's so unfair. Do you think Lewis will understand, will do something about it?'

'I was going to ask you that. You were always such friends, you two.'

'When we were children. Yes.' She drank coffee. 'Now it's hard to know what is going on behind all that beard. Maybe Frank could speak to him?'

'I doubt he'd take it from him.'

'Greville then?'

'He's in his employment, now, remember? It's not easy.'

'Then let's hope he thinks of it for himself,' said Hetta briskly, rising. 'Now I promised Aunt Caterina that I would see the silver counted back into its cases.'

Greville and Caterina were also discussing Madame Fonsa's Will. His disappearance from the party was quickly explained. 'Forgive me,' he said. 'It was a question of getting your picture on to the packet before she sailed. Who knows when there will be another one? We can't be sure of anything these days. I thought it essential.'

'You were sadly missed, but I am sure you were right. Now, what are we to do about Lewis and the estate?'

'Let him make the first move,' he said at once, proving that he had been thinking about it too. 'In my opinion, it will be time enough for changes when the war is over and he comes home to settle down. If he does.'

'He talked about Coimbra University.'

'And a very good idea, too. But in the meantime something must be done to regularize your position, Caterina. You cannot go on forever living as unpaid housekeeper. I've said all along you should take an allowance from the estate, now it is more essential than ever. You ought to be saving out of it, against the day when young Lewis brings home a bride to turn you out. You could hardly live on your earnings from your painting if you did not have a roof over your head.'

'How unkind of you to remind me. But you are quite right, as usual. My vulgar picture of the governor's daughter bought the taffeta for my gown last night, but it would hardly have paid for the party itself. And at the moment I see no chance of another commission.'

'No. The nobility are getting out of town as fast as their carriages can take them. It's not just the vote of confidence in Dom Pedro that one would have liked to see. Seriously, Caterina, have you thought of what the future holds for you and Lewis if the Liberator should fail in his attempt?'

'Yes,' she said soberly. 'I have indeed. Exile. I love and respect Lewis for joining Dom Pedro, but it has clarified our position in a very drastic way, has it not?'

'It certainly has. That is why I made a point of catching the packet with your picture last night.'

'Well, let us devoutly hope that good comes of it. Do you know,' thoughtfully, 'it surprises me to say it, but I can bear the idea of having to leave Porto. Do you think old Madam Trellgarten would welcome me to Wales more enthusiastically than she did Lewis? She's never answered a letter of mine yet.'

'Let's hope it doesn't come to that,' he said. 'Have you heard from Lewis today?'

'Not a word. Nor yet from Dom Pedro. Which I hope means that they have started for Lisbon.'

'Or at the very least are clearing the Miguelites from the south bank. I have to confess that I quite long for a clean shirt.'

'Greville, what a selfish brute I am! I never even thought to ask you where you were staying. You should have come here.'

'I wouldn't dream of it. I've been at the Wares' so far, but it's no problem finding accommodation in town; enough people are running, I am sorry to say. I've found temporary quarters over a goldsmith in the Rua Caterina – your street. It's handy for every-thing and tucked well away from the river front, where I am afraid it is going to be uncomfortable living until Dom Pedro clears his enemies from the south bank. I trust you won't dream of letting Harriet and Hetta go home before that.'

'No; Frank asked me to keep them. But is it really so dangerous, Greville? Ought he to be there?'

'Can you imagine him leaving?' It was unanswerable. He rose. 'You'll be thronged with grateful callers soon. That's settled then. I'll open an account for you and pay in your back earnings. Lord knows the estate can stand it after the frugal way you have lived all these years.' And before she could protest. 'Did you manage any work this morning?'

'Oh, yes, I never miss that.' Her early hours in her studio were the high point of her day. 'I wish I had time to show you, but there's the first caller now.'

It was only after he had left that she realized that his questions about her work had pre-empted the protest she had meant to make about his high-handed behaviour over her finances.

Sweating in hot morning sun, Jeremy Craddock was making his way reluctantly up the steep lanes to the well-remembered house where Rachel Emerson had her apartments. She had seized an opportunity, while Frank was concentrated on her daughter the night before, to demand that he call on her today. 'It will be to your advantage to do so,' she had said. 'You will regret it bitterly if you do not.'

He had spent the night arguing with himself about what to do. He knew her for a dangerous woman and one-time French spy. She had fooled him to the top of his bent when he was young. He had thought himself in love with her. It was hard to believe now, seeing the waning of her beauty, in such sharp contrast to Caterina, whom he had once neglected for her. Every instinct warned him to keep away from Rachel now, but could he risk it? Better the danger you know, he told himself.

Climbing the steep stairs to her rooms, he was not surprised to find her alone. 'I have sent my beloved Ruth out shopping,' she told him. 'What I have to say to you is not at all for her innocent ears. Is she not a delight, Mr Craddock? The daughter every mother longs for. And such a success last night, carried all before her, and not a bit proud about it, just pleased and surprised and grateful to everyone for being so kind. My only aim in life, now, is to see her well established, and that is where I need your help.'

'Mine? What can you mean?' He had refused to sit down, was standing at the window looking down at the wide view it commanded of the upper river and the bridge of boats across it to the south bank.

'I wish you would sit down, Mr Craddock.'

'I prefer to stand.'

'If you insist.' She plunged straight in. 'I have followed your career with great interest. You are a rich man now, since those years in Brazil, and a successful one, Palmerston's emissary to report on what the misguided Portuguese are up to. And with plans, I am sure, for a high-level career in politics: foreign minister, perhaps, when Palmerston himself reaches the highest office? Believe me, I respect you for it. I am ambitious too, but it is not so easy for a woman. And it's not for myself, it is for my little Ruth. She knows nothing, of course, about your and my interesting pasts, nor do I intend her to do so. She is innocence itself. In the bad years, when my husband was still alive – you see I am keeping nothing from you – when he was making my life a hell, I saw to it that Ruth knew none of it. She was safe in a dame school in Boston, getting the accomplishments of a young lady and learning to be a good Christian and a better woman than her mother. And she is. I, her mother, can tell you so, and prove it, for your ears only, by telling you she bores me to death. It is more than high time that she was married, before she drives me to say something I regret, and before she is tarnished by my company. I told you I was going to speak frankly, as to an old friend, and you see I am doing so.'

'You most certainly are. But why?' He turned from the window to stare at her.

'You aim at a career in politics, Mr Craddock.'

'What's that to the purpose?'

'Everything. A politician needs a wife. My Ruth would make you an admirable one. You saw her success last night, drawing all eyes. I have told you about her character. Talk to her, and you will recognize her intelligence. She is an open book for who will to write on. Believe me, you could do much worse. And all the slander stopped.'

'Slander?'

'Those tales about beautiful young blacks in Brazil. Black men, Mr Craddock. I told you I had followed your career with interest.' She had silenced him and knew it. 'So – I have a choice to offer you: either marry my Ruth or stand her friend and provide her dowry. I don't much care which, but if I were you I would go for marriage. It would solve so many problems for you.' She paused, looked at the clock. 'Now, she will be back any minute. Will you stay to meet her, or would you rather take a day or two to think it over?' Raising a warning hand. 'I beg you not to lose your temper, Mr Craddock. The last thing we want is for Ruth to come back to the sound of angry voices. I do urge you to keep your options open.'

She had him by the short hairs, and he knew it, controlling rage with an effort. 'I'm a busy man,' he said. 'With a report to write for the next packet. I will give myself the pleasure of waiting on you when it has sailed. But I make no promises of any kind.'

'I count on your good sense.' She had risen to say goodbye, now turned to the window, her attention drawn by increased noise from the river. 'There is something for your report, Mr Craddock, Dom Pedro is moving south at last.'

Unlike the Wares' house, the offices of Gomez and Daughter were on the land side of the Rua Nova Dos Inglesas, not far from the English Factory, the social and business centre of Englishmen in Oporto. As a result, Greville, busy trying to work out some kind of financial security for Caterina, was not aware of the movement of troops across the river until a clerk came in to announce a visitor.

'Mr Craddock to see you, sir. And, sir, Dom Pedro's troops are crossing the river.'

'Are they, by God! That's wonderful news. Yes, show Mr Craddock in, Wells, and send me up a bottle of best white port.' It was odd to realize how little he was looking forward to this meeting with his old friend.

'Craddock! It's good to see you!' He felt his greeting a little too warm, but Jeremy Craddock seemed to notice nothing, returning his handshake with an equally firm one.

'I'm delighted to find you here still, Faulkes. I confess I never thought to do so.' They had been on christian names, old school friends, when Jeremy persuaded the younger Greville to undertake the management of Caterina's affairs over twenty years before, but had hardly met since, and not at all for the last ten years, during which Jeremy had made great strides in the world and Greville had stayed quietly in Oporto.

'I like it here and, besides, Caterina has needed me.'

'You were always a good fellow. I knew she would be safe with you at her side. Though, mind you, I have heard some disquieting rumours since I've been here this time. Can those old brutes really have died without making provision for her?'

'It's public knowledge.' Greville made a little business of pouring white port for them both. If his old friend had come to pump him about Caterina's affairs he was going to get nowhere.

'Monstrous. Your very good health. What does Lewis say about it all? And how much does he know?'

'There's been no time to talk to him. And if they have really marched south today, there won't be for a while.' He did not propose to answer the second question. How could he? He knew so little. Caterina never spoke of Lewis's father. Indeed it had been Jeremy himself who had told him of the rash teenage marriage, in England, when he asked him to take little Lewis out to Oporto. And what a hideous journey that had been. And plenty of gossip at the end of it, of course, but he had always refused to listen.

'I'll believe in a march south when I see it,' said Jeremy. 'And as for Lewis, he was always a spoiled, turbulent boy and it didn't look last night as if the man was much different. You weren't there for the dancing, were you, so you didn't have the pleasure of seeing him competing with Dom Pedro for the favours of young Ruth Emerson. Not the way to endear himself to his chief. And if I were Caterina I would not much like the idea of Ruth Emerson as a daughter-in-law either. I could tell you things about her mother—'

'I would much rather you did not,' said Greville. 'And the girl seemed well enough, and modest too, for such a beauty.'

'You were always too tolerant for your own good. Delicious port. Is it true that you and young Frank Ware got most of your stock across river the other day?'

'Yes, Frank's idea, and a very good one.'

'I should say so! There was talk in England before I came away of a loan to Dom Pedro secured on the wine stocks here in Oporto. It would be a disaster for the liberal cause if they were to fall into Miguelite hands.' He rose. 'Thanks for the port. Do you fancy strolling down to the Wares' with me for a view of what is happening across the river? I hardly had a chance to speak to young Frank last night, though I danced with that poor pretty scarred sister of his. Now that was young Lewis at his worst, if you like.'

'He was very young,' said Greville. 'And he regrets it bitterly.'

'That don't help the girl much. Pity she's not a Catholic really, then she could go into a convent and be done with it. If you and the Wares are the only ones with wine on this side of the river you are going to be on to a good enough thing so you can fund Caterina, and Frank can look after his sister.'

'Caterina would never take such funding. No, I won't come, Craddock. I have work to do here.'

Left alone, Greville drank another glass of port without even noticing that he had done so. Then he went back to thinking angry, constructive thoughts about Caterina's finances.

Jeremy Craddock did not go to the Wares' house either. He had much to think about. Rachel Emerson's threats had caught him between wind and water. He had thought that old scandal safely left behind in Brazil, now he had to calculate, fast, how much harm she could do him. There was no real evidence. He had seen to that, ruthlessly. It would come down to her word against his. He thought about this, with cold intensity, for some time. Nothing was going to make him marry Ruth Emerson. He had decided that at once, but was marriage perhaps the answer? Marriage not to Ruth, but to Caterina. Intolerably, Rachel Emerson had been right in a great deal of what she said. He did intend a career in politics, always had.

And the right wife would make a vast difference as well as helping to scotch any rumour that Rachel Emerson might try to put about. Besides, as a married man, could he not, perhaps, do something quietly for the daughter? Or at least let Rachel Emerson think he meant to do so? It should do well enough after all: an elegant, intelligent wife who adored him, and his long, frustrated passion for her to explain his failure to marry before, to excuse any small side slippings in the meantime. It would do very well, and, he congratulated himself, he had made a good beginning with Caterina yesterday without realizing he was doing so.

His mind made up, he went down to the waterfront to pick up the latest word on the quay. 'They've got them on the run, sir.' An old fisherman looked up from the net he was mending. 'I doubt they'll stop this side of Coimbra. Folk in the big houses up the hill will be able to sleep snug in their beds tonight.'

'Are you sure?'

'Certain sure. It was warm work over there for a while, but, see, all's quiet now and our flag flying from the Serra and the fort at San Antonio downriver.'

It was true. Straining his eyes, Jeremy could see the blue and white flag of the liberals flying from the fortress monastery high up on the other side of the river from which Wellington had launched his attack on the French over twenty years ago.

'That's good news indeed,' he said. 'Are the liberals following them?'

'I'm not just so sure of that, sir. Evening will tell us. But at least with both banks clear a man will be able to fish again. That's what I care about. A man must live. Oh, thank you kindly, sir.' He took the handful of small coins as Jeremy turned away to walk uphill to the Sanchez Palace.

He found Caterina and her two friends surrounded by callers, and was glad of the forethought that had equipped him with the latest news. Inevitably it propelled the group from the comparative coolness of Caterina's saloon to the afternoon heat of the terrace. The Serra was not visible from here, but the flag on San Antonio was there for those with sharp eyes to see.

'That's wonderful!' exclaimed the plump, cheerful middle-aged

English woman who had been introduced to him as Mrs Procter the day before. 'I really wonder if I do not dare go home and unpack. I've been under starting orders for the English ships for longer than I like now, with everything at sixes and sevens in the house. It will be good to be able to settle down again. You must come and dine with us just as soon as the roads are safe, Mrs Fonsa. Dear Harriet will show you the way, I am sure. And my good friend Hetta must come too, and Frank if he can spare the time.'

'I am sure we shall all be delighted,' said Caterina with grave courtesy, concealing her amusement at this surprise invitation. Was it the return of her son or entertaining Dom Pedro that had suddenly made her respectable?

Mrs Procter's departure started the other guests moving, all except Jeremy Craddock. 'May I take the liberty of an old friend and stay a while to hear all your news?' He hesitated, wondering if he dared call her Caterina and equally doubtful if he could get the right note of calm conviction into using her adopted name of Fonsa, since they both knew, and knew the other knew, how little claim she had to it. Marriage would be a good thing for her too, he thought. It was really all very promising. But how was he going to get rid of the Ware women, who were, after all, his hostesses as well as Caterina's guests?

'Yes, do stay a while, Mr Craddock,' said Caterina. 'But it's too hot out here at this time of day. Let's move back in, and, Hetta dear, would you ask Carlotta to send us some iced lemonade? Unless you'd like something stronger?' To Jeremy.

'No, lemonade would be delicious. Just the thing.' He was pleased and surprised to see Hetta murmur something to her mother and the two women move away together to deliver the message. He would have been less pleased if he had heard what Hetta had said.

Left alone with him, Caterina led the way into a small, cool room on the north side of the house, where the first thing that caught his eye was a portrait of a much younger, beardless Lewis.

'But that's brilliant! Yours?' He regretted the hint of a question the moment it was spoken.

'You doubt it?'

'It looks like man's work. I thought for a moment it might be a late Lawrence.'

'Why, thank you. I'm a little ashamed of the Byron touch now. But Lewis was rebelling against everything when I painted it. Against being painted, among other things. I've never had such an impatient subject, nor painted so fast.'

'It's brilliant,' he said again, and meant it. She had painted her son full length, standing on a high place, the wind against him, hair and cloak blown back, right hand raised.

'What's he doing?' Jeremy asked.

'That's what I didn't understand. He was throwing a stone, Mr Craddock. I thought it a salute of some kind, boy's play, it was something much more dangerous. Next day he was arrested. You know what followed. I'll never forgive myself for being so stupid.' She had not meant to tell him this.

'You're incapable of stupidity.'

'You say that to me? Well, I do thank you. Ah, here is our lemonade.' They were silent as the maid filled glasses tinkling with ice and passed the inevitable little too-sweet cakes.

'Caterina,' he took the plunge as he had planned. 'It has been so long. Too long, I know. But what could I do, impoverished adventurer that I was? I did not even feel I had the right to tell you that all my work, all my thoughts were for you. And, besides,' ruefully, 'you had told me that all yours would be concentrated on bringing up your son. He's a man now, and you must be proud of him, but it is time to be thinking of yourself a little, and of me, Caterina, who have thought of you all these years. And I have heard a piece of news since I came that gives me selfish pleasure.'

'Oh?' She looked at him thoughtfully over her glass.

'That neither of those old wretches left you a scudo, after all your pains for them. I have been making my fortune so I could match it to yours, ask you as an equal. Now, when at last I am free to speak, when I come here to do so, I find that you have none, that it is all left to that impulsive son of yours. My foot is on the ladder now, I am promised office in London when I return, and, forgive the boast, I'm a rich man. I did not waste my time in Brazil; there was money there for the making, for a man with his wits about him.'

'Which you always were.'

Something in her tone alerted him. 'Caterina, I am doing this all wrong. Forgive me. I've rehearsed this scene in my mind so often, and now I find myself doing it all back to foremost. The important thing, the only thing is that I love you, have always loved you—'

'Oh, Mr Craddock—' She put out a hand to silence him. 'What a whopper! What would Rachel Emerson say about that?'

'Young man's moonshine.' Impatiently. 'And just look at her now! An old woman while you are more beautiful than ever – a woman to be proud of—'

'A Catholic. Had you perhaps forgotten that? Not the ideal wife for a man making his way in politics.'

He had forgotten, and cursed himself, but made a good recovery. 'Everything has changed since the old king's death and the Act of '49. Tolerance is the word now—' Again something in the quality of her silence warned him that he was on dangerous ground. 'You'd have to tolerate me, Caterina. I've not much faith left after the life I have led, but I would be happy to respect yours. And – as to children – I long for children [and there was a lie if ever there was one] – perhaps a division by sex?'

'You mean, boys Protestant and girls Catholic?' It was exactly what he had meant. 'You are going entirely too fast for me, Mr Craddock. You give me no time to answer. If you have been planning these pretty speeches for twenty years, it is more than I have imagined. You took your own path, and I am sure you were right to do so when you accepted Wellington's offer and persuaded Greville Faulkes to bring little Lewis to me instead of coming yourself. That changed everything, did it not, though perhaps we did not realize it at the time?'

'But, Caterina, be fair. You had asked for a year to think my proposal over. And interpreting for Wellington was the chance of a lifetime.'

'And next year you were involved in that bloody, unsuccessful siege of Burgos and quite rightly thought you could not ask for leave of absence, even to propose to a lady.'

'I wrote to you.'

'A most moving letter. I have it still. Somewhere.' For a while, she had known it by heart. 'But by then I knew what a problem I had with little Lewis, after those first dreadful years in the orphanage. Poor little thing, he had just learned to speak dreadful cockney English and fight for every crust he needed, and then he found himself plunged into Portuguese and a battle between two selfish old grandparents as to who could spoil him worst.'

'I'd have been a father to him, Caterina. What he needed. Still does. But it's not too late. Give me the right and I'll be able to show him that he's not the only grape on the vine, teach him to be a man among men.'

'I think the army will do that, if it is needed.' Caterina had remembered Jeremy's letter now. There had not been a word about little Lewis in it from start to finish. It had made answering it much easier, though she had cried, she remembered, at the time.

'Of course he can do no wrong in your eyes,' said Jeremy. 'Just returned to you after so long. It is longer still since I have seen you, but, Caterina, not a day has passed when I have not thought of you, dreamed of you, dreamed of doing this—' He meant to pull her to him, but failed somehow.

'Too quick, Mr Craddock. You go too fast for me. Remember, it is ten years since we met and I have to say I have not spent them dreaming of you. I've been too busy.' She poured more lemonade for him. 'But I do thank you for finding me Greville Faulkes. He has been a tower of strength to me.'

'He was always a good fellow.' He considered, and dismissed, the idea of putting on a jealous scene and did not at all realize that she had recognized this.

'The best,' she said. 'He's been my right hand, both in the business and over my work.'

'Your work?' Surprised.

'Yes. Lewis is not my only subject. I've turned portrait painter while you have been making your fortune. It's not making mine, I can tell you, but it has kept me sane during these last years when Lewis has been in exile. It's raised some eyebrows, here in Porto, as you will imagine, but Greville has helped immensely by acting as my agent, dealing with the business aspect of it for me.'

'You mean you paint for money?' Now she really had shocked him.

'Yes.' Cheerfully. 'But not nearly enough. I don't command the prices Mr Lawrence got, but it pays for my materials, and a little bit over. I cannot begin to tell you how I enjoy it. That picture of Lewis has been worth its weight in gold – well,' laughing, 'in scudos, in commissions. All the noble mothers wanted their sons to look like him. And I have a good line in charming young ladies, too.'

'You will hardly have used young Hetta Ware as your model for those. Caterina—' He had no idea how furious this had made her. 'We have strayed from the point. Of course, you must go on with your painting. I know a coming young man called Landseer who might give you some hints. In London, of course, where you will be safe. I am afraid you are going to rue the day when young Lewis plunged himself and you into the liberal camp. Frankly, Caterina, nothing I have seen so far fills me with much optimism for their future.'

'I hope you are not going to write in those gloomy terms to Palmerston.'

'It may be my duty to do so. As it will be my pleasure to offer a home in London to you and Lewis, and all your friends, if, as I expect, Dom Pedro is soundly beaten by his brother Miguel and leaves Oporto with his tail between his legs. I promise you, Caterina, my house and my heart are large enough to have a welcome for you all.' He put down his glass. One more try. 'Think again, Caterina. Make me the happiest of men; say you will be mine, and I'll write by the next packet to order a studio with a north view.'

'And lessons from Mr Landseer? You go altogether too fast for me, Mr Craddock. We are strangers now, you and I; we have both changed. You are on the path to fortune. I am a woman in her middle years with a grown-up son. You may well be right about Lewis; perhaps he does need a father. Perhaps I do need a husband. Jeremy,' she used his first name at last, 'I do not know you. Let us make friends again. Give me time, as I asked you before.'

'If you insist,' he said. 'But this time, Caterina, I shall come back.' He took her hand and was about to kiss it when the door of the room was thrown open and Lewis burst in. 'Mother, I'm back! I've seen active service at last— Oh, I beg your pardon. How do you do, Mr Craddock? We sent them packing, I can tell you. They must be halfway to Coimbra by now. The duke sent me to thank you for yesterday, Mother.'

'He is in full pursuit of the enemy then?' asked Jeremy.

'Well – no. Some of us did wish to go on, while we had them on the run, but more cautious councils have prevailed. Sometimes I wish the duke had left his band of greybeard councillors behind on Terceira.'

'He might not thank you for saying so,' said Jeremy dryly.

'Of course not. Only among friends, Mr Craddock. Mother, I have another message from the duke. He asks for linen—'

'Linen?'

'Old sheets, anything, for bandages.'

Chapter 4

Jeremy Craddock walked back into town feeling satisfied with a start well made. Caterina had not said yes, but she had not really said no either. He rather thought that the irruption of young Lewis had been well timed from his point of view. They had all been subdued after that by the sudden reality of bloodshed; it had been no time for talk of marriage. And he was most certainly in no hurry. He had to decide what to say to Rachel Emerson before he announced his engagement to Caterina. It must be bribery, he thought, unless he could find some secret of hers to hold in exchange. Granted her past, this was a hopeful enough possibility. He must play for time, and look about him.

It was pleasant to be able to walk along the Rua Nova dos Inglesas without worrying about rifle fire from the opposite bank. He passed the Wares' house and went on to the English Factory, where, as he had expected, he found the arcaded loggia crowded with merchants eagerly discussing the events of the day. Frank Ware was there in animated talk with a group of older men. Joining them, Jeremy heard Frank's voice rise: 'Even if it does mean it's not the best vintage ever, at least it will be there for the drinking. Or the selling!'

'Like yours, you mean,' said an older man Jeremy recognized as John Procter. 'Shaken and stirred and tasteless. You want us to imitate your rashness so that we are all in the same boat. Is that not it, my boy?'

'No need for panic,' said another man. 'The Miguelites are pretty well down to Coimbra tonight, by all one hears. We shan't see them back in a hurry.'

'I do hope you are right,' said Frank. 'I'd agree with you if Dom Pedro and his men were camped behind them, but they are back in town congratulating themselves on a glorious victory. It's not what Wellington would have done.'

'We all know who is your hero,' said Procter. 'Even if he did disappoint you over the Reform Bill you were so mad for. You'll be glad to be able to get your womenfolk safe back home tomorrow, I'm sure. A splendid party, mind you—' There was a little pause while everyone wondered just what he was going to say next.

'I've just come from the Sanchez Palace,' Jeremy intervened. 'I met your wife there, Mr Procter.'

'That's right, she said she'd be calling today. Splendid party,' Procter said again, rather more as if he meant it. 'An old friend of yours, I believe, Madame Fonsa?'

'A relation, Mr Procter. We are cousins. And a good friend too, I hope I may say. A most talented lady.'

'She needs to be,' said a voice from the crowd.

'I beg your pardon?' Jeremy was aware of Frank, rigid at his side. 'You have something to say about my cousin, sir?' There was a little silence. 'No? Good. I'm the head of her family, I suppose, since her father died. Anyone who has anything to say about her, should say it to me. Frank, shall we go? As to the wine these gentlemen mean to leave at risk on the wrong side of the river, that is strictly their own affair.'

'Parcel of ignorant buffoons.' Frank had waited until they were further down the street to explode. 'Thank you, sir, for intervening, or I might have said something I'd have regretted. I have to do business with them after all. Josiah Bankes was there. In fact I rather thought—'

'Best not to,' advised Jeremy. 'Gossip's a curious thing. Once started, impossible to stop. So, best not started. Specially not with a powder-keg like young Lewis ready to go off at the slightest touch.'

'Goodness,' said Frank. 'I had not thought of that.' He laughed, surprising Jeremy. 'And I wager nor had Josiah Bankes.'

'If it was Josiah Bankes.'

'As you say.' They had reached his house now and the conversation ceased as the door was flung open to receive them. Indoors, over a glass of wine, Frank reopened it. 'Sir, I had forgotten you were Aunt Caterina's cousin. She told us not to call her that,' he remembered.

'No, you are grown up now. It's a surprise. I remember you all as children, you and Lewis and your delightful sister.'

'Dear Hetta. But the thing is, sir, there's something I have always wanted to know, but it's not just what one could ask one's mother, specially when she's such a good friend of Caterina's. But you're her cousin, you were here, all those years ago when it happened, weren't you?'

'I was indeed.' Jeremy was thinking hard. 'It's a long time ago.'

'Yes, but it still casts its shadow. Well, you heard Josiah Bankes—'

'If it was Josiah Bankes—'

'Oh, it was, but let's not go into that. But the case is, I'd be able to deal with that kind of smear so much better if I knew what the real facts of the matter were.'

'Yes, I can see that.' This was a young man to be reckoned with. No use hoping to fob him off with a lot of easy lies. 'The thing is, I had left Oporto when it all came out. Wellington sent for me to act as his interpreter, it was not something one could refuse.'

'I should rather think not. I cannot tell you how I envy you working for him. But didn't he have something to do with it all? I've heard some extraordinary tales of a party at our house, and an assassination attempt. All connected, somehow with my poor grandmother's madness. And all hushed up because of it.'

'Poor old lady.' Jeremy saw his way. 'That's the difficulty, Frank, your grandmother was involved in the plot against Wellington, I am sorry to say. It was a crowning mercy that her mind went when it did; it made it much easier to hide her away and hush things up. I'm sorry—' He could see how hard this had hit the young man. 'You can see why people are reluctant to talk to you about it.'

'My grandmother involved in a plot against Wellington? I can't believe it.'

'True, I am afraid, but she was a stupid woman; she really had no idea of what she was doing. She had fallen into the toils of her dressmaker, who was a French spy. She simply let herself be black-mailed and used. It was Caterina's courage that saved the day. She was kidnapped from a party, you see, here in this house, held as hostage in the attics, Wellington to give his life for hers.'

'Good God! But what happened?'

'We couldn't stop him; you're quite right to admire that man; but Caterina talked her way out of it. That's a remarkable woman.'

'Oh, I know that. And the kidnappers?'

'Were arrested, but the leader escaped. I always wondered whether that was not perhaps connived at. It was immensely awkward, you see, he was old Madame Fonsa's grandson, Luiz da Fonsa y Sanchez. He had thrown in his lot with the French as some young liberals did. You cannot imagine what an upheaval it meant. All kinds of things came out as a result. Everyone had thought that Madame Fonsa was in her dotage, but it turned out that she was very much in command of herself, it was her son-in-law, Sanchez, who was in the last lunatic stages of the pox, poor fellow. She had been trying to conceal it, keeping things going, building all her hopes on her grandson.'

'Oh, the poor woman,' said Frank. 'I liked her, you know, we used to enjoy going up there to play with Lewis; you could talk to her. She listened. Not like old Gomez, Caterina's father. He was a curmudgeon if ever I met one.'

'That was the trouble,' said Jeremy. 'I brought Caterina back from school in England, you know, on his instructions. He was hell bent on having an heir for his vineyards; told Caterina she must marry or be put in a convent. The silent sisters.'

'No!'

'Yes. What we none of us knew was that Caterina was married already, an idiotic boy and girl affair, back in England, and a child there.'

'Lewis!'

'Precisely. Don't ask me who the father was; that is Caterina's secret. The old lady decided to adopt Lewis as her heir, disinheriting her grandson. All the money was hers by then, you see. Her son-in-law had squandered the Sanchez estate, but she had managed to keep the Fonsa money intact. She always had the best lawyers in town. I was away, of course, campaigning with Wellington while all this was going on. The next thing I knew was that Caterina had become Fonsa instead of Gomez and her little Lewis was being brought up as Lewis da Gomez y Fonsa, heir to both estates.'

'What about Gomez?'

'He wanted the boy, too, once he knew about him, hence the Gomez. Well, you must remember what it was like for Lewis when he was a boy. Caterina used to write me about it, but there wasn't much she could do between those two formidable old tyrants, not even Caterina.'

'But what about his father, sir?' Frank asked the question Jeremy had hoped to avoid.

'Caterina never mentions him. I have always assumed he was dead. Killed in the war no doubt. I am counting on you not to say a word of this to anyone, Frank, not even to your mother and sister. Caterina has trodden a difficult enough path all these years without having the old stories raked up now. You know what Oporto is like for gossip, and she is particularly vulnerable, living as she does between the Portuguese and English communities. And then her painting—' His eye had been caught by a portrait of Hetta hanging over the chimney piece.

'I know,' said Frank ruefully. 'She's too good at it, is the trouble. The old tabbies would forgive her if she did pretty little daubs, views of the harbour or the sunset across the bay, but when she catches their character, or their daughters', they don't much like it. You can't go wrong with Hetta, of course, the face is the character.'

'It was brave to show the scar.' Jeremy was glad of the new direction the talk had taken.

'Hetta made her. Clever to do it three-quarter view like that, so it doesn't dominate the face as it does in real life. Poor Hetta. And poor Lewis too,' he went on surprisingly. 'It changed him, I think.'

'For the better, I hope.' He rose, seizing the moment to escape before Frank asked any more awkward questions. 'This isn't getting my report written.'

'I am glad you have good news for it. There's talk that Mendizabal is in London trying to raise a loan to fund troops and supplies for the liberal cause. Good news from here will make all the difference to his chances of getting it.'

'I just wish it was better. And I must write as I find. You were absolutely right about that wine across the river, Frank, but I didn't feel it my place to say anything, neutral as I am supposed to be. Must be seen to be. That wine of course is the security on which any loan would be based, and what kind of security is it while it is so exposed to the enemy?'

'Not our enemy, remember,' Frank intervened. 'I'm supposed to be neutral too, but it is difficult. Specially when I think about my father's death.'

'I know. Would you feel you could stay here if the Miguelites were to take the city?'

'Let's not think about that. Thank God, it seems much less likely today than it did yesterday, as one dodged rifle shot in the side streets.'

'Yes. Now that threat is lifted, I feel I can thank you for your great kindness and say I must find rooms of my own. It seemed craven to do so when you were actually under fire, but I am sure you will understand that as a government representative I must be on my own ground.'

'Not staying with visibly unneutral neutrals like us? Yes, I do see, though we will be sorry to lose you. Let's just hope that this enemy retreat is the beginning of the end.'

'Did I interrupt something?' Lewis asked, when Jeremy Craddock had left and his mother had rung to tell Carlotta to start getting out linen. 'You looked very serious, the two of you.'

'He was offering us hospitality in case we should find ourselves in exile.'

'What an idiotic idea! There's a kind of caution about that man I don't much like, Mother, even if he is an old friend of yours. Anyway, he's gone, thank goodness. He did have the sense to see he wasn't wanted. There's more to the duke's message, but I didn't want to go into it with Craddock there listening and ready to report straight back to England. Which he will, don't ever forget. It's what he's here for.'

'What's wrong with that?' But she had thought of this herself.

'Nothing, if he does it fair and square. Well—' He thought about it. 'I'm not so sure, actually; there are things might put volunteers off coming, and we do need every man we can get. The thing is, it's not just bandages they need at the hospital down the road, they need everything. Half the staff ran with the Miguelites.'

'Nuns,' said Caterina, 'of course. What did Dom Pedro expect after that proclamation of his against the religious orders? But is it very bad there, Lewis?'

'Terrible! Filthy. Disorganised. No food, no bandages, nothing. Mother, I told the duke I was sure, when you heard, you would go and see what could be done?'

'Oh, you did, did you?'

'What's Lewis done now?' Hetta asked the question as she and her mother came into the room.

'Only suggested to the Duke of Braganza that I might take an interest in affairs at St Antony's Hospital. Apparently everything's at sixes and sevens there, and the wounded beginning to come in.'

'I know,' said Hetta gravely. 'Carlotta told me. I'm so glad to see you safe, Lewis. Was it very dreadful?'

'Yes,' he said, and there was a little silence. 'It's not glorious at all,' he went on. 'War. Specially not when you are all the same really. I had no idea. We took some prisoners. I knew one of them. He's wounded; he's in the hospital. Mother—'

'We'll certainly go and see how things are there, when the linen is ready. Hetta, be a love and see how Carlotta is getting on. And tell Tomas we'll need men and handcarts to take it. But, Lewis, I cannot promise to take charge there; I have my own work, after all.'

'Your work?'

'Yes, my painting. I live by it.'

'What in the world do you mean? Your painting more important than St Antony's, than the wounded, than the duke's request! He thought you the ideal person, said so himself.'

'Aunt Caterina—' Hetta had returned from her errand to hear the end of Lewis's increasingly furious speech. 'Suppose you let me act as your secretary, your second in command? Please? You are the perfect person, you know, both English and Portuguese. And

Catholic. I know of several nuns who are hiding, probably starving here in Oporto since their convents were closed. They are of liberal families, they can't throw in their lot with the Miguelites—'

'And I suppose their families don't want them back on their hands,' broke in Lewis savagely. 'There's loving Catholicism for you, Mother. But it's a wonderful idea, Hetta. If you know some, they will know more. It's a vast barrack of an unfinished building, St Antony's, I'm sure the duke would arrange living-quarters there for nursing nuns if you could find them, Hetta. And you would take charge, Mother?'

'What do you say?' Caterina asked Harriet, who had been a silent but deeply concerned listener. 'It would mean that Hetta would have to stay here with me, I think, handy for the hospital, and you know how delighted I would be to have her.'

'If Hetta really wants to do it,' said Harriet. 'Who am I to object? And of course she must stay with you, Caterina. I'd been meaning to ask if she might anyway. The waterfront is all very well for an old widow like me, but I doubt it's the place for her.'

'Oh you'll be all right down there, now, Aunt Harriet,' said Lewis comfortably. 'I don't think the enemy liked the reality of war any more than we did. Bit of luck it is all over now bar the negotiating between the two brothers, but it's best to be prepared just the same. I can't tell you how grateful the duke is going to be, Mother.'

'Good. Then tell him there is one condition: if he stays in town, I want to paint his portrait.'

'You have agreed to take over the hospital.' Calling next day Greville was appalled. 'You are off your head, Caterina!'

'I do so agree with you, but there seemed to be nothing else for it. And Hetta undertakes to do the real work, bless her. She has got together a skeleton staff of nuns already. I had no idea she was so active among the poor. She seems to be in touch with women all over town, on every level of society, who will be glad to help. I'll just be the figurehead, the respectable old lady in charge. I won't let it interrupt my morning's work, I promise you.'

'That's a relief. And, of course, we all hope the hospital won't be seriously needed. I know the duke hasn't received the overwhelming welcome he hoped for, but supplies and volunteers are beginning to come in, and there's not been a move from the Miguelites.'

'No offer of negotiations?'

'Well, no. I did hear a rumour that Miguel himself was on his way from Lisbon to join his troops. If he is, they would be bound to wait for him.'

'Yes, indeed. But, Greville, I've been thinking; if talk about the Miguelites reaches us, is the same thing happening the other way? Will they know how disorganized things are here?'

'Bound to soon enough, I am afraid. There are plenty of fishermen on the river who don't much care on which bank they land their catch. That's why it's such a good thing the Miguelites have been cleared from the south bank. But there are market-women coming in with supplies too. There are bound to be some spies among them. I just hope we have some of our own, going out.'

'Horrid,' she said. 'But I suppose you are right.'

Lewis paid a call that evening. His knowledge of the city made him invaluable to the duke as a kind of high-level errand boy and he had spent the day on a series of not very successful missions to such of the nobility as had not actually fled. They were all delighted to see him and hear his news. Some, but not many of them, had been at Caterina's party and sent civil messages to her. They all read the duke's offers of high office with calm courtesy and with equal courtesy made it clear that they were still hedging their bets. The last of these frustrating missions left him with a little time on his hands. He was up near the cathedral, and, as always, an open market was in full swing on the bare rock just below it. He stopped and bought two little nosegays, thinking how odd it was that market-women were still bringing them in from the country to sell in this time of war. Then he ran a repressive hand through his unruly black hair and beard and strode swiftly down the steep alley to the house where the Emersons lived.

Knocking on the door of their apartment he was surprised and not pleased to have it opened by Frank Ware, who had obviously also brought a bouquet, since Ruth was arranging flowers in a vase.

'Mr Fonsa.' Rachel Emerson greeted him warmly. 'Or must I call you *senhor*? Either way, how good of you to have come to reassure us that you are none the worse for yesterday's gallant action. We held our breath for you, my Ruth and I, when we saw your gallant little band marching out across the river. Mr Ware says you have sent those Miguelite rascals packing clear down to Coimbra. It's wonderful news. We can all sleep easy tonight.' She had taken the flowers from him as she spoke and handed them to her daughter. 'You are too good to us, both of you, and both of you with so much on your hands. Mr Ware was telling us he has quite failed to persuade the other merchants that now is the moment to get their wine across river as he did his and your clever mother's. Do please tell her how infinitely grateful Ruth and I were for her invitation to that delightful party. I am ashamed not to have called yesterday – she will think me quite a barbarian – but dear Ruth had one of her heads and I could not possibly either take her with me or leave her alone in this dangerous city. You will make our apologies to your mother, Mr Fonsa?'

'Yes, indeed. She will be so sorry. But you mustn't think it a dangerous city, Mrs Emerson. I was just thinking as I bought the flowers for you in the market how peaceful it all seems.'

'Seems, yes, but what is the reality? Mr Ware has been telling us a sad tale about the hospital out beyond where your mother lives. He was commissioned by his sister to ask if Ruth and I felt we could help in any way, which of course we mean to do just as soon as Ruth is well again. And that puts me in mind of an old friend of mine, who lives down by the river, near the bridge of boats. If I were to scribble a quick note to her, would you perhaps be so good as to deliver it on your way home, Mr Ware? I am sure Francesca would be more than happy to join in the good work, and it does sound as if dear Madame Fonsa is going to need all the help she can get.'

'I'm afraid so,' said Frank. 'I'll be delighted to take it for you.'

'I knew I could count on you. Then, if you will excuse me, gentlemen, I'll leave my daughter to entertain you while I write dear Francesca. Show them your drawings, Ruth. I can tell you two good friends that I was quite surprised when I fetched her from school this spring to find what a talented child I had.'

'Oh, Mother!' protested Ruth. 'It's only what we all did.' But her mother had picked up a portfolio from the corner of the room and plumped it down on the central table. For Ruth, embarrassment at her lack of skill as an artist was lost in the disconcerting experience of finding herself entertaining two handsome young men single-handed. She was glad enough to let them riffle through her drawings of school friends and exclaim over her little sketches of buildings in Boston, where she had been to school.

'I like drawing buildings best,' she confided shyly, when Frank praised a sketch of what she told him was Faneuil Hall in Boston. 'They don't move for one thing. I don't know how your mother does it, Mr Fonsa. That picture of you that hangs in her parlour – it's wonderful! Did you sit for hours – or stand rather?'

'Nothing of the kind. I was the devil of a sitter – forgive me, Miss Emerson. Always wanting to be off with my friends – you remember, Frank—'

'I do indeed.' There was a little silence as Frank remembered his father's death, and Lewis, sorry at having blundered, turned back to the portfolio. 'Why, here's the bridge of boats, and a speaking likeness if ever there was one. I am glad you are turning your pen to our sights, Miss Emerson. But you've not got the fortifications on the Serra quite right, you know. It's a very interesting study in perspective. Come and look.' He reached down a masterful hand to draw her up from her chair and lead her out on to the balcony to see the bridge of boats and the Serra monastery beyond and above it, lit up by the setting sun. 'Do you see?' Returning to the table he picked up a crayon and made a few bold corrections. 'There and there—'

'What in the world are you doing?' Mrs Emerson returned to the room.

'Giving your daughter a lesson in perspective, ma'am. I hope you don't mind.'

'You inherit your mother's talent then? But I am afraid I have let you tire out my invalid. Here is my note for dear Francesca if you would be so good, Mr Ware? I suppose in fact you two gentlemen go the same way, do you not? How are you finding life at the Franciscans', Mr Fonsa?'

'The very walls seem to hate us,' he said, surprising himself.

'I'm sorry. Perhaps I should not have asked. I remember the church there so well, and all that extravagant gilding. I just hope the Duke of Braganza does not decide to go one step further and strip that to pay for his campaign. Or the silver altar in the cathedral that escaped the French all those years ago.'

'What an appalling idea! He's still a Catholic, Mrs Emerson, but a liberal one. Anyway, there is talk that Palmela is going to England to help Mendizabal arrange for funds. I am sure our churches are safe.'

'Of course they are. I was only teasing. Which reminds me of something I meant to say to Francesca and quite forgot. Give me my note again for a moment, Mr Ware. And, tell me, are your mother and sister back home with you yet?'

'Not yet. My sister stays with Madame Fonsa so as to be handy for the hospital. It is just along the road from them, if you remember.'

'No. I don't think I have ever seen it.' She had opened the note and added to it as he spoke. 'There, Mr Ware. Can you read the direction? It's in one of the alleys just above the bridge of boats. Anyone will tell you. I'm most grateful. It has been such a pleasure to see you two gentlemen, and we count on you, Ruth and I, to come and cheer up two lone ladies when you have the time, busy as we know you both are.'

'Charming women,' said Lewis, as they made their way down the dark stair.

'Yes, but what bad luck to find themselves in Oporto just at this moment. Mrs Emerson was telling me, before you came, that she had planned this European tour as a little treat for her daughter on leaving school, and they came here first because of all her happy memories of the place. With no idea, of course, of what was brewing here.'

'Well, few people had,' said Lewis. 'I suppose she means to make a good European marriage for the girl. Lord knows she's beautiful enough to catch herself a duke if she wants one.'

'Which I doubt.' Frank looked at the note in his hand as they reached the bottom of the steep lane down from the Emersons' building. 'Not a very salubrious address for a friend of Mrs Emerson's. I thought it was all shacks and tenement living above the bridge of boats.'

'An old servant, I expect. Working women are what we are really going to need up at St Antony's, not ladies who swoon at a little blood.'

'You won't find Caterina swooning,' said Frank. 'Nor Hetta either, I can tell you.' He was suddenly out of patience with his old friend, and was glad, when they reached his house, that Lewis refused his inevitable offer of hospitality.

'No, no, I must get back to barracks, thanks.'

'Odd to think of the Franciscans' as barracks.'

'Yes, even the troops are a bit subdued. Long may it last.'

Frank was delighted to find his mother at home before him, but when he told her where he had been it got him an anxious look. 'Frank, dear, you know I wouldn't dream of interfering in your affairs—'

He smiled at her lovingly and poured her a glass of wine. 'But you are going to just the same.'

'I wish now I had spoken sooner. It was such a shock, having Rachel Emerson turn up like that, and there had been so much to do, but I have to tell you, Frank, that when she was here before we thought nothing of her, Caterina and I. She was posing as a healer of some kind and that husband of hers was a terrible man. I never quite knew the rights of it, but in the end I know Jeremy Craddock got them out of town by paying their fares to America, and we were glad to see them go.'

'And not best pleased to see Mrs Emerson back,' said her son. 'I grant you she is a bit of an antidote – I hate gushing women. But the daughter is something else again. She seems to have spent most of her time at boarding-school, away from her parents' influence. Shy as be damned – Lewis came in while I was there, by the way. Bearing flowers.'

'Did he so? I wonder what Caterina will say to that.'

'We're grown up now, Lewis and I,' her son reminded her. 'Mother, I have something to tell you. I hope you don't mind. I got

Craddock to tell me about the plot against Wellington all those years ago and how splendid Caterina was. And about my grand-mother.'

'Poor woman,' said Harriet. 'Her madness was a crowning mercy.'

'That's what Craddock said, but it must have been terrible for Father.'

'Yes, it was. He went to see her every Sunday of his life. She never knew him, but he went just the same. When those brutes put him in prison she just pined and died. I went every Sunday, of course, in his place, but it was no good. She never did like me. I have to tell you, Frank, that I was relieved when she died. I'm ashamed to confess it, but I was. What else did Craddock tell you?'

'A little about Caterina's secret marriage in England. That was why I asked him, really. Josiah Bankes made one of those malicious remarks about her when I was at the Factory with Craddock this morning. You know the kind of thing; you must have heard them often enough. Not saying anything, but implying everything. It makes me furious. I wanted to know what ground I was on to resent them. Craddock was splendid, Mother. He took it up; said he was her cousin and head of her family. Bankes kept quiet and we all pretended we didn't know who had spoken. Craddock told me to go along with it; scandal more easily started than stopped in his opin-ion. I'll tell you one thing, Mother, the day I am twenty-one I am going to dismiss Josiah Bankes.'

'I can't say I shall be sorry to see him go. But in the meantime, do please remember there's almost a year to go until your birthday. Make the best of things, Frank, try not to let him see how you feel.'

'I'll do my best. But tell me, Mother, what are things like up at St Antony's?'

'Much worse than we had expected. Sometimes I despair of the Portuguese, Frank. A splendid new building, admirably planned—'

'By an Englishman,' interjected her son.

'That's true. I wonder if that was resented. I hadn't thought of that. It's not been finished; it's not been looked after; and it's not been cleaned. Caterina took one look at the main ward, if you can call it a ward, and sent Tomas back to fetch her entire staff of servants. When I came away, fires had been lit, water was boiling and a start was making on the first of the wards. With Hetta in charge,' she added, with justifiable pride. 'Most of the helpers who weren't from the Sanchez Palace were women she knows in the town, and very good workers they are too.'

'And Caterina?'

Harriet smiled at him. 'Caterina had to hurry home for Dom Pedro's first sitting. She made a portrait a condition of agreeing to take over at the hospital and he is actually complying.'

'Wise man,' said Frank.

Chapter 5

The duke was not an easy sitter. Still in his early thirties, he had lived hard and it was beginning to show. Caterina's keen eye took it all in: the hair carefully swept across the balding patch; the beard masking lines of dissipation on the face, the increasing girth concealed by a well-cut uniform. Worse still, from her point of view, was his awareness of all this. While treating her with what she felt was slightly excessive gallantry, he kept a sharp eye on the progress of the portrait. She was glad indeed that she had decided to paint him downstairs in her parlour where servants came and went, though callers were banned for the duration of the short sittings that were all he could give her.

He had struck, from the first, an heroic pose for her and she had been happy to go along with this. No need to let him know that upstairs in her studio she was working on another version that his wife or mistress might have found more like him.

'Admirable.' It was his third sitting and he had come round, as he so often did, to stand just too close behind her and study her work. 'It's going to be my ugly phiz to the life. Had you thought at all about the background? It's to be outdoors, I take it, like your admirable picture there of your son? And what am I holding?' His hand brushed her shoulder as he pointed at the picture and she was glad of her painting uniform of high-necked brown holland dress and heavy apron.

'I was going to ask you about that.' She moved a little away from him. 'In the main square, perhaps, with a crowd of suppliants around you? So, maybe holding the charter?'

'Or a sword?' He thought about it. 'No, I think you are right as always. The charter would be best; I come to bring not the sword, but peace. I am sure that my brother Miguel will understand that and give way now I am here in the flesh. Have you ever seen my brother?'

'I've not had that pleasure.' She picked up her brush as an indication that she would like to get back to work. It was unsettling to have him loom so closely behind her, exuding his own kind of rank male magnetism.

To her relief he took the hint and moved back to the improvised rostrum on which she had posed him. 'They used to call him the handsomest man in Brazil,' he told her. 'You'll do your best by me, won't you, brilliant lady? Make me the soldier I am, but no uglier than you must, and tell me, while you do so, why a lady of such charm and talent has never remarried.'

How do you snub royalty? She did not at all like the line the talk was taking and was more relieved than was quite comfortable when a servant burst into the room with a messenger close behind him.

'The enemy are across the Douro, sire, upriver, in strength. They have occupied Penafiel and are threatening our lines of communication. You are needed most urgently at the palace.'

Caterina was glad not to understand Dom Pedro's roar of what were clearly Brazilio-Portuguese imprecations. Recovering himself, he took his leave with swift courtesy, urging her to make what progress she could with the picture while he dealt with the enemy. 'I have no doubt we will find that the news is greatly exaggerated as always,' he told her. 'Some kind of skirmish upriver and the old women who come to market blowing it up out of all proportion.'

'I devoutly hope so, sire.'

'Oh, I am sure of it,' carelessly. 'My brother Miguel does not want it to come to serious blood-shedding any more than I do. We shall settle things admirably between us, I am sure.' He kissed her hand with a flourish. 'And all your sterling work at St Antony's wasted.'

'I should be happy to find it so.'

A few days of bloody fighting on the Vallongo road to the east of the town proved her right and Dom Pedro over optimistic. The hospital was filling with wounded men, each with his own story to tell. Friars and even women were fighting for the Miguelites, Hetta told Caterina, and the peasants, too, were proving unenthusiastic for the liberal cause, if not actually hostile. Acts of great individual gallantry were wasted because of an element of muddle in the high command.

'It sounds as if the only thing that saves the day,' said Hetta ruefully, 'is that the same is true of the Miguelite army. I really think this war is going to be won by the side that first gets properly organized – or maybe the one with the best spies. Someone told me that the Miguelites thought us much stronger than we actually are until a message reached them across the river, just the other day, telling the true state of the case. Hence this attack.'

'I wonder who sent it,' said Caterina a trifle vaguely. She had seized on Dom Pedro's absence to work ferociously on the cartoon of him upstairs in the studio and it occupied all her mind.

'It's formidable.' As always Greville Faulkes was the only person to see it. 'Can you finish it in time for the next packet? I wrote Mrs Wallis by the last one asking her to stand by for a quick engraving job next time. Prints of this in her bow window in St James's Street will do more for the liberal cause than enough bandages to stretch from here to Coimbra. It's masterly.'

'Mistressly?' Smiling at him. 'I do confess that I am pleased with it myself. I find I can do him so much better in cartoon than in straight portrait. In portrait the weaknesses of the man will out and I keep fighting it, and he notices, and it is all a little awkward, whereas up here I think of him as a symbol, not a mere man, and it practically draws itself. You don't think I have overdone it?' Anxiously. He was her only critic and she trusted his judgement.

'Not a bit. Have you ever seen Dom Miguel? You have made a wonderfully convincing devil of him.'

'No.' She smiled. 'Never. I asked his brother about him. The handsomest man in Brazil, he told me. That's why I have done him with his back to the audience, and I am afraid I have simply given him his brother's rakish characteristics.'

'While making an angel of Dom Pedro!' In her picture, the two figures confronted each other across a writhing, distorted map of Portugal. Dom Pedro, with just the hint of a halo from the sun behind him, held the charter. Miguel, a dark and louring figure, had the corpses of tiny hanged men dangling from his fingers.

Greville looked at it for a long moment, soberly. 'You do realize, don't you, Caterina, that if this is published in England and has the effect I expect, and Dom Miguel wins, your life is not worth a scudo.'

'If they find out I did it. You're right, though, one must remember that. But, think, Greville. For myself I don't much care, and Lewis is involved already. If Miguel should win, we are dead or exiles anyway. But none of that is to the purpose. I do this for Harriet's dead husband and all the other innocent victims of Dom Miguel and his butchers. Would you think me very pretentious if I said I did it for Portugal?'

'I would think you a wonderful woman. Caterina—'

'Something's happening downstairs,' she interrupted him. 'We'd better go. I don't want anyone coming up here.'

'No indeed. We'll keep your secret so long as we can, Mr Forsyte.'

Coming down the last flight of stairs, with Greville just behind her, Caterina saw her son in furious altercation with old Tomas. 'I must see her,' Lewis was shouting. 'What nonsense is this? Her studio indeed! My house. Let me by, or regret it.'

'Here I am, Lewis.' Caterina paused where she was, still above him on the stair. 'What is so urgent?'

'Panic in the town, Mother. I hate to say it, but I think you should be packing your bags.'

'I can't believe it. But, Lewis, you're wounded!' He was white with fatigue, his arm in a sling.

'It's nothing. A scratch, but the duke sent me back on an errand and to get it dressed. I can't imagine what has happened since I have been gone; things were going splendidly when I left Ponte Ferreira where the action was. We were carrying all before us. I thought the day was safe or I'd never have come away, and now I hear the duke has sent orders to embark his treasure and baggage. Governor Mascarenhas has panicked and ordered the town's

paving stones pulled up to strengthen the defences, and people are
running in crowds for Foz. I'm surprised you haven't heard them
passing the gates. I don't know whether to advise you to run, too,
or suggest you go down to the Wares and make interest with Frank
to get you on to a British ship. No relative of mine will be safe if the
Miguelites take the place.'

'And what will you do, Lewis?'

'Rejoin the duke, of course. I wish I had never left him.'

'Then I stay here,' she said. 'I couldn't go without Hetta anyway
and she is at the hospital. Don't argue, Lewis, there's not time. I
doubt if you should have wasted it coming here anyway.'

'Very well, ma'am. On your head be it.'

'You made him very angry,' said Greville after Lewis had left.

'He made me quite cross. Did you hear him? His house indeed.
I know it is true but he should not be saying it to the servants.
What am I going to do, Greville? No, don't answer that. Carlotta!'
Raising her voice.

'*Senhora.*' Carlotta must have been hovering just outside the
door.

'Put our plans for a siege into operation.'

'They are already started, when I saw the crowds passing the
house, running for Foz, but I didn't like to disturb you. Not when
you were working. You mustn't mind the young master, *minha
senhora*. It's all gone to his head a bit, and no wonder. Errands for
the duke indeed! It's only the other day I was smuggling him good-
ies when you locked him in his room to cool his temper.'

'Oh dear,' said Caterina ruefully, when Carlotta had left them.
'Was I really such a tyrannical parent? No wonder he is turning on
me now.'

'Nonsense,' said Greville. 'You were doing the best for that boy,
and you know it.'

'I meant to,' she said, 'but the trouble was I was always thinking
of my work, too, and sometimes I am afraid it got in the way. I
certainly didn't know Carlotta smuggled him in luxuries when I
put him on bread and water. That's what comes of taking your
mind off your household. What's this? Another messenger?'

'The duke sent me.' If Lewis had looked exhausted, this man

seemed dead on his feet. 'He's back in town, quelling the rumours. All's well. Mascarenhas is dismissed and Bernardo de sa Noguieira is governor in his place. The enemy are retreating and our troops are withdrawing in good order.'

'A nice distinction,' said Greville, when Caterina had thanked and despatched the man to Carlotta for food and a new bandage.

'Yes, I wonder what it really means.'

They found out next day when the liberal troops marched back into town with green branches in their caps in token of a victory nobody quite believed in. Stories of panic and the disastrous results of divided command seeped through the town, and worst of all was the sight of the enemy established once more across the river. They had retaken Vila Nova when the panic-stricken governor dismantled the bridge of boats.

'We could actually see it all from our balcony,' Ruth Emerson told Lewis when he called on them next evening. 'It was like a play, only real. Horrible. Men falling; the flashes of the guns; the sound; the smoke. I couldn't bear it, I'm afraid, I hid my eyes, but Mother watched it all.'

'I felt I must,' said Rachel Emerson. 'We had our things packed, of course. One sign of the enemy crossing and we'd have been off, my Ruth and I. I can't risk her with those brutes of Miguelites.'

'I should rather think not,' said Lewis. 'Nor yourself, either, Mrs Emerson. Tell me, I heard a rumour that the enemy actually took the Serra and held it for a while.'

'Quite true,' she told him gravely. 'They caught the garrison unawares, I think, and took it by storm. That's when I began to think seriously of flight, but then our gallant soldiers rallied and retook it. A crowning mercy. I doubt if Oporto would have been tenable if the enemy had got their cannon up there.'

'I am afraid you are right,' said Lewis. 'Not much use building defences if they can throw cannonballs down into the town at will. It's going to be bad enough having them across river again. I am charged by my mother to call on the Wares on my way back to barracks and urge Mrs Ware to go back to my house. But I couldn't resist calling on my way to make sure that you ladies were none the worse for the alarms of the last few days. I can see you have taken it like Trojans.' With an admiring glance for Ruth who blushed becomingly and wondered who Trojans were.

'Don't hurry away,' begged her mother, before Ruth could betray her ignorance. 'We are quite longing, Ruth and I, to hear all the details of the gallant action at Ponte Ferreira, and to be reassured that your wound is only the scratch you claim. I am afraid I did hear a hint from someone of a little difficulty among your brave leaders. The duke's a lion, we know, but an impulsive one— But then,' she had seen him stiffen at the hint of criticism, 'what is a poor woman to understand about the drama of the battlefield? We would so much like it, Ruth and I, if you would explain to us what really happened so we can deny any damaging rumours we may hear.'

'I wish I could.' They could hear the great bell of the cathedral. 'But if I am to do my errand and be back in barracks on time, I must leave you, much though I hate to do so.' He had been sitting on a small sofa, close to Ruth, now rose and looked down into her eyes.

'Must you really?' She smiled up at him.

'I really must.'

'But Mr Fonsa,' intervened Rachel. 'I have a favour to ask of you before you go. An urgent message for your mother. You'll be sleeping at home tonight, surely?'

'Leaving my men to their own devices? I should rather think not, ma'am. But I'll give your message to my mother on my way to the palace tomorrow.'

'No matter, I'll send my man. Give our kind regards to Mrs Ware and tell her how much all her friends hope she will remove herself from the line of fire. These have been a bad few days for Oporto, I am afraid, Mr Fonsa.'

'Oh, all's well again now,' he told her cheerfully, pressed Ruth's hand in a long farewell and left.

He found Harriet Ware obdurate in insisting that her place was in her own house, with her son. 'You'd not expect Caterina to abandon you would you, Lewis?'

'The case is very different, ma'am.' There was a little silence while Harriet and Frank wondered just what he meant by that. 'Hetta asked me to urge you to come,' he went on. 'What a girl she is! Not an ounce of fear in her. When I went to the hospital to get this wretched arm of mine dressed they were all talking about her. There was panic there, you know, when the fugitives to Foz started streaming past the gates, and some of the staff wanted to cut and run. She jumped on a bloodstained table and gave them a piece of her mind in that street Portuguese of hers. I won't sully your ears by telling you some of the words she used, but they had their effect. When they were needed, the nurses were all there. She should have been a man, your Hetta.'

He turned again to trying to persuade Harriet to leave her exposed house, but to no avail, and he was very nearly late back to the crowded barracks that had been the Franciscans' monastery, stepped up from the river a little further downstream, and masked by a rise in the land.

The Wares were still arguing. 'Mrs Bankes is back on board ship.' If Frank had thought this would influence his mother she made it clear that he was mistaken.

'You expect me to join her there? If I go anywhere, it will be to Caterina in her fortress house, but for the moment I do not intend to move.'

'You don't think you should perhaps go to Caterina's to act as chaperon while she is painting Dom Pedro, Mama?'

It got him a quick, sharp look. 'I have to say that is the most powerful argument you have advanced so far, but I also think Caterina well able to look after herself. And then there is Hetta.'

'A tower of strength,' agreed Hetta's brother. 'But she's only there at night.'

'Well, Dom Pedro is going to be quite busy in the daytime.'

'Not too busy for his sittings, it appears.'

His mother laughed. 'Caterina is making quite a hero of him; it's no wonder he is enjoying it.' She looked up sharply. 'Do you smell burning, Frank?'

'No?' Since the Miguelites were back in control of the south bank all the shutters on the river side of the house were tightly closed. Now he moved to open one and peer out cautiously into the darkness. 'Nothing to be seen, but, you're right, I can smell it. A big fire, downriver, don't you think?' They moved with one accord to the front of the house where an anxious servant was peering out into the street.

'What is it, Simpson?' asked Frank.

'I don't rightly know, sir, but a big fire. Down river.' They could see red light now, gleaming above the bluff that masked the next reach of the river.

'The Franciscans'?' asked Harriet. And then, 'Lewis?'

'Fetch a cudgel, Simpson,' said Frank. 'I'm armed. Lock up behind us, Mama, and don't worry.'

'I'll try not to. And I'll have the girls heat up some soup. Be careful, Frank.'

Left alone, Harriet was surprised to find how badly she missed Hetta. Servants were chattering in the kitchen quarters on the lower level at the back as they blew up the fire, but the rest of the house seemed hugely empty and silent. For the first time in her life she found herself thinking homesick thoughts of a snug little cottage in an English village. She had grown up in Bath, would it perhaps be pleasant to go back there? Extraordinary to be thinking like this. She shook herself and went to look out of a street-facing window. There was more activity in the street, now, and shouts of 'fire' and 'the Franciscans',' confirmed her worst fears. She had never paused to weigh the difference in the love she felt for her son, Frank, and her nursling, Lewis; now they were both at risk. And Hetta not here. Her thoughts kept circling back to Hetta.

Half an anxious hour later, Frank arrived with Lewis, both of them smoke-blackened and scorched as to the hair and, in Lewis's case, beard. Blood was seeping again through Lewis's filthy sling and they were both in a state of post-action euphoria.

'All's well, Mama,' shouted Frank. 'But it was a near thing, and lucky Lewis got back when he did, and with his wits about him too. He caught the fire-raisers in the act—'

'Well, the second act,' interrupted Lewis. 'If I had got there sooner the damage would have been less and we would not have lost the men we have.'

'Lost?' asked Harriet.

'Three men killed. And we have lost the colours of the regiment, too, which is almost as bad. And one whole building unusable until we can make some repairs, which is why I am here to beg your hospitality, Mrs Ware.'

'Of course. But who—?'

'Three friars, I am sorry to tell you. One was killed on the spot, but the other two are taken and will stand trial for their lives. From what one of them said I think there was more to it than arson.'

'More?' asked Harriet.

'They had meant to fire all the barracks in town, and actually hoped for a chance to assassinate Dom Pedro. You know how he is always to the forefront in any emergency. If the fires had taken more hold he'd have been bound to come and they hoped to kill him under cover of the confusion.'

'Barbarous,' said Harriet. 'What are we all coming to? And friars – holy men!'

'Not so holy as they should be,' said her son. 'Or rather, worse still, holy bigots, convinced of the justice of their cause. Their trial will be an awkward enough business, I am afraid. It will stir up all the passions that were aroused when Braganza issued his edict against the monasteries.'

'Yes,' said Harriet, 'but on the other hand their behaviour proves his point for him. But what are we doing standing here talking, Lewis is exhausted. Look at his poor arm. I do wish Hetta was here.'

'Don't we all,' said Frank.

Caterina heard of the fire at the Franciscans' when she came down from her studio for breakfast next morning. Two messengers were awaiting her, one from the duke, cancelling his sitting, and the other from Harriet, telling her that she had Lewis in bed with a high fever. There was no need for alarm, Harriet wrote. The doctor had been and said that all he needed was a few days' absolute rest. 'Positively no visitors,' Harriet wrote, 'so don't you and Hetta think of leaving your duties. I promise to take the very best care of him.'

'And so she will.' Hetta was eating a hasty breakfast, prior to leaving for the hospital. 'Don't worry, Aunt Caterina, Mama will make him mind her better than either you or I could. If it's rest he needs, and I believe her, she will see he gets it.'

Caterina sighed. 'I believe you are right, Hetta dear, but I do hate not to go to him. The only thing is' – she looked down at the two notes in her hand – 'the duke says he will drop in for a sitting if he has a spare moment. He expects me to be here.'

'He would,' said Hetta. 'And in fact I think you should, don't you? I believe in the long run this war is going to be a matter of international propaganda as much as action in the field. Your picture will be a weapon in Dom Pedro's hands. I can't tell you how brilliant I think it is, if you will forgive my saying so.'

'I most certainly will.' Caterina was tempted to tell Hetta about the other picture up in the studio, but the fewer people who knew about Charles Forsyte and his cartoons the better. 'The man's waiting for an answer to your mother's note,' she said instead. 'I'll send your love, shall I?'

'Yes, indeed, and tell Lewis, from me, to be sensible.' She rose. 'I must be off to the hospital. I have to tell you, Aunt Caterina, that I am glad Lewis isn't being looked after there. We are short of everything.'

As soon as she could, Caterina hurried back up to the studio. The packet was due any day and she must have her cartoon ready for shipment, concealed as usual among Greville's office correspondence. Later, when she heard the sounds of an arrival, she hurried downstairs expecting to find the duke come for a quick sitting, and was taken aback to find the two Emerson ladies instead.

'We had to come,' explained Rachel Emerson. 'We are so anxious, both of us, about your dear son. There are the wildest rumours in the town about his heroism last night and his illness today. We thought he looked very far from the thing when he called on us yesterday, did we not, Ruth?'

'His poor arm. They say he and Mr Ware were absolute heroes.' Ruth was blushing irretrievably and alarm bells rang in Caterina's mind.

'And now a raging fever, I understand,' said Rachel. 'We are so concerned about him, my Ruth and I, we wondered if there was anything we could do to help. Reading aloud, perhaps? I cannot imagine that he would be an easy invalid.'

'He never was,' said Caterina. 'You're quite right about that. But he's not here, Mrs Emerson. He took ill at Mrs Ware's house and she has undertaken to look after him.'

'Oh! Nobody told me that!' Rachel sounded furious. 'I took it for granted that he would be at home. But then, you are so busy with the great portrait, are you not? Everyone is talking about it. May we be privileged to see it?'

'I am afraid not. I am showing it to no one until it is finished.' Caterina was actually glad to hear sounds of another caller. 'Mr Craddock!' she welcomed him. 'How good to see you.'

'I came as soon as I heard.' He pressed her hand, but was looking beyond her at the Emersons. 'Mrs Emerson, Miss Emerson, your servant. But how is he, Caterina, I do hope it is not so bad as they say?'

'Just a fever,' she told him. 'The doctor says there is no cause for alarm. Some badly needed rest, and he will be as good as new.'

'I'm delighted to hear it. I might have known that the Portonian grapevine would make the most of a wounded hero. But if he is no worse, may I see him? I brought some books I thought might help to keep him amused.'

'Too kind.' Caterina could not quite keep the amusement out of her voice. Books had never been her son's long suit. 'But he is not here, Mr Craddock. I was just telling Mrs Emerson that he took ill at the Wares' and dear Harriet has kept him there.'

'And you are resisting the temptation to hurry down and smooth his fevered brow?'

'I do seem to be. The doctor says absolute rest and no visitors.'

'But you're his mother,' said Ruth Emerson, surprising herself as much as the rest of them.

'Why, so I am.' She smiled at the girl, finding it impossible not to like her. 'But I am also a woman with work to do. The duke promised me a sitting today if he could manage it, and here, if I mistake not, he is. If you will excuse me?'

Greeting the duke she found herself wondering what Rachel Emerson would have to say to Jeremy Craddock, granted the past that lay between them. But she would have been surprised if she had heard her challenging tone. 'Well, Mr Craddock, I hear the packet is due any day now.'

'Yes.' He had remained standing, now moved as if to go. 'I have been kept immensely busy with my report, as you can imagine, with things developing as rapidly as they have. I had hoped for a few words with young Lewis about the fire last night. If you ladies will excuse me, I must go and look for another source.'

'It will hardly make encouraging reading for Palmerston, I am afraid,' said Rachel Emerson. 'Don't forget, Mr Craddock, that we are counting on a visit from you when the packet has sailed. We shall be so much looking forward to it, my Ruth and I.'

Chapter 6

Hot July drew into hotter August. Sweating volunteers laboured on the defences of the city, which were to extend upriver as far as the Quinta do China and down to the sea at Foz. The duke was out every day, riding the rounds of the new fortifications, pausing here and there for a quick word of encouragement, a glass of wine in a friendly farmhouse, a smile for a pretty girl. In the afternoon, he sat with his council, and, when he could, he came to Caterina for a quick sitting. He often arrived seething with rage, straight from the council table. She was reduced to giving absolute orders that no one was to come near them when he was sitting, for fear of what might be overheard. He was beyond discretion.

'I wish I'd left the lot of them behind on Terceira,' he told her one heavy August afternoon. 'All but Vila Flor and Palmelia, that is. The rest are concerned about nothing but jobs for themselves and their friends. And intrigue! How is Mendizabal to get us the English loan we need so badly if I can't even stir my pack of wise old fools into fetching the stored wine over from Vila Nova before the enemy are too strongly entrenched there? It was even a struggle to persuade them that the Serra must be defended at all costs. Torres and Bravo are there now, and will hold it to the death, but old Freire and his cronies say there is no way we can retake Vila Nova. And they won't agree to a raid to fetch the wine. They say they are afraid of rousing my brother into action before our defences are ready. Pack of fools. No wine, no loan, but they won't see it.'

'Cannot you override them, sir? You are in command, after all.'

'I'm paying the price of my own liberal ideas,' he told her ruefully. 'If I had it to do again, back on Terceira, I think I'd set up for a tyrant like my brother. I begin to think there is something to be said for absolute rule after all. But I've given them the power to tie my hands, and by God they are using it. I'd mind it less if it weren't for the intrigue. They've made Vila Flor so angry with their caballing against him that he actually came to me and offered to resign. I talked him out of it this time, but God knows how long he'll hold steady in the teeth of their malice. I begin to think I'm going to have to give him a chance to show his mettle.'

'And fetch that vital wine?' Caterina picked up her paint-brush as he took his pose. 'Sir—' she hesitated.

'Say what you please!' With a savage laugh. 'Everyone else does.'

'It's everyone else I am thinking of. You don't talk like this to everyone, I hope.'

'Only to those, like you, whom I absolutely trust. I am glad to hear that your son goes on so well.'

'You have seen him?'

'Not yet, his dragon of a hostess keeps us all at bay. I've taken your advice by the way, about those vile friars. We are going to lose them in the penal system and let them rot in gaol untried. It is thanks to your son that the damage they did was no worse. You can tell him, when you see him, that his new quarters are ready for him as soon as he is fit to move.'

'Thank you, sire. I know how impatient he is to do so.' She had started a new cartoon upstairs in her studio, showing Pedro and Miguel as good and bad boys on a seesaw, with Pedro, of course, uppermost, and it had kept her so busy that she had not been down to the Wares' house for a couple of days. 'I will go and see him this evening,' she promised herself as much as the duke.

She found Lewis up and dressed but confined by the doctor to a sofa in the upstairs street-facing room where Harriet had installed him. The windows were wide open to the evening air, but the room still struck her as too hot and too full of people. It was disconcerting to find the Emersons there, Ruth sitting very close to the sofa with a book in her hand and Rachel deep in talk with Jeremy Craddock by the window.

'I'll tell the mistress you are here,' said the servant who had showed her up, with a rather helpless glance around the room.

'Thank you.' She moved over to greet her son. 'You are holding court today, Lewis.'

'I do hope we have not been tiring him.' Ruth Emerson had leapt to her feet, book in hand, blushing furiously. 'Mrs Ware said I might read aloud for a little while, and then Mama came to fetch me, and then Mr Craddock—'

'So not much reading,' said Caterina. 'What is your book?'

'It's *Count Robert of Paris*, Sir Walter's latest—'

'And not a patch on *Ivanhoe*,' put in Lewis. 'Have you seen the duke today, Mother?'

'Yes, he came for a quick sitting this afternoon, and says your quarters are ready for you at the Franciscans' when you are fit to move back there. He misses you, but you are not to hurry back too soon.'

'He seems to be managing excellently without an interpreter.' Lewis seemed to aim the remark at Ruth, who blushed more than ever.

'Fancy the duke calling on poor little us in our attic rooms.' Rachel Emerson had crossed the room to greet Caterina. 'My Portuguese is not much better than his English, I'm afraid, but I was able to reassure him that we were suffering no kind of inconvenience where we live. Not like poor Mrs Ware and her closed shutters. It's hardly the drastic ending to the affair that we had all expected, is it, if we are really going to dig ourselves in for a winter's siege here in Oporto? I do begin to wonder whether I ought not to take my little Ruth away while it is still possible. What do you think, Madame Fonsa? Surely the duke must have given you some idea of what he means to do.'

'Good gracious no.' Caterina lied with some emphasis.

'I suppose you are too busy with your work to talk. I have been asking Mr Craddock for his advice.' Turning to Jeremy. 'But he is the perfect diplomat. Not a straight answer to anything.'

'Well, I suppose the less talk the better,' said Caterina. 'Ah, here is Mrs Ware. Harriet dear, I am afraid there are far too many of us wearing out your invalid. Though I must say his looks do you great credit.'

'Thank you.' Harriet had her bonnet on and had obviously just come in from the street. 'This is a surprise.' Looking at them all. 'And I rather think not one of which the doctor would approve. I do not wish to seem inhospitable, but—'

'Of course, we must go.' Jeremy Craddock looked as if he was pleased to.

'Not before I have heard the end of the chapter,' protested Lewis. 'How can you expect me to rest, Aunt Harriet, if I don't know whether Count Robert is going to be rescued?'

'I should think you could be fairly sure of that,' said Harriet. 'Since I see Ruth is only in the first volume of Sir Walter's book.'

'Sad to think there will almost certainly be nothing more from his pen,' said Rachel. 'Has anyone heard news of his health?' And then, when nobody spoke. 'But, Ruth dear, we have our orders, we must be going. Perhaps I can prevail upon you to see us home, Mr Craddock? The streets seem unusually full today. It's the work on the defences, I suppose. A most dispiriting thought.'

'Then let's not think about it,' said Harriet briskly, moving to usher them out. 'And I think we should leave Lewis alone too, Cat.' She smiled down at the invalid. 'I leave it to you whether you choose sleep or Sir Walter.'

'Thank you, Aunt Harriet. I am a little tired.'

'I'm sorry about that.' Harriet led the way into her own small sitting-room. 'I have to go out sometimes, and the servants will ask him if he'll see people, and, of course, if it is Ruth Emerson, he says yes. I am afraid you won't much like it, Cat dear.'

'No,' Caterina said bleakly. 'I don't.' And she liked still less the fact that her friend's story differed from Ruth Emerson's. 'I can't tell you how tempted I was to tell Rachel Emerson a great tale of the horrors of a siege and persuade her to leave on the next boat.'

'But would she? And who else would hear of it? And assume it came straight from the duke.'

'Exactly. Hetta says there are the most extraordinary stories going round at the hospital. Even tales of that lost medieval prince Sebastian coming back. Honestly, Harriet, the Portuguese will believe anything.'

'Or pretend to.' Harriet was amused to hear her friend sound so British. 'How is my dear Hetta? I do miss her.'

'I'm sure you do, but so do I, come to that. She's hardly ever at home. You should just hear the things the duke says about her, but, Harriet, just the same, I did want to talk to you. I wonder if you should not seriously consider going back to England and taking her with you. And Frank, too, if you can persuade him to go. And promise not to tell a soul that I've suggested it.'

'Not even Frank and Hetta?'

'Not even them.'

'And will you come, too?' It was the crucial question and they both knew it.

'I can't, Harry.'

'Well, that settles it, and we won't talk of it any more. But I'll tell you what I am doing, and I hope you or Carlotta are thinking about it too, I am laying in basic supplies. Quietly.'

'Yes, so are we. But let's hope it doesn't come to it. I was surprised at Rachel Emerson's talk of a siege. Gloomy thinking, surely. From what she hears at the hospital, Hetta is convinced that one really strong push could rout the Miguelite army and leave the way clear to Lisbon, and then what a couple of old women we would think ourselves.'

'Have you told the duke Hetta says that?'

'No. Should I, do you think?'

'Well, if he thinks she is so wonderful,' said Hetta's mother.

Two days later, Ruth Emerson roused her mother very early, just as the dawn was breaking. 'Mother, wake up, something's happening down on the river. Listen!'

Great swathes of dawn mist masked the Douro below and at first the two women, shivering on their high balcony, could see nothing, though they could hear sounds of intense activity. Then the mist parted for a moment. 'They are replacing the bridge of boats!' exclaimed Rachel.

'It must be the attack at last. Just think, by tonight it may be all over.'

'One way or other,' said Rachel. The mist was clearing rapidly now, as the sun rose, and they could see the last link in the bridge of boats lashed into place, and, almost at once, troops appearing from behind the bluff and beginning to march across.

'The *caçadores*,' breathed Ruth. 'How splendid they look. Oh, Mother, I am glad Lewis is still confined to his room.'

'He won't be glad,' said Rachel. 'Be careful what you say when you see him. If this is the beginning of the march on Lisbon he will never forgive himself for missing it.'

'Men are so strange,' said Ruth. 'Goodness, there is someone at the door. It's very early. The girl is not even up yet.'

'It's a very strange day.' Rachel opened the door. 'Good morning, gentlemen, you are early callers,' she greeted Frank Ware and Jeremy Craddock.

'We hoped you would be up,' said Frank to Ruth. 'I thought the noise from the river would have roused you as it did me, knowing what a light sleeper you are.'

'And I was waked by the troops moving through the streets,' put in Jeremy. 'We both had the same good idea that this would be the place, if you would allow it, Mrs Emerson, from which to watch what I hope will be the beginning of the end for Dom Miguel.'

'Do you really think so, Mr Craddock?' Ruth asked eagerly. 'You mean by tonight the road to Lisbon may be open?'

'It's common knowledge that Vila Flor has been chafing at the bit since the shambles at Ponte Ferreira,' Jeremy told her. 'Standing siege here in Oporto was never his idea of how to liberate the country, and it looks as if he has carried the day with the duke and his council at last. May we stay and watch the outcome, Mrs Emerson?'

'We shall be glad of your company,' said Rachel. 'Wake Susan, Ruth, and tell her to put the kettle on.' And then, when Frank had followed Ruth on her errand. 'I am glad to see you at last, Mr Craddock. You have fobbed me off for quite long enough. It is time for a straight answer: is it to be the girl, or the dowry?'

'I've not known what to say,' said Jeremy, with absolute truth. And then, inspired, 'But the situation seems to me to be changing. Your daughter is enjoying a great success.'

'Astute of you, Mr Craddock. That option may not be open to you any longer. I shall expect to hear from you.'

Caterina was in her studio looking with satisfaction at her drawing of Dom Miguel falling off the seesaw, a ludicrous upside-down figure, entirely devoid of dignity.

'Yes?' She looked furiously at the servant who had disturbed her.

'It's the duke, *minha senhora*. He asks for a sitting. And Vila Flor has marched across the river. We didn't like to disturb you with the news.'

'Thank you, Tomas. I'll come.' She followed him downstairs and greeted the duke warmly. 'I hear great news, sire. You have decided to attack?'

'At last? Yes, Vila Flor and I carried the day with my council yesterday, to win or lose it all. I am come to bite my nails in your company, since my pack of greybeard councillors would not let me risk my precious life at Vila Flor's side. The waiting is the worst of all.'

'I am glad you came.' She was busy preparing her brushes. 'But you cannot mean that if Vila Flor should fail today you are thinking of withdrawing from Porto?'

'*I'm* not. But whether I would be able to hold the others steady . . . let's not talk of failure; Vila Flor has taken the flower of our troops. He is confident of success.' He mounted the rostrum and struck his pose, then added, 'But I wonder if you should not be thinking of packing up a few possessions, just in case.'

'No,' she said. 'The head a little higher, Your Grace. That's better.'

'Have you noticed that you call me "sire" when you think my star in the ascendant and "your grace" when you are not so sure?' he asked, disconcerting her.

'Forgive me for an ignorant woman—'

'Who doesn't much care for such niceties? And why should you, when you paint like a man?'

'I can't paint at all if you will not keep still.'

It was not a satisfactory sitting and she was glad when he left. It was still early, much too early for any chance of news from across the river, but she picked up her parasol and walked down through streets buzzing with apprehension to the Wares' house.

'I am so glad you are come.' Harriet greeted her. 'Frank went out at first light and Lewis is neither to hold nor to bind.'

'Where's Frank gone?'

'To the Emersons'. He said their apartment has the best view across the river of any place in town. I hope that is all his reason.'

'Do you think he is beglamoured too?'

'I'm very much afraid so. Lewis, what are you doing?'

'Going out, Aunt Harriet.' He had his hat in his hand. 'Good morning, Mother. Do you bring news?'

'I've had the duke, on tenterhooks, for a sitting, but he couldn't stay still. He's gone into town now, for news, but, of course, it is too early.'

'We must certainly hope so,' said Lewis. 'News now would be bad news. I don't know how I can bear not to be there, whatever happens. I'm going to the Emersons', Mother. Frank said he'd be there. I went up to your top floor and opened the shutters, Aunt Harriet, there's no sign of life in Vila Nova. Miguel's commander, Povoas, must have withdrawn all his troops there to face the challenge from Vila Flor. If the wine masters over here had any spunk they'd be across there now fetching their stock.'

'But that would be to assume defeat, Lewis,' said his mother.

'You are absolutely right.' He looked suddenly young and vulnerable. 'How could I not have thought of that? I'll give your regards to the Emersons?' He had established that neither of them was going to challenge his right to go out.

'Yes, but do be careful, Lewis,' said his mother. 'Come back the minute you are tired. The duke was saying how much he misses you; you don't want to make yourself worse.'

'Staying here would make me worse than anything.'

★

'I think he's right about that,' Caterina told Harriet after he had left. 'He was never one to endure uncertainty.'

'Or being crossed.' They looked at each other. 'I do wish the Emersons had never come,' said Harriet. 'You don't think he and Frank—'

'They are too good friends to quarrel. I just wish I did not dislike and distrust Rachel Emerson so thoroughly.'

'And with cause. Have you said anything to the duke about her?'

'No. Do you think I should have? It's twenty years ago, Harry, and surely it was her husband was the spy?'

'She had Jeremy Craddock well and truly in her toils for a while.'

'Yes, but that's different. And that's just why I couldn't talk about her to the duke. I'd seem just another jealous woman. But it's true, I was a little anxious, the other day, when Ruth said the duke had called on them. It's awkward, isn't it? He talks so freely among friends.'

'Let's just hope he is safe on the road to Lisbon by tomorrow and the problem solved for us.'

'Yes.' Caterina rose. 'No use sitting here worrying. I think I shall go home and do some work.'

'How is the portrait coming?'

'Well, I think, if only the great man will sit still.' She had it much on her conscience that she had not told Harriet about her cartoons, but knew that Greville was right in insisting on absolute secrecy. 'Have you seen Greville Faulkes today?' she asked now.

'No. He often drops in first thing to enquire after Lewis, but there's been no sign of him today. Maybe he is up at the Emersons' too.' She picked up her bonnet. 'I think I'll walk up with you, Cat, go to the hospital and see how Hetta is. I've not seen her for days. I do hope she isn't working herself too hard.'

'She thrives on it. The duke says she is worth her weight in rubies. I wonder what she will do when this is all over.'

'Oh, so do I,' sighed Hetta's mother.

When they reached the Sanchez Palace, Harriet only stayed for a moment to admire the duke's portrait. 'It's splendid,' she said, 'and

I know you when you want to get back to work. I'm off to the hospital.'

'Bring Hetta back to supper if you can. Maybe we will be celebrating.'

'Oh I do hope so. I just wish Saldanha was here.' They exchanged a long look. Neither of them, in fact, was very hopeful. There had been too much confusion, too many changes of plan. 'I'm glad Lewis is safe,' said Harriet, and left.

Up in the studio, Caterina took a long look at the princes on the seesaw, and decided that they were finished. Greville could take them away for dispatch by the next packet. Where was Greville? A sudden sharp stab of anxiety caught her in the ribs. Ridiculous. She had worried irrationally like this about Lewis when he was a boy and had always been wrong. Time to get to work; something Harriet had said had given her an idea, not for one but for a whole series of drawings. She found a piece of charcoal and began rapidly to sketch. A council chamber; a group of grey-bearded old men would sit, obviously arguing, and where the council table should have been an immense cauldron at which they were all busy stirring, with clashing spoons. *Too many cooks*. Did it need the caption? She would ask Greville. Where was Greville? The anxiety was back, sharper than ever.

She locked the studio door behind her and hurried downstairs. 'Is there any news?' she asked Tomas, who was lurking in the hall.

'Rumours, *minha senhora*. Not happy ones. They say the noise of battle is getting louder.'

'A retreat?'

'That's the talk, but, it may well be a pack of lies like last time, remember.'

'So it may. Thank you, Tomas.' Smiling at him. 'I saw my son this morning. He is much better, but he is safe here in town. Tell the other servants, will you?'

'Thank you, *senhora*.' He smiled back, a rare event. 'Carlotta will be glad to hear it. The young master safe and well.'

'Yes.' She went back upstairs to her studio. She had wondered what Hetta would do when the crisis was past. More immediate was the question of what she herself would do when the war was over and Lewis installed in her place. No use worrying. She looked at her drawing and saw what it needed. A column of steam rising from the cauldron, with Saldanha's unmistakable face.

She had told Tomas to let her know as soon as there was real news and he came tapping at the door just as she had satisfied herself with Saldanha's likeness. 'The Senhora Ware has returned, *minha senhora*. She says the first wounded have just reached the hospital.'

Early news was bad news. She knew it was true. 'A retreat?' She was following him downstairs.

'It sounds like it.' Harriet answered her. 'A confused story. I could not make head or tail of it, but I'm on my way home, just in case—'

'Yes, but Harry—' They had talked of this before. 'If it should come to an enemy attack, you do promise to come back here, don't you? You are so exposed down on the waterfront, and this place was built to stand siege.'

'I have to talk to Frank,' said Harriet, 'but I told Hetta to come to you if the worst came to the worst.'

'It would have to be very bad indeed to make her leave the hospital,' said Caterina.

'It may be. Jeremy Craddock told me the other day that he thought one reason the duke had not insisted on taking the offensive was that he was afraid of the consequences if he did so and failed. That old hypochondriac Freire and the others would insist on evacuating the town.'

'Leaving the Portonians to the tender mercies of Dom Miguel?'

'Exactly. You would have to get out, Cat, you and Lewis.'

'Well, I suppose Lewis would go with the duke.' She faced it bleakly. 'I wonder if Craddock is writing to Palmerston in this dismal vein,' she went on after a moment's thought. 'Because if he is it can hardly be improving our chances of British aid.'

'You speak like a Portuguese.'

'I am a Portuguese – no, that's not entirely true. I wish I knew what I was. Must you really go, Harry?'

'You know I must, though I hate to leave you here all by yourself. Shall I ask Lewis to come home?'

'When he tears himself away from the Emersons? No, if he's well enough to come here he's well enough to return to his duty.'

'You are absolutely right. I must go. Take care of yourself.' A long kiss and they parted.

Impossible to settle to anything. Caterina went out on to the terrace, but there was no sign of action in the part of Vila Nova that she could see. No use trying to work. She went back indoors and sought out Carlotta for a discussion on the supplies they had laid in against a siege: salt cod and rice, flour and sugar, garlic and onions, and great sides of home-cured pork hanging from their hooks in the cool dark storeroom. The onions gave her an idea.

'We should make ourselves a vegetable garden,' she told Carlotta. 'I know the men are all busy working shifts on the fortifications, but surely they could find time to dig one for me? For extra money, of course?'

'You pay them very well already,' said Carlotta. 'I'll talk to them. The lower terrace, you mean?'

'Yes.' She was remembering a secret meeting, years ago, in another of the family's palaces, where she had discovered the old caretaker happily growing his own vegetables in what had been the terraced garden. Most of the time, she managed not to think about Luiz da Fonsa y Sanchez, the lover who had betrayed her, but now she suddenly found herself remembering that dangerous assignation with him, and the instinct of caution that had kept her out of his arms. I hope he is dead, she found herself thinking, and was ashamed.

She had not been listening to Carlotta. 'I'm sorry? No, of course, I would not insist on their doing it. Would it help if I were to do some digging myself?'

'But—' Carlotta's shocked reply broke off. 'Someone's come—' She followed Caterina up the steep flight of stairs from the subterranean larder. 'You should take off that apron, *senhora*.'

But Caterina's fingers fumbled helplessly on the knot, making her realize just how tense she was. 'Greville! I'm so glad to see you! But what is it? What in the world have you been doing?' She had never seen Greville Faulkes anything but impeccably clad in whatever best suited the occasion, a man whose clothes you did not notice, because they were just right. Today, he looked like a beggar off the streets, rumpled, shabby and sweatstained. Bloodstained?

'Forgive me.' A dirty hand pushed filthy hair back from his brow. 'I came to warn you, Caterina. It's bad. The duke is in council now. If he can't hold them steady, those old men may insist on evacuating the town.'

'It's defeat?'

'A shambles! And all going so well, too, at first. Vila Flor drove Povoas out of Feria with heavy losses. He was pursuing them, the road open before him, when Captain Rebosa sounded the retreat. He thought, he *said* he thought, that the enemy's horse were upon him. Treachery? Or just panic? Who can tell, but the result was the same, the fifth *caçadores* panicked too and fled, and the rest of the army followed them. Vila Flor could not hold them, but he managed to get some of his staff and a few of us together and we stopped them in the end at the entrance to Vila Nova. The duke met us there. He'd heard the bad news from the first fugitives. Mercifully, the Miguelites were as surprised as we were and did not try to follow up their advantage, or I am afraid Oporto would be in their hands now.'

'But, Greville,' Caterina could not believe her ears. 'You say "we"? What do you mean?'

'What else could I do? I went along as an observer. Vila Flor invited me himself. He was so confident of victory. He said I would find it interesting. Well, I certainly did! And when it came to the crunch, what could I do but fight? Just to stand and watch would have been obscene. It was touch and go there for a while, I can tell you, every hand counted. I'm proud to have been there.'

'But—' She hesitated among all the questions. 'I always thought you a man of peace, Greville.'

'Why, so I am, but there is a fighter in all of us men, I think, just waiting for the blast of war. And you're forgetting, Caterina, that all my generation grew up during the long war with France. We served in the militia from our early teens. I may not like to fight, but I know how. I promise you I didn't disgrace the firm of Gomez and Daughter.'

'As if I was thinking of that! But you're hurt!' Some of the stains were blood, she was sure of it now.

'Bruises only.' He looked down at himself ruefully. 'The blood's from my horse; it was killed under me, poor brute. No one asked it whether it wanted to go on active service. But, Caterina, there's no time for talk. I am afraid what I have done has only served to make your position more dangerous. If the duke and his council decide to evacuate the city you must go with them. You remember what happened to the liberals last time Oporto rebelled. They were hanged in the great square.'

'Yes, I do remember.' She thought about it, both of them silent. 'Would you come?' she asked at last.

'To see you safe, certainly. And, remember, there is nothing to stop you serving the cause with your cartoons, back in London. It would be easier in fact; no need to keep your secret, unless you wanted to.'

'Which I would. I am sure I am more efficacious as Charles Forsyte than I would be as Caterina Fonsa. Both as British and as male.'

'You're right, of course.' He did not try to argue the point. 'I think you should be packing up, Caterina. As little as possible. It will be mayhem, if we go. Every man for himself. Is Lewis at the Wares' still?'

'I don't know. He was at the Emersons' – watching. But he'll know now. What will he have done?'

'Joined the duke, for a certainty, so you don't need to worry about him. But the Wares are another matter. Hetta's at the hospital, I suppose. Would you like me to go and warn her?'

'Oh, yes, please, but she'll know, won't she?'

'With the wounded coming in? You're right, of course. But will she leave them?'

'Of course she won't!'

'If it comes to an evacuation, you will have to take her, by force if necessary. No foreigner, and no woman, will be safe if it should come to a sack.'

'But Greville, a negotiated withdrawal?'

'Think, Caterina. Think about Dom Miguel. The negotiated terms would be broken the moment the withdrawal was complete.'

'You're right.' She faced it. 'We will all have to go, and you will have to help me persuade the others, Greville.'

Chapter 7

For two long, desperate days Dom Pedro and his councillors argued, and the streets seethed with grim rumours. Many of the English merchants and their families were already huddled on board the British ships moored in the river, while others were living in intense discomfort at Foz, hoping to get on to the packet, due any day. Work on the town's defences went on, but half-heartedly. What was the use of digging up one's garden for a gun emplacement if the town was going to be given up anyway? Besides, people did not much want to be publicly associated with the defence if it was going to be abandoned. Everyone was remembering the twenty liberals hanged in the great square by Dom Miguel's usurping government after the failed rising of 1828.

For the first time, Caterina had packed the smallest possible bag and had seen to it that Hetta did likewise. The Wares, too, were ready to go, and Lewis, on a quick visit from the palace, where he was back on duty, confirmed to his mother that he would be going with the duke, if he should yield to his councillors and agree to a withdrawal.

'I actually find myself wishing Dom Miguel was with the absolutist army,' he told her. 'There might be some chance of an agreement being honoured if Miguel were to commit himself in person.'

'Perhaps that is why he is staying away,' said Caterina. 'So that he can claim not to be responsible for any violation.'

'You may well be right.' They exchanged a gloomy look. 'I will get news to you the minute the retreat begins, if it does, and you must not lose an instant. I know you have Captain Thompson's promise of accommodation on the *Squirrel*, but it will be easier for him to hold it for you if you are there in person. It will be bad, I am afraid, very bad. One more thing before I go, which I must, do you know what arrangements Mrs Emerson has made? It's been so desperate up at the palace; I've not been able to get away; this is the first time, and I must get back. Mother, will you find out for me? Make sure they get safe away?'

'Lewis, what are you saying?'

'That I love Ruth Emerson. She's the woman for me, my other half. I know it, I feel it, but I've not had a chance to speak. Look after her for me, Mother? Go and see them. Make sure they are safe? Please? When I saw them, the day of the battle, her mother seemed strangely doubtful about what they would do. Imagine Ruth exposed to the horrors of a sack!' He looked at the clock. 'I must go. They will be reconvening and I must be there. I think they will decide tonight, one way or the other, but don't say I said so. Only, go to the Emersons, Mother?'

No time now for discussion, even if she knew what to say. 'Of course I'll go.'

'Thank you.' He bent to kiss her, a rare event. 'Take care of yourself.'

Left alone, she thought for a moment, then rang for Tomas. 'I have to go into town. The litter, I think, and two men as escort.' The carriage horses had all been requisitioned for the army.

'But, *minha senhora*—'

His protest was interrupted by Carlotta, closely followed by the Emersons themselves. 'We are come to throw ourselves on your protection,' said Rachel. 'The arrangements I thought I had made have broken down. I was quite in despair until I thought of you.'

'They have brought their luggage,' said Carlotta.

'I am so glad.' Caterina took Rachel's outstretched hand, smiling at Ruth. No need to say anything about Lewis. 'I have been anxious about you,' she told them. 'Of course you shall share my fortunes, whatever they are. I have accommodation arranged on the *Squirrel*. I am sure you can share it if the worst should come to the worst.'

'Which we all hope it won't,' said Rachel. 'Perhaps you have news from the palace?'

'My son has just been here. They are still talking.'

'Is it true that the Miguelite fleet has sailed from Lisbon and we can expect to be blockaded from the sea any minute now?'

'Lewis said nothing about that.' This at least was true. 'But I am sure we can have the greatest confidence in Admiral Sartorius and his ships.'

'I do so hope you are right. I've heard some tales about them. Now, you must not let my little Ruth and I be the slightest trouble to you. Just a tiny corner where we may lay our heads. I know what a responsibility it is to keep house – and such a house – in such times, but any little thing that we can do to help. . . .'

'Thank you. Carlotta, rooms in the guest wing, please.'

'Oh, just a room, my little Ruth and I like to share.' Caterina saw a shade of something flash across Ruth's face. 'Oh, one other thing,' Rachel went on, a dramatic hand to her brow. 'Something I clean forgot. My friend Francesca down by the river; I should have written her a note to say we are coming to you, but did not like to take you for granted. If I wrote a quick scratch for her would one of your men be going into town perhaps? Take it for me? Dear Francesca lives down by the bridge of boats, she'll know the latest from the river.'

'Yes, of course. Tomas will see to it. And now if you will excuse me—' She had a new cartoon, just started, up in her studio and longed to get back to it. If they had to run for it, she meant to take it with her, whatever else she left behind. The duke could worry about the fate of his portrait.

There had still been no news from the palace when Hetta came home from the hospital at supper-time.

'Things are dreadful at St Antony's,' she told Caterina. 'Some of our nurses have run and the others are quarrelling in whispers, behind our backs. Some of them are Miguelites at heart, I am sure. Oh—' She broke off, surprised, as Rachel and Ruth appeared.

'Forgive me, I do hope we are not late, dear Madame Fonsa.' Rachel Emerson had changed her travel dress for a becoming dark silk. 'And dearest Miss Ware—' holding out a friendly hand. 'Are things so very bad at the hospital?'

'Oh, not really,' said Hetta with ill grace. 'I was just grumbling. I did not know we had guests.'

'Not so much guests as grateful refugees from the horrors of war. Have you had any word from your family today, Miss Ware? They are very much in the front line, are they not, down there by the river.'

'Not a word,' said Hetta. 'I imagine my brother is busy trying to persuade the city fathers to fetch their wine across river while this breathing space lasts. All was quiet at Vila Nova, thank goodness, the last I heard.'

'I suppose Povoas is regrouping his forces for an attack,' said Rachel.

'Let's imagine no such thing.' Caterina spoke more sharply than she had intended. 'But here is Tomas to tell us our supper is ready. Any news, Tomas?'

'They are still talking at the palace, *minha senhora*, and things are quiet now in town, Tonio says.'

'He found your friend all right, Mrs Emerson?' Caterina had risen to lead the way to the dining-room.

'Yes, in a great panic about me, and I am afraid about things in general. She says they expect the worst down there in the lower town. Since the disaster the other day no one trusts Vila Flor as a commander any more. If it hadn't been for the gallant duke hurrying across river to steady the troops all might have been over with us then and there. There's talk, Francesca writes, that he will take over the command himself, but even he can't be everywhere at once. If he is in the field, who is to keep his council steady?'

'They keep talking about Saldanha at the hospital,' said Hetta. 'I don't remember him; I was only little when he was governor here. Was he such a special person, Aunt Caterina?'

'Oh, yes,' said Caterina. 'I've been lucky enough to meet two heroes in my life, and he is one of them.'

'I wonder what the trouble is between him and the duke,' said Rachel. 'Do you know, perhaps?' Turning to Caterina. 'I was way off in America, and knew nothing until I got here and found that Saldanha had been left out of the liberating army. It seems so very odd. To let him sit sulking in Paris with the little queen while it is all being fought for here.'

'Whatever Saldanha is doing,' said Caterina, 'I am sure he is not sulking. Let me help you to some fish, Mrs Emerson.'

'I wish you would call me Rachel. Delicious fish! We had better enjoy it while we can. If it should come to a siege, and the Miguelite fleet blockading the harbour, it will be a choice of salt cod or salt cod.'

'Better a siege than flight,' said Caterina. 'But no reason why you and your daughter should stay to endure one. I don't in the least wish to seem inhospitable, but surely if the duke decides to stay and defend the city your best plan is to be off on the next packet.'

'Always so practical, my dear. You're right, of course. Two more idle mouths to feed, and yet how shameful to run for it and leave all our friends in such danger. What do you think, Ruth?'

'I?' The girl looked astonished, as well she might, at being consulted by her mother. 'I want to stay. But not to be useless. I've been longing to ask you, Miss Ware, if there isn't something I could do at the hospital?'

'Nonsense,' said her mother. 'You faint at the sight of blood.'

'But I write a clear hand.' She was still addressing Hetta. 'Surely there must be letters to be written.'

'There certainly are, and records to be kept.'

'Don't be so absurd,' said Rachel Emerson. 'You know no Portuguese, goose.'

Caterina had been battling with herself during this exchange. Lewis would want Ruth to stay. And it was his house. 'There must be some letters to be written in English,' she said. 'And linen to be sorted, that kind of thing.'

'Goodness, yes,' said Hetta. 'Don't think we couldn't find work for you, and hard work too, quite away from the sight of blood. Do stay, Ruth, I'd be glad of the company.'

She meant it, to Caterina's slight surprise. 'Hetta!' she exclaimed. 'I'm ashamed. I should not have been letting you go to and from the hospital unaccompanied.'

'Just think of having to wait around for an escort. But it's true, two would be better than one. Ruth and I will do very well together, I promise you, Mrs Emerson.'

'She'll stay here, of course.' There was nothing else Caterina could say. But how to avoid inviting Rachel Emerson too?

'You are too good,' said Rachel. 'But are we not going a bit fast? Francesca seems sure that Dom Pedro will sail away in the *Stag* and leave Oporto to its fate. And in that case, we will all be on the *Squirrel* tomorrow, I do trust. And now, if you will excuse us, my little Ruth and I are for our beds. It's been a hard day.'

Left alone, Caterina and Hetta exchanged a long, thoughtful glance. Then, 'I hope I did right, Aunt Caterina,' said Hetta.

'So do I.'

Lewis arrived, breathless, just as they were sitting down to breakfast next morning. 'All's well,' he told his mother, then looked beyond her. 'You found them. Bless you, Mother.'

'They came. The duke's staying?'

'Yes. He's taken over the command from Vila Flor. It's all hands to the fortifications. Palmela goes to England to drum up international support and help Mendizabal over the loan. The duke refuses to treat with his brother, is hopeful of international intervention. He sent me to you, Mother, to tell you this and to say he will be too busy for a while to sit.'

'I should just about think so. The supreme command himself? It's a lot to take on.'

'Yes, he knows it. Palmela is to look out for a tried man to take over from him, Portuguese or foreign.'

'Why not Saldanha?'

'God knows. There's some prejudice—' His bright glance swept the little group of women. 'I do not need to tell you that this is all deeply confidential. It's good to see you safe here, Mrs Emerson.' He spoke to her, but looked at Ruth.

'Your mother has been kindness itself, as always. But, dear Madame Fonsa, now we know where we stand I must give you my thanks and go home to my little eyrie over the river. I cannot tell you how much happier I shall feel knowing that my Ruth is here with you, safe in your fortress of a house. But you will not forget to visit your old mother, Ruth. How strange it will seem to be on my own again, but I am sure I shall find useful work to do down in the

town, while you are doing your share at the hospital.' But Ruth was
not listening, busy explaining her plans to Lewis.

'I must go to work,' said Hetta. 'How much of what you have told
us is to be public knowledge, Lewis?'

'Oh.' He was taken aback for a moment. 'Just the fact that the
duke takes over from Vila Flor. And that he stays of course.'

'The rest of it will be out soon enough,' said Rachel. 'You know
how talk runs through the streets, here in Oporto. I must be off,
dear, dear Madame Fonsa, with a million thanks for all your kindness. I don't want to find that my landlord has thought me gone for
good and rented my rooms. I have a sentimental fondness for them,
you know, because of having shared them with my Ralph. Will you
come with me and fetch the rest of your things, Ruth dear, or shall
I send them up to you?'

'I don't know—' Ruth looked doubtfully at Hetta. 'Should I
come with you today, Miss Ware?'

'Call me Hetta for goodness sake, if we are to work together. No,
better not, I think; let me explain about you first. See you tonight,
Aunt Caterina.' And before Caterina could suggest that she send a
man with her, Hetta was gone.

'I'm on my way into town on the duke's business,' said Lewis.
'May I have the pleasure of escorting you, Mrs Emerson?'

In the end, Ruth went too, and Caterina was left alone with her
anxious thoughts. For once in her life she had missed the morning
time in her studio, but when she went up and tried to go on with
her picture of the Braganza brothers playing at blind man's buff,
she found she could not work. Had she been mad to invite Ruth
Emerson to stay? But how could she have helped it? She sighed,
gave up trying to work and went downstairs to find Carlotta and
Tomas, most unusually, out on the terrace. 'Listen, *senhora*,' said
Tomas. 'We just heard them. Big guns.'

Now she too heard the dull boom from across the river. 'It's
begun.' She looked from one to the other.

'Yes, *minha senhora*, it's begun,' said Carlotta. 'And Admiral
Sartorius has sailed downriver to challenge the Miguelite fleet. We
must all pray for his success, or we shall find ourselves cut off from
the sea too. *Senhora....*' She and Tomas exchanged glances.

'Yes?' What was coming now?

'Did the *senhor* tell you, when he was here?' asked Carlotta.

'Tell me? About the duke? Yes, of course.'

'No.' Another exchange of glances. 'We wondered,' went on Carlotta, 'whether he told you he had given orders for all the men to go and work on the defences.'

'No, has he?' So far they had worked only on a rota system. 'And quite right too. I should have thought of it. Well, I hope you will be able to persuade the girls to take over my vegetable patch, Carlotta. I think we are going to be glad of that this winter. There are the guns again. How far off do you think?'

'Not in range yet,' said Tomas.

Caterina went back to work with a will after that, and when Greville called late in the afternoon her game of blind man's buff was almost ready for him. She was working faster now, each cartoon going more swiftly than the last since she had established the ground rules for them. And Greville had good news for her. 'The packet's in and Mrs Wallis writes that Charles Forsyte is the talk of London. She wants as many and as fast as you can send them. Can this one go as well as your seesaw?'

'I don't see why not.' She stood back to look at it. 'Do you think they are really being useful, Greville?'

'They are most certainly selling, and their message reads clear enough for all to see. Let us just hope that they help to back up Palmela's mission. Do you realize, Caterina, how very bad things look, now Dom Pedro has refused even to negotiate with his brother? Listen to that!' The gunfire across the river had stopped for a while, now resumed. 'They've not got the range yet, but they will, and then nowhere will be safe. And rifle shot across the river too. I called on the Wares this afternoon.'

'They are staying.' It was not a question.

'Yes, but you are a different case, Caterina. They are British through and through, protected by the crown, you are half Portuguese, and then there is Lewis.'

'There is indeed. And you are suggesting that I go off and leave him? Not to mention Hetta. And,' she could not help smiling, 'no way you could know it, but I have Ruth Emerson staying with me too.'

'What?' He quite visibly could not believe his ears. Then, characteristically, he went straight to the point. 'Do you want her to marry Lewis, Caterina?'

'He's too young to marry anyone. But, no, of course I don't. As to her staying here, I had no choice.' She explained swiftly how it had happened. 'I can hardly go back on it now, besides, Lewis would be furious. And he is master here, I do find myself coming back to that.'

'As well you might. I'm not sure I don't wish there had been an evacuation after all, and you safe off to England. There's still time, the packet does not leave until tomorrow. I wish you would. Why do you smile?'

'You're not thinking, Greville. If I were to go, I would be leaving Hetta and Ruth alone in what we keep remembering is Lewis's house. Besides, I don't want to go. Quite aside from any question of the heroics of the case, I have the strongest feeling that Charles Forsyte might find he could not work in England.'

'Ah.' Now he was smiling. 'There is an argument.'

After he left she settled down with Carlotta to discuss how they were to replace the men Lewis had ordered out to the fortifications. 'I am afraid our new garden is going to suffer,' said Carlotta. 'The girls are going to be as busy as sparrows.'

'I shall tend to it myself,' said Caterina. 'I shall enjoy that. Oh, who now, Serafina?' she asked the girl who was replacing Tomas.

'It's the Senhor Craddock, *minha senhora.*'

'Oh.' She sighed and rose to her feet. 'Wine and cakes, Serafina.' And, when the girl had left, 'Carlotta—'

'Yes?' With a quick, intelligent glance.

'Give us ten minutes, and then disturb us. I don't care why.'

'Very good, I'll think of something.'

'Caterina!' Jeremy came towards her, both hands outstretched. 'I cannot tell you how I admire your courage and how deeply I deprecate it. I met Faulkes on my way here; he tells me you mean to stay and face the chance of a siege. Dear friend, let me beg you

to think again. I would not say it to anyone but you, but I am
convinced that Dom Pedro's cause is doomed, has been ever since
he failed to march at once on Lisbon. You have seen how divided
his councillors are, and how he fails to control them. And he's
such an obstinate fellow. I am afraid this winter is going to see all
the horrors of a siege: the starvation, the sickness, plague perhaps.
And, at the end of it, worst of all, a sack. There is a rumour going
about that Dom Miguel has promised his men a free hand here in
Oporto when they take it, and you know what that means. I have
watched you with such admiration Caterina: your magnificent
portrait of the duke; your work for the hospital. All of it your
death warrant at Miguel's hands, if you were even to survive the
sack, which I doubt. And the two girls in your charge, think of
them. This is no time for romantic gestures, this is the time for
hard sense. If you won't think of yourself, think of Hetta Ware
and Ruth Emerson. Imagine them in the hands of Miguel's
soldiers.'

'I know,' she said. 'I do. But there is Lewis—'

'Lewis is a man, able to take care of himself. And, think,
Caterina. What do you owe him? Nothing. You sacrificed me, our
happiness to him, brought him up, loved him, managed his estates
for him, and what has he done in exchange? Vanished without a
word, compromised you by his service to Dom Pedro, and taken
control of things here without so much as a thank you. I'm not
blind, Caterina, I have seen what has happened here; the high-
handed orders to servants, discounting you. It is more than time to
start thinking of yourself at last. Better still, think of us, Caterina.
Think of the happiness we have put off for so long. The packet sails
tomorrow; I know the captain; he will make room for us, and for
the two girls, if you wish. No time to marry before we go, but once
in London a special licence will see us right. You are laughing?' He
was outraged.

'I'm sorry, but haven't you forgotten something? Two things in
fact: what about your own work here, and where is the love in all
this? You don't love me. I don't love you. That is an old story, best
forgotten. I thank you for your flattering offer, Mr Craddock, but
must decline it.'

'Nonsense.' He pulled her fiercely to him. 'You're mine! I'll show you—'

'The Duke is here,' said Carlotta. 'He says he has half an hour for a sitting.'

After Jeremy Craddock had left, in some disorder, Caterina was surprised to find that the duke really was there, and she was too busy adding final touches to his portrait to think about Jeremy Craddock. Leaving, the duke took her hand, held it for a long moment. 'You are not proposing to leave on the packet tomorrow, *senhora*?'

'Should I be?'

'I hope not.'

Much later, in bed that night, she lay, restless, thinking of what Jeremy Craddock had said. Nothing would induce her to marry him, that was certain enough, but there was a horrid element of truth in what he had said about Lewis. It did not make her like Jeremy any better. But it took her a very long time to get to sleep.

Chapter 8

August drew into September. Admiral Sartorius and his handful of ill-equipped ships had sent the Miguelite fleet packing, while Torres and Bravo beat off two desperate attacks on the Serra. The Portonians were working with a will now on the defences of their city. Everyone knew that Dom Miguel had promised his troops the sack of Oporto if they took it. The knowledge concentrated minds wonderfully. Far up the Douro the grapes ripened untended. Men who would normally have been working on the harvest and its shipment were hard at work digging trenches alongside their own servants.

Greville Faulkes had been working his shift on a gun emplacement below the bluff. Now, stiff, tired and filthy, he returned to the office of Gomez and Daughter. 'Any word of the packet?' he asked his one remaining clerk, Sam Wells.

'Not yet, sir. She should be in any day now, but it's been proper stormy with the equinoctial gales and all. There's a man come in from upriver, though. Slipped through the enemy lines last night. He says it's going to be the best grape harvest for years. Seems a shame, don't it, all going to rack and ruin.'

'It certainly does. Let me know the minute there's news of the packet. I have a couple of things for her.' He shut his office door and sat down to write his weekly letter to his mother. As a boy, he had not known she existed. Brought up a lonely orphan in his dead father's home on the Welsh border, he had learned about her when the bullying began at Rugby. 'Whore's brat,' had been the best of what they called him. It was his first friend, Jeremy Craddock who told him about his actress mother, Jenny Forbes. 'Nothing to be

111

ashamed of,' Jeremy said. 'She's the talk of the town, outshines the Siddons and the Jordan. Why don't you write to her?' And Greville had done just that, and then been terrified at what might happen. Suppose she came to Rugby and made a scene? It did not bear thinking of. But she had simply answered his letter as if it had been the most natural thing in the world, and they had been corresponding ever since. On her advice he had decided to say nothing about her to his cantankerous grandfather until his education should be finished. 'The old man owes you that at least,' she had said.

He had looked forward to confronting his grandfather when he was ready, but a gossipy neighbour saw him in his mother's box at the Haymarket Theatre in his last term at school and the fat was in the fire. The Faulkes might not have a title, his furious grandfather told him, not for the first time, but they were one of the oldest families in England. Now they had been disgraced by father and son in succession. His only comfort, said old Mr Faulkes, must lie in his younger son, Greville's uncle, and his sons. It had seemed an odd kind of comfort to Greville, since they never came to Faulkes Abbey. He had met his cousins in London and thought them over-rich and underbred. He said so to his grandfather when the old man called his mother a mercenary bitch, and the result was inevitable. He was thrown out of the house there and then; all his plans for university and a career in politics gone in a flash. It had been lucky for him that he had already had Jeremy Craddock's proposition about Oporto.

Twenty years ago. He picked up his pen. No use trying to pull the wool over his mother's eyes. Things were bad in Oporto and he would tell her so, knowing her absolute discretion. He had complimented her on this once and she had laughed and said she had suffered enough from gossip herself: 'I'll never add to the sum of human misery.' And she never did. But he had not told her the identity of Charles Forsyte and that was why he was biting his pen now. She had written in her last letter that she had just bought the first two Forsyte cartoons and thought them brilliant. 'Do tell me if he is by any chance a friend of yours, dear Greville. He seems to think along very similar lines.' He was immensely tempted to tell her, but must not. It was not his secret. For once, this made his letter difficult to write, and in the end he put it aside and strolled over to the English Factory in search of news. He found the arcade seething with talk: the packet was in, and Palmela back.

'He's got the loan,' John Procter told him. 'But it's secured on the wine at Vila Nova.'

'Which means he hasn't got it.'

'Precisely. And there's worse. Neither Dom Pedro nor Dom Miguel seems to give a rap for the rights of us neutral Britons. The Miguelites stop our ships at sea, and the Pedroists destroy our houses and gardens outside the walls here. In the name of defence! Monstrous! And Braganza speaks slightingly of our brave British soldiers. Why do you smile?'

'I was thinking just how odd the whole business of British neutrality is.'

'You're a fine one to talk. I heard about your exploits after the reverse at Feria. Not much neutrality about that.'

'Nor can you expect cannon balls to be respecters of nationality. I was so sorry to hear about the Jones's house.'

'Yes. Totally destroyed. It was a merciful thing they were safe on board ship at the time. The Taylors have lost their prize magnolia, too, and even Dorothy and I have had a cannon ball in our vegetable garden, all among our melons and cucumbers.'

'I am so sorry. Please give my sympathies to Mrs Procter.'

'I certainly will. It's what she needs. She wouldn't have minded if there had been some official form of condolence.'

'For melons and cucumbers?' Greville could not help asking.

'It's the principle of the thing. You know how short of supplies they are at the foreign hospital, and British troops not paid nor clothed while the Portuguese want for nothing. It's all of a piece. And losing the loan won't help to mend matters.'

'No, I am afraid it won't.'

Greville had been fighting all day against a longing to go and call on Caterina. Now he felt he had a reason. He found her in her studio, putting the finishing touches on her latest cartoon. 'The packet's in,' he told her, looking at it. 'I hope it's ready.'

'I think so.' She stood back to look at the tug of war between the

Braganza brothers, Portugal stretched helpless between them.

'So do I. You get better and better, Mr Forsyte, but I have to say that I don't think Dom Pedro will like this one much better than his brother does.'

'No.' Thoughtfully. 'I do see what you mean. Let's hope he does-n't see it. Have any of my cartoons come back here do you know?'

'Not that I have heard of, but I suppose it is bound to happen sooner or later, with the packets still sailing so regularly, thank God. Caterina, how is the portrait? Are you still seeing the duke?'

'Not often, he's been so busy, but he does drop in for a moment or two when he can. He wants it finished just as much as I do. Why do you ask?'

'There is something needs saying to him, and I can't think of anyone better than you to do it.'

'Oh?'

'I've just come from the English Factory. There's a lot of angry talk there, about discrimination against the British. On all kinds of levels.'

'Yes, I've heard some tales, too. Hetta came home in a rage the other day. She had been on an errand to the Foreign Hospital and found things as bad there as they were at St Antony's when she first went there. All the supplies are being channelled to the Portuguese.'

'Yes, and it's the same in the army. Causing a lot of feeling. Of course some of the grumbles are totally unreasonable. Dorothy Procter thinks she should have had a visit of condolence from Dom Pedro because of a cannon ball among her cucumbers. Yes, you may laugh, but this is going to be a bad winter, and we don't want to start it in a state of friction among ourselves.'

'You're absolutely right. But what's to do?'

'Would you think me mad if I suggested a party of some kind?'

'No, very sensible. There's nothing like a party. But it wouldn't be easy. Oh, my goodness, that reminds me of something I have had it in mind to say to you. It's St Bruxas' Eve next week, and you know what that is like, here in Porto.'

'Yes, licensed mayhem.'

'I've been wondering what will happen this year. What might be best to do about it. If the duke should come I'll try and put it in his head that he should mount some kind of celebration then.'

'What if he doesn't come?'

'Then I'll do it by way of Lewis, which might work as well or even better, come to think of it. He comes here all the time.' Smiling. 'Not for my sake. He's head over heels in love with Ruth Emerson, you know. There's not a thing in the world I can do about it except stand by and watch. It's impossible not to be fond of Ruth, but I can't say she is the girl I would have chosen for a daughter-in-law. It does worry me, Greville. But I still like the child. You couldn't have an easier guest, and she and Hetta seem to get on admirably.'

'Hetta is a girl in a million.'

Jeremy Craddock was relieved at the comparatively reasonable sum Rachel Emerson had agreed to accept for her silence. It was strange to be walking up the steep stairs to her apartment with a bag of gold again as he had done years ago when he was a young man pretending to be healed by her. They had fooled each other then, and he had no doubt that they were doing their best to fool each other now, but secrecy was in both their interests. This payment would keep her quiet for a while, and in the meantime he must set about finding some secret of her shady past that would shut her mouth for good.

'You are prompt to your time, Mr Craddock.' She smiled the smile that had once bewitched him. 'Thank you.' Taking the heavy little bag. 'I am sure there is no need for me to count it. Now the past is past and we are to be friends, are we not, as we used to be?'

'I would like that.'

'I'm glad. So I shall confide a little idea of mine to you. I'm sure you know as well as I do how awkwardly things go on just now in the British community here in Oporto. Especially among the women. All very well for you men to go navvying it on the fortifications, making a kind of boys' school outing of it, but what about the wives and daughters at home with cannon balls landing in their cabbage beds and shattering their windows? Worst of all for the daughters, of course. Not a young man in sight. They are all out playing soldiers. Now, I had a little idea about that. Suppose we were to get up a party of pleasure, while the good weather still holds, to ride around the fortifications and see the great defence works for which the men have been neglecting us. I can't suggest it, an American rebel, as your good English ladies like to remind me, but if you were to put it into Dorothy Procter's head, for instance? She rather fancies herself as a kind of leader among the English ladies.'

'What an odd idea.' He thought about it, wondering, inevitably, what advantage was in it for her?

'Odd if you like, but it's a good one just the same. Think about it a little. It would make the English ladies feel they had a stake in the work that is going on, and imagine the pleasure to the workers to find themselves admired by charming young ladies like my Ruth and that formidable Miss Ware.'

So that was what she wanted, an outing for her daughter. 'It might not be such a bad thing at that,' he said rising. 'I'll certainly think about it.'

'Do. And thank you.' She patted the bag of gold she had still not counted.

Jeremy met Colonel Hare, the British military representative, just outside the English Factory and on an impulse put the idea to him.

Hare's first reaction was as adverse as his own had been. 'A pleasure outing with things as they are? Absurd!' Then, visibly, he thought about it. 'But there might be something in it, just the same. I'll certainly have a word with Dolly Procter. A remarkable woman that. Always ready with a smile and a glass of wine. Braganza likes her, I've heard. One of the English he is prepared to talk to.'

'Is that so? Well, I'll leave it with you, then, Hare.'

Hare told Jeremy next day that Dorothy Procter had greeted the idea with enthusiasm, and he went off at once to call on Caterina. He had kept away since that disconcerting day when she had rejected him. She would come round in the end, of course. He had taken it all too fast, and thought the best thing to do was to leave her alone, let her wonder whether he had given up entirely. With penury staring her in the face, she should find this quite sobering, or so he hoped. To his own surprise, the fact that she had refused him had given him a new enthusiasm for the project. But he would take it slowly from now on. He had silenced Rachel Emerson for a while; he need not rush things.

He found Caterina busy with domestic affairs. She and Carlotta were taking an inventory of the household linen. It was a fine, gusty, late September afternoon and they had spread sheets and blankets out on the top terrace to air, be checked for moth holes, and counted. Caterina's sleeves were rolled up, she was wearing one of her painting aprons and her black hair had escaped from its braids.

'Mr Craddock.' She held out her hand, smiling. 'You take us quite by surprise. We are taking stock, Carlotta and I, to see how much we can spare for the Foreign Hospital. But come into the cool of the house. You can finish here, Carlotta, can you not? And ask one of the girls to bring us cakes and lemonade?'

She was beautiful, he thought. There was a glow about her. It was all very satisfactory. And she listened to his description of the projected outing with flattering interest. 'It seems a mad enough idea at first,' he concluded, 'but I really think there might be something in it.'

'Not mad at all.' She poured lemonade for them both. 'Funnily enough, I had thought very much the same thing myself, or rather Greville Faulkes suggested it to me. We had thought of some kind of Anglo–Portuguese party on Bruxas' Eve next week, and I've been meaning to have a word with the duke or Lewis about it but haven't had a chance yet. We had imagined some kind of informal ball, but I can't see why that could not be combined with a tour around the fortifications, which I think an admirable idea. And refreshments, of course. That won't be easy, but if we all sacrifice some of our winter supplies we ought to be able to manage. No problem about drink. I'll supply it from my stores downriver.' And then, flushing, 'I mean Lewis will. I'll send a messenger to the palace, asking Lewis to call when he has a moment. And shall I ride over and call on Mrs Procter? What a good thing she decided to forget my shady past and come to my party. I like her, you know, she is a sensible woman.'

'Remember to condole with her on the cannon ball that fell among her cucumbers. But this ball, Caterina: were you thinking of the English Factory, because I do wonder if the old fogies there would agree.'

'It would certainly take them for ever to decide. No, no, I had thought of the Carrancas Palace. That's why I need Lewis, or best of all the duke, but he hasn't been for a sitting for days. And I am not brave enough to ask him to come, in case you were thinking of suggesting it.'

'I think you are brave enough for anything, Caterina,' he said, and realized that he meant it.

'What an extraordinary idea.' Lewis had not liked being summoned. 'It's hardly a time for parties, surely. Still less for using up scarce food supplies! But then,' he thought about it for a moment. 'There might just be something in it.' He had looked hopefully about him when he arrived, now asked, 'How are the girls? I suppose they are still at the hospital?'

'They don't usually come home till supper-time. They would enjoy a party, I'm sure. And deserve one!'

'I'll certainly put it to the duke, Mother.' He picked up his hat. 'I must do so, to explain my absence, but I do not hold out high hopes. It's a crying shame that they treated him so cavalierly when he was in London. It's not something he is going to forget in a hurry.'

'Whether he can afford to remember it so publicly is the question right now. I wish you would ask him to come and see me.' What hope of Lewis persuading the duke when he was less than lukewarm himself? 'Tell him I need a quick sitting and then think I could finish the portrait. It has the advantage of being true.'

'Very well, but I doubt he will come. Or that you will be able to persuade him to hold this party. And on St Bruxas' Eve, too. Asking for trouble. Give my love to the girls.' Carefully casual. 'Tell them how sad I was to miss them.'

'You would see them at the party, Lewis.' She could not resist it.

The duke came next day. He looked haggard and harassed, she thought, and promised herself not to let it show in her picture of him as hero. 'What's this mad idea for a party?' he asked, striking the familiar pose as she picked up her brushes.

'Not only my idea, Sire. That's what is so interesting.' She had called on Dorothy Procter the day before and was very glad that she had. 'Several people seem to have thought of it at the same time, which must surely mean that there is something in it? I called on Mrs Procter at Entre Quintas yesterday. They have had a Miguelite cannon ball in their vegetable garden and she is very angry, but she is a sensible woman too and has been thinking, as I have, about what this winter is going to be like. If we are all going to suffer together in the cause of Portuguese liberty, we will do it much better if we suffer as friends. Your Grace must see that.'

'You are doing it again,' said the duke.

'Doing what?'

'You called me Sire to begin with, because you thought I would back your mad scheme, then you began to wonder, and I am back to being My Grace. Well, I am going to surprise you. I do think it is a mad scheme, but I also think there is something in it. You shall have your ball at the Carrancas Palace, always providing that the enemy do not choose that day to attack us. You seem to have left that rather out of your calculations.'

'Well, they do seem to be taking their time about it. Are they really going to try to starve us out?'

'They won't succeed,' he told her, and she hoped he was right.

Preparation for the party went on apace. Dorothy Procter could provide *chouriço* sausages for the refreshments; Caterina had plenty of *almaça* cheese, and wine was no problem. A suggestion that the evening should end with fireworks was vetoed by the duke, while the all-important question of dress was hotly debated among the women. In the end a kind of compromise between day and evening dress was decided upon and seamstresses all over Oporto were hard at work.

'At least it is good for business.' Hetta had come home from the hospital to find Caterina at work on her own dark-blue costume. 'For those who aren't clever with their fingers like you and my mother, Aunt Caterina. What are you going to wear, Ruth?'

'I don't know yet. My mother said she would find something for us both. Her friend Francesca is a great needlewoman, she says. She has some idea of what she calls the lady patronesses all dressing in the same colour. Would you mind if I were to tell her that you are wearing blue, Aunt Caterina?'

'Of course not.' Caterina could not quite get used to the way Ruth had slipped into calling her 'Aunt Caterina' as Hetta still did. 'I got the material from Senhor Chaves in the Rua das Flores, and practically had to go on my knees to him to get him to sell it to me. He's hoping to hold out for rising prices if it comes to a siege. But he had several rolls of it and I persuaded him at last. It seems odd to be troubling about dress at a time like this.'

'Yes, I do agree,' said Hetta. 'Ridiculous.'

'But Mother says that it's important we all look our best,' said Ruth. 'For the sake of morale, you know.'

'The effect on the licentious soldiery.' Caterina's smile took any sting out of the words. 'And she is absolutely right. If a thing is worth doing it is worth doing well. I just hope the weather holds. Just suppose the October rains begin early.'

'We won't suppose any such thing,' said Hetta. 'If I really have to abandon my patients and dress up I mean to enjoy myself.'

'And quite right too,' agreed Caterina. 'Something to think about when things get bad this winter, as I am afraid they will. Are you and your mother really going to stay, Ruth dear?'

'She says she wouldn't feel right leaving.' Ruth sounded surprised herself. 'I'm so glad. I know I wouldn't. I've been so afraid she would decide to go, but I think she has quite made up her mind now. She was saying last time I saw her that it is more than time we put my visit to you on some kind of a business footing.' She was blushing to the roots of her hair with the effort of saying it.

'Nonsense,' said Caterina. 'We love having you, Hetta and I.' And then, 'But, in fact, it is Lewis you should speak to.'

'Oh, I couldn't possibly do that. Please, Aunt Caterina – oh—' Her colour was higher than ever. 'Someone's coming.' They could hear a man's voice.

'But it's Frank,' said Hetta. 'Not Lewis.'

Frank had a message from his mother for Caterina. 'She has

found a secret hoard of ratafia cakes for the party.' He smiled at them all. 'No need to ask how you are, I can see you are in the best of health and looks. You are not letting my sister work you too hard, I hope, Miss Emerson?'

'No, indeed,' said Ruth. 'I love it. I don't think I have ever been so happy in my life.'

'Scrubbing filthy sheets and writing dull letters,' said Hetta laughing. 'What odd notions of happiness you do have, Ruth dear.'

'Ah, but scrubbing them among friends,' said Ruth.

She was in quite a glow of looks, Caterina saw, and was ashamed of herself for being glad that Lewis was not there to see. 'Tell your mother we are all to wear dark blue,' she told Frank. 'What Ruth's mother calls the lady patronesses.'

'I wish we could wear masks,' said Hetta and caused a little silence.

Then: 'But why not?' said Caterina. 'St Bruxas' Eve, after all. Not for the tour of the fortifications, of course. But when we get to the palace and take off our jackets or shawls to reveal the elegance beneath? Then we whip our masks out of our reticules and become the fair unknown.' She laughed. 'The duke was telling me that they are devilish short of candles, as he puts it, at the palace. We are to be dancing in the half dark, he says, and masks will add to the spice of the thing.'

'Why, Aunt Caterina,' said Frank, 'I'm surprised at you. But what a splendid idea. I promise you,' turning to Ruth, 'I will recognize you behind a dozen masks, Miss Emerson.'

The weather held. Day after day, thick morning mist gave way to blazing autumn sunshine only to close in again as the sun went down. All over Oporto blind eyes were turned as owners borrowed back their own horses or mules for the ride around the fortifications. The band of the 5th *caçadores* practised waltzes as a change from military marches, and Lewis offered to teach Ruth and Hetta the latest dance steps.

In the end it was only a small party that set forth for the tour of the entrenchments, most of the ladies preferring to go in all their finery straight to the palace. On Colonel Hare's advice, the little group of riders simply took the Foz road to look at the new defences protecting the two castles at the river's mouth. There had been a sharply fought action at the other side of town recently, and, he said, there might still be sights and smells that would offend the ladies. Going this way he could promise them a fine view of the open sea. In fact, they did not get even that far. Caterina had rather expected this when Rachel Emerson joined the little party, riding a mule with a limp. When they reached the Arrabida Battery, halfway down to Foz, Caterina was in the lead, with Jeremy on one side and Greville on the other. Reining in her horse to acknowledge the cheers of the defenders, she turned as Colonel Hare drew his cavalry charger to a halt beside her.

'I'm afraid Mrs Emerson is feeling the heat,' he told her. 'And that poor beast of hers is suffering. Do you think we should call a halt here?'

'I'm sure we should,' she agreed warmly. 'Look at the splendid view one gets of the river all the way down to the bar, and if you ask me, one battery is really very like another. Besides, wouldn't you say that the mist was beginning to come upriver? You know how fast it closes in at this time of year.'

'You're absolutely right,' he said. 'That settles it. I'll pass the word.'

'Well that's a relief.' Rachel Emerson pulled her skinny mule up beside Caterina's horse. 'I shall be stiff as a board tomorrow. I can't think why I was so mad as to come. Lord knows, my Ruth is well taken care of.' She looked back down the rocky track to where Ruth was loitering in the rear with Hetta, Frank and Lewis. 'Help me down, please.' She appealed to Jeremy. 'I really must rest for a few minutes before we start back.'

'Not too long,' Caterina warned. 'The mist is coming in from the river.'

'No, no, trust me to keep clear of the mist.' Rachel handed her reins to Jeremy. 'I'll just get one of these delightful men to give me a glass of water and be with you.'

Caterina was glad to set forward with Greville, having found the ride out with the two men competing for her attention a trifle exhausting. By the time they got back to the Bicalno Battery, the mist was lying so thick below them that they could not see the water at all. 'I do hope the others don't linger,' she said to Greville. 'This is no track to be riding blindfold.'

'I am sure they won't,' he said reassuringly. 'Jeremy Craddock is far from being a fool, and Lewis and Frank grew up here after all. They know the risks.'

'Of course. I am being stupid. It's so hard not to worry.'

'I'll give you something else to worry about,' he said. 'Do you know that Braganza had to preside over the court martial of an old friend from the Azores this morning? Fellow deserted and was caught. Not a hope for him, I'd have thought, but if he is condemned to death I do wonder if the duke is going to feel able to attend our party.'

'Oh dear, that is a worry!' Caterina turned at the sound of a horse behind them, but she was surprised to see Jeremy alone. 'Where's Mrs Emerson?'

He pulled a face. 'At the devil for all I care. She said she would wait for Mrs Procter and Colonel Hare.'

The duke had set aside a suite of rooms at the Carrancas Palace for the ladies to tidy themselves after their ride, and Caterina, making the necessary adjustments to her own dress, was glad to see Hetta and Ruth come in soon after her.

'We're late,' said Hetta. 'The dancing has started already. I can hear the music. I don't think we should wait for the others, do you, Aunt Caterina? Colonel Hare was having the devil of a time getting Ruth's mother going when we came away. She was too tired to stir, she said.'

'I knew it would be too much for her,' said Ruth apologetically. 'I did try to persuade her to come straight here in a litter like your sensible mother, Hetta, but she said it was her duty as one of the lady patronesses. She sent you her apologies for being so slow, Aunt Caterina, and please don't wait for her. I will, of course.'

'Yes, I do think we should go on,' said Caterina. 'If you are sure you don't mind, Ruth?' The room was crowded with women, English and Portuguese, busy tidying themselves. 'I do rather feel I owe it to the duke to get there as soon as I can. So, on with your mask, Hetta dear, and let's go.' She was amused and a little touched to see Ruth put hers on too, as if she felt it some kind of protection in this room full of strangers. 'It's amazing what a disguise it is,' she went on, looking from one girl to the other.

'It certainly is,' said Ruth, with one of her rare laughs. 'If I didn't know you two so well I'm not sure I'd know which was which.'

'I told you the lighting was going to be terrible,' said Caterina. 'Come along, Hetta, let's take the plunge.'

The high, sparsely furnished rooms of the Carrancas Palace were already thronged with people, and Caterina paused on the threshold of the ballroom looking about her doubtfully. The band of the *caçadores* was playing a waltz and the floor itself was not crowded yet, but she looked in vain for the little knot of people that always indicated the presence of the Duke of Braganza.

'We must pay our respects to our host,' she told Hetta. 'I imagine he must be in the cardroom. Oh – what a relief.' She turned as Greville came up to them. 'I'm so glad to see you, Greville. Can you tell us where the duke is?'

'Not here, I'm sorry to say. They found his old acquaintance guilty this morning and the execution was carried out on the spot. Braganza did not feel he could come tonight and I cannot say that I altogether blame him.'

'Perhaps not,' she said. 'But it's a pity just the same.'

'Yes. Rather defeats the purpose of the operation, you might say. I think the more visibly we all enjoy ourselves the better, don't you? Will you do me the honour of dancing with me, Caterina?'

She turned rather doubtfully to Hetta, but saw that Frank and Lewis were both advancing on her, smiled and let herself be led on to the floor. 'You seem to have recognized me easily enough behind the mask.'

'Of course I recognized you.' He steered her expertly into the middle of the room where the floor was emptier. 'What are you looking for?' he asked after a few swift turns. 'You are supposed to be entertaining me with agreeable conversation and instead you are peering about the room like a modern Argus from behind that idiotic mask of yours.'

She smiled up at him. 'I do apologize. To tell you the truth I am just a little anxious about Rachel Emerson. Have you see her since we got back?'

'No, I can't say that I have, but that is a woman who can take care of herself if ever there was one. If you want to worry about anyone, worry about poor Colonel Hare, last seen with her. But if it makes you feel better, I can see two other of your distinctive blue dresses whirling about the room.'

'One of them is Hetta, of course. Can you see who she is dancing with, Greville?'

'Her brother,' he told her. 'That's a good lad.'

'Yes. Is Lewis dancing?'

'Not that I can see.'

'Oh dear.' No need to share with him her recognition that Lewis had left it to Frank to take pity on his sister and dance with her.

The firm arm round her waist gave her a small, reproachful squeeze. 'You are supposed to be visibly enjoying yourself, remember.'

'Yes, that's all very well, Greville, but suppose some accident has befallen Rachel Emerson. The mist was getting very thick when we came in. Could we take a turn towards the garden entrance and see what it is like now? Poor Ruth is waiting for her mother in the cloakroom and must be worried to death.'

'Anything to stop you worrying, Caterina.' He took them in a series of swift swoops across the floor to the curtained doorway that led out into a formal garden. Like the rest of the palace, which belonged to an absentee nobleman but was used by the Braganzas when they were in Oporto, this showed signs of neglect. The mist was lying patchily here too, but it was still a little lighter outside than in. They could see a couple moving away from them down one of the hedged walks. 'That's Lewis,' said Caterina with absolute certainty.

'Yes.' There was laughter in his voice. 'So the lady in blue must be Ruth Emerson, who is no longer in the ladies' cloakroom worrying about her mother. Are you happy now, Caterina?'

'Not very,' she told him.

She might have been happier if she had heard what they were saying. Rachel, arriving late and breathless, had been furious to find her daughter waiting for her, and had sent her straight into the ballroom with instructions to try and behave as little like a fool as she could manage. Entering nervously, Ruth had been pounced on by Lewis, who had taken her for one giddy swirling turn of the room before whisking her out through the curtained doorway into the quiet of the garden. 'At last.' His arm firmly on hers he led her through a gap in the myrtle hedge to a secluded walk leading to a dimly seen fountain.

'But, Lewis!'

'Don't "but Lewis" me. This is our chance at last. I thought I'd never get you alone, have a chance to say it. You are mine, Ruth, and you know it. We've both known it since that first day when our eyes met. You are my life, my other half! I've told my mother. I was beginning to think I would never get the chance to tell you, but there's no need is there? You know it too. Ruth, my darling, my own, my wife!' He pulled her to him muttering Portuguese endearments.

'No.' She pulled away. 'I'm sorry, Lewis, but you're wrong. It's not like that. Oh, for a minute, that first day, I did have the strangest feeling. I do know what you mean. I feel I have known you forever, understand you maybe better than you do yourself. But, Lewis, I don't love you. Not like that. Not marrying love.'

'I don't believe you!' He snatched off her mask, cupped her face in ungentle hands and bent to kiss her.

'No!' She snatched herself from his grasp, surprising him by her sudden burst of strength, and dived through a gap in the further hedge.

'Ruth!' He still did not believe it. She was playing with him, teasing him. But when he entered the next alley there was no sign of her. 'Ruth!' he called again, angry now, but keeping his voice low. There was another gap in the next hedge. 'Don't torment me!' Which way would she have gone? Not back to the house. She was merely playing hide and seek with him. He plunged through the further hedge and was rewarded by the sight of a blue dress whisking around a far corner and out of sight. He had not thought she could run so fast, but everything about her was surprising him today. And it made him mad for her. He ran swiftly down the alley, turned the corner, saw the blue figure not far ahead, caught up with a few rapid strides, put his hand on her shoulder, swung her round and looked down into the masked face of a total stranger.

He had known from the moment of touch. His hand on the shoulder became a vice. 'Who in God's name are you?'

'I might say the same to you.' It was no surprise that this was a man's voice. 'But need not.' He was making no attempt to escape from the grip Lewis still kept on his shoulder. 'You are Lewis da Gomez y Fonsa. The very man I need. You serve the duke, do you not? I am here at the risk of my life with overtures from his brother. It's more than time this madness was stopped, friend against friend, cousin against cousin. I've been mixing with the dancers, hoping for a word with Braganza, but there's no sign of him.'

'No,' said Lewis. 'He's in his own apartments.'

'To which you have the entré. Fetch him for me, quick, without telling a soul. You know what old cravens his councillors are. I tell you, boy, it's a chance in a million, for peace, for Portugal.'

'Who are you? Why should I trust you?' Lewis did not much like being called 'boy' and his grip on that muscular shoulder tightened.

The stranger used his other hand to whip off the mask. 'Look at me, Lewis! Know me. I am your father, Luiz da Fonsa y Sanchez.' And then, 'Your mother never told you?'

'No!' In the moment of absolute astonishment Lewis's grip had slackened, but the other man made no move to escape, merely stood there exchanging look for look. His father? He would not believe his ears. He knew the name, of course: old Madame Fonsa's grandson who had gone with the French, years ago. His mind reeling, he gazed at that strange face that was also so familiar that he was horribly sure of one thing: this was his father.

'Don't stand there gawping, boy. There's no time to be lost. Fetch the duke. Quickly. Secretly. I have his brother's token, but must show it to none but him. If we succeed, we save Portugal. But if I am taken, unsuccessful, just try and imagine the disgrace to your mother – and to yourself, my poor bastard.'

Lewis hit him. He had not intended to. It simply happened, and in the short, savage, silent fight that followed he was inevitably worsted, despite the handicap of his opponent's dress. He had been brought up to fight fair, and this was not a fair fight. Winded by one last ferocious blow to the chest, he lost consciousness for a few seconds, recovered to find himself alone, the black mask lying beside him. Half-consciously he picked it up and put it in his pocket before getting unsteadily to his feet. What in the world should he do? Give the alarm? But that would be to precipitate the scandal his father had predicted. He still believed that it had been his father. The very fact that he had not been killed, nor even seriously injured went to prove it. If he gave the alarm, the duke's ball would be ruined, its purpose destroyed. But was this special pleading because he so badly wanted not to give the alarm?

'Lewis!' Jeremy Craddock had come through the gap in the thick hedge. 'What in the world has happened? Are you hurt?'

'No, it's nothing.' He was dusting down his uniform as he spoke. 'You're the very man to advise me, Mr Craddock. I don't know what to do.'

Chapter 9

'I think you are absolutely right. Say nothing.' Jeremy Craddock had listened impassively as Lewis poured out his story, passing lightly over the encounter with Ruth Emerson. 'Whoever he was, the man is gone. To raise the alarm now would achieve nothing and cause infinite embarrassment to your mother as well as to yourself. You believed him when he said he was your father?'

'Yes.' Through gritted teeth. 'And you are not surprised. You knew all the time?'

'Nobody ever told me, but, yes, I thought he must be. You will have to tell your mother. Warn her. I am sure she hoped him dead. But not tonight. The duke's absence from the party has been bad enough without an alarm like this. And Sanchez must be long gone. I take it there are ways out of the gardens?'

'Yes, out though not in, because of the lie of the land. He must have come in with the other guests.'

'All those women dressed alike. Whose idea was that, do you know?' Jeremy was thinking hard.

'Lord, no. Some female nonsense cooked up among them. All the women in Oporto probably knew about it. You know how they talk. Sir, what am I to do?'

'Nothing. Tell your mother, no one else. You can rely on my absolute silence. And now, we should get back to the party. You will be missed.' He held out his hand. 'I'm so sorry, Lewis. Anything I can do. . . .'

'Thank you, sir.' They moved back in silence towards the sounds of revelry.

★

Dancing with her brother, Hetta saw Lewis swoop on Ruth and sweep her off into the garden. 'You missed your step,' Frank reproached her. 'Pay attention, Het, or I'll drop you off with the wallflowers.'

'I'm sorry, I was thinking.'

'Well, don't. A ballroom is no place for thought. Or if you must think, tell me what I am to say to Maria Bankes when I take the floor with her, as I must, heaven help me.'

'You won't need to say anything. She'll tell you all about how uncomfortable it has been staying on board ship, and how she wishes herself safe in England, and how dreadfully her husband is overworked.'

'You're right, of course. How well Aunt Caterina dances!' She had just swept past them in Greville's arms.

'She wants us to call her Caterina but I do find it difficult. Ruth is calling her Aunt Caterina now.'

'Is she? I like that. You're fond of Ruth, aren't you, Het?'

'And sorry for her. Do you know, Frank, sometimes she says things about her childhood that put me in a rage with her mother. I cannot like that woman.'

'It's not like you to take against people.'

'It's not just dislike. I almost think I hate Rachel Emerson. She's false right through. And to see her fawning on Aunt Caterina— Oh, there is Ruth all by herself—'

'Where?'

'Just come in from the garden. That's right—' He had made a swift turn and was steering her towards the garden entrance. 'Can you see her?'

'Yes, she looks distracted, poor girl. Did that mother of hers teach her nothing about how to go on in company?'

'You'd be surprised how little time she has spent with that mother of hers.' They had reached Ruth now. 'Ruth dear, what is the matter?'

This was a mistake. Ruth burst into tears.

'Back to the garden.' Frank took one of Ruth's arms while Hetta took the other. 'Or would you like me to fetch your mother, Miss Emerson?'

'Oh, no, please don't! She'll be so angry, but I couldn't help it, really I couldn't.'

'Help what?' asked Frank.

Hetta thought she knew. 'Ruth dear, come and sit on this convenient bench,' she said. 'And, Frank, could you brave the dragon in the ladies' cloakroom and fetch our shawls for us, do you think? Ruth should not be sitting out here in the evening chill after the fright she has had.'

'But who did it?' asked Frank savagely. 'Who frightened you? Let me just get at him!'

'Oh, no,' said Ruth, appalled. 'It's not like that, Mr Ware. It's all my fault, every bit of it, and Mother is going to be so furious.'

'Off you go, Frank, this is women's work,' said Hetta. She guided Ruth firmly to a marble bench that commanded a view of the garden's long central alley.

When she took that tone, Frank always obeyed his sister. 'I'll be as quick as I can.' He turned away towards the house.

'So we must be quick too.' Hetta settled her friend beside her on the bench and kept the comforting arm firm round her waist. 'It's Lewis, isn't it? Do you want to tell me about it?'

'Oh, yes! Mother will be so angry. She's been counting on it so. I'm sure that's why she was so eager for this ball. She keeps saying how rich I will be, and how powerful, and I really meant to say yes, but when it came to the point and he was taking it so for granted, Hetta, I just couldn't!'

'So what happened?'

'I ran away. It's all alleys and statues down there. It was easy to hide from him and come back the other way, and then I began to think how angry he'd be, and what I was going to tell my mother, and, oh Hetta, I can't face her.'

'Don't tell her anything,' said Hetta bracingly. 'You can be sure Lewis won't say a word, he's much too much the gentleman for that. But I'm afraid he is going to be very angry and very surprised. Stupid of him to try and rush you like that. Don't you think, Ruth dear, that maybe if he had gone about it differently, more gently?'

She could imagine the scene all too easily.

'But he isn't gentle,' said Ruth, and it was unanswerable. 'And Mother will want to know all about everything. She always does.'

'Then I am afraid you will have to learn to lie to her,' said Hetta. 'Does she know he swept you out into the garden like that, which was most improper of him, by the way.'

'No, she doesn't. That's true!' Ruth was beginning to revive. 'She was still up in the cloakroom. She was furious when she found I had waited for her. She sent me down, and Lewis was waiting.'

'Yes, I saw, but I doubt if anyone else did. He wasted no time! So forget it ever happened. You were alarmed at finding yourself all alone among so many strangers, Frank and I came to your rescue, and here we are. And here is Frank with our cloaks. That was quick,' she smiled at her brother. 'But we have changed our minds. You are going to take Ruth on to the floor and I am going to return our cloaks to the ladies' room. And nothing more is going to be said about this.' She was looking down the long alley as she spoke. 'Quickly, Frank, take her in, she's getting cold. I'll sit here a while longer, I think. It's a restful place for a wallflower. Get along with you, do,' she urged, as Frank hesitated. 'And indifferent topics, remember!'

'If you say so.' Frank was too pleased at the way things had turned out to object to being dragooned by his sister. He took Ruth's arm and led her back to the house, neither of them noticing the two figures Hetta had seen at the bottom of the long alley.

She had known Lewis at once, but it took her longer to recognize Jeremy Craddock as his companion. She sat relaxed, waiting for them to reach her, wondering how to deal with them, unsure whether she wished to speak to Lewis alone or not. But as they got nearer she jumped to her feet. 'Lewis!' she exclaimed. 'What's happened? What's the matter?'

'The devil! Is it so obvious?' The two men exchanged a rueful glance as Lewis spoke.

'You've been in a fight.' She had expected him to be angry after Ruth's rebuff, but not visibly dishevelled like this. What in the world could have happened? Surely not a fight with Jeremy Craddock? They seemed on the best of terms now.

'We had hoped it did not show,' said Jeremy. And then, smiling, 'Not a fight with me, Miss Ware, in case you were wondering.'

'If it is not to show, allow me, Lewis.' She twisted his left epaulet back into place, and made a swift, firm adjustment to his stock. 'You're always so point-device in your appearance, that anyone would notice so much amiss. And there is a stain on your elegant new inexpressibles, too. Perhaps you should just admit to having had a fall? Though it is hard to see quite how.' As she ministered to him, she felt how he seethed with pent-up rage. 'But the worst of all is the way you look, Lewis dear. You're the duke's aide. If you go into the ballroom now, looking as you do, the world will jump to all kinds of desperate conclusions, which is not the purpose of this party at all. Do you think perhaps the best thing you can do is to plead illness and let Mr Craddock make your apologies? I am sure you must know some convenient side entrance by which you could return to the palace.'

'I'd rather die than cry craven like that. I tell you what, Hetta, you had better dance with me.'

'And let the world think you have taken pity on me and wished you hadn't?' She regretted the words as soon as they were spoken, but they seemed to have a bracing effect on him. 'I've lost my mask, Lewis.' She had dropped it when she was comforting Ruth.

'No matter, I have one here.' He produced it from his pocket. 'Not that you need one. 'Specially not when dancing with me, of all people.'

Jeremy Craddock, watching this exchange, had come to a conclusion of his own. 'I have it,' he said. 'Lewis, you rescued Miss Ware from the unwelcome advances of a stranger, who found her alone in the garden and took advantage of it. You really should not be out alone here in the dark, you know, Miss Ware.'

'Which has to explain why your stranger even thought of molesting me.' Hetta put on the mask Lewis had handed her and took his arm. 'Thank you, Mr Craddock, for a most flattering notion. Let's go, Lewis; they are just striking up a new dance. And let's not say anything unless we have to.'

'No,' Jeremy agreed. 'The less said, the better. Is that your cloak, Miss Ware? Would you like me to take it indoors for you?'

'Oh, thank you.' She had forgotten the two cloaks lying on the bench. 'That would be kind.' As he picked them both up without comment she was sure that he had seen Frank and Ruth while Lewis, deep in talk, had not.

'What in the world were you doing out in the garden all by yourself?' Lewis asked, as he led her back into the ballroom.

'Hiding my shame at my lack of a partner, of course. As an occasion to promote friendship between English and Portuguese I am afraid this party is not being an outstanding success. We need the duke here to sweep protocol away and dance with everyone.'

'He saw an old acquaintance shot this morning,' Lewis told her repressively.

'I know, but isn't it royalty's job to tie a knot, however painful, and go on?' She was glad to feel some of the tension in him begin to ease as he turned his mind to the duke whom she knew he loved.

'He's so lonely, Hetta! I suppose he had to send his wife and daughter to safety in France, but do you know, I sometimes wish he had not left his mistress behind on Terceira. I hate to see him with no one to turn to after his battles with those greybeard councillors of his.' He swept her round in an expert turn and looked down at her ruefully. 'Forget I said that, Hetta. Inexcusable!'

'But flattering!' She smiled up at him. 'This mask is a most desperately bad fit. Do you mind if I take it off? I feel like a horse in blinkers.'

'Of course I don't. I'm proud to be seen dancing with you, Hetta.'

'Well, you aren't going to be seen so for long,' she told him. 'I see a grateful patient approaching, and since he is Portuguese I think I had better accept his flattering offer, don't you?'

'Damnation,' he said, and turned as an elegant young Portuguese *fidalgo* touched his shoulder.

'I am so glad you removed the mask, Miss Ware,' said Almeida Garrett. 'You cannot monopolize our angel of mercy, da Fonsa. I have been looking for you everywhere, Miss Ware, in the hope that you will do me the honour of joining me for the supper that is now ready in the next room.'

'*Chouriço* sausages and *almaça* cheese,' said Hetta, smiling at him. 'I will be delighted, Senhor Garrett. At least we know the wine will be delicious. A thousand thanks, Lewis.' They had not discussed the suggestion that he had rescued her, but the thanks would cover it.

Caterina was in the refreshment room with Greville on one side of her and Jeremy on the other. 'We do sadly miss the duke.' She accepted a piece of her own cheese from Jeremy. 'Oh, there is poor Harriet stuck with the Bankeses. Do let us join them. If Ruth is dancing with Frank, as you say, Greville, and Hetta with Lewis, I am absolved from all duties as chaperon and can feel free to enjoy myself.'

'By rescuing Mrs Ware from the Bankeses!' But Greville had already taken her arm to guide her across the room to where Harriet was making heavy weather with Mr and Mrs Bankes.

'Oh, Caterina, I am so glad to see you.' She meant it. 'Have you seen Lewis? Mr Bankes has the oddest tale of some kind of struggle in the garden.'

'I was taking a breath of air,' said Bankes pontifically. 'Enjoying the quiet of the night. Do you realize there has been no bombardment of any kind all day? I was thinking about that, and regretting the duke's absence, when something – a cry perhaps? – drew my attention to the alley that leads down to the fountain. One of the young ladies in blue was struggling with a man there, very unwelcome attentions by the look of it. I am sorry to tell you, Madame Fonsa, but I rather thought it was your son.'

'Impossible,' said Caterina. 'He is in the ballroom, dancing with Miss Ware.'

'Ah,' said Bankes with obvious satisfaction, 'but this was a little time ago, you must understand.'

'I take it you did not think fit to intervene?' Jeremy Craddock surprised Caterina by his own intervention. 'In fact, it was your son who did so, Caterina. He found Miss Ware being molested by a stranger and went to her rescue, as one would expect of him. No need to look so anxious, Mrs Ware, here she comes to tell you she is none the worse.' He turned to Hetta, who was approaching with Almeida Garrett. 'I'm afraid your little misadventure was observed after all, Miss Ware, so I have not been able to respect your wish for silence. Mr Bankes saw Lewis rescue you, and rather misinterpreted the situation.'

'Oh dear, I do feel such a fool.' Hetta put up a hand to the scar on the side of her face. 'I'd gone out into the garden for a little peace and quiet, masked of course, and some gentleman the worse for drink decided that I was fair game. Fancy me, of all people! I was so grateful to Lewis for coming to my assistance, Aunt Caterina. I am afraid there was a bit of a fight. I suppose that was why you did not feel just like intervening, Mr Bankes?'

'I was too far away,' he said swiftly. 'And besides, my wife was waiting for me. I would very much like to know, Miss Ware, whether the inebriated gentleman was English or Portuguese?'

Trouble either way. 'That I am afraid I cannot tell you, Mr Bankes. A drunk is a drunk in any language. Perhaps Lewis will know. Here he comes. Lewis, our little secret is out I am afraid. Mr Bankes saw you rescue me out there in the garden and wants to know whether my drunken assailant was English or Portuguese. I had to say I had no idea. It all happened so fast. But I was telling your mother how gallant you were.'

'It was nothing. And, frankly, Mr Bankes, I think the less said about the whole thing the better. The man was someone I have never seen before and do not wish to see again. Mother, I am come to offer you my escort home. I am sure that Hetta would be happier there after her unfortunate experience.'

'And you want to change your dress,' said Caterina, looking him up and down. 'If you look like that, one can only wonder about your opponent. Perhaps we should survey the room for a black eye and a broken nose as we leave. Come along, Hetta, we must find Ruth and our cloaks, and, Harriet, what a comfort that you agreed to spend the night with us.'

As she had intended, this broke the group up. Only, parting with him at the gates of the Sanchez Palace, she held Lewis's hand for a moment. 'Give our grateful thanks to the duke, Lewis, and come tomorrow and tell me the real story.'

'Believe me, Mother, I will.' His words echoed in her head all night. Was there a threat in them, or was she imagining things? She was worried, too, about Ruth, who had looked wretched and hardly spoken a word as she came back on Frank Ware's arm.

Chapter 10

Caterina had been convinced from the first that whatever had happened in the garden, Ruth had been involved in it as well as Hetta, and one look at her next morning confirmed this. She looked heavy-eyed, close to tears. Hetta urged her to take a day off from her duties at the hospital. 'I will make your excuses for you.' But Ruth looked frightened and insisted on going with her.

Left alone, Caterina decided not to try and do any more work on the rather unsatisfactory cartoon she had started before breakfast. Today was bound to bring a crowd of visitors and she very much wished she thought that Lewis would be the first of them. But he had his duties, and she was less surprised than sorry when Rachel Emerson was announced.

'How is my poor child today?' Rachel asked at once. 'She looked dreadfully last night, I thought. I am sure you have not let her go to work today.'

'I am afraid I could not stop her. She did not look quite the thing this morning, it is true, but felt it her duty to go, and I respect her for it.'

'But what happened last night? There have been the most extra-ordinary rumours going round the town.'

'It is an extraordinary town for rumours. One simply has to live with them. And try not to add to them.'

'Oh, that's of course. But between old friends like you and I, Madame Fonsa, I think there is room for a little straight talking. And more than time for it, too. My Ruth was in high good looks when she ran down to join the dancing last night, and looking forward to it. Well, you remember what a success she had at that little affair you gave for the duke when he first came. No reason to expect anything different yesterday; so what happened while I was still up in the cloakroom, that's what I want to know! When I got down there was no sign of her and when I next saw her, dancing with young Ware, she looked like the wrath of God. What did she say when she got back last night?'

'Nothing.' It had the virtue of being true. 'We were all tired and went to bed at once.' Caterina had been both surprised and relieved that Rachel had not, as she had feared, invited herself to spend the night. 'I am afraid we both seem to have failed poor Ruth as chaperons last night,' she went on. 'And the masks were a complication were they not? And all the dresses alike. That was your idea, I believe?'

'I regret it now. My poor little Ruth, such an innocent child as I have always wished to keep her. Are you sure you do not know what happened to disturb her so last night?'

'I have already said so, Mrs Emerson.'

'And what does your son say? He saw you home last night, did he not? I was a little surprised when I learned that my beloved child had gone off without even saying goodbye to me, but you and I know his devotion – and his overbearing ways, do we not?'

'I have not talked to my son since last night, Mrs Emerson, and, in fact, it was Frank Ware who danced the last dance with your daughter and saw her home. Lewis was with Hetta. I do not believe he and Ruth exchanged a word.' And this too was true enough. It had surprised her at the time.

'Can that be it?' Rachel Emerson pounced on this. 'Can he really mean to play fast and loose with my little girl, after all the significant attentions he has paid her? Was that what distressed her so? I warn you, if your son has been trifling with my child, and so publicly too, and now means to abandon her, he will have me to reckon with.'

'If there should prove to be an engagement between them, of course Lewis must honour it, but, frankly, Mrs Emerson, I know of nothing of the kind. It is quite true that all the young men lost their heads over your beautiful Ruth when she first came, but – how shall I say this without offending you? Ruth is a delightful child, but she is a child still, and I imagine that some of her cavaliers have begun to find her perhaps a little young for them. I cannot speak for Lewis, mind you; we have not discussed the matter at all.'

'Then it is high time you did.' Rachel rose and picked up her gloves. 'If he has tampered with my daughter's affections, I will go straight to the duke, and so I warn you. We will talk more of this.' She flounced out of the palace, leaving Caterina more anxious than ever. If only Lewis would come.

Rachel Emerson found a caller waiting for her at home. 'I took the liberty of telling your girl I would wait.' Jeremy rose to greet her. 'We need to talk today, you and I.'

'Do we? I cannot begin to imagine why, but, of course, I am always delighted to see you, Mr Craddock.' She made a little business of taking off hat and gloves and ordering wine and cakes, and he had time to notice that she looked tired this morning, lines showing where they should not.

It gave him confidence. 'No need to beat about the bush with you, Mrs Emerson. You were painfully frank with me a while ago, I am going to return the compliment now. How much have you managed to learn about what happened at the Carrancas Palace last night?'

'Very little. I have just come from Caterina Fonsa, who seems to know nothing. Or that is what she says.'

'If she has not seen her son yet, it is almost certainly true. So I shall give myself the pleasure of telling you. I found young Lewis in the garden, recovering from a blow. It had knocked him out for a minute and his assailant had escaped, presumably over the wall somewhere. The interesting thing about him was that he was disguised as a woman in one of those fetching blue dresses all you lady patronesses wore. More interesting still, from Lewis's point of view, was that he claimed to be his father, Luiz da Fonsa y Sanchez.' He was watching her very carefully and saw the reaction he had expected. 'And convinced him, too. He is a very unhappy young man today, I suspect, Lewis da Gomez y Fonsa. Well, that is his problem. I am come to tell you of yours, Mrs Emerson.'

'Mine?' She tried to sound both surprised and puzzled.

'Yes, yours. I talked to a few people last night and was not altogether surprised to learn that the idea of the similar blue dresses was yours. You learned that Caterina Fonsa had bought hers from Senhor Chaves and managed to persuade him to sell you the rest of the cloth. A great deal of it. Enough for an extra dress perhaps? And then you came to our outing on a limping mule, which made you dally behind the rest of us on the way home. I am really thunderstruck at my own stupidity that I did not realize you and Luiz da Fonsa y Sanchez might be old friends from the time of the plot against the Duke of Wellington all those years ago. Was there a fond farewell before I put you and your husband on the boat for America? And have you been in touch ever since? And does that explain your surprising appearance here in Oporto just before the outbreak of hostilities? I suppose once a spy always a spy. Well, now your teeth are drawn. I am glad to see you do not try to deny it.'

'What do you propose to do?' She went straight to the point, and he found himself respecting her for it.

'As little as possible. I am not even going to ask for all that gold back that I gave you the other day, but I suggest you use it to pay for passages back to the United States for yourself and your charming daughter.'

'And keep my mouth shut.' She was visibly hard at work assessing the new situation in which she found herself.

'Well, of course. I am acting as Caterina's friend in this. Just imagine her situation if all the old stories were to be revived by the reappearance of Lewis's real father. It might even upset his inheritance of the two estates, and you are the last person to want that, granted young Lewis's passion for your daughter.'

'But I thought you wanted me to take her away?'

'Not if she has better things to do here. She is a surprisingly harmless young thing, considering that she is your daughter. It is only you that I want away from here, or I would not be able to reconcile it with my conscience not to speak up about what really happened last night.'

'You have not so far?'

'Oh, no. You've not heard? The story is that Lewis found Hetta Ware being molested by a stranger. Bankes had seen something of the struggle between Lewis and his father and it was the best I could think of to account for it. So Lewis is a hero, Hetta a romantic heroine and your daughter quite out of the picture. And Lewis's father, too, and, for everyone's sake, I would much rather it remained that way. And so, I am sure, would you.'

'That's all very well, Mr Craddock, but you have not thought about the talk that would be generated if I were to abandon my daughter here before her marriage. You are absolutely right, my teeth are drawn. Sanchez did use my help to get into the palace last night. He said he wanted a chance to persuade the duke into an accommodation with his brother.' Something in her tone told him that she had known this for a lie, his intention much more sinister. 'He was supposed to come here afterwards,' she went on. 'I had made arrangements to get him back across the river. It can still be done, you know, under cover of darkness. But – he never came.' He had been aware, throughout the interchange, of strong emotion in her, now recognized it as rage, pure, simple rage. 'He has used me, and dropped me. I should have expected it. It was always his way.'

'So you mean he is still in town, hiding somewhere?'

'Oh, I doubt that. He is not such a fool. No, he probably managed to cross the lines somewhere down towards Foz. It's easy enough, if you have friends. And, remember, he grew up here in Oporto. He'll be long gone by now, and so much the better for Caterina Fonsa. If you have her best interests at heart, you must see that. Mr Craddock, let me stay, and I promise you, if he should by any mad chance get in touch with me again, I will let you know at once.'

'You'll turn your coat?'

'Why not? I have had enough of Luiz da Fonsa y Sanchez. He has let me down once too often. And I know you for a good payer, Mr Craddock, which is more than one could say of him. Promises were always his line. All I want is to get my little Ruth well married, of which I have every expectation, and, believe me, I'll be off as soon as the knot is tied. If you think starving in a besieged city is my idea of how to spend the winter you are very much mistaken. The bombardment is heavier this morning, had you noticed? Making up for yesterday.'

'You mean it was stopped to protect Sanchez?'

'So I assume. He is one of Dom Miguel's most trusted advisers.'

'Is he so? Do you know, Mrs Emerson, I believe that we may be able to be of use to each other. Mutual silence, and mutual aid?'

'And payment for services rendered?'

'When they are. I am sure you will find the British Government a more reliable paymaster than Dom Miguel.'

'It's a bargain.' She poured wine for them both. 'Friends and allies then, Mr Craddock. And not a word to a soul.'

Greville Faulkes was Caterina's next caller, and she was glad of the chance to ask him what was being said in town about the party the night before.

'It's a thousand pities the duke did not feel able to attend,' he told her. 'It has caused a good deal of bad feeling among the British. Dolly Procter was certain he was going to dance with her – you know the kind of thing. And there are some strange stories going, Caterina, about your Lewis and his gallant rescue of Miss Ware. Josiah Bankes is full of hints and insinuations. He's a deplorable fellow. I am afraid he has never forgiven Frank – and his family – for that successful action of his in getting the company wine across the river when he himself was hiding under a bed somewhere.'

'Oh, dear,' said Caterina. 'What is he saying?'

'Nothing direct. Just nasty little hints about poor Hetta Ware's scarred face and the improbability of an attack on her. And some curious talk about the lady patronesses and their blue gowns. All very unpleasant and not at all what the party was supposed to achieve. But otherwise I am happy to tell you St Bruxas' Eve seems to have passed off calmly enough. The lack of bombardment was a bonus, of course, but it has resumed with double strength today. There! Did you hear that?'

'Close,' agreed Caterina. 'I do hope not among my vegetables.'

'Further off than that, I think. Caterina, did you hear the other main subject of talk last night? Some kind friend in England has sent the Procters a great batch of Forsyte cartoons and they are all agog to know who is Charles Forsyte's informant here in Oporto. If you want to keep your secret, you are going to have to be more careful than ever both in what you say and what you put into your splendid drawings. It had not struck me, as it should have, how full of solid local detail they are.'

'Oh dear,' she said. 'No, it had not struck me either. I will be careful, Greville. I have the most horrid feeling that Lewis would absolutely hate to have the truth come out.'

'He does not know?'

'I should rather think not.'

'And you don't think he will like it?'

'I am absolutely sure he won't.'

'And why should you care a rap for that?' he said robustly, surprising her. 'Caterina, does it not occur to you that you have concentrated all your heart and thought on that son of yours for quite long enough? Think of yourself for a change. Things are going to be bad here in Oporto this winter. I don't think anyone is quite facing how bad. Caterina—' He broke off. 'Damnation!'

Carlotta had entered the room. 'The *senhor* is here, *minha senhora*; he says he has very little time, must see you at once.'

'Then I must leave you.' Greville rose. 'Till another time, Caterina.'

He said a friendly word to Lewis in the doorway, but Lewis took no notice, concentrating a dark look on Caterina. 'Mother.' Looming over her. 'The duke has sent me with his apologies for not appearing last night. He says he knows you will understand. I have very little time, but we have to talk.' She could feel fury boiling in him. 'Mother, is Luiz da Fonsa y Sanchez my father?'

'Lewis!' She looked quickly at the door, but Greville had closed it behind him. 'Who told you that?'

'He did. Last night.'

'What?' She could not believe her ears.

'It was with him I fought. I took him for Ruth. He was disguised.' Impatiently. 'In one of those blue dresses you all wore. When I challenged him he said he was a secret envoy from Miguel, seeking peace – and told me he was my father. Tell me it's not true. Tell me he was trying to scare me into silence.'

'Lewis, I can't. It's true. I had so hoped he was dead, that I would never have to tell you.'

'So all the story of the English marriage was a pack of lies?'

'Told for your sake, Lewis. I'm so sorry—' She looked up at him pleadingly, feeling their positions suddenly and irrevocably reversed.

'You were not married to Sanchez.' It was not a question.

'I was a child, Lewis. I loved him so. You remember your Grandfather Gomez. Imagine what it was like to grow up in his house. I was so lonely. And then, I met Luiz. You know the summer-house down in the gorge, on the Gomez side where I lived then? He lived here, came across to me. It was boy and girl, Romeo and Juliet. That's what I thought. I only learned the truth about him much later.'

'The truth?'

'He was every woman's Romeo. How was I to know? I thought him the great love of my life, would have done anything for him.'

'Did,' he said savagely. 'You are telling me I am his bastard, Mother.'

'Yes. What use to say I am sorry? I did not discover my condition until I was at convent school in England. The nuns were good to me, sent me to a place in Bath for unfortunates like me. It was run by Harriet's mother.'

'What? Aunt Harriet?'

'We have been dear friends ever since.' She was not going to tell him any more about Harriet than that. 'When my father suddenly sent for me, there was nothing for it but to leave you behind. It was the worst day of my life, Lewis, but what could I do? Harriet came with me and I knew that so long as I managed to scrape together the fees and send them to her mother you would be fed and housed. It was not easy. Well, you remember what your grandfather was like. He just wanted me married, a son-in-law to run the firm. But, Lewis, I still hoped that your father would come back; we'd be married; you'd be acknowledged.'

'Acknowledged a bastard! Thank you, ma'am. You say "come back". Where was Sanchez?'

'Disinherited. Disgraced. When Wellington drove Soult out of Oporto, Luiz went with the French. And when he did come back it was in secret, as their agent, but I was older by then, wiser, sadder. I loved him still, but something in me did not trust him.'

'So you did not fall into his arms again?'

'No.' This was worse than anything she had ever imagined. But she must not cry. 'By the goodness of God, your great-grandmother, old Madame Fonsa got in touch with me, told me the truth about Luiz. His father, her son-in-law, was a wastrel and a womanizer. He squandered his wife's fortune, but could not get his hands on Madame Fonsa's. When I told her about you, she put her lawyers to work and they did a good job. You are her legitimately adopted great-grandson, Lewis, and there is nothing wrong with your title to her estate.'

'Thank you for nothing. And I suppose your father welcomed the little bastard with open arms too?'

'As a matter of fact, yes, Lewis, he did. Like her, he was mad for a male heir. Don't you remember how they used to fight over you when you were little?'

'I hated it. I always wished I had a proper family like the Wares.' She had thought for a moment that he was softening towards her, now his tone hardened. 'How many people know this sordid story, Mother?'

'Only Harriet. And the lawyers, of course, but it is their job to stay silent.'

'Jeremy Craddock seemed to know. He promised his silence.' The fury was back in his voice. 'What do you expect me to say to you, Mother? When I think of all the lectures I have endured from you about my behaviour! My behaviour! And you – no, I won't say it. I must return to my duties. Let us meet as little as we can manage, ma'am.'

'But, Lewis—' There was so much that still needed saying.

'Not now. If I stay longer, I shall say something we shall both regret.' And he was gone.

Left alone, Caterina sat for a while, staring into space, the tears now streaming down her cheeks. At the sound of yet another caller arriving she jumped up and fled into the garden. She had to be alone, to recover herself and dry these unwonted tears. One of the girls was working in the vegetable patch on the second terrace, so she hurried on down, calling a greeting as she went. She did not often come down to the bottom of the gorge that divided the Sanchez and Gomez estates. It still held memories for her of those long ago secret meetings with Luiz da Fonsa y Sanchez.

Lewis and the Ware children had loved to play here when they were young. She had had a bridge built across the gorge itself, and the little summer-house on the Gomez side, where she and Luiz had once made love, had been their headquarters. They had not used it since Lewis went away, but she had had it looked after, though the bottom terraces of both the Sanchez and Gomez estates now showed signs of wartime neglect. Since all the men were away working on the fortifications there had been no autumn pruning this year and laurel and myrtle and jasmine were growing rampant across the path. Pushing her way through them she emerged on to the bank of the gorge. It was dry still, since the autumn rains had not yet started, and she was glad to see that the bridge was in good condition. She would cross it and inspect the summer-house while she was here. It would be as good a reason as any for having come down here when she ought to have been at home to callers.

Honeysuckle and jasmine twined across the handrail of the bridge, and the paved area in front of the summer house was grown up with luxuriant weeds. She stopped, rigid, still holding the handrail of the bridge. The weeds showed a clear path where some-one had recently walked. Across the river, a cannon boomed, but here it was very quiet. Too quiet. Too solitary. Absurd. Her house and servants were within call. Her son's house and servants. Idiot. The servants had always used this path as a quick way between the two houses. But the trail she was looking at led to the summer-house.

Its door opened. 'How very convenient,' said Luiz da Fonsa y Sanchez.

'You!' She had to believe her eyes. She had not seen him for twenty years, but there was no mistaking him. Handsomer than ever, dark brown from long sun, tough and wiry, with all the deceptive gentleness that had charmed her quite gone. An entirely ruthless man.

'Yes, me, Caterina, come to make an honest woman of you.'

'What?'

'Not what I had meant at all.' His smile had lost its magic. 'I could not believe my eyes last night. Still my beautiful Caterina, my only real love, the mother of my son. And what a young ruffian that is! I tell you, Cat, he needs a father's hand.' He was holding his hand out to her, taking her response for granted.

She withdrew a step. 'What are you doing here, Luiz?'

'Has the boy not told you? I came on a secret mission of peace for my good friend Dom Miguel. Just like that old fool Pedro to stay away on some sentimental pretext or other last night and deprive me of my chance. But think what a means for good our marriage will be, Cat. You, hand in glove with Pedro and I Miguel's right-hand man.'

'You are well informed.' She must keep him talking while she racked her brain for some way out. 'Rachel Emerson, I suppose.'

His laugh grated on her ear. 'And what a disappointment she was! Can you wonder that I expected to find you a fat, black-clad old lady? And here you are a beauty still, and a painter, too. I want to see this portrait that has made Dom Pedro your slave. But there will be time for that. The question is, what's best to do now, before tongues start wagging too hard. Can the boy be relied on to keep silent?' And then, alerted by something in her look. 'What's the matter, Cat? You can't be blaming me for getting in touch with Rachel Emerson first. How was I to know you had waited for me all these years?'

'You must have known I had not married.' She must be infinitely careful.

The laugh again. 'I thought it was because no one had asked you. One look last night and I knew better than that. Do you know, I think I have it! We have been secretly married all the time. The papers will have to be conveniently lost in the chaos when Miguel takes the city. The boy will like that. I could see it hit him hard last night. Well, he hit me hard! What a farce. Father and son at it hammer and tongs, and me in fancy dress too! There was a moment when I thought he might even get the better of me, and was proud of him. I didn't hurt him, did I?'

'Only his pride.' She must at all costs go on listening. The more she heard, the more she was afraid. For a moment, she had actually been tempted. A secret marriage all those years ago would mean legitimacy for Lewis. For her it would mean bondage to this stranger she had once loved too well. 'You talk of Miguel taking Oporto. What kind of peace terms does that imply?'

'A politician too! What a creature you have become, my Caterina. The terms, of course, are what they have always been. Dom Miguel to marry the young queen and all is right again. Shall we celebrate our remarriage at the same time?' Now he was holding out both hands to her. 'Come, Cat my love, enough of this talk. If you have really stayed single for my sake all these years you must be as mad for me as I am for you. And if you have not, well, I have a peccadillo or two to be forgiven. Let's cry quits and start again.' He had her right hand now, meaning to lead her into the summer-house. 'I am glad you kept the place up for us,' he said.

'You're mad.' She knew now what she must do. 'Had you not wondered why I am here, so conveniently, as you say? I am meeting my man of business here, and a carpenter, to discuss what repairs we must do before the autumn rains begin. They should be here by now.'

'That fellow you were dancing with last night?' To her relief he accepted it without question. 'Pity. To business then. I have to see Braganza. In secret. Can you get him down here to me?'

'No. Impossible. The portrait is finished.' She looked anxiously about as if expecting Greville Faulkes and the imaginary carpenter.

'Then get the boy to bring the duke to the Fonsa Palace. It's mine now. Ours, Caterina. Those old Fonsa cousins died of idleness in Brazil. I've my headquarters there, and damned uncomfortable it is too.'

'Luiz, you must go. To be caught here would be fatal.' She managed to sound anxious for him. 'Can I send a message to the Fonsa Palace?'

'Take it yourself. It's a ruin now; there's a broken window by the front entrance. Drop a note through. I'll get it. And mind you come with Braganza and the boy.'

'Someone's coming!' she lied, and was relieved to see Luiz vanish swiftly round the side of the summer-house. Would he risk staying to eavesdrop? She thought not, but was already moving quickly across the bridge and up the overgrown path to the upper terrace, and safety.

The girl was still working in the vegetable patch and it was infinite relief to see her there. It also reminded her that up at the house there would probably be guests waiting for her. She found a secluded bench at the far end of the top terrace and sat down to catch her breath and ask herself what in the world she should do. Did she believe what Luiz had told her? She thought not. And even if she did, what kind of peace proposals were these? The time for talk of marriage between Miguel and his young niece was long past. And there had been something sinister in the casual way Luiz had referred to the taking of Oporto. He had not come, disguised, to the party last night to talk peace, he had come to kill Dom Pedro. It was clear in her mind now. But what in the name of God could she do about it?

Interrupted just as he had gathered up his courage to propose to Caterina, Greville Faulkes did not mean to give it up. Lewis had been in a great hurry, would not stay long. He went down to the open market and bought a little nosegay of late summer flowers for Caterina, noticing that the market-women's supplies of fruit and vegetables were scantier and poorer looking than they had been when last he had been there. More and more he wanted Caterina and her dangerous talent safe out of the city before the inevitable winter siege began. And the sight of Lewis, so visibly boiling with rage, had encouraged him. Perhaps Lewis himself would succeed in convincing his mother that it was time they parted company.

Thinking these hopeful thoughts as he walked back up the road towards the Sanchez Palace he did not notice Jeremy Craddock approaching from the other direction, looked up with a start at his greeting.

'If those are for Caterina,' Jeremy looked at the flowers, 'I am afraid you are wasting your time. That old besom Carlotta told me her mistress was tired out from yesterday's party and not to be disturbed. Just between ourselves I met young Lewis coming away in one of those towering tempers of his. I never saw a boy in worse need of a father's hand.'

'Hardly a boy now,' said Greville.

'He behaves like one. Are you coming my way, Greville? I wanted to ask you about those remarkable Forsyte cartoons that Dolly Procter has been showing everyone. My masters in London are bound to want to know about them. I agree with Dolly that there must be someone here sending information or even perhaps sketches to this Charles Forsyte. You have been here longer than anyone. I don't suppose it is you, by any interesting chance?'

'Lord, no. But another time, if you don't mind. Having bought these flowers for Caterina I will at least leave them with Carlotta for her. Tell me, though, this fight of young Lewis's last night. Did you actually see it? And who was the other man, do you know? I thought the invitations were strictly limited.'

'I know. Very odd, but, no I didn't see it, just came on Lewis afterwards. And really for everybody's sake I think the less said about it the better, don't you?'

They parted, mutually dissatisfied, and Greville returned to the Sanchez Palace, where he was surprised to be greeted warmly by Carlotta, who took the flowers from him and told him that Caterina was out in the garden. 'She and the young *senhor* had words, I think, and she went out to collect herself. I have been turning people away, but I am sure she would want to see you.'

Encouraged by this he went out on to the terrace where the light was beginning to change towards evening. The bombardment which had slackened while he was walking up the hill had started up again and now a cannon ball fell, too close, somewhere down towards the Gomez house. He quickened his step, and was relieved to see Caterina sitting on her favourite bench with its view down-river towards Foz and the sunset.

'Caterina,' he said urgently, approaching her. 'You ought not to be out here. That last ball was too close for comfort.'

'Greville—' She rose to face him and he saw with a lurch of the heart that she had been crying. 'I told Carlotta—'

'I'm sorry. I had to see you. Lewis interrupted me earlier, but I must say it even if it is a bad moment. I cannot go on like this, watching that son of yours browbeat you, treat you like some kind of housekeeper. Caterina, we are such old friends, such good ones.

Say you will marry me, give me the right to protect you, to take you away from this dangerous city. He's made you cry, that young devil, I can't bear to see it. Let me look after you, Caterina. Please. I can, you know, I've been wanting to tell you; I heard from my grandfather's man of business the other day; a terrible thing, my cousins both killed in a street brawl – some nonsense about the Reform Bill – and their father is dying. The estate is entailed; I could almost feel sorry for my grandfather. He has actually commissioned his agent to ask me to come home. But I can't go, Caterina, and leave you here. Listen!'

Another ball had fallen, a little further away this time, down nearer to the river.

'This winter is going to be terrible, supplies are running short in the market already, and all that outing yesterday served to show was the way the siege lines around us are tightening day by day. Worse still, Dom Pedro's behaviour last night must have convinced you as it has me that his distrust of the British is getting worse rather than better. I have heard some disquieting rumours about his treatment of Colonel Hodges. If he lets those councillors of his persuade him to get rid of Hodges, Lord knows what will happen. And, if it should come to a sack, imagine your position, both as Lewis's mother and as Charles Forsyte. It does not bear thinking of. Caterina, give me the right to take you away from here, to look after you at last. My mother will love you, I know; we could live with her at first, if you liked; she is always saying her house is much too big for her. There's bound to be room for a studio and you could work just as well, maybe better, as Charles Forsyte there as here. And portraits too—'

Caterina had had a hard day and this echo of Jeremy Craddock's proposal was suddenly too much for her. 'Thank you for nothing!' She turned on him furiously. 'You all seem to think me nothing but a pawn, to be pushed about at your will! And if you have discussed this kind offer with your mother, as by the sound of it you have, give her my humble thanks and tell her Charles Forsyte prefers to stay here in Porto with his friends.'

'Caterina, I never— Oh I have done this all wrong—' But she had swept past him with a furious rustle of skirts and he found that he did not dare follow her into the house. Nothing he said now could do anything but make matters worse. Following at last a few minutes later he found Carlotta in the hall. 'I'm sorry, *senhor*,' she said.

Chapter 11

To Caterina's relief, the duke's cutting his own party interested the gossips more than the fracas in his garden. The October rains began in good earnest a few days later and this combined with an increasingly heavy bombardment of the town to keep the talkers at home. It was becoming uncomfortably obvious that while the duke's forces had been carrying out their unsuccessful sorties across the river, the enemy had been quietly building new batteries to control its mouth. It was no longer possible to bring supplies upriver to Oporto itself. Everything, even the mail, had to be off-loaded at Foz and slipped upriver in small boats under cover of darkness. Supplies, and tempers, began to run short. Colonel Hodges was manoeuvred into a hasty resignation as commander of the British contingent and it was instantly accepted. Conditions among the foreign volunteers were so bad that 400 English soldiers marched on the Carrancas Palace demanding their back pay.

'They were fobbed off with promises again.' Hetta had brought the news back from the hospital. 'Do you know some of them have actually had to sell their uniforms to buy food.' And then, 'Good gracious, Caterina, what has happened to the duke's portrait?'

'He asked for it. I had it taken over to the palace.'

'He's paid for it, of course?' And then, reproachfully, 'Oh, Caterina!'

'I have his promise to pay when the war is over.'

'And you accepted it? He has also promised pay to the British troops and supplies to the Foreign Hospital. I was there yesterday; they've still not repaired the bomb damage; you never saw such a shambles; it's shameful. But have you heard the other news? Dom Miguel has arrived at last to take command of his army.'

'No, I hadn't heard.' Caterina had it on her conscience that she had done nothing and told no one about her encounter with Luiz da Fonsa y Sanchez. She had neither spoken to the duke nor gone near the Fonsa Palace, and, hearing nothing further from Luiz, had assumed with relief that he had managed to get clear away back to the enemy army. Lewis had not come near her since the scene on the day after the party or she thought she would have told him. Greville and Jeremy had kept away, too, and she blamed the rain, and missed them. It was not at all the same thing to send her latest cartoon down to the office for shipment as to have Greville come and comment on its progress. She needed his friendly, constructive criticism, and was angry with him for the absurd proposal that threatened to spoil their happy relationship.

It seemed to her that the cartoons were getting almost too savage these days, but Greville's brief notes reported a continuing enthusiastic reception in England and she knew that Dorothy Procter and her friends were hot in search of Charles Forsyte's presumed informant in Oporto.

'I'm sorry, what did you say?' She had let her attention wander.

'I said I hoped Dom Miguel's arrival would concentrate Dom Pedro's mind a little,' Hetta repeated it. 'So far the bombing and the casualties seem to have improved morale in town, but I do wonder if it will last if supplies get really short. We had a poor young Portuguese lady in today; she had been sitting on her balcony to catch a breath of sunshine between showers and had her arm shot off.'

'Oh, the poor thing!'

Hetta had Caterina's full attention now. 'I'm sorry the portrait is finished,' she went on. 'I had been rather hoping you might say something to the duke; he seems to listen to you. He needs to face the fact that his only hope of success now is through foreign intervention. It would have been another matter if he had carried things with a high hand to begin with, but now he really cannot afford to alienate the people whose help he needs. Mr Craddock was at Mrs Emerson's when Ruth and I went to see her the other day, and something he said made me wonder just what he was saying in his reports to England. It will do the duke's cause a lot of harm there if Craddock plays up his anti-British behaviour. Caterina, if you're not seeing the duke any more, do you think you could suggest that Lewis says a word? When he next comes home?'

Was there a question in her voice? 'He's not been since the party,' said Caterina. 'He's angry with me, Hetta.' It was an immense relief to admit it to this good friend. 'I can't talk about it. I wish I could. But it's my fault, it's all my fault. He has a right to be angry.'

'I find that hard to believe. But he seems to be angry with everyone just now, poor Lewis. I worry about him.'

'Oh, so do I.' They looked at each other, sharing visions of forlorn hopes and suicide attacks. 'But there's nothing I can do. Hetta, do you think that Ruth—'

'I just don't know.' Hetta sounded deeply doubtful.

'Something happened at the party, didn't it?'

'I think a great deal happened at that party. None of it good. And as for the duke's not even turning up! Sometimes I have no patience with that man.'

'I know just how you feel. But then one has to think of the alternative.'

'His brother. Yes.' She paused. 'Caterina, there's something I've been wanting to say to you.' She went to the door, opened it, looked out and shut it again. 'You're Charles Forsyte, aren't you? No, I haven't been spying on you, I promise, but all that work you do upstairs – and I know you so well. I recognize you in those brilliant drawings. Of course, I have said nothing to anyone, but it does make me anxious for you. Frankly, I don't know which of those brothers is going to dislike you most when the truth comes out.'

'Then I must make sure it doesn't. I hope no one else is as acute as you, Hetta dear. And thanks for the warning. I really will be more careful. Greville said very much the same thing to me a while ago and I can see I should have paid more attention.'

'He knows, then.'

'Oh yes, always. He has made all the arrangements for me, found the cover in England. I couldn't have done it without him.'

'I like him so much,' said Hetta.

'And so do I. God knows how I would have managed without him all these years. Or how I shall when he leaves.'

'But he'll never do that, surely?'

'His cousins have died. He's heir to the family estate now. He really ought to go home.' She suddenly had a bleak picture of Greville going home. And taking Hetta with him?

'Pour me a glass of wine, love.' Rachel Emerson turned leisurely on her side, her bare breast brushing Jeremy's. 'You get better and better.'

'And so do you.' He leaned across her to reach for the decanter and pour Madeira for them both, still electrified by the slightest touch of her. 'I had no idea it could be so good.'

'No more black boys?' She could tease him now.

'Good God, no.' He laughed, cupping a well-formed breast in his hand. 'I have put away childish things.' That first day, when he had found himself, so surprisingly, in her bed, a still greater surprise had been to find that while her face had aged, her body was still young, active and infinitely satisfying. 'You're all I need,' he said, and meant it. 'Damnation, the bombardment is beginning again.'

'Thank God for granite houses. But maybe we should get dressed, love. The girl, Susan, tends to panic. We don't want her bursting in on us.'

'I don't care who knows,' he said, surprising himself as much as he pleased her. 'I want to marry you, Rachel.'

'That's nice.' Standing naked beside him, she bent down for a slow, luxurious kiss. 'But not now, not yet. I've been meaning to tell you, I heard from Luiz this morning.'

'At last! What did he say?'

'A lot of lies about why he didn't come back here after the party. And how much he misses me. And how badly he wants to see me. He's planning something, I don't know what. But to know about us would frighten him off for ever. We must be much more careful. I didn't have the heart to tell you when you came, but this will have to be your last visit for a while. Luiz is bound to have other contacts in town as well as me. If he were to learn about us, it would spoil everything.' She laughed. 'At the moment, he thinks he has me totally in his thrall.'

'I'd like to kill him.' Jeremy surprised himself again.

'Nonsense! You're not thinking, love. He can be far too useful. I shall write him a loving answer, fooled by all his lies, tell him how dreadfully I miss him. He'll come, because he wants something from me, and what he wants will tell us a great deal about Dom Miguel's plans.'

'I don't like it. You won't—' How could he ask it?

'Of course I shan't. How could I? I shall have the headache, or Ruth coming, or something. And that reminds me, have you been up at the Sanchez Palace lately?'

'No.' Having so suddenly transferred his allegiance from Caterina back to Rachel he had felt it simpler just to keep away.

'I wish you would go, and tell me what is going on there. So far as I can make out, young Lewis hasn't been near the place since the duke's party. I don't find Caterina very welcoming these days, and Ruth won't say a word about what happened that night. Mind you, I do see your point: the poor boy is bound to be upset about finding he's a bastard. But just the same he should have proposed by now. You're sure that his title to the estates is sound, despite the illegitimacy?'

'What a good mother you are! Yes, absolutely sure. Old Madame Fonsa had the best lawyers in town, and Gomez was no fool. Besides, there is no one to question Lewis's claim. I heard the other day that the Fonsa cousins are all dead in Brazil, and they were the last kin on that side. And as to the Gomez estate, can you imagine Caterina disputing her son's claim?'

'No, of course not. She dotes on the boy, spoils him rotten if you ask me. I hope she has the good sense to go back to England when once they are married.'

'If they are married,' he reminded her. He had always wondered what exactly had taken place between Lewis and Ruth on the night of the party. 'Your Ruth is such a quiet child.' He thought it best to warn her. 'Still waters run deep, remember.' They had both dressed by now and he moved to the window. 'It looks as if a bomb has fallen upriver from where the bridge of boats used to be. I hope it hasn't inconvenienced your friend Francesca.' He kept hoping to find out more about Francesca, still only a name to him.

'Oh, Francesca can take care of herself. But I must be thinking what to say to Luiz. Do go and call on Caterina for me, Jeremy love, and tell me how the land lies there. And for my sake be careful in the cross streets. One of my neighbours was killed going to market the other day, poor woman. Her family are desolate.'

'It's odd how little one hears about the civilian casualties,' said Jeremy.

'Yes, quietly buried and forgotten unless one actually knows them. We need some kind of local paper, or our own Charles Forsyte, better still. Have you managed to find out any more about him? Luiz asked in his note if I knew who his informant was here. If I could give him a hint about that it might be useful—'

'In pulling the wool over his eyes? Yes, I see your point. But it is the strangest thing, I still have no idea.'

'Ask Caterina, why don't you? And the two girls might know something; they see a great deal at that hospital. I suppose I am right to let Ruth go on working there.'

'Could you stop her? Must I really stay away from you? How can I bear it?' He pulled her into his arms for a last, long passionate kiss.

'How can I!' Smiling up at him. 'I'll send you a message, just as soon as I hear from Luiz.'

It was raining again, and Jeremy was glad of his English umbrella as he walked up steep alleys that were doubling as rivulets. At least, his drenched condition should mean that Caterina would feel she must ask him to stay for supper, which would give him a chance to see the two girls when they got back from the hospital. Thinking it over, he had decided that he wanted Ruth to marry Lewis just as much as her mother did, but he was a great deal less sure that it would happen.

It was disconcerting, dripping his way into Caterina's salon, to find Greville Faulkes there before him. He, too, had just arrived, and Caterina turned from him to Jeremy.

'Well,' smiling at them both. 'Two strangers at once; what a happy day for me. I have seen neither of you this age. I was wondering whether it was the bombardment that kept you away, or the weather.'

'Oh, the weather,' said Jeremy. 'I never could bear to get wet. We are all used to the bombardment, though I am afraid there are more deaths than we are quite aware of. Someone was saying to me that we need our own local cartoonist, our own Charles Forsyte to tell us what is really going on. Isn't it amazing that after all this time no one has any more idea of who his informant is here in Oporto.'

'Yes, extraordinary,' said Greville. 'I was just saying to Caterina that it is hard to say which of the contending brothers would most like to know his identity.'

'Yes, neither of them has much to thank him for, but his message is clear enough just the same, he's a savage liberal, is Charles Forsyte.'

'Savage?' asked Caterina. 'What an odd word to use.'

'It's the right one just the same. I received a whole batch of his recent work by the last packet, and some of them are formidable. Have you seen the one of the duke as an avenging angel? Not an angel I'd like to meet on a dark night. Besides, vengeance is the last thing anyone here in Oporto wants to think of, exposed as they are to the threat of a sack.'

'That's quite true,' said Greville. 'But I suppose Mr Forsyte is thinking rather to influence opinion in England than here.'

'You're right as usual, Faulkes. It's a trait I remember finding particularly irritating in you when we were at school together. What's the news of your wonderful mother, by the way?'

'Wonderful,' said Greville. 'In fact that is just what I came to see Caterina about. I had a letter from her by the packet. I can hardly believe it. She plans to come out here for the New Year.'

'Good gracious,' said Caterina, and, 'Good God, she's mad,' said Jeremy. 'How in the world are you going to stop her, Faulkes?'

'Oh, I shan't try,' Greville told him. 'I met my capable mother much too late in my life to expect to have the slightest influence over her. And besides, she has it all arranged. She seems to have made friends with Saldanha on one of his trips to London and he has fixed it up for her. As you know his name is an open sesame here in Porto. So, believe it or not, she is coming to give a solo performance at the opera house here on New Year's Day.'

'Can she do it?' asked Jeremy.

'I think she can do anything,' said her son. 'If you mean is she too old for it, in a sense I suppose you are right. I wouldn't dare ask her age, but I suppose she can't be less than fifty, but she still thinks nothing of taking breeches parts when she fancies them, and she has kept the figure for them, unlike poor Dorothy Jordan. And you know how she can hold an audience.'

'Yes, I was there that time during the Reform Bill riots last year when she came on stage and stopped the house booing Wellington. They'd not have taken it from anyone else. But does she know any Portuguese?'

'I don't suppose so, but who ever expects to hear a singer's words? If I know her she'll do a mix of serious and comic songs, from Handel to Rossini, and have her audience laughing and crying without quite knowing why.'

'I do long to meet her,' said Caterina. 'And it's splendid of her to want to come; it should do wonders for Anglo–Portuguese relations, if it is handled right.'

'That is why I have come to see you,' said Greville. 'Saldanha has organized it for her and we all know of the difficulty that exists between him and the duke.'

'Yes, but I never did understand it,' said Caterina.

'It goes way back,' Greville told her. 'And Braganza is not a man to forget or forgive. If her coming is not to do more harm than good someone has to persuade him not to behave as he did over that unlucky party.'

Caterina smiled at him. 'And you want me to bell the cat? I'm sorry, but I don't see the duke any more, not since the portrait was finished.'

'Has he paid you for it yet?' asked Jeremy.

Caterina did not like the question, but answered it. 'I said there was no need until after the war, but it does make it more difficult for me to get in touch with him. I would not for the world have him think that I was dunning him.'

'No,' Greville agreed. 'But, surely, Lewis—'

'I don't see him either,' said Caterina bleakly.

This was news to both men, though Jeremy understood it better than Greville did. 'Surely you could send for him,' he said. 'If he's in one of those sulks of his he would probably be glad of an excuse to come out of it. And Faulkes is right; he would be the one either to speak to the duke himself or ask him to call on you, Caterina.'

'You might be right at that,' she said thoughtfully. 'I'll certainly send him a note. But, Greville, have you thought where your mother is to stay? You can't possibly expect her to live in your rooms above the goldsmith's shop, and we all know what the hotels are like here in Porto. I do hope we will be able to persuade her to come and stay here with me. If you will give me her direction I will write her a note by the next packet.' She smiled at them both. 'It's a little awkward, isn't it? One can hardly urge her to stay as long as she pleases, when it means all the danger and discomfort of a siege, but do you think we could persuade her to stay for the Twelfth Night celebrations, Greville? I have been thinking what a sad business it is all going to be this year, and having her here would make all the difference.'

'Thank you, Caterina,' said Greville. 'I have to confess I hoped you would invite her. She is a hardened campaigner, of course, after years in theatrical lodgings, but the case is that my landlord's son and his family have had to come and live with him. Theirs is one of the houses outside the walls that Colonel Hodges had pulled down. I know he was right to do it, but it has come hard on the people involved. And it means we are so hugger-mugger in the house already that I do not like even to mention the possibility to my poor landlord. Harriet Ware would have Jenny, I know, but their house is most dreadfully exposed to fire from across the river.'

'You call your mother Jenny?' asked Caterina, surprised.

'I always have. You'll understand when you meet her. But here are the girls home and hungry from the hospital. Time we were going, Craddock.'

'No, no, stay to supper,' urged Caterina. 'I am quite sure Carlotta has included you in her calculations, and the menu will be no surprise to you. Should we warn your mother that it will be a choice of salt cod and rice or rice and salt cod, do you think?'

'No need. She writes that she is an avid student of the Forsyte cartoons and knows all that there is to know about life here in Porto. How good to see you,' he turned to greet Hetta and Ruth. 'It's been too long.'

'Much too long,' agreed Hetta, then turned to Jeremy. 'And Mr Craddock, too. Carlotta says to tell you that the boys went fishing last night, Caterina. It's fresh fish for supper, and plenty of it.'

'Oh dear,' said Caterina. 'It's terribly dangerous on the river these days.'

'But they enjoy it. It makes a change from digging gun emplacements, they say.'

'I can understand that,' said Jeremy. 'There's something so basically dull about defensive warfare. We need a gallant sally to liven us all up.'

'And kill some more young men?' said Caterina, a new cartoon flashing into her mind. And then: 'Forgive me! We have splendid news tonight, girls. May I tell them, Greville?'

'Of course, but I think it should go no further until you have managed to square the duke.' He turned to Jeremy. 'Do you mind, Craddock? A secret, for the time being?'

'We're all agog,' said Hetta. 'Aren't we, Ruth?'

'Indeed we are. What is it, Aunt Caterina?'

'Greville's mother is coming to give a performance at the opera house on New Year's Day,' Caterina told her. 'But it's the deepest of secrets for the time being.'

'Jenny Forbes!' exclaimed Hetta. 'Oh, I have always so much wanted to see her; She holds the audience in the palm of her hand, they say. But why the secrecy, Caterina? Looking forward is half the pleasure, and her coming will be just the kind of morale booster we all need just now. It's odd how much worse bad weather makes things seem.'

'You're quite right,' Caterina agreed. 'But, you see, Saldanha helped her with her arrangements. He is a great friend of hers, Greville says, and you know how the duke feels about him.'

'Oh dear yes. Shall Ruth and I have a word with Lewis, Aunt Caterina? Next time he drops in at the hospital?'

'Oh, does he?'

'Yes, several of his friends are in our hands just now and he is very good about visiting them. We would tell him it's for his and the duke's ears only, of course, but don't you think he is probably the best person to say something about it?'

'I'm sure he is,' said Caterina.

'But how odd it is,' Jeremy said. 'The great liberal leader to be handled always with such kid gloves. Don't look so shocked, Caterina. I wouldn't say it anywhere else, but you must admit that our noble duke is not the easiest of men! Oh, now I am in disgrace with you all, and must take my diminished self away. It's good of you to invite me, Caterina, but I have an errand I must do in town this evening. I cannot tell you how I look forward to seeing your mother perform, Faulkes. If there is anything I can do to make her life more agreeable while she is here you have only to say the word. It is good to see you young ladies in such splendid looks. Don't work too hard, Caterina.'

There was a little silence after he had left and then they all started talking at once.

The excuse to call on Rachel was too good to be let slip. It had stopped raining and Jeremy walked briskly across town, grateful for an evening pause in the bombardment that made it comparatively safe to take the most direct route. It had been six whole days since Rachel had told him he must stay away and they felt like six ages. He had spoken more truly than he realized when he told her he needed her. She was a fire in his bones, pre-empting his thoughts and interrupting his sleep. Climbing the stairs to her apartment with impatient strides, he was enraged at being held at bay by her black maid, Susan.

'The mistress is not well today. She gave orders that no one was to be admitted, sir.' The solid figure blocked his way.

'I'm sure she will see me, Susan. Tell her I have news for her.' He pressed a lavish handful of coins into her receptive palm.

'But she is laid down on her bed, sir, with the migraine.' She weighed the coins thoughtfully in her hand. 'I will tell her, of course, and maybe she will see you. Why don't you step down to the market and buy her some flowers? She was saying only this morning that she missed the flowers you bring her. Come back in half an hour, and maybe I will have a better welcome for you? But not a minute sooner, mind. She don't like folks about when she's dressing.'

'I'll do that, and thank you, my dear.' He pinched the glossy black cheek and turned away, thinking how much he would have liked to help Rachel dress.

He had forgotten how late it was. When he reached the marketplace on the rock below the cathedral he found it closed and silent, the market over for the day. Stupid of the girl to have forgotten, but then what else did one expect of someone like her? He went down to the Rua Caterina and spent lavishly on a fine gold chain instead, and the inevitable haggling meant that it was more than half an hour before he presented himself once more at the familiar door. This time Susan let him in, all smiles. 'Milady is waiting for you.'

'But I have to scold you, just the same.' Rachel extricated herself from his first, passionate embrace. 'I have missed you terribly, hence the migraine, but I did tell you not to come until I sent for you. But you have news, Susan says?'

'Yes, and this, to show how I have missed you.' He dropped the gold chain over her head.

'Beautiful, and I thank you.' She turned so that they could both see her reflection in the huge looking-glass that almost covered one wall of the room. 'But the news that is important enough to make you disobey my orders, tell me that. No!' He was trying to steer her towards the bedroom door. 'I have the migraine, Jeremy. I have got myself up, though my head is killing me, to hear your news, but that must be all. I am ill today.'

'You are pale,' he said solicitously. 'My poor darling. What can I do for you?'

'Tell me your great news, and leave me to rest. I am cross today, my dear, you must bear with me. Forgive me!' She laid a loving hand on his sleeve.

'Of course! I am so sorry. As to the news. Two things. I went to Caterina's as you asked me, and stayed until Ruth and Hetta came home from the hospital. Your Ruth is more beautiful than ever, but she looks older, I think, as if the world was being hard on her. But

Hetta mentioned that Lewis is a frequent visitor at the hospital. Several of his friends are there, apparently. He seems not to be going to Caterina these days. I thought she looked older too.'

'They have quarrelled, of course, over the bastardy. He was bound to take it hard, that spoiled young man. I could almost find it in my heart to be sorry for Caterina.'

'Not quite?'

'No, there is something in the way she treats me that I find hard to bear. I wonder if the trouble between her and Lewis is not really that she has forbidden the match with my Ruth? She is quite capable of it.'

'But he wouldn't obey her,' said Jeremy. 'And he holds the purse strings, remember. There is nothing in the world she can do if he insists. But that is not all my news,' he went on, aware of impatience in her. 'Greville Faulkes was there too. Believe it or not, his mother is coming to give a performance at the opera house on New Year's Day.'

'The great Jenny Forbes! There's a turn up for the books. I wonder how she has managed that, and why she wanted to.'

'To see her son, I suppose. She always seemed a devoted mother.'

'You have met her?'

'Yes indeed. Greville took me several times to her box in the theatre, and then to supper afterwards. A delightful woman and remarkable for her age. Better at a distance than near to, of course,' he hastened to add. 'But I would expect her to cause quite a stir here in Oporto, if the duke can just be persuaded to behave civilly to her.'

'Why should he not?'

'Greville says she's a friend of Saldanha's. He fixed the engagement for her. Braganza won't much like that.'

'No he won't, will he? But if he has any sense at all he will behave. There's still feeling among the British about that party he cut.'

It reminded him of something. 'Have you heard anything more from Sanchez?' he asked.

'Not a word, but I am sure I shall. Communication is not easy, as you can imagine, across the lines, 'specially now the market is so ill attended. But I am glad you reminded me. You have stayed quite long enough for a casual visitor, my dear, particularly when I am known to be ill. I won't scold you this time for flouting my commands, but don't do it again. There is too much at stake. The sooner this war is over, the sooner our happiness begins.'

'You're right, and I love you for it.' One long lascivious kiss and he left her.

'Hetta, you know I can't speak to Lewis about it.' Ruth had been appalled at the idea that she should approach Lewis about persuading the duke to behave like a gentleman to Greville's mother. 'He would be bound to misinterpret it. You know what he is like!'

'But would he be wrong to misinterpret it, Ruth?' asked Hetta. 'I have wondered a little whether you might not have regretted being taken so by surprise that night, being so definite.'

'Oh, no, Hetta. Never think that. Please. I love Lewis dearly, it's so strange, and yet the very idea of marrying him fills me with a kind of horror. I think it must be because I know I couldn't cope with him, manage him. Do you know what I mean?' They were nearly at the hospital now and she paused on the question to gaze at Hetta.

'Oh, yes,' said Hetta. 'I do know. Very well, in that case I'll just have to speak to him. Help me to get a chance, Ruth.'

She got it next morning when Lewis came in on his way into town on an errand for the duke. She had to tell him that one of his friends had died in the night and it hit him hard. 'He was doing so well!' he protested.

'I know. He was on the mend. It happens all the time; they seem to be recovering and then suddenly slip away. I'm so sorry, Lewis. Come in here a moment, would you?' She led him into a small room used as an office. 'We need an end to this war,' she said.

'It's not a war.' Furiously. 'It's shadow boxing. Do you know what we are doing tomorrow, Hetta?'

'No?' A quick look at the door showed it securely closed.

'Launching an attack across the river to secure the wine your brother Frank talked about from the very start of things. The duke's wise old men have suddenly discovered just how badly they need it as security for the loan from England.'

'Oh, Lewis, are you going?'

'Of course.'

'Please be careful!'

'I'm a soldier, Hetta.'

'But you're a man too, a man we all love. Be sensible, for all our sakes. And, Lewis, it seems trivial, absurd, but if you have the chance, there's something the duke needs to know.'

'Yes?' He was relieved at the change of subject.

'Greville Faulkes came to the house yesterday. His mother is coming to give a performance at the opera house on New Year's Day.'

'What a splendid thing! I've never seen her, have you?'

'No, but the thing is, Lewis, she's a friend of Saldanha's. He made the arrangements for her. We're all a little anxious about what the duke might do. You know how he feels about Saldanha.'

'And with how little reason. Thanks for telling me. I love Saldanha too. I've tried often enough to change the duke's mind; perhaps Jenny Forbes will manage better than I have. And I will certainly say a word to the duke about her. She's just what we need. Where's Ruth, Hetta? She's not in her room.'

'No, she's visiting her mother today. I know.' He had pulled a face. 'But her mother sent a message that she wasn't well.' She paused for a moment, gathering her courage. 'Lewis—'

'Yes, what is it, Het?'

'Do come and see us. It's been ages. Caterina doesn't say anything, but I know she minds dreadfully. She seems very much alone, somehow, these days.'

'We're all alone, Hetta,' he said. 'It's the human condition.'

'Oh, Lewis. I can't bear to see you so unhappy.'

'These are hardly happy times. Look after Ruth for me, Hetta.'

'She's like a sister to me; we look after each other. And you, Lewis, be careful tomorrow, for all our sakes; don't do anything wild. Please? And come and tell us about it afterwards? When you can?'

'Of course I will. Don't fuss, Hetta. I'm sorry now I told you.' He had pulled open the door as he spoke and found himself facing Jeremy Craddock. 'What brings you here, Craddock?'

'The same as you, I imagine. The death of a friend. But I'm interrupting – forgive me. I just wanted to ask Miss Emerson if she had any messages for her mother. I've an errand to do up by the cathedral.'

'Thank you, but Ruth's with her mother today,' Hetta told him. 'Mrs Emerson isn't well.' What could he have overheard? Nothing of importance, she was sure, and anyway, why should she worry about what Jeremy Craddock heard?

Leaving the hospital, Lewis hurried into town, dispatched his business as quickly as possible then yielded as he had known he would to irresistible temptation and went to call on Rachel Emerson. He found her and Ruth on the point of going out, but Rachel swiftly changed their plans at sight of him. 'All I need is a breath of air to cool my poor head,' she told him. 'I shall leave my Ruth to entertain you, if you will forgive me, and just go up to the cathedral square to see if the women have any flowers today. Even dried ones are better than nothing and they sometimes have them despite this terrible weather. No, no,' Ruth was trying to protest. 'I am better alone. You will stay, Ruth.' There was a note in her voice that Ruth always obeyed.

'At last.' Lewis plunged straight in. 'I thought I'd never see you alone. I've wanted so much to tell you how sorry I am that I frightened you so that night, Ruth. Going too fast for you: I can see that now, such a child as you are. Stupid of me, but you are mine; you know it as well as I do. I am going into danger tomorrow, Ruth, to death perhaps. Let me go knowing you are here, loving me, waiting for me. That will be the talisman I need, to keep me safe.'

'Oh Lewis!' She looked up at him, eyes full of tears. 'I tried to tell you. I'm so sorry; I do love you, but not like that, not marrying love. Don't look like that, Lewis, I can't bear it; I'm so fond of you; I'd do anything for you—'

'Then marry me! I'm a bastard, Ruth, did you know that? Is that why? A rich bastard, mind you, I've been talking to the lawyers, and the fortune is all right and tight. My bitch of a mother can't take that away from me—'

'What did you say?'

Her tone should have warned him, but he was too deep in his own grievance to notice. 'Whore if you'd rather. I'm sorry to use the word to an innocent girl like you, Ruth, but if we are to marry, you have to know the worst of me. And of my high and mighty mother, Madame da Fonsa, the great lady, the arbiter of morals—'

'Stop it! You ought to be ashamed of yourself. To speak of your mother like that. All your life she has thought of nothing but you, and this is how you thank her! If I had had any thoughts of marrying you, Lewis da Fonsa, which I haven't, the way you speak of her would have ended them. Now go away, before I say something I shall really regret.'

'But, Ruth—' Her colour was high, her eyes sparkling; he had never seen her so beautiful. She had moved away from him as she spoke, now he took a long step forward meaning to sweep her into his arms.

'No! If you touch me, Lewis da Fonsa, I shall hit you.'

'Ruth—' He stood for a moment, looking at her, uncertain, then turned at a scratching at the door. It was the maid, Susan, with wine and cakes, and he was not sure in his rage whether he was relieved or not. 'Thank you, but I'll not stay,' he told her brusquely. 'I have errands to do for the duke.'

'Lewis,' now Ruth held out her hand to him. 'Please, be careful tomorrow.'

Chapter 12

Walking home from the hospital, Hetta promised herself that she would not tell even Caterina about the next day's attack on the south bank. Lewis should not have told her. Surprise must be the very essence of such a plan; the fewer people who knew of it the better. She was glad that Ruth had not been there. She loved Ruth dearly but discretion was not her long suit. As for Jeremy Craddock, if he had heard anything he could surely be relied on to say nothing, except to his masters in England.

She reached the Sanchez Palace at the same time as Ruth, in a litter with Susan's tall black husband walking beside it. 'Mother wouldn't let me walk.' She jumped out to hug Hetta.

'And quite right too. How is she?'

'Much better for seeing me, she said. Her migraine has quite gone; a long night's sleep will complete the cure.' Ruth had been surprised and relieved that when her mother returned from her walk she had asked no questions about Lewis's visit. And instead of pressing Ruth to stay, she had seemed anxious to have her go, insisting that all she needed now was quiet. Riding home in the jolting litter, Ruth had congratulated herself on not having had to parry questions about Lewis. She must not even tell Hetta or Caterina about tomorrow. But she would pray for Lewis. She turned to Hetta as they entered the courtyard of the palace.

'How were things at the hospital today? I did feel guilty about leaving you on your own.'

'Quiet enough.' Hetta thought how different they would be after the next day's raid. 'Lewis dropped in, hoping to see you, so I told him about Jenny Forbes.'

'Oh, good.' It would be easier not to mention his visit.

They were both glad to find Frank sitting with Caterina in the saloon. 'There you are at last, Hetta. What hours you keep!' He pecked a brotherly kiss on her cheek and turned to Ruth. 'And Miss Emerson. I hope they are not working you too hard at the hospital. You look to be thriving on it anyway.'

'I had the day off.' She was blushing furiously, Hetta noticed. 'My mother's not well; she sent for me.'

'Nothing serious, I hope?' Caterina had heard stories of cases of cholera, and death, quietly concealed.

'No, just one of her migraines. She's better now, said all she needed was a good night's sleep.'

Watching him, Hetta caught a very odd look on her brother's face. 'Lewis called in at the hospital.' She broke a little silence. 'I told him about Jenny Forbes, Caterina, and he was delighted. Says he has always longed to see her and will do his best to persuade the duke to give her the welcome she deserves.'

'Oh I am glad,' said Caterina. 'Bless you for a capable girl, Hetta. And now here is Carlotta to say our supper is ready, and the boys have been out fishing again.'

'What a treat!' But it made Hetta think about what was to happen across the river next day and she was very quiet for a while, leaving Frank to entertain the other two with stories of jealousies among the English colony.

'There's this terrible competition,' he told them. 'As to who gets invited to dine on board the British ships in the harbour. No short commons there, of course; no salt cod for them. You have to admit it's an extraordinary situation having those neutral ships right here in the harbour, watching everything but unable to intervene.'

'But at least they report it all back in England,' said Caterina. 'And the stories of high-handed Miguelite behaviour, too, which must surely help to sway English opinion.' Could she use the British ships in a cartoon? She rather thought she could. It made her suddenly wish very much that Greville would call again when she was alone. It had been maddening to have Jeremy interrupt them the other day. 'We must start thinking how best we can entertain Mrs Forbes,' she said, surprising the others by the sudden change of subject.

'I thought she was going to entertain us,' said Frank.

'Yes, but don't you think a party afterwards? Here, of course, and I think I will boldly invite the duke.'

'It's the least he can do to come,' said Frank. 'By the way, I heard down town that the new French commander, Marshal Solignac, is due about then. The man who is going to reform the liberal army. You'll have to ask him too, Aunt Caterina.'

'I wish it was Saldanha,' she said. 'But of course I must invite him. Does the duke's army need so much reforming, Frank?'

'You do hear stories, but the less said about them the better, I think. You're very quiet, Hetta. Mother says it's high time you came to see us.'

'We're so busy at the hospital.' And would be busier still next day. But she must not say that. 'Tell her I will come just as soon as I can.'

Hetta's bedroom was on the river side of the house and she woke early, after a restless night, to the sound of military activity from below. She hurried next door and roused Ruth.

'Isn't it very early?' Ruth protested, coming up from deep sleep.

'Yes, but we're going to be busy today. An attack has started across the river. They are trying for the wine again.'

'You knew?'

'Yes.'

'You said nothing last night?'

Something in her tone alerted Hetta. 'You knew too!'

'Yes. Lewis came to my mother's.' Ruth was out of bed now, pulling a dressing-gown round her. She moved to the window. 'Yes: boatloads of men. Oh, Hetta, I'm so worried about Lewis.'

'I begged him to be careful. For what that's worth.'

'So did I. But he doesn't know the meaning of the word. Besides – oh Hetta, I made him so angry. And then we were interrupted— If anything happens to him it will be all my fault.'

'Nonsense!' Hetta said it with more confidence than she felt. 'Don't think like that.' She longed to know more, but must not ask. 'They are beginning to land. We must get to the hospital. Dress quickly, Ruth. I'll tell Carlotta we want breakfast early.'

'Will you tell Caterina?'

'Not till she comes down from her studio. She'll have enough time for worrying.'

'You're so sensible, Hetta.' Was it admiration, or criticism?

'You knew last night, didn't you, Hetta?' said Caterina. 'That's why you were so quiet.'

'Yes. I'm sorry.'

'No need to be. You were quite right to say nothing. Is Lewis with them?'

'Yes. I begged him to be careful, for all our sakes. I think he listened. And he really was pleased about Jenny Forbes.'

'Something to look forward to? We all need that. I do bless the woman for coming. But I mustn't keep you girls talking. You'll need to be getting ready at the hospital, won't you? What a blessing you came home last night, Ruth dear.'

'Yes, wasn't it,' said Ruth, something niggling at the edge of her mind.

After they had left and Caterina had swallowed a tasteless roll and drunk some strong coffee she found she could settle to nothing. Idiotic to try. 'I am going down to the Wares,' she told Carlotta. 'The attack is downriver from where the bridge of boats used to be, towards the Franciscans'; they should be able to see it all from their upper windows.'

'Do you want to see it?' asked Hetta.

'No, but I feel I must.' As Charles Forsyte she had a duty to do so, whatever the outcome. 'Besides, it will be better in company.'

'I thought you'd come,' Harriet greeted Caterina warmly. 'It's going splendidly. They have taken the high points at the Quinta da Cavaço and San Antonio and are beginning to get the wine across already. Is Lewis there?'

'Yes. He told Hetta yesterday, but she said nothing.'

'And quite right too.' Frank made room for Caterina by the window. 'No wonder she was so quiet. But it does all seem to be going like clockwork. We shan't be the only ones with wine on this side of the river any longer. The boats that took the men over are coming back loaded with it already. If only they get enough really to secure the British loan.'

'You speak like a Portuguese.'

'I want it over.'

'Don't we all.'

'It's horrible!' exclaimed Harriet. 'Watching it like this as if it were a theatrical entertainment. I can't bear it. I'm going to go and sort linen in case they need more at the hospital. Are you coming, Caterina?'

'I know just what you mean, but I think I'll stay. They are watching from the British ships, too, have you noticed?'

'Yes, ringside seats,' said Frank. 'And a glass of wine in their hands, no doubt. I wonder if they are inviting friends to dine and watch the fun. I hate this war, it is doing dreadful things to us all.'

'War does,' Caterina told him. 'I remember the last one. I'll tell you one thing, when this is all over I think I am going to go home to England and grow cabbages.'

'I believe you really mean that.'

'I believe I do. Isn't the bombardment getting worse?'

'I hope not.' He turned as Jeremy Craddock entered the room. 'Come to join the audience, Mr Craddock?'

'Yes. It seems to be going brilliantly. Your two firms are losing their monopoly by the look of it.'

'I do hope so,' said Caterina.

'I came by the quays,' he told her. 'They have drafted every able-bodied man in town to the unloading. The boats will be going back for more any minute now. The *caçadores* are holding the heights and they are working like beavers down on the quays on the other side. Look.' He passed his spy glass to Caterina. 'You can see them piling casks up on the wharf ready for when the boats return. It actually looks like a well-planned operation for once.'

'Yes.' Caterina was peering through the glass. 'But what is happening up at San Antonio? Look! It's on fire!'

'What?' He snatched the glass. 'You're right, by God! Idiocy! Or treachery? You can see them retreating. The enemy are after them!'

'They are beginning to retreat from the Cavaço heights too,' exclaimed Frank. 'And no sign of the boats coming back yet from this side. If they can't hold the enemy, they will be cut off on the quays over there.'

'Lewis!' said Caterina. She wanted to go away, join Harriet, count linen, anything, but must stay and watch.

Nobody said anything for a little while; there was nothing to say as the disastrous retreat continued. Impossible to make out faces, or even uniforms, but it was becoming horribly obvious that the liberals had fallen into what looked like a well-laid trap.

'There are a few boats on that side still,' said Frank, reaching for comfort.

'Yes,' said Caterina. 'And the cowardly first fugitives are cramming into them.'

'Fighting each other for places,' he said. 'Lewis won't be there.'

'No.' Silence fell again as they watched the débâcle continue. As the boats pulled away from the far shore men who had failed to get on to them plunged into the water, hoping to swim to safety. 'They'll never make it,' Frank said. 'Not in uniform.'

'No,' said Jeremy. 'Look! They are heading for our ships. Fools! There is no way our people can help them!'

'They won't let them on board?' asked Caterina.

'How could they? It would be a total breach of neutrality. Leave our ships wide open to bombardment by the Miguelites.'

'Thank God I'm not on board,' said Caterina. Men were clinging to the tackle of the ships now, and as they watched, silent with horror, the Miguelites began to fire at them from the far shore, and they dropped off, one by one, to certain death.

'I can't bear it,' said Caterina. 'I'm going home. If there is news, it will come there. If you hear anything, let me know.'

'I wonder where Greville is?' said Frank.

'Oh, didn't I say?' said Jeremy. 'He's down on the quay, helping with the unloading of the wine. Too late, alas.'

'But he is helping,' said Caterina.

Back at home, she locked herself in her studio and began frantically to draw with great black strokes, a cartoon headed simply: 'Neutral!'

★

'The waiting is the worst.' Ruth had met Hetta in one of the hospital's long, bleak corridors.

'Yes, I wish we could see the river from here. But no news has to be good news. Maybe we will be celebrating tonight.'

'Please God. Oh, Hetta, I do pray Lewis does something splendid and comes back a hero. He needs it. I'm so worried about him.'

'Oh, so am I,' said Hetta, and they exchanged a long, thoughtful look. 'What's that?' Her head went up, listening to sounds from the front of the hospital.

'Bad news,' said Ruth. 'We must get to our stations.'

They did not meet again until late afternoon, when the full tale of the disaster had come out in broken sentences from one half-drowned, gravely wounded man after another. Almost too busy to think, Hetta began just the same to realize that she had seen none of Lewis's troop of *caçadores*. Was this good news, or the worst? Hurrying to the store room for more of the dwindling supplies of linen, she met Ruth on the same errand and remembered with a little jolt of surprise that she had been supposed to faint at the sight of blood. Now her sleeves were stained with it and she was quite unconscious of a smear on her face.

'Hetta.' She reached out a dirty hand. 'Have you heard anything of Lewis?'

'No, nor of any of his men. We are going to run out of linen.'

'I know. Should we send to Aunt Caterina?'

'And my mother. Oh, thank God, there's Frank.'

'Both of you! Good.' But there was nothing good about the way he looked. 'I've been looking for you, Hetta. I've brought more linen; Mother said you would need it. Caterina is sending some, too. But the way things are here I think you had better take charge of the distribution.'

He was right. There was panic and confusion all round them as more and more wounded men poured in.

'Yes,' Hetta said. 'But, Frank, is there any news of Lewis?'

'It's bad.' He spoke to her, looked at Ruth. 'I've been helping out on the quay. Mayhem! You never saw such scenes. Aunt Caterina went home. Mother's been making bandages all day. Jeremy Craddock went on taking notes,' he said savagely.

'Well, it's his job,' Hetta told him. 'And Greville?'

'He's been on the quay all day, helping unload the wine and get the boats away. He helped a man out of one of the last of the boats and recognized him as one of Lewis's troop. Hetta! Ruth! It's bad.' It was hard to tell them.

'Yes?' Hetta reached out to take Ruth's hand.

'They were making good their defences in San Antonio when fire broke out all round them. He thinks it has to have been laid.'

'A trap?'

'That's what he says.'

'And Lewis?' Hetta tightened her grip on Ruth's hand.

'They had to retreat. He was rallying his men just below the bluff, hoping to hold the enemy there. They were coming on in force, the man says. It was hand-to-hand, savage. Lewis was shouting, urging them to stand fast, then, suddenly, silence. He had fallen, and it was every man for himself, panicking down the hill to the boats.'

'You mean they left him?'

'Yes. Shameful. Don't look like that, Ruth. He may not be seriously hurt; he may have managed to hide; he may be a prisoner. We must not think the worst.'

'What does Caterina say?' asked Hetta, tight-lipped.

'That we must wait for news. I wanted her to go to the duke, but she would not. "What's the use", she says. It's hit her hard. I wish one of you could be with her.'

'We'll both go,' Hetta told him, her mind suddenly made up. 'When we have seen to the sharing out of this linen, and God bless you and Mother for that, Frank. We've been here with hardly a break since first thing this morning, tending a lot of soldiers who behave like that.' She was very white, her eyes blazing, the scar standing out on her cheek. 'I've had enough. Stay with us, Frank, help us give out the linen. They are capable of anything. And then we'll go to Caterina. That's where the news will come.'

'He's dead.' Ruth spoke for the first time. 'I feel it, here,' with a filthy hand on her heart.

She was swaying where she stood. Frank put a firm arm around her. 'You've had enough, both of you. I'm taking you away now. Let the Portuguese share out their own linen.'

'Oh, Frank, don't!' But Hetta's eyes were full of tears and she let her brother take command.

Caterina was prowling around the house with Carlotta anxious at her heels. 'Any more news?' she asked them eagerly.

'Nothing.' Frank shook his head. 'Caterina, the girls are exhausted. They have been working like Trojans all day among the wounded.'

'I can see—' Caterina looked at them for the first time, forgetting her own anxiety. 'Carlotta, water to the young ladies' rooms and the best meal you can find for us. We all need it. Thank you for reminding me, Frank. Making ourselves ill will help no one. Come and drink a glass of wine with me, while the girls change their dress. You look exhausted too, but clean.'

'Mother made me change before she would let me come.' He smiled at her, feeling at ease in her company for the first time in his life. 'Caterina, don't worry too much. We always used to say that Lewis had nine lives; he can talk his way out of most things.'

'If he can talk.'

'Don't! That's not the way to think.'

'You're right, and I know it, but it's not easy. I wish Greville would come.'

'I'm sure he will if there is any news.'

But the long evening dragged by with no word from anyone.

At first Lewis and his *caçadores* had carried all before them at San Antonio, then, suddenly, had come the cries of 'Fire', the smell of burning and panic among the men. Rallying them as best he could, he was managing to hold them steady, just below the burning fortress, when he was stunned by a glancing shot.

Coming to himself, he had no idea how long he had been unconscious. The sounds of battle had receded. He seemed to be alone. His head throbbed. Worse still, he could not move. He was lying on what must be a bale of straw, his hands and feet lashed down.

'Don't move.' A hand came down to close his mouth. 'Well, you can't. But don't speak either.' He knew the voice. 'Lie quiet. I've no time for you now,' said Luiz da Fonsa y Sanchez, 'but you'll be safe enough here. My man will keep watch; we'll talk tonight when it's all over. You shall take a message to your mother for me. Don't try anything. José here would dearly like to kill you, but I have told him he must not. He will probably obey me unless you try anything foolish. Now, I must leave you to bless your luck that it was I who found you. Guard him well, José, but don't talk to him. And don't forget I need him alive.'

The answer was something between a growl and an oath from somewhere out of Lewis's line of vision. Tethered as he was, all he could see was the roof of what must be a barn. He heard the door close behind his father.

'Filthy liberal!' The man moved into view with a waft of sweat and garlic. 'He's right, the master. I would enjoy killing you.' He bent over to spit in Lewis's face. 'Just give me the excuse, do.'

It was the hardest thing he had ever done, but Lewis closed his eyes, pretending unconsciousness, and soon drifted off into something between that and sleep. When he woke, the light in the barn had changed and everything was quiet. He stirred a little, testing the bonds that held him, aware of throbbing pain in his head, but nothing more. Bless your luck, his father had said. Where was his guard? He held his breath, listening, and was rewarded by the sound of heavy breathing. He rather thought José was asleep. His head was clearing by the moment and he was aware of every possible kind of discomfort, major and minor. No time for that. He was not going to be lying here, trussed like a fowl for the slaughter, when his father came back. Not his father, his enemy, the man who had seduced his mother. He began, very quietly, to work at the stake that held his right wrist. The earth floor of the barn was dry and friable. Gently moving his wrist, so far as he could, this way and that, over and over again, he felt the stake begin to shift.

The stertorous breathing continued. He freed his right hand at last and began to work on the other one. Outside, all stayed quiet, the battle must be over, and the very silence seemed ominous. But freeing his left hand was easier. Sitting up stiffly, he turned to see his guard lying dead to the world, an empty wine bottle beside him. It was getting darker by the minute. He worked frantically to free his feet and was beginning to rub them back into some kind of life when he heard the sound of horses. Five minutes more and he would have had a chance of defending himself. As it was, an instant decision had him lying back on the straw bale in the position in which his father had left him.

Desperately listening as the men dismounted outside, he thought it a small party. Three or four horsemen? Four or five? 'Wait here.' His father's voice. 'I'll call if I want you.'

The door of the barn was behind Lewis. He heard it swing open; saw the glimmer of torch light on the roof; made himself lie still.

'Damnation!' His father must have seen José's sleeping form. Not his father, he reminded himself, his enemy. Sanchez came to stand at his feet, shining the torch on his face. Flexing feet and ankle muscles, Lewis felt them respond, made himself lie still.

'You're awake. That's good. I'm sorry to have left you so long. I meant to be back sooner, but we've run into a bit of trouble. Dom Miguel has a better idea than mine. You're to be a hostage, not a messenger. I do hope, for your sake, that your mother does what she is told, though I have to say it will be most unlike her if she does. And I am afraid that if she refuses, your end will not be a pleasant one. My master has always been a man of his word. But no need for you to be uncomfortable in the meanwhile.' He moved nearer.

Now or never. Lewis brought both his feet up into the air, caught his father squarely in the chest and sent him flying backwards to land with a satisfactory thud.

Too good to be true. He had hit his head on something and lay still. And Lewis's feet were working now. He rose, picked up the smouldering torch from the floor, helped himself swiftly to his victim's sword and pistol, and moved over to the closed door to put his head against it and listen. Several men were talking outside, standing at ease, waiting for orders. Further off, horses moved restlessly, harness jingled. Again, the element of surprise would be all-important. He found the latch on the barn door, doused the light, threw open the door and flung himself on the little group of soldiers. For a few moments, the surprise complete, he had it all his own way and thought he might be able to burst through them and take his chance in the darkness beyond. But there were more of them than he had thought, the fight was beginning to go inexorably against him when he heard a shouted command and another group of men threw themselves into the fray.

Sleeping fitfully at last, Caterina was roused at first light by Carlotta. 'One of the men found this pinned to the back door.' Handing her a note. 'They must have come up from the Gomez palace. I don't like it, *senhora*.'

'No.' After all these years she still knew the writing. She opened the note with a hand that shook. It was short and to the point.

He is alive, and well for the moment. Dom Miguel sets the terms for his release: our marriage, and a meeting with his brother. Arrange it fast. He is in some discomfort in the meantime. It will get worse. The bombardment will stop at dusk tonight. When it does, have yourself rowed over, alone, to the quay above the Serra. I will be there, also alone. If you bring the duke's written promise of a meeting, Lewis will return in your boat. Unless of course, he prefers to throw in his lot with us, stay and witness our marriage.

There was no signature. It needed none.

'But I can't.' She read it through again, then spoke. 'Carlotta, wake the young ladies and send a man to fetch the Senhor Faulkes. Urgently.' She began to pull on her clothes, hands shaking, her mind scurrying around in useless circles. The very fact that the note said nothing about secrecy underlined the absurdity of the demand. Even if Dom Pedro were prepared to consider such a promise to his usurping brother, there was no way he could keep it without the consent of his council, and not the slightest chance of their agreeing to anything in less than several days. And in the meantime, Lewis would be 'in some discomfort'. She was actually wringing her hands as she hurried downstairs to where coffee was ready on the big table.

'What is it? There's news?' The two girls had obviously slept as little as she had herself, and dressed as hurriedly.

'Yes, a note. I think you should read it. He's alive; a prisoner. I don't know what to do.'

'That's not like you.' Hetta was reading. 'Marriage?' She looked up to meet Caterina's eyes.

'Oh, yes.' Impatiently. 'I had forgotten you don't know. It hardly seems important now. The note is from Luiz da Fonsa y Sanchez. Lewis's father. He wants to make an honest woman of me. I don't like to think what their plans are for the duke.'

'You can't do it,' said Hetta. And then, 'And it wouldn't legitimize Lewis.'

'No, nothing can do that.'

'Oh, poor Lewis.' She thought for a moment. 'What do you think he would want you to do?' She passed the note to Ruth.

'I don't know,' said Caterina slowly. 'Suddenly I don't feel I know him at all.'

'But anyway, that hardly matters,' said Hetta. 'You can't do it and you know it. Just think what a weapon you could become in the hands of the enemy, Caterina. You've not been thinking of the implications, and I don't blame you.'

'Oh!' It was true. Thinking only of Lewis's plight and the horror of marriage to his father, Caterina had forgotten about Charles Forsyte. She exchanged a long, thoughtful look with Hetta as they both imagined the inevitable discovery.

'I can't believe it.' Ruth was a slow reader and had only just digested the contents of the note. 'Have you sent to Dom Pedro, Aunt Caterina?'

'Not yet. Only to Greville Faulkes. I wish he'd come.' Somewhere in that silent exchange she and Hetta had agreed that they were not going to mention Charles Forsyte in front of Ruth.

'He has been so miserable, poor Lewis.' Ruth was beginning to take it in. 'But it will be all right now, won't it, Aunt Caterina? It's quite a romance really! Fancy his father being faithful to you all these years. And surely Dom Pedro will agree at least to a signature?'

Once again Caterina's eyes met Hetta's in a long look of comprehension. 'I wish it was so simple,' she said. 'Oh, if only Greville would get here.' But the servant returned soon afterwards with the news that Faulkes had not come home the night before.

'Frank said he was working on the quay all day,' said Hetta. 'Perhaps he went to our house, Caterina. Should you not send there? I know Mother would want to be with you.'

'Yes, I should have sent in the first place, but I hardly knew what I was doing.' She looked up at the clock. 'Should you two not be going to the hospital?'

'I've been thinking about that,' Hetta said. 'We came away without leave last night and they are bound to be busier than ever today. Ruth dear, do you think you could go and make my apologies? Someone ought to stay with Caterina.'

'And you'll be much more use.' Ruth got up. 'Of course I'll go. I know you will save him somehow, Aunt Caterina. I'll be praying for you.'

The other two were silently relieved to see her go. 'You've eaten nothing.' Hetta poured coffee for Caterina and passed her a roll. 'Do you think you should wait for Greville? Suppose he's not at our house? It seems to me that you owe it to the duke to let him know about this at once. Lewis is his man. It has to be his decision as well as yours.'

'Even though we know it will be impossible for him to decide?'

'Just because of that. You can't afford the slightest delay.'

'You're right. Should we copy the letter for him to see?'

'I think so, if you can bear to. He needs to know it all. I'll do that while you write to him.'

'Not about Charles Forsyte. That must stay between you and me, Hetta, please. I'm grateful to you for reminding me.' She was remembering some of her more ruthless caricatures of Dom Miguel.

For the first time, Hetta smiled. 'I think you are absolutely right about that. You need to be safe in England before that tale is told. I don't think it is exactly going to endear you to Dom Pedro either. But what will you do if he agrees to promise a meeting with his brother?'

'God knows. I must be thinking. If it was my death, it would be nothing. I would gladly die for Lewis.'

'This is so much worse?'

'Oh, yes.' Memory of her meeting with Luiz was dark in her mind, but there was no time to tell Hetta about that now, even if she wished to. She finished her coffee without tasting it, handed Hetta the letter to copy and moved over to her writing desk to try and write to the duke.

A few minutes later, Hetta put down her pen and looked at Caterina, who had not got beyond the address of her letter. 'It can't be done, can it?' she said. 'You'll have to ask him to come here and tell him yourself.'

'But will he come?'

'He must.'

Chapter 13

Rain fell in torrents. The morning dragged on. The first of Caterina's messengers reported that the duke was in council, not to be disturbed. The second returned a little later with Harriet but no news of Greville.

'He wasn't with us last night,' Harriet said. 'Frank's not at home either; he's been out since dawn helping deal with the shambles on the quay.' She kissed her friend, holding her tight. 'I'm glad you've got Hetta here.' She was reading the note. 'You can't do it, Cat! He must mean that deserted quay from which Wellington launched his surprise attack on Soult all those years ago. It can't be seen from anywhere. Anything could happen to you.'

'I suppose that's the whole point,' said Caterina.

'What does the duke say?'

'He's in council.'

'He must be disturbed.'

'That's why I need Greville. What can have happened to him, Harry? I'm frightened for him, too. Do you remember that other time, back in the autumn, when he joined in the fighting? I am so afraid he has done it again, may have drowned, and we will never know.'

'I've been thinking about that.' Hetta had come back into the room with fresh coffee for her mother. 'And I begin to wonder if Greville's vanishing isn't the most encouraging thing that has happened. He was working on the quay, remember, yesterday, the last anyone saw of him. It was he who learned the bad news about Lewis. And after that he vanished.'

'You mean he's gone across there, too?' Caterina looked at her wide-eyed.

'It would be like him to go,' said Hetta. 'If he thought there was a chance.'

'But he's not come back,' said Caterina bleakly.

'Not in the daytime. How could he? Or they? Caterina, send a boat tonight as you are told to, but don't go yourself. Just send a note, asking for more time. After all, it is Lewis's father we are talking about. Surely he'll do nothing too dreadful to him?'

'No, it's not,' Caterina told her. 'It's Dom Miguel.'

'And we all know that his word is like water. And you have not even got a direct promise from him, have you? Only from Sanchez.'

'That's perfectly true. Oh, God, what am I to do?' Never in her life had she felt so helpless.

'Wait,' said Hetta. 'But arrange for the boat.'

'It will need the duke's authorization.'

'Of course. But not much use getting the authorization and finding there is no one willing to go. Besides, the way things are, here in Oporto, I am sure the news that such a boat is being got ready will leak across the river somehow. That can only be good for Lewis, if he really is still in their hands.'

' "In some discomfort",' quoted Caterina.

'You must send again to the duke,' said Harriet urgently. 'Absurd to let ourselves be fobbed off with his being in council. I wish Frank was here to go for you, Cat, but he's got his own problems today. Josiah Bankes and his wife were on the *Squirrel* yesterday, dining with Captain Thompson and watching the show.' Her tone was savage. 'It has decided Bankes to cut and run for it, and I don't know whether to be glad or sorry. He and his wife are at home today, packing up their effects ready to take the next chance of a passage to England.'

'Good riddance,' said Caterina. 'Frank will be pleased. But, yes, I can see he will be busy picking up the pieces.'

'Not too busy to arrange for a boat,' said Frank's sister. 'That at least would be making a start.' She paused at the sound of a voice outside. 'It's Mr Craddock. Perhaps he would go to the duke for you.'

But Jeremy Craddock, full of sympathy, explained that it was quite impossible for him to do so.

'Don't say the word "neutral" to me, Mr Craddock,' said Caterina dangerously. 'Please.'

There was a little awkward silence, broken by Hetta. 'Idiotic,' she said. 'I shall go.'

'No, we will go together. Thank you, Hetta. Absurd not to have thought of it myself. This is hardly the moment to be standing on female ceremony.'

Luckily, their arrival at the palace coincided with the break up of the duke's council and he was surprised into seeing Caterina at once. In the heat of her anxiety for Lewis she had not realized just how awkward a tale it would be to tell, and found herself wishing she had stuck to her first intention of simply sending Braganza a copy of the letter. It was more than disconcerting to see his expression change as he took in the fact that she was nothing more nor less than a mother without a husband. And in the end, it was all to no avail.

'I am more sorry than I can say.' He sounded as if he meant it. 'You know how fond I am of your son, but it has been borne in on me today that I must not act without the consent of my council. And they have just dispersed.'

'To meet again?'

'Tomorrow.' He let his surprise at the question show.

'Then may I send a note across, as instructed, asking for twenty-four hours to think it over?'

'My dear madam, you hardly need my permission to do that.' The interview was over.

'But who are you going to send?' Harriet went straight to the heart of the matter. 'You can hardly ask one of your servants to risk his freedom, his very life among the enemy.' She thought for a minute. 'It will have to be Frank. I'll send for him; this is much more important than the firm's affairs, however chaotic Bankes has left them. No need to look so bothered, Cat dear, Frank's a neutral, remember, he'll be perfectly safe.'

She hoped it was true, but her main concern was for her friend who had come back from the palace looking both distraught and somehow diminished. 'No need for Frank to know the whole story,' she went on. 'The fewer people who do the better for everybody's sake, 'specially Lewis's. Do you think the duke will be discreet, Cat?'

'He said he would, but, oh, Harry, if you could have heard his tone. Lewis is never going to forgive me for this.'

And there was a grim little silence as all three women wondered if Lewis would be alive to forgive or not to forgive.

Ruth had made her and Hetta's apologies at the hospital, and then demanded the day off. 'I'm sorry.' She was adamant in face of outraged protest. 'I am, after all, a volunteer.' And got her way.

'I have to see my mother,' she told Susan's surprised face at the apartment door. 'Tell her so, Susan, would you?'

'But she's so upset today—'

'I expect she is. So am I, Susan. Tell her that. So are we all. Ask her if she would rather see me or the duke's officers. You listened, didn't you, at the door the other day? Told her everything Lewis said. I was a fool not to understand that. I have been all kinds of fools, but I am none of them any more. Tell my mother that, and she will see me.

'I hope you are pleased with yourself,' she greeted her mother, lying in elegant decline on the sofa. 'You and your spying! How could I have been such an idiot? I suppose I don't know you very well, really. What were you doing all those years when you left me at school? Living by your wits, you and my father, one way and another. And that's what you were doing when you were here before; that's why Caterina has never liked or trusted you. I've wondered so much about that. Well, now I understand. And you are going to tell me how you managed to get word across to the other side of the river, after Susan listened at the door and heard Lewis tell me about the planned attack. You never took time to think how your spying might affect him, did you, clever Mother?' She had no intention of telling her mother about the letter Caterina had received. 'If they kill him over there, maybe have done already, it will be all your fault. But I think there may be hope for him yet.'

'Why so?' She had her mother's full attention now. She was sitting up, the invalid pretence forgotten.

'Because Greville Faulkes has vanished too. He was on the quay yesterday, helping with the wounded, then suddenly he wasn't there any more. Why? Because some of Lewis's men must have got back with a story he thought worth investigating. Very few of Lewis's men have turned up at the hospital. I expect many of them are dead – your doing – but I am hoping that some of them are back on the other side now, with Greville Faulkes, a rescue party. But even if they manage to free Lewis how are they going to get him back across? That is where you come in.'

'I don't understand.'

'Oh yes you do. Tell your friend Francesca, whom I have never met, to arrange something, whatever it is she does. Or is it a he? Another of the lovers I am not supposed to know about? Your innocent little Ruth. We are at the parting of the ways anyway, but it is up to you to decide how we part. Do your best for Lewis, get him back safely, and I will say nothing, merely drench several pocket handkerchiefs in public when I see you on board the next packet. Fail in this, and I go to the duke with the whole story.'

'You mean it!' Rachel looked as if the earth had opened under her feet.

'I am glad you see that. I will leave you now to make your arrangements. If Lewis is safe back tomorrow, I will see you on to the next ship like a dutiful daughter, with nothing said. If not, I go to the duke.'

'But what will you do, by yourself here?'

'From now on, that is my affair.'

'For Lewis? Of course I'll go.' Frank had listened intently to his mother's brief explanation. 'It's wonderful news that he is alive. But absurd of Dom Miguel to imagine that the duke could give an immediate answer; everyone knows how his hands are tied by that greybeard council of his. And, Mother, Caterina, there is not the slightest risk to me. I shall go under British colours, a visible neutral, there's no need to fret. Nothing the least heroic about it. I just hope the bombardment does slacken; it will be hard to decide what to do for the best if not, but you must leave that to me. I'll go and have the boat made ready at once. Try not to worry.' He kissed his mother and was amazed to find himself being warmly embraced by Caterina. 'See me out, Hetta?'

'Of course.' Standing on the steps to the palace gate, Hetta kissed him warmly. 'Be careful, Frank.'

'Believe me, I will, and, Hetta—'

'Yes.' She knew what was coming.

'Give all my love to Ruth.'

Left alone, Caterina and Harriet discussed without deciding where they should pass the endless time of waiting. Then another thought struck Caterina. 'Oh, my goodness,' she exclaimed. 'It's the least of our worries, but I sent off my invitations to my party for Jenny Forbes yesterday. Lewis's party! Greville's mother! Oh, Harry, tell me that tomorrow will see them safe home.'

'At least we know Lewis is alive. And, think, Cat, every minute that passes must increase his chances. Imagine the scandal that would arise if anything happened to him, a prisoner, half English and English educated. Just the kind of bad publicity Dom Miguel knows he cannot afford. Think what Charles Forsyte would make of it.'

'Goodness me,' said Caterina. 'I hadn't thought of that.'

'What hadn't you thought of?' asked Hetta, rejoining them.

'Your mother was saying what a weapon any ill treatment of Lewis would be in Charles Forsyte's hands,' Caterina told her, images flashing through her mind. Would she be able to do it, if the worst happened?

'That's perfectly true,' said Hetta. 'Clever of you, Mother.'

'But I wish there would be news of Greville,' said Caterina. 'Let's go down to your house, Harry, it's nearer for news. We'll leave a message for Ruth to join us there when she gets back from the hospital. I know how anxious she will be.'

'We all are,' said Hetta.

It had rained on and off all day, but towards evening the clouds gave way to a brilliant sunset.

'It postpones the dusk,' said Caterina, gazing down the flaming path across the river.

'Not for long,' Harriet told her. 'Listen! The bombardment is slackening.'

'You're right. And the light is going.'

'So it won't be possible for anyone on the other bank to make out whether it is a man or a woman in the boat,' said Hetta. This had been worrying her, but she had spared the other two the anxiety. 'Ah, here's Ruth at last. Were things dreadful at the hospital that you had to stay so late?' she asked as Ruth joined them.

'It's mayhem there.' Ruth did not tell them that she had stayed to make up for the time spent with her mother. The less said about that, she felt, the better. 'The bombardment is slackening.'

'Yes.' Hetta told her. 'Frank will be setting off now.'

'Frank?' Ruth gripped her hand. 'What do you mean?'

'Of course, you don't know. Frank offered to go in Caterina's place, bless him. He said there would be no risk to him as a neutral. He goes under British colours,' she explained, aware of something rigid about her friend. 'There he goes!' They could see the Ware boat now, coming out from the quay and catching the evening breeze to move steadily upriver and out of their line of vision. Ruth and Hetta went on holding hands, and nobody said anything.

When the Ware boat rounded the Serra point it slid into shadow, the sun cut off by the towering bluff above. They had lost the wind too, and Frank's two crewmen unshipped their oars. 'Not a word now,' he said softly. They already had their instructions, and their oars slid in and out of the water almost soundlessly. He wanted to maintain as much of the element of surprise as possible. It was quiet as well as dark, now they had rounded the bend away from Vila Nova and the sounds of the enemy camp. No light showed on the shore. Frank had fished from this deserted quay as a boy and it seemed to have fallen into even more disrepair since then, but he was able to find the familiar mooring in the half-light and jump ashore, leaving his crew to lie off and wait for him.

He stood quite still for a few moments, getting his bearings, listening intently. Nothing. If someone was there to meet him, they might well be doing the same thing, trying to make out who he was in the half light. But at least his sharp hearing reassured him that there was no concealed body of men awaiting him, some sound would inevitably have betrayed their presence by now. Memory still serving him, he moved quietly forward to a little ruined chapel at the back of the quay. When he was a boy, there had been one service a year here, on the saint's day, and he and Lewis had rowed over to attend it together.

'Is there anybody there?' He was at the chapel door now. 'I am Frank Ware, come with a letter for Luiz da Fonsa y Sanchez from Caterina Gomez. I am quite alone.'

'And where the hell is she?' A tall figure emerged from the chapel. 'I am Luiz da Fonsa y Sanchez. You had best tell me what the letter says. It would be asking for trouble to show a light here.'

This was the best of news to Frank, since it seemed to imply that the meeting was secret even from the Miguelites. 'She asks for twenty-four hours' grace,' he said. 'The duke does not feel he can promise the meeting his brother asks without the consent of his council, and they don't meet until tomorrow morning.'

'Pack of old fools,' said Sanchez. 'Will they manage to decide tomorrow, do you think?'

'I doubt it,' said Frank honestly. 'A pity. I do feel that a meeting between the two brothers is the best hope for an end to this unspeakable war.' And how odd to be saying that to this enemy stranger, but there was something curiously liberating about the silence and darkness that surrounded them.

'You're right there, one way or another. But what of my other request, what did Caterina Gomez say to that?'

'She told me nothing of another request. I am only authorized to ask for twenty-four hours' grace, and to remind you, on her behalf, that Lewis Fonsa is her only son.'

'*Her* only son? She did not choose to tell you that he is mine too?'

'Good God, no!' A kaleidoscopic movement took place in Frank's mind as the whole of his and Lewis's past changed shape and resettled into the new pattern. 'I see!' he said.

'And the odd thing is, so do I,' said Sanchez. 'She's a much cleverer woman than I understood, Caterina Fonsa, as she chooses to call herself. It's really a pity she didn't come today; we might have made something of it yet, she and I. Tell her I said so, will you, Ware? As it is, I shall have to change my plans quite drastically. You're not the slightest use to me as a hostage.'

'I am glad you see that. But what of Lewis?'

The other man actually laughed, a low chuckle that sounded strange in the darkness. 'That's the cream of the joke. I thought him a negligible young fool, expendable, a pawn in my dealings with Dom Miguel. I left him securely guarded, as I thought. When I got back, he had freed himself. He took me by surprise, knocked me out and escaped. A son to be proud of.'

'Does Dom Miguel agree with you?' This was the oddest conversation Frank had ever held with anyone.

'I doubt he will. That's why I've not told him; why I am here alone. If Caterina had come, she would have been my hostage, and all well. She's beaten me, I never thought to have to admit it. Tell her so, from me, and tell her that I am cutting my losses and going back to Brazil. And tell her something else, because I rather think she is the only woman I have truly loved. Tell her, from me, to go home to England. There is going to be no peace here in Portugal for years to come; these two idiotic brothers have lit a fire they will find it hard to put out. Now I must go. I have my arrangements to make.'

'But Lewis? Where is he?'

'God knows. I told you. He knocked me out. When I came to myself there were the signs of a savage fight outside the barn where I had hidden him. Several dead Miguelites, one dead *caçador*, no Lewis. If he is lucky, he will be slipping back across river tonight; if not, he may never be seen again. Dom Miguel will not be pleased. That is why I mean to make the best of my way out of this.'

'Can I help at all?' Frank was amazed to find himself asking this.

'Handsome of you, but, no, thanks. I am still capable of making my own arrangements. But give a father's blessing to my son, if he should chance to get back across in one piece. Not that he will be grateful for it.'

'No, I don't suppose he will.' Frank held out his hand. 'Goodbye, sir, and good luck.'

His hand was taken and strongly wrung. 'And give my love to Caterina, and no hard feelings.' He moved swiftly away into the darkness.

The wind was against them on the way back so it took longer, but the bombardment was not resumed and Frank found himself safe once more on his own quay in the early hours of the morning.

As he had expected, he found all four women still up, waiting for him. 'All's well so far.' He spoke to Caterina but looked at Ruth. 'He was there, Luiz da Fonsa y Sanchez, alone, in the dark.' He handed the letter back to Caterina. 'He couldn't read this, said we must not show a light. Lewis has escaped, and Dom Miguel does not know it yet.'

'Escaped!' exclaimed Caterina. 'Thank God! But how?'

'It was the strangest thing,' Frank told her. 'It seemed to me that Sanchez was actually pleased about Lewis's escape. He took him by surprise, knocked him out, was gone when he came to himself.' He explained about the signs of a rescue.

'It must have been Greville,' said Caterina. 'God bless him. But where are they now?'

'Trying to get back across the river,' said Frank. 'It won't be easy, I'm afraid.' And then, to distract her. 'But, something else, Caterina: Sanchez told me to tell you he is abandoning the Miguelite cause, returning to Brazil. He advises you to go back to England. This war will go on for ever, he thinks. The brothers have started something they can't stop.'

'I wonder if he is right,' she said. 'Thank you, Frank, a thousand times, for doing this for me. And now, we must go home.' To the two girls. 'We will all be better working.'

The little party lay huddled in the black darkness among the huge wine vats. The cellar was dug deep into the cliff and the air was cold and damp and heavy with the smell of fermentation. When their guide had left them there, urging quiet and no lights, they had all slept, they did not know for how long, exhausted by the day's narrow escapes. Lewis had taken the lead all day and Greville had been glad to let him. He was on his own ground after all. It was Lewis who had found them their guide, whom they must trust.

'You think he will come back for us?' Greville whispered.

'Unless someone offers him more. What I cannot understand is why there is no general search, but it's a blessing. I think it gives us a chance. I don't know about you but I have to say I would much rather not be taken. I've not thanked you properly, sir.'

'Nonsense. And I wish you would call me Greville. It's a long time since those trips to school.'

'How I hated them. And it. I'm sorry. Looking back, I must have been a dead bore with my tantrums and carrying on.'

'You were a very unhappy boy. But your mother was right, you know, you would have got no proper schooling in Oporto. I was bullied at school too. I always wondered whether to tell you about it.'

'I wish you had. But it wasn't just the bullying. Are they still asleep?' They were both quiet for a moment, listening to the sounds of snoring from where the three *caçadores* lay concealed between the next rows of great vats.

'Yes. Long may it last. Have you any idea what the time is?'

'No way to tell night from day here. I've no idea how long we slept, have you?'

'No. And he said he wouldn't be back for us until the small hours.'

'If he comes. I have to tell you I didn't quite like the feel of him. He may be out there selling us to the highest bidder.'

'Not much we can do about it. What else beside bullying?' The darkness made it possible to ask the question and hope for an answer.

Lewis moved impatiently beside him. 'Those last years at Stonyhurst, when I was in the Philosophers'. You were more or less your own man there, able to go and come as you pleased, without one of the old fathers hanging around you all the time. I really thought things would be better there.'

'And they weren't?'

'My fault. It was all so boring, Greville. Prayers, Virgil, healthy exercise, Homer, Virgil, prayers, more exercise. We used to go for these long walks over the moors. There was a set of fellows used to cut off for a house . . . a kind of inn . . . there was a woman there. . .'

'Of course,' said Greville.

'I made such a fool of myself. She made such a fool of me. They all did; they were all laughing at me. And then, naturally, I was the one who was caught. I'll never trust a woman again. Least of all my revered mother!'

'Lewis!' And then, 'What do you mean?'

'Don't you know? You amaze me! Jeremy Craddock does. I expect by now everyone in Porto does. The man I escaped from yesterday was my mother's lover, my father, Luiz da Fonsa y Sanchez.' And suddenly he was pouring out the whole tale, in a kind of savage whisper, the darkness making it just possible to tell it. 'I know you saved my life,' he said at last, 'but don't expect me to be too grateful, Greville. What in God's name am I to do with it?'

'Make the most of it.' Greville had listened in appalled silence. 'Hush! There's somebody coming.'

Frank was trying to apply his mind to clearing up the muddle Bankes had left when his clerk came in with a scrap of paper. 'Delivered by hand, sir. It's good news. The best.'

'Oh, thank God!' He snatched and read it quickly, recognizing Lewis's hand: *Frank, come to our rescue, we're held as spies, here at Foz by the* [here he used a Portuguese adjective] *French. Greville says get the duke*

Get the duke. Well, why not? 'Run to the house, Simpson. Give my mother this.' Handing back the note. 'Tell her I've gone to the duke.'

Braganza was in council again, but emerged on receiving Frank's urgent message. 'An international incident, in fact,' he said, after Frank had swiftly told his tale. 'Greville and Fonsa and we don't know how many of my *caçadores*, all held by our enthusiastic French allies. Maybe I had better come myself.' At least it got him away from his council. 'You had better come too, Ware. It's a fine day for a ride.'

'Thank you, Your Grace, I would like to.'

'And we will send a message to . . .' a slight pause, 'Madame Fonsa, to tell her we are going to the rescue of her son, who does seem to have a genius for getting into trouble.'

Frank opened his mouth to protest, but thought better of it. Lewis must fight his own battles.

The French commandant at Foz was, in fact, relieved to see the duke. He had begun to have second thoughts about the shabby group of fishermen his men had arrested that morning as they landed surreptitiously on the little beach below Foz Castle. The Cabadello Battery across the river had opened fire on his position soon afterwards and he had not had time to reconsider his decision to keep them incommunicado until he could interview them. Now, with the bombardment easing off as it usually did towards the siesta hour, he shrugged off the smuggled message that had brought the duke so speedily.

'Maybe they are what they say after all,' he conceded. 'Sit down, Your Grace, have a glass of wine, while I send for them.'

They did indeed look a group of filthy fishermen, but there was no mistaking Lewis and Greville despite the disguise. Lewis was in a raging temper, Greville looked both relieved and amused.

'Good of Your Grace to come so swiftly to our rescue,' he greeted the duke. 'There was no convincing your people here that we were anything but dastardly Miguelite spies, and really I don't blame them. As you can see, we were most efficiently disguised.'

'Yes,' said the duke. 'And what I want to know is, by whom?'

'That, Your Grace, we have undertaken not to say.' He met the duke's outraged glare steadily. 'The men know nothing, and Fonsa and I have given our word of honour.'

And from that nothing would shake either of them. Mounts were found for Greville and Lewis, the *caçadores* were left to make their own way back to town, and the duke promised himself that he would get the whole story out of Lewis as soon as he had him alone. No use trying to pump him in front of Greville, who had made their position so firmly clear, and with Frank Ware present, who had witnessed this. The other three men were also aware of so much to be said, that in fact they said very little, the roughness of the going providing a good reason for silence. When they reached the Carrancas Palace, the duke reined in his horse.

'You had best go straight home,' he told Lewis. 'Madame—'

Something very odd in his tone. 'Your mother will be anxious about you. Report for duty tomorrow. I will hear your story then.'

Chapter 14

The three men rode the short distance to the Sanchez Palace in a heavy silence, each of them drawing his own conclusions from that odd tone of the duke's.

'We'll leave you here,' Greville told Lewis when they reached the palace gates. 'Your mother will want you to herself, and I must reassure my landlord that I am still alive before he throws my things into the street and relets my rooms. I don't need to remind you of the promise we gave our friends on the other side. Tell your mother I will call on her tonight.'

'And so will I,' said Frank. 'What a happy day, Lewis.' But it did not feel like one. Riding on with Greville he turned to him impulsively. 'Something is the matter,' he said. 'What is it, on this happy day?'

'It's a long story,' said Greville. 'And not mine to tell. What has been happening here, Frank?'

Caterina was alone. When the good news had come, the two girls had gone to the hospital and she, too, had decided to try and do some work on her cartoon about neutrals. But she could not concentrate. All she could think of was what she was going to say to Lewis. What was he going to say to her? She almost hoped Greville would come in with him. But when he came at last, Lewis was alone. She heard the servants' tumultuous greeting, made herself wait for him in her parlour. Could she be afraid of him?

'Mother!' He closed the door behind him. 'I am glad to find you alone.' Even through the filthy disguise she thought he looked older, savage. 'What have you been saying?' he asked. 'What have you told the duke?'

'Lewis!' He had not even touched or kissed her. 'I had to tell him. Look!' She handed him his father's note.

'You showed him this?'

'What else could I do, to persuade him?'

'Which you failed to do. I take it you did not go to this dangerous assignation?'

'No use without the duke's answer. Frank Ware took a note instead, asking for twenty-four hours' grace. And, I have to tell you, Lewis, I would have died for you, gladly, but I would not have married Luiz da Fonsa y Sanchez.'

'You may be going to find that death would be the easier option, ma'am, judging by the duke's tone when he spoke of you just now. A fine winter we are going to have of it here in Porto, with you the butt of every scandalous tongue in town, and my name gone with yours. I begin to think I may yet be sorry I survived the last two days.' They had still not touched each other. 'I knew you for a whore, ma'am, but I did not think you a fool until today.'

'Lewis!' Absorbed in each other, they had not heard the door open. Now both swung round at sight of Hetta, white with rage. 'I'm ashamed of you!' She came into the room and faced him, a small fury. 'Have you any idea what your mother has gone through, what we all have, while you have been lost to us? And now you come back and behave like a child in a tantrum. So the story is out at last! If you ask me, everyone has known the gist of it for ever, but everyone has chosen to pretend not to. Why? Because they loved your mother, maybe were a little fond of you too. I can't think why. And as for her, what has she thought of all these years but you? And this is her thanks. You had better go and wash your face, and your mind with it, Lewis, and come back and beg her pardon.'

'What do you know about it?' He faced her, as angry as she.

'Not much. Nor want to. But I know Caterina. And so should you. And now, if you don't want to be caught by her first visit of congratulation on your safe return you really had better clean yourself up, Lewis.' Her tone softened. 'You must have had a terrible time of it over there; no wonder if you are not quite yourself today.

We have two of your men in the hospital, by the way, who would be glad of a visit. To know you are safe. They seem to like you. Or do you have to go straight back to barracks?'

'No, the duke has given me today off duty. Is Ruth at the hospital still?'

'Yes, she is on late shift tonight. If you went to visit your men later, you could see her home; the streets are sometimes a bit lively at night.'

'I'll do that. Thank you, Hetta.' He turned to his mother, could not think what to say, and left the room.

'I'm sorry.' Hetta was appalled to see tears in Caterina's eyes. 'And so will he be. You mustn't take it so hard, Caterina.' She took out a large, nurse's pocket handkerchief and handed it to her friend. 'He's not grown up yet, that's all.'

'He's older than you.'

'I didn't get sent to boarding-school.'

'But, Hetta, I had to.'

'Oh, Caterina, I know that. He grew up so fast, poor Lewis. I thought you very wise. It was getting dangerous, him and Bess, you know, but I'm not sure how much sense they taught him at Stonyhurst, and the army's not much better, if you ask me. All those men's rules. He'll learn about the real world in the end. But don't you think you should tell him about Charles Forsyte, Caterina? He is going to feel a terrible fool when he finds out, and he won't like that either. Don't you think it's maybe time you broke through the veil of secrecy altogether? It can't hold forever and I am sure it would be better if you came out with it, rather than being unmasked. Maria Bankes is bound to put her inquisitive nose to the ground when she gets back to England. How closely is the secret guarded there?'

'I don't know. Greville looks after all that. Hetta, do you realize that his mother is due on the next packet, and I have this party planned for her, and now I begin to wonder if the duke will come.'

'He'll be a fool if he doesn't,' said Hetta robustly. 'But then I often think he is a bit of a fool.'

'Hetta!'

'No use trying to sound shocked. You think the same thing yourself; it shows in your cartoons sometimes. It's the one good reason I know for not revealing your identity so long as you are here in Oporto.'

'You sound as if you thought I was leaving.'

'Haven't you thought of it? Things you have said lately have suggested it. About England, and growing cabbages. I wonder where you are thinking of growing them.'

'Trellgarten,' said Caterina instantly. 'It's a funny thing, Hetta. I've never met my grandmother, but she has been there at the back of my mind all my life, and now I find myself thinking about her more and more. It's odd, Lewis didn't like her, but everything he said about her made me do so.'

'I know just what you mean,' said Hetta. 'She was friends with the Ladies of Llangollen and wanted the surviving one to come and live with her. It makes her sound interesting, doesn't it? And it does make one think that she might welcome you with a good deal more enthusiasm than she did Lewis.'

'Yes, I'd thought that. And, don't you see: if I went there, I could go on with the cartoons—'

'From another safe and secret base! I do believe you are almost serious about this.'

'Do you know, I believe I almost am. I've always known I must move out when Lewis marries, and it does begin to look as if he was going to, doesn't it?'

'Lewis!' Ruth had been just ready to leave the hospital when he came knocking on the door of her office. 'I am so glad to see you safe! Have you been to see your two men?'

'Yes, I had to give them sad news of some of their comrades, but they seem to be doing well enough.'

'If we only had proper food and medicine for them, they would be doing better. But those two are tough, I think they will survive hospital life.'

'They are certainly grumbling in a very healthy way. Come along, Ruth, I am going to see you home. Hetta says the roads are risky at night.'

'Does she so?' But she let him help her into her cape. 'Is it raining still?'

'No, it has stopped, thank God.' He opened the door for her. 'I thought we might go by way of the market. You look as if you could do with a breath of air; nobody could say your hospital smelled sweet.' He had opened the outside door for her now and they moved out into a golden afterglow.

She could feel the tension strong in him as he took her arm and guided her into a secluded corner off the road, with a fountain and a statue of a saint. 'Ruth.' He stopped, turned to face her. 'I have to tell you! You must stand by me now: I don't think I can face it alone. I told you I was a bastard, but it's worse than that. Far worse. I'm the son of a Miguelite traitor, and, worst of all, the whole world is going to know it. My fool of a mother has blown it to the duke. I am going to be a public laughing stock, Ruth.'

'I doubt that,' she said. 'It would be a brave man who laughed at you, Lewis. And your mother is no fool. If she showed the duke your father's letter, it was because there was no other way of getting him to help save you. Are you not a little grateful that you have survived?'

'No thanks to my mother and her revelations.' But he had not realized how much she knew, and it shook him. 'I rescued myself, thanks in part to Greville, who arrived in the nick of time with some of my men. And my mother would not even keep the assignation my father proposed; she sent Frank instead.'

'Having it both ways, aren't you? Or rather not having it! If she had gone, she'd be a hostage now. And probably married out of hand to that villain, your father. Which would have killed her and done you no good at all. Think of the talk then! What is going to be said now will be nothing compared. Besides, the world has more important things to talk about just now, than whether you are legitimate or not, Lewis da Fonsa. Has no one told you just what a disaster that cross-river attack was? A shambles. If talk about your little problem distracts any attention from it, I think you should look on it as a blessing. And after all, Lewis, nothing has changed. It's not who you are but what you are that counts.'

'Ruth, *you've* changed! What's happened?' He did not give her time to answer, but rushed on, 'I knew I had to come to you. With you at my side, I can face anything. It's a dishonoured name I offer you, Ruth, but take it, and we will make it honourable again between us.'

'Lewis, I'm sorry.' She withdrew her hand from his, faced him squarely. 'I told you before; I can't. You should have believed me. Being sorry for you changes nothing. Now, I want to go home. No need to escort me. Hetta should have had more sense.' And she turned and walked swiftly away into the gathering dusk.

Back in the office, Frank found it hard to concentrate on the problems that faced him. Considering how little business there had been for Ware and Son to do since the war had started, it was amazing what a muddle Bankes had managed to make of it. But when he tried to apply his mind to it, that scene outside the Carrancas Palace played itself over and over again in his imagination. Up to now, he had simply not had time to think about the implications of Sanchez's announcement that he was Lewis's father. Growing up with the story of Lewis's dead father in England, and away at school in England himself for long periods, he had remained unaware of the whiff of gossip that had reached his sister's more receptive ear. Now it all hit him as suddenly as it must have hit the duke, and he understood that strange hesitation when Braganza spoke of Caterina, and Lewis's reaction to it. Greville's too, so Greville must also have known the story.

What was he going to do about it? What could he do? Nothing. He wanted ferociously to strangle the gossips with his bare hands. Which would merely make matters worse. How odd to find himself thinking of his own father, traces of whose ineffective, gentle hand he had been finding here and there in the office files. His father had gone to Lewis's defence, and died for it. And here was something he could do, and should have thought of sooner. He must tell Lewis what Sanchez had said about him. More than that, he must tell Lewis that he had found himself actually liking Sanchez. A father one need not be altogether ashamed of. Perhaps that would help to dispel the black cloud that had hung over his friend as they rode down to the Sanchez Palace. And then he found himself wondering

just what Lewis had said to Caterina when he got there, picked up
his hat and told his clerk he was going out.

Striding uphill towards the Sanchez Palace, he met Lewis in the
market place. 'Lewis!' He put out a hand to stop him as he would
have walked straight by, blind to everything but his own misery. 'I
wanted to speak to you. '

'Why?' said Lewis.

'There's something I need to tell you. Let's go into the market
tavern; the wine's not good, but if we talk English no one will
understand us. Come along. You look as if you could do with a
drink.'

'Hemlock,' said Lewis.

'As bad as that? I'm sorry.' He fetched two beakers of rough local
wine and sat down on the bench beside his friend. 'I want to tell
you about your father,' he said.

Wine spilled from Lewis's beaker. '*You* know?'

'I didn't. He told me. Lewis, it was the strangest thing; he told
me about how you had bested him. He wanted to; he was proud of
you, boasting. We had to talk in whispers, without a light shown.
He couldn't even read Caterina's note. He hadn't told Dom Miguel
about your escape, you see. I imagine that is why you managed to
get clear away. There was no hue and cry. Miguel will be furious
when he finds out, but your father is abandoning his cause. He says
this war is going to go on for ever and he is going back to Brazil.
Told me to tell your mother that. I should think it must be an
immense relief to her, don't you?'

'I don't give a damn,' said Lewis savagely. 'Why did she have to
blab the whole thing to the duke? You heard how he spoke of her,
Frank. Her name's gone, and mine with it.'

'Oh, names,' said Frank. 'Don't you think people are more
important? You're beginning to sound like a Portuguese *fidalgo*,
Lewis, and that I never thought to hear. Besides, I believe the duke
is going to have to think again about Caterina. He will, if he has any
sense. She has made an interesting place for herself here in Oporto,
as a bridge between British and Portuguese society, and she has
been a good friend to him. Think of that portrait. And, something
else.' He had just thought of this himself. 'Think of Jenny Forbes's

visit and Caterina's party for her. The duke can hardly cut that. I don't think even he would commit so grave a social error, and from all one hears Mrs Forbes should be able to charm him out of any Puritan sullens he may have got himself into. I do long to meet her, don't you?'

'No.' Lewis drained his beaker, picked up Frank's and pushed his way to the corner of the room where the villainous looking landlord presided over the cask. Returning, he handed Frank his drink and raised his own in a toast. 'I wish I was dead,' he said.

'You ought to be ashamed.' Frank did not drink. 'If you don't care about yourself, with all the future holds for you, think of your mother, think of the rest of us, think of Ruth—'

'She refused me tonight.' Lewis had not meant to say this. 'I never thought she meant it till now, but she does. So what in hell's name does the future hold for me, tell me that?' Exhaustion and wine were having their way with him and his words were beginning to run themselves together.

'You're worn out. Tomorrow will look better, I promise you. Now I'm going to take you home.'

'I have no home,' said Lewis with difficulty. 'Take me back to barracks, Frank, and thank you for a good friend. Tell me,' with a sudden gleam of intelligence, 'what did you really think of my father?'

'Lewis, I liked him.'

Caterina had been busy with congratulatory callers all afternoon and it was almost a relief when a message summoned the two girls back to the hospital after their early, silent evening meal. She needed time alone to think about her son, to face her future, to let her wounds quietly bleed.

She was not going to get it. '*Minha senhora*,' Carlotta caught her just as she was going upstairs to her studio. 'The duke is here.'

'The duke?'

'Yes. He says he has to see you.'

She owed it to Lewis to see him. 'Very well, Carlotta, and we must not be disturbed, whoever comes.'

The duke looked exhausted, sallow with fatigue and, she

thought, anger. 'Good of you to see me.' He kissed her hand and something uncomfortable stirred in her. 'So late. I had to come; the only place I could think of, for comfort. I've been in council with my old men all afternoon. They scolded me, *senhora*, for wasting my time on your son. May I congratulate you, by the way, on his safe return?'

'Thank you.' Mechanically. He had not let go of her hand, and she wished he would.

'They scolded me,' he said again. 'Like a bad boy who has played truant from his lessons. How am I to endure it, beautiful lady?'

'They are a rod you made for your own back, Highness. It was you gave them the power they use to thwart you.'

'And what comfort is that supposed to be to me? I tell you I cannot go on, facing both disaster and their carping criticism alone. I need someone behind me, to love me, to care for me, to stand by me. Then I could bear it, then I could carry on to the end, to the freedom of Portugal and my daughter its queen. Lovely lady, you who are so intelligent must know how I have admired, no, loved you since we first met, how I longed to touch you, to caress you when you were painting that brilliant portrait. Then, I did not understand your situation, now I do. Now all is open before us. You shall be my dear friend, my support, my councillor, above suspicion and beyond reproach as my dearest companion. And I will be a new man as a result, master of them all. Come!' He was pulling her to him. 'We've wasted too much time. You're human too; I've felt it. I feel it. It is not good for man to be alone. I shall make you so happy!'

'No!' But the protest was lost in his ferocious kiss.

His hands were all about her. 'I need you!'

'No!' But she could feel it and, worse still, feel it begin to have its effect on her.

'Your Highness!' The icy voice from the door had them apart on the instant.

'Greville. Thank God!' Caterina turned to him, colour high, hand outstretched. 'The duke does not understand—'

'I can see that. May I remind Your Highness that the Senhora Fonsa is a valued member of the English community.' He stressed the word English. 'And her son in your service.' He was talking to give the duke time to control rage that had almost burst out in violence. 'Things are bad enough, here in Oporto, after the other day's disaster. You cannot afford a rift between the two communities.' He could understand the Portuguese obscenities the duke was muttering under his breath, hoped Caterina could not, and actually found himself wondering whether to throw the identity of Charles Forsyte in the duke's furious face, when Braganza made a tremendous, visible effort and spoke.

'I am not accustomed to being interrupted, Faulkes.'

'I think the *senhora* will tell you she was glad to see me.'

'Yes,' said Caterina. 'You were acting under a misapprehension, Highness, and I think we had best decide it never happened.' It was clear in her tone that this was as much threat as promise.

'I am your servant to command. As always.' And he withdrew in as good order as he could manage.

'Greville, I do thank you!' Caterina's colour was still high, her breathing rapid. 'But how in the world did you get past Carlotta?'

'By brute strength, I'm afraid. I'll apologize to her presently, don't worry, and she'll forgive me.' He saw tears standing in her eyes, and longed to take her in his arms and comfort her, but must not. 'Let us count our blessings,' he said instead. 'I rather think that little scene is going to be one in disguise, Caterina.'

'Well disguised,' she said. 'What can you mean?'

'Braganza's not going to put a foot wrong where you are concerned from now on, so all we have to do is persuade that volcanic son of yours to take things quietly and you may be out of the woods yet. Was he very tiresome, Caterina, poor Lewis?'

'Tiresome! He called me—' She could not say it, but he could guess. 'Then Hetta came in and went for him like a fury and I've not seen him since. I'm so worried, Greville.'

'No need to worry about him tonight at least,' he told her. 'I met young Frank taking him home to barracks, drunk as a lord. Just what he needs. And Frank told me something I know you will be glad to hear. One of your problems is solving itself. Sanchez told Frank he was leaving Dom Miguel and going back to Brazil. Told him to tell you so. He seems to have taken something of a fancy to young Lewis, actually enjoyed being knocked out by him, and did not report his escape to Dom Miguel. Doubtless why we got away as easily as we did, thank God. But you can see that when Miguel learns about it, he is bound to be furious. I imagine that by now Sanchez is well on his way to Lisbon and the next boat for Rio de Janeiro.'

'You're right, that is the best of news. But, Greville, you mean Frank knows now?'

'Yes, Sanchez told him. He was boasting of his son's prowess. That brings me to what I have really come to say. I think you have to face it that what has been tacit knowledge for all these years is going to be open from now on. The duke's muzzled, but there are the rest of the gossips to be thought of. Caterina, I have left you alone to think about it, but you know what I said before. Please, dearest Caterina, marry me, let me take you home to England, out of all this, to a new name, a new life, new hopes. Please—'

He would have taken her hand and the touch might have changed everything, but she had had too much for one day. She moved a step away, swept him a ferocious curtsy. 'You are too good, Mr Faulkes, and I thank you for the offer of your name to hide my shame, but I'll fight my own battles, in my own way, as Charles Forsyte, if necessary. And here, in good time, are the girls home from the hospital.'

Chapter 15

Turned away twice from Rachel Emerson's apartment by Susan, Jeremy Craddock was finally reduced to writing her the news of Lewis's safe return, and the revelation about his father. This got him a summons at last, several days later.

He climbed the familiar steps, burning for her.

'She's not been at all well, *senhor*,' Susan warned him at the door. 'If you can, tell her only good news.'

'I've brought her a present. I hope she'll like it. Do you realize it is almost Christmas Day, Susan? The Portuguese may wait till Twelfth Night for their celebrations, but there's nothing to stop us behaving like Christians. And a very happy Christmas to you, too.' He handed her a little packet of coins neatly wrapped in a scrap of scarlet paper.

He had bought Rachel a gold bracelet to match the chain he had given her, but the Christmas greeting dried on his lips when he saw her. She had aged ten years. Red spots burned in her cheeks, and even her hair had lost its lustre. 'You've been ill, Susan says. I am so sorry.' Desire ebbed away at sight of this wreck of a woman. 'You must take better care of yourself.'

It was the cue she wanted. 'I intend to, dear friend,' she told him. 'This illness has been a warning to me. My health is too delicate to endure the privations of a siege any longer. I am making my arrangements to go home to America.' She smiled, a travesty of the smile that had enslaved him. 'And you are relieved to hear me say so. It was a splendid dream while we dreamed it, but it is over now, is it not? But we shall part the best of friends, and I shall wear this always,' putting on the bracelet, 'in loving memory of our happy days. I shall never forget you, dear Jeremy.'

'Nor I you.' Already he was busy replanning his life. Caterina, perhaps, after all?

'Tell me, have you seen Caterina and Lewis since this scandal broke?' She might have taken the thought out of his mind. 'How are they bearing up?'

'I've not seen Caterina.' Some instinct had kept him away. 'But Lewis goes about the town looking like death, and losing his temper at the slightest cross. It's a miracle he's called no one out yet. Talk about making bad worse! Tell me, what have you heard from Sanchez? Is it true that he has abandoned Dom Miguel and is going back to Brazil?'

'I've not heard a word.' She spat it out. 'But I imagine he has gone. He was never one to linger at the scene of his failures. And that brings me to a favour I have to ask you, dear friend. You were right when you warned me that English gold was more reliable than the Miguelite kind. All I ever had from Sanchez was promises, and now I find myself hard put to it to find my fare to America. Once there, I am my own woman again, but how to get there? Do you think that your masters could be persuaded to make me one last payment?' The large, shadowed eyes met his in something between a plea and a challenge. She was promising a closed book on their relationship in exchange for this last payment, however obtained.

'I believe they might,' he said slowly. Best she think it came from the British Government, though it would not.

'Thank you. That's a weight off my mind. I'll arrange for my passage.'

'Does your daughter go with you?'

'I don't know.' Slowly. 'I wanted to ask you about that. I had hoped by now to have heard news of an engagement, which would take care of everything, but if you say Lewis is going round town in a passion it hardly sounds like it, does it? I wish I knew what is happening up at the Sanchez Palace.'

'If you wish it I will go and find out.'

'I knew you were a good friend.' She held out her hand and he kissed it for the last time, marvelling at how little he felt.

*

The Wares and Caterina had always shared their Christmas celebrations, and this year it was the Wares' turn to go to the Sanchez
Palace for the festive *bacalhau*. 'Is Lewis coming?' Harriet asked her
friend, when they were discussing the arrangements two days
before.

'I wish I knew. He's not been near me, Harry!'

'Oh dear. I'll get Frank to have a word with him.' She was more
and more worried about Caterina. 'I'm going to be indiscreet,' she
said, 'but I think you should know: Lewis told Frank that Ruth
had refused him.'

'Oh my goodness,' said Caterina. 'My poor Lewis! The last straw
for him! And I have just asked Ruth's mother to join us for
Christmas dinner! I thought it the least I could do. Ruth tells me
she has been ill. And Greville's not coming. What a dreadful party
it looks like being. Can she really have turned Lewis down?' She
came back to the subject that concerned her most. 'I have to say
that a while ago I'd have been delighted, but now I'm not so sure.
I've grown so fond of Ruth since she's been living here.'

'Hetta loves her,' said Harriet.

'Yes, they are like sisters. Oh, poor Lewis. And he hasn't even
told me!'

'He was drunk when he told Frank.'

'Is that supposed to comfort me? But I do bless your Frank for
being such a good friend to him.'

'We all love him, Cat.'

'Except Ruth apparently. I find it so strange. I was sure she
meant to have him.'

'And her mother is not going to be pleased,' said Harriet.

'No she isn't, is she? What a horrid party this is going to be. Shall
I ask Jeremy Craddock just to make it worse?'

'No, don't.'

'I think you are right.' They exchanged a thoughtful look.

In the end it was Hetta who persuaded Lewis to come to his
mother's Christmas dinner. She met him in the hospital corridor

on Christmas Eve and congratulated him on the good progress his two men were making. 'I look forward to seeing you tomorrow,' she said.

'Tomorrow?'

'Your mother's Christmas dinner.'

'I shan't be there.'

'Nonsense. Think a minute, Lewis. Think of the servants. Your servants. Your house. Your Christmas dinner, come to that, though your mother has done all the work, as always. Just stop being sorry for yourself for a moment, Lewis, and think what the world will say if you do not appear in your own house, for your own Christmas celebration. They will say you are ashamed, can't face it. And they will be right.'

'Hetta, you're formidable; what's happened to you?' Oddly he remembered saying much the same thing to Ruth.

'I've grown up, Lewis. Watching people die does things to you. Surely you've found that? One's own problems seem less important, somehow. Do come, Lewis. We'll all be miserable without you. And I'm afraid the servants will talk.'

'How am I to forgive you for being so absolutely right, Hetta?' But he was smiling as he said it and she felt a great leap of relief. 'Tell my mother I'll be there, would you? And, Hetta—'

'Yes?'

'I've had it on my mind – the duke sent her a message the other day, at least, I think he meant it for a message. It seemed so odd. He said he hoped he was still welcome at her party for Mrs Forbes.'

'And you haven't told her?'

'I've not seen her.'

'Isn't it more than time that you did?'

He looked suddenly rueful, the guilty boy that she remembered from so many childhood scrapes. 'You're right again, confound you, Hetta. I'll call in on my way back to barracks.'

The joint Christmas had always been an Anglo–Portuguese mixture and this year with everything in such short supply, Caterina and Harriet had agreed to keep it as simple as possible, but when they learned that Lewis was coming, the servants turned to with an extra will so that the palace smelled and shone as it had not done since the summertime party for the duke's arrival.

'Lord, what a long time ago it seems,' said Harriet, elegant in the grey dress Caterina had designed for her.

'Yes, an age. I wish Greville was coming. It doesn't seem right without him. He says he is too busy getting ready for his mother.'

'Which is ridiculous, since she is going to stay with you,' said Harriet.

'Yes, we shall miss him sadly.' Caterina had written Greville to tell him of the duke's message, and urge him to come, but had had no answer, and minded. 'Ah here are the girls. How nice you look, both of you. But where is your mother, Ruth? I expected her before this?'

'I don't know.' Ruth looked worried. 'She's not been at all well.' She turned her head at the sounds of rejoicing from the hall. 'That must be Lewis, at least.'

Lewis and Frank had arrived together and in the little commotion of their greetings, Hetta was able to see how much better Lewis looked. They had always begun their Christmas celebration with a particularly potent form of sangria made with either Ware or Gomez wine, depending on whose house they were in, and now Carlotta brought in the gleaming silver Sanchez bowl with its matching ladle and placed it firmly in front of Lewis. 'Mother?' he asked. She had always served it in the past.

'Of course. Your turn now, Lewis. And you'll find it hard work, I promise you.' He had actually kissed her when he arrived, and if only Greville had been present she thought she would have been perfectly happy. 'You will forgive us, Ruth, if we don't wait for your mother?'

'Of course, she'd not want it.'

Lewis was already ladling out fragrant goblets of wine while servants passed round spicy *petiscos*, the *hors d'oeuvres* that traditionally accompanied it. When everyone was served, the servants left the room to share their own similar bowl in their quarters. His duties done, Lewis moved over, glass in hand, to where Frank was talking to the two girls.

'I want to thank you, Hetta,' he began, but was interrupted as the door swung open to admit Rachel Emerson.

She was wearing low-cut black velvet, which made her look white as a ghost and showed too much of a neck that should have been hidden. 'I have come to say goodbye,' she announced, as Lewis moved back to the silver bowl and filled her a goblet. 'I have booked my place on the packet; they say it will likely be in tomorrow, so this is our last meeting. Thank you, Lewis.' She took the glass, and he realized she had been drinking already. 'Here's to you all.' She raised it and drank, her eyes travelling slowly round the silent group until they settled on her daughter. 'And goodbye to you all. Especially to you, Ruth, my dear. I had hoped to leave you settled, but since you have chosen to go your own way I mean to leave you in Caterina's charge. If I may call you Caterina this once?' Something mocking in her tone. 'We have shared so much, you and I, though I'm the only one to know it. To my cost. Luiz da Fonsa y Sanchez was the love of my life, too, Caterina, and his daughter Ruth is there to prove it. My husband never forgave me her birth and Sanchez never gave me anything but her – and promises. Enough of that. I'm not well. I must go home. You will look after your son's half-sister for me, will you not, Caterina? Try to behave yourself, Ruth.' And she turned and swept from the room.

There was a long, stunned silence. Frank had a supportive arm around Ruth, while Lewis, white-faced, gazed at her with a mixture of shock and comprehension. 'You felt it,' he said at last. 'The kinship. So did I, but I did not understand.'

'And she would have let you two marry.' Caterina's voice shook as she understood it all.

'I think she is capable of anything.' Ruth needed Frank's support. 'I'm ashamed. I have known for a little while that she was a spy, but this I did not know. It makes me understand—' She paused. 'I was going to say, "about my father". Not my father, poor man. No wonder he disliked me so.' She had been very white, now she blushed crimson.

'Don't,' said Lewis gently. 'Don't mind it too much. It's not so bad when you get used to it, and at least we have each other, Ruth. I never thought to have a sister.' He held out his hand. 'We'll look after you. Let her go, forget her. We're your family now.' He turned to Caterina. 'Aren't we, Mother?'

'Of course.' His intervention had given her time to control the first blinding flash of pure rage, and she was grateful. 'But the less said about it, the better, don't you think?' Her eyes swept the shocked and silent group. 'This really would be one scandal too many. We must all go on as if nothing has changed. Please.' And then, 'Ruth, forgive me for asking, but will your mother talk?'

'Not if you pay her not to,' said Ruth, white again. 'I know she was worrying about her fare on the packet.'

'Then she must have it.' Lewis took charge. 'I think we should send it at once, don't you?' He turned to Caterina. 'With a note, explaining our terms.'

'I'll take it,' said Frank. 'It's not a job for a servant, and I have an idea of something that might help to keep her quiet. Forgive me, Ruth?'

'Nothing to forgive. Promise her my silence, too. She'll know what I mean. Caterina, I don't know what to say—'

'Dear child. No more do I. So let's not try. I'm not much of a mother, but I'll do my best.'

'We all will,' said Lewis. 'Best write the letter, Mother, and I'll tell Carlotta to delay dinner until Frank returns. And, thank you, Frank, for going. I'm grateful. I don't think I could keep my hands off her, even though she is your mother, Ruth.'

'She has never been a mother to me,' said Ruth. 'And it's a relief to admit it. I suppose it is understandable enough if my birth really destroyed her marriage. Oh, please, let's stop talking about it. What are you doing, Hetta?'

'Finding the counters.' Hetta emerged flushed from the chest in which she had been rummaging. 'Before Lewis went away we always used to play loo at Christmas, and that is just what we are going to do now. A rousing family game. Hurry back, Frank, you were always lucky at loo.'

'Believe me, I shan't loiter,' said her brother.

Walking quickly through the quiet Christmas streets, Frank was glad that the bombardment had stopped. He needed a clear head and quiet time to arrange what he would say to Ruth's mother. Even today there were a few old women at stalls in the little market below the cathedral and he paused to look at their shabby wares, then stiffened at sight of a familiar figure emerging from the alley that led down to Rachel Emerson's apartment. 'Craddock,' he went to meet him. 'What brings you here?'

'I could ask the same of you,' said Jeremy Craddock. 'I thought Ware and Company would be celebrating up at the Sanchez Palace. Comforting your friends there. But the less said about that, perhaps, the better.'

'I do so agree with you,' said Frank. 'I am on my way to Rachel Emerson with her packet fare as a parting present from Caterina Fonsa.' He stressed the surname. 'And I plan to take the opportunity to say to her that the less she says about any of the events of the last few weeks, the better for her. If she talks, I shall be compelled to mention the affair she has been conducting with you, Mr Craddock, and I do not think either of you would like that much. You have presumably been paying her off, too.' It was not even a question.

'Yes. Dammit, how did you know?'

'Mr Craddock, I live here in Oporto, have done all my life. There's not much goes on here that I don't hear of. If you plan to stay, I would try to remember that, if I were you. While forgetting a good deal else.'

'Is that a threat, Ware?'

'Oh, no, just a warning. Happy Christmas, Mr Craddock.'

'A message from the Senhora Fonsa,' he told Susan, and was admitted at once.

'You?' Rachel looked surprised. 'I had expected Lewis.'

'You will have to make do with me.' He handed her Caterina's note, kept the little bag of gold in his hand. 'I shall need your promise of silence about Ruth before I give you this,' he said. 'For what it is worth. And before you waste both our time on protestations I should tell you that I met Craddock outside, coming away from a similar errand. I warned him that I knew about his affair with you and got a promise of discretion out of him. I think you should be grateful to me for that.'

'Perhaps I am. Who else knows?'

'No one that I know of. Have I your promise?'

'Of course. What else can I do?' She put down Caterina's note and reached out her hand for the little bag of gold.

'And you'll be on the packet without fail?'

'Nothing would keep me here. And my farewell message from my daughter?'

'She promised you her silence. That is all. She is out of your life forever and you will oblige us all by not making a melodrama of it. They are waiting Christmas dinner for me at the Sanchez Palace.' He put the bag into her hands, bowed formally and left her.

Striding swiftly back, he paused at the corner of the road where Greville Faulkes lived above the goldsmith's shop, thought for a moment then turned down it and knocked at the door. As he had expected, he found Greville alone, surrounded by piles of papers.

'Frank! What brings you here? Not more trouble for Caterina?'

'Well – a surprise. I'm sworn to secrecy, but I know it does not apply to you.' He swiftly described the scene at the palace, and explained his errand, leaving out the meeting with Craddock.

'Brother and sister!' said Greville. 'Well, I'll be damned. And she'd have let them marry. What a woman! But, Caterina, how is she taking it?'

'I have never seen her so angry,' said Frank. 'I thought for a minute that she was going to burst out with something we would all have regretted, but luckily Lewis spoke up, gave her time. But you can imagine how it has hit her, Greville. I think you ought to come back with me. She needs all her friends around her now. Not saying anything, just being there.'

'I can't, Frank. There's something else going on. Another threat to Caterina's peace of mind. I can't tell you about it. That really is her secret.'

'You mean Charles Forsyte, I suppose? And the Bankes have found out? Or are coming close? I was afraid of that. I think they are hoping to find out and then go back to England and dine out on the story of their cleverness. It's exactly what Caterina could do without just now.'

'How long have you known?'

'Since she did the one of the two boys on the seesaw. I remembered the scene from our childhood and, did you not notice, Pedro had something of a look of Lewis? I'm afraid she must have cast me as Miguel.'

'And you've said nothing.'

'Well, of course not. Her secret. Her affair. But what has Bankes got, do you know?'

'A batch of originals, stolen from my English contact. They are bound to provide a clue. And they are coming back on the packet that is due tomorrow. I have been trying to get on to the customs officers to induce them to impound the whole cargo with a tale of contraband, but you know the Portuguese "tomorrow".'

'The duke could do it.'

'But we can't tell him why.'

'No, it's difficult. Lewis could persuade him, I think, but Lewis doesn't know about Charles Forsyte either. I wish he did, Greville, it worries me.'

'Me too, but that is absolutely Caterina's affair. Don't you think you could persuade Lewis to speak to the duke without telling him, Frank? You and he seem to be very good friends these days.'

'Yes, thank God. I think he is beginning to come to terms with himself, with it all. And, yes, I think he would speak to the duke as a favour to me. He's' – he searched for the word – 'gentler, somehow. More approachable. Do come to Caterina's Christmas dinner with me, and see.'

'I still can't do that, Frank.' He gestured at the piles of papers on his desk. 'It's not just the Forsyte affair; I'm clearing my desk. I think I shall go back with my mother when she leaves. I'm finished here. Lucky for me I've got a future waiting for me in England. And you're wrong, you know; I'm the last person Caterina would want to see on this bad day. Now, be off with you, and don't keep them waiting for their Christmas *bacalhau*.'

Left alone, he returned with grimly renewed energy to his attempts to secure a reasonable subsistence for Caterina from Gomez and Daughter's funds. Half of him longed to be at the Sanchez Palace, being silently close to Caterina in her time of need. But what comfort could he, the twice rejected suitor, give to her at this moment when she must face it that the love of her life had been unfaithful to her all along – and with Rachel Emerson of all people. In his heart, he was sure that Caterina still loved Sanchez. Her first, her only love. He could not bear it for her. He could not bear it for himself. And what in the world was he going to tell his mother, who was to stay with Caterina?

Chapter 16

A gale blew up on Boxing Day and the packet did not arrive until the end of the month. Greville rode down to Foz to meet it through squalls of rain blown on a blustering wind, and the intermittent thud of shells from the Miguelite batteries south of the river. It was going to be a rough enough arrival for his indomitable mother, but at least a note from Frank had told him that the duke had listened to Lewis and ordered a customs seizure of the packet's cargo. Caterina's original drawings, and her secret, were safe for the time being.

Reaching Foz, he found a gloomy little group of people sheltering from the worst of the rain in the castle precincts. As he had expected, Rachel Emerson was there and he saw with a little tweak of apprehension that she was deep in talk with Josiah Bankes.

'I'm here to meet a precious consignment from England,' said Bankes importantly. 'And here, in good time, comes the packet.'

'Making heavy enough weather of it,' said Greville. 'You'll have to resign yourself to being taken out by boat, Mrs Emerson.' He gestured to the chattering crowd of stalwart fishwives standing ready on the tide line. 'With their help.'

'Frightful! And my baggage?'

'Don't worry. They will see to everything; they know their business. It's the price you have to pay, I'm afraid, for travelling at this time of year.' He actually felt sorry for her as she stood there gloomily contemplating the prospect before her. 'You'll find things snug enough on board, once you get there.' He was afraid for a moment that she might change her mind and refuse to go. 'And think of the comforts of London.'

'London!' She spat it out. 'I'm not staying a moment more than I must in England. It's home to the United States for me just as soon as I can get passage. But aren't you worried for your poor old mother, Mr Faulkes? How is she going to endure this barbaric treatment?'

'Oh my poor old mother can take care of herself,' he told her cheerfully. 'She'll be on the first boat, I promise you, and the life and soul of the party.' It was beginning to rain harder. 'And if I were you, Mrs Emerson, I would get down to the foreshore now and make interest with one of the women there to get you on board for its return journey. You don't want to stand around in this weather any longer than you must. Let me find you a reliable giantess.'

By the time she had agreed terms with the strapping young woman he found for her the packet had anchored and the first boat was being lowered. A shell fell somewhere beyond the castle and Rachel Emerson gasped with terror, but Greville held up a hand.

'Listen,' he said. 'What did I tell you? She's on the first boat.' As it pulled away from the ship they could hear the strains of *Bony was a Warrior* growing in strength as voice after voice joined in, one, obviously a woman's, rising above the rest.

Another shell fell, nearer, as the boat was hauled up on to the little patch of sand hemmed in by jagged rocks. Greville saw Rachel Emerson picked up bodily by her amazon as he pushed his own way through the crowd to where another one was depositing a slight figure on the sand as delicately as if it were made of crystal.

'There she is, *senhor*,' the woman beamed at him toothlessly. 'They told me to take good care of her and I have.'

'Thank her for me, Greville.' Jenny Forbes raised a laughing face for her son's kiss. 'What a dramatic arrival! I couldn't have staged it better myself. But do you not think the cannonading almost excessive?'

'It's so good to see you, Jenny!' He hugged her again. 'But you're soaking! We must get you to town and a fire as fast as possible.'

'Not before my costumes come safe to shore, love. A little wetting never did me any harm; think of all the times I've ridden outside on the stage coach, and enjoyed it. This was better still. And wasn't that a rousing chorus!'

'Yes,' he said. 'They've stopped now.' The boat was on its way back to the packet already.

'There was a very frozen-faced woman being loaded in my place. I don't just think she'll have put much spirit into them. Who was she, Grev?'

His heart warmed at the pet name. 'That was Rachel Emerson,' he told her. 'I've written you about her.'

'You certainly have. I wish I'd known. How long till the baggage comes ashore?'

'Any time now.' He turned to ask a customs officer whose face he knew.

'No use waiting, sir,' the man told him. 'Orders from the duke. The whole cargo is under embargo, to come into town and be claimed at the customs house there. Tomorrow or the next day when it's been inspected. I'm sure the lady will have no trouble, but you'd best get her back to town and a hot drink now, hadn't you?'

'Thanks, I will.' He turned as Bankes plucked at his sleeve.

'What did the man say?' Bankes asked.

'The cargo all has to go to the customs house in town to be cleared there. The duke's orders. Tomorrow or the next day, the man says. I'm sorry, Jenny.' He should have expected this.

'No matter, so long as I get my things in time for the performance. I'm sure Caterina will lend me something in the meantime. Am I to call her Caterina, Grev?'

'Oh, surely.' There was so much to tell her, but how to begin? Certainly not on the awkward mule ride back into town. Bankes inevitably joined them, paying eager court to the visiting celebrity, and Greville listened with a mixture of irritation and remembered amusement as his mother expertly parried the flattering speeches. But when they reached the Arrabida Battery Jenny pulled her mule to a willing standstill.

'Am I imagining things, Grev, or is that not an ale house over there?' It was little more than a hovel but it had a green branch hanging outside it, a sure sign of an inn. 'Because if it is I am going to plead female frailty and ask for a short rest. It's raining harder than ever.' Pulling her cloak more closely round her. 'And visions of hot toddies are filling my head. You must not let us keep you.'

She turned to Bankes who had also reined in his mule. 'I know how worried your wife will be about you with this bombardment going on.' Another shell landed inland as if to oblige her. 'Grev will look after me. He always has.'

'But it will be barbarous,' protested Bankes. 'A soldiers' pot-house, not fit for a lady.'

'I'm no lady, just an old campaigner. I wish you a very good day, Mr Bankes. It has been a pleasure to meet you. Now, Grev, for my hot toddy.' She turned to her son as they entered the tavern. 'Was that not well done?'

'Admirably. I like the idea of your female frailty, Jenny. Just the line for Bankes.'

'Terrible fellow.' She dismissed him and moved nearer the fire that burned in the centre of the room, its smoke finding most of its way out through a hole in the ceiling. At sight of her, throwing back her hood and brushing raindrops from her dark curls, the group of soldiers who had been steaming around it uttered exclamations of delighted surprise and made way for her. One of them found a stool, another took her drenched cloak, a third moved to the back of the room to shout for the landlady. She smiled impartially at them all and murmured '*obrigada*' to each. 'Tell them it is my only word of Portuguese, Grev, but my intentions are honourable.'

'So I am glad to see are theirs,' said Greville, smiling at the easy way she had taken charge.

The landlady was soon promising eggs and mulled wine and the soldiers withdrew to the far corner of the room with instinctive courtesy.

'Good.' She settled herself by the fire with one more grateful comprehensive smile for them all. 'Now, tell me all about it, Grev.'

It was the phrase she had always used when he came to her in London with a tale of some schoolboy disaster or other and it warmed his heart. 'Oh, Jenny, it's so good to see you!'

'I knew it was time I came. I've read it in all the things you haven't said in your letters. It's Caterina, isn't it?'

'Yes.' It came out as almost a groan. 'It's always been Caterina.'

'I thought so. That's why you stayed.'

'Yes, but I am leaving now. I think I shall come back with you, Jenny.'

'And cherish your grandfather? That *is* a surprise. And here in good time comes our hot wine. Tell her she is a ministering angel, Grev.'

His translation got a hoot of delighted laughter from the toothless crone who had served them, and she soon returned with an earthenware dish of spicy scrambled egg, which Jenny pronounced the best food she had eaten since she left England. 'I wonder what they feed the hens on,' she said thoughtfully, and then, without change of tone, 'So, have you asked her, Grev?'

'Twice, and been summarily rejected each time. It's a long story.'

'Then you had better start telling it. Your letters have been full of the most amazingly echoing silences. That's why I'm here.'

'God bless you.' He drank some more wine and began. When he finished the soldiers had gone and the fire had burned low. 'So you see why I think I must give up and come home,' he said in conclusion. 'She has her memories of Sanchez, her work, and her son, and that is all she wants.'

'I can understand about the work, and the son.' She smiled at him. 'But Sanchez? Even after this last revelation of Rachel Emerson's? I do wonder. And I do hope that woman is even more uncomfortable on the packet than I was!'

'I can tell you one thing: she won't make the best of it as you did.'

'No, poor woman, she did look cross. Well, Grev, all I can say is that I long to meet them all. 'Specially Caterina.' She rose. 'Tell the old lady her reward will be great in heaven. Goodness!'

'What—'

'I suppose your Caterina is a Roman Catholic.'

'Not *my* Caterina alas, and, yes, she is.'

'And her son too.' Thoughtfully. 'Oh well, it's more interesting really when things are complicated. Bless the woman, this cloak is almost dry! Have at you for the Sanchez Palace, Grev.'

It was late afternoon by the time they passed the Carrancas Palace and started down the sloping hill towards Caterina's house. 'We're late, I'm afraid,' said Jenny. 'Will she be worrying, Grev? Is it a bad start?'

'Not a bit,' he told her cheerfully. 'Working, more likely, and surprised when we get there. The girls will be at the hospital still, so you two will have a chance to get to know each other. Shall I plead work and leave you to it?'

'Oh, I don't think so.' She very much wanted to see the two of them together. 'Unless you think you will catch pneumonia in those wet clothes.' It had started raining again.

'Lord, no. And in fact I do want to tell Caterina that her drawings are safe in the hands of the customs officers.'

'But only for a few days, you say.'

'I'm afraid so. It's hard to see how they can be kept out of Bankes's hands any longer. It couldn't be a worse moment for Caterina's identity as Charles Forsyte to be revealed. But here we are.' Servants had been watching for them and the great gates of the Sanchez Palace swung open as they approached.

'Gracious.' She looked about her, smiling at the servants. 'It's not just a palace, Grev, it's a fortress.'

'It needs to be in this beleaguered city. We all have standing invitations, in case the impossible should happen and the enemy storm the city.'

'Impossible?'

'Well, no,' reluctantly. 'It very nearly happened last autumn. But here we are.' They had reached the main entrance of the palace and he jumped down to help her alight.

Carlotta was there at the top of the steps to greet them and take Jenny's sodden cloak from her shoulders with sympathetic noises in the international language of women. Then she turned and spoke to Greville.

'I was quite right,' he told his mother. 'Caterina is working. Carlotta has sent to fetch her. She'll be down directly. There is a fire in the saloon.' But Jenny was already following Carlotta. The hem of her plum-coloured habit was soaking, he noticed. 'You ought to change,' he said.

'Into what, love?' she reminded him. 'Anyway, not till I have met my hostess. And here she is.' She turned, smiling, as Caterina came hurrying through the far door of the room, welcoming hands outstretched.

'You poor thing, you must be drowned.' She took both Jenny's hands in hers. 'I do hope you have been drinking hot wine somewhere on the road.'

'Of course we have. And the best scrambled eggs I ever ate.' The two women were exchanging long enquiring glances, and Greville, watching them, thought that they looked alike, both dark, both slim, both with faces where beauty fought with character. Jenny was the taller, he saw with surprise. 'I am come as a beggar to you,' she was saying now. 'The customs in their wisdom have impounded all our baggage so here I am in what I stand up in.'

'And taller than me, too.' Caterina smiled back. 'But much the same size otherwise. Carlotta shall take you up and give you the run of my wardrobe. You will be much better out of those wet skirts. And I expect Greville will have told you why it's good news about the baggage. It's such a comfort to think you know my guilty secret.'

'Bankes was at Foz,' Greville told her. 'And very put out indeed when he learned of the baggage impoundment. I'm afraid it means only a few days' grace, Caterina.'

'Yes. I'm glad to have you here to stand by me in my hour of shame, Jenny. May I call you Jenny? It's how I think of you.'

'Of course. And why shame, for goodness sake? I have been longing to tell you how brilliant I think your pictures are, and what a powerful effect they have had on London opinion.'

'Why, thank you. But you don't understand our Portonian society. I shall be in disgrace on two counts: first, because I am a woman, and women don't do these things; and, second, much more serious, because I have kept them in the dark about it all this time, and this they will bitterly resent. And, of course, they don't much like me anyway.'

'I wonder you stay,' said Jenny.

'Well, do you know, sometimes, so do I. But this isn't changing your dress.' She rang the bell. 'You won't mind if I let Carlotta take you— And I'm sure I don't need to remind you that only Greville knows my scandalous secret.'

'Ridiculous,' said Jenny. 'But of course. You had better go and find some dry clothes too, Grev. Is it too much to hope that he will sup with us?' she asked Caterina.

'Indeed he must. You call him Grev. I like that. Greville always seemed a bit portentous somehow. Like an elder statesman. But before you go, Greville, tell me, did Rachel Emerson leave on the packet?'

'Yes, she did.'

'And looking very Friday-faced too,' said Jenny. 'I caught a glimpse of her as I was hauled ashore. Lord, I shall dine out on my arrival here in Oporto for the rest of the winter.' She sneezed. 'Maybe I will go and change. I can't tell you how happy I am to be here, Caterina, or how grateful I am to you for having me. Tell your Carlotta how sad I feel not to be able to speak Portuguese.'

But in fact she and Carlotta seemed to understand each other remarkably well.

'The house feels different.' Hetta and Ruth had come home as early as they could manage from the hospital.

'It smells different too. Carlotta must be making one of her special rices.'

'So she must like our guest.'

'Yes, but there's something else. A perfume. Ah—' They had dropped their wet cloaks in the hall and followed sounds of life to the saloon where a fire always blazed in the evenings. 'Caterina?' But Ruth's voice was doubtful as she looked at the slim figure who stood with her back to them gazing down into the fire. She was certainly wearing Caterina's crimson velvet dress.

'No,' said Hetta, before the stranger turned a smiling face to greet them.

'No, indeed,' said Jenny, 'but wearing her dress since the customs have seen fit to impound my baggage. You must be Hetta, I think. And Ruth.' Shaking one hand after the other. 'You must forgive me for feeling I know you so well, but my son is an admirable correspondent. Up to a point. And here he is.'

When Caterina joined them a few minutes later, she found them all talking at once like old friends.

Ruth had made a discovery. 'It's her perfume,' she said aside to Hetta. 'Delicious.'

'I'm glad you like it.' Jenny had sharp ears. 'It's my trade mark.

I found a little man in Paris when I was there after the Peace of Amiens and he's been making it up for me ever since. It used to be smuggled during the war in exchange for roses for Josephine's garden at Malmaison. And that's a long time ago.' There was a little silence while they all did sums in their heads and found the answer impossible to believe.

It was broken by a stir in the hall and Lewis entered the room and crossed straight to where Jenny sat close to the fire. 'I am sent by the duke to bid you welcome,' he said. 'And to apologize on his behalf for the inconvenience caused you by the baggage seizure. A mismanaged business if ever there was one!' With an angry look for Greville. 'I'm ashamed to have taken part in it.'

'But why, *senhor?*' She smiled what Greville recognized with amusement as her professional charmer's smile. 'Surely any small inconvenience to me must be outweighed by considerations of state. And as you can see the inconvenience is small indeed, thanks to your mother.' She extended a slippered foot to the fire. 'It gives me a chance to show off my ankles, which I always enjoy. Almost as good as a breeches part. I do hope the duke your master has given you leave to sup in your own house tonight and let me tell you how grateful I am to you for your hospitality? As to my baggage, it is a matter of no moment whatever, so long as I have my costumes in time for my performance.'

'To which the duke says he is immensely looking forward. And, yes, of course, your effects will be brought up to you here first thing tomorrow morning. And here is Carlotta to tell us dinner is ready.' He took her arm to lead her into the dining-room where he seated her at his right hand, visibly enslaved.

Following, Caterina and Greville exchanged a glance of rueful if slightly anxious amusement. They did not see Hetta and Ruth doing very much the same thing, behind them.

Briefly alone with Greville over a ritual glass of port, Lewis returned to the subject of the baggage seizure. 'I feel wretched about the nuisance to your mother, Mr Faulkes. I'm sorry now that I let Frank talk me into approaching the duke about that wretched cargo. I'm sure nothing will be found; just one of Frank's mare's nests, but he's a good friend.'

'One of the best,' said Greville. 'And you are forgetting to call me Greville. Shall I start calling you Senhor Fonsa? Though, of course, as your employee that is what I ought to be doing, but I confess I'd find it difficult after all these years.'

'Impossible,' said Lewis. 'Especially after what we have been through together. Have you forgotten that you saved my life? I certainly have not. But—' He hesitated. 'Greville—'

'Yes?'

'There's something I wanted to ask you. I dropped into the office this morning.' He coloured and Greville was sure he had been drawing money. 'Sam Wells said something that puzzled me. You can't possibly be meaning to leave us?'

Damn Sam Wells, thought Greville, but that was unfair. He should have expected this. 'It's true, I've been having a bit of a spring clean,' he said. 'It was more than time, particularly now you are back.'

'But I can't think of taking over. Not till the war ends. Besides, I'm not at all sure that I want to. I have all my life to rethink, Greville.' He found the name easier this time. 'Now I know I can never marry Ruth! I don't want a sister, I want a wife. I'm thinking of asking the duke to send me on a diplomatic mission. Anywhere in the world so long as it's not here, where I have to see her every day. Maybe London? I should dearly like to escort your mother back, when she goes. What an amazing woman! Why have you not said more about her, Greville?'

'Because she's my mother, I suppose.'

'You're so lucky! A mother with all that talent, charming the world.'

'I think we should join the ladies.' Greville rose.

Harriet had entirely understood Caterina when she said that she did not intend to invite her and Frank to meet Greville's mother on the first night of her visit. 'But just the same it seems odd not to be there,' she said to Frank as they finished their solitary meal.

'Yes, all wrong. Specially with Hetta there. And Lewis, I'm glad to say.'

'Oh, really?'

'Yes, I dropped into the Franciscans' on my way home for a word about that detained cargo and his man told me the duke had given him leave to go home and entertain his guest. Her baggage got held up with the rest of it, by the way.'

'It all sounds a great fuss about nothing. Do you really think they will find anything?'

'Well, there are certainly spies all round us. Rachel Emerson is safely gone, by the way. I met Bankes, in a great rage about some packet that was held up in the Customs, and he had seen her go. He seemed to have lost his heart to Greville's mother. She must be quite a charmer!'

'I can't wait to meet her. Listen, the bombardment is getting worse.'

'It's been bad all day. I'm glad Greville's mother is safe up at Caterina's house.'

'I think we should learn to say Lewis's house,' his mother warned him.

'Yes, you are absolutely right. Mother, what in the world is Caterina going to do?'

'I wish to God I knew,' she said.

'That was a close one.' Frank went to the window as a shell fell downriver, much too near for comfort. 'I think we had better sleep downstairs tonight, Mother, just in case. I wish you were up at Caterina's.'

'Lewis's,' she reminded him.

Chapter 17

'I bring bad news, I'm afraid.' Lewis had interrupted his mother and Jenny at their leisurely breakfast next morning. 'I am so very sorry, Mrs Forbes, but the enemy scored a direct hit on the customs house last night. It has burned to the ground.'

'With everything in it?' asked Caterina. He looked exhausted, she thought, and smelled faintly of burning.

'I'm afraid so.'

'Were there people there?' asked Jenny. 'Was anyone killed?'

'We don't think so. But your costumes, Mrs Forbes! All your baggage is gone, I'm afraid, with the rest of it. And your performance in two days. What in the world will you do?'

'Well, tie a knot and go on, I suppose,' said Jenny cheerfully. 'I was afraid you had news of a real disaster. Can you recommend a good dressmaker, Caterina? Or have you perhaps an attic full of antique finery that I could plunder? The beauty of a performance like mine is that I do it all *ad lib*. I was waiting to find out how things felt here, before I decided on my programme. This just means a little more thought. But I am most grateful to you, Lewis—' She smiled at him. 'May I call you Lewis? For letting me know at once. I shall need every minute of these two days to arrange my costumes and my thoughts.'

'You don't mean to cancel?'

'Good God, no. Not unless the duke wishes it. If there had been loss of life, it would be different, but if it is merely things, surely we should go ahead? It's a challenge, that's all, and I enjoy them. Everything was destroyed, you say?'

'There is nothing but blackened ruins this morning.'

'And you have been up all night, fighting it by the look of you. I thought I smelled burning when you came in. I am so glad you were not hurt. I suppose you are on your way to the palace now.' And when he nodded. 'Would you give the duke a message for me? Tell him I am his to command. If he thinks the performance should be cancelled, I will be happy to do so, but if he wishes it to continue, tell him I will do my poor best.'

'Your rich best,' he said, and left them.

'So much for Mr Bankes.' Jenny smiled at Caterina. 'What a passion he must be in this morning, poor tiresome fellow. And now, Caterina, I am going to demand your services for the next two days. I do hope Mr Forsyte's schedule can afford it, because I need him.' She laughed. 'You notice that I am taking the duke's answer for granted.'

'I am sure you can do so.' And, in fact, Lewis was back half an hour later with an offer of any help the palace could provide, and his own services if she needed them.

'You could arrange for two days' leave of absence for the girls,' Jenny told him. 'We are going to rifle your grandmother's closets. Your mother has promised to be my designer, and Harriet Ware will join us, but I shall be busy arranging the music, with my volunteer accompanists. You will not mind if we turn your house a little upside down for the next couple of days? I thought if they could work with me here, I would be available whenever I was needed for fittings.'

'My house is yours to command.' He said it from the heart. 'I'll fetch the girls at once.'

Two extraordinarily happy, chaotic days followed, with Jenny oscillating between the saloon, where the four women were sewing her costumes, and the music room, where she was teaching her accompanists English songs and learning Portuguese ones from them in exchange.

'You can tell where she is by the gales of laughter,' Hetta said to Ruth.

'Yes, but did you ever see anyone capable of such hard work?'

'And getting it out of others, too. Have you noticed the way

Carlotta and the maids are working with the preparations for the party?'

'Yes, Caterina says Carlotta keeps coming up with delicacies she didn't know existed.'

'I'm finding just the same thing,' Harriet joined in the conversation. 'I don't know whether it is a spirit of competition or just that word has got around that this is to be a very special occasion. I only hope it isn't too much for Jenny having the party right after the performance.'

'I don't think anything is too much for her,' said Ruth. 'There, that's done.' She set the last exquisite little stitch in the hem of a scarlet skirt and stood up rather wearily to hang it on its hanger. 'Won't she look splendid in it?'

'Yes, but you look worn out, Ruth dear,' said Harriet. 'Have you two girls been out at all today?'

'There's not been time,' said Hetta.

'Well, make some now and go and walk on the terrace. I rather think it has stopped raining. Off with you!' When they had left, protesting but relieved, she turned to Caterina, who had just joined them. 'Forgive me for interfering, but the child does look so wretched. One forgets how she must be missing her mother. Do you know, Cat, I didn't like her at first, but now I am getting fonder and fonder of her.'

'So am I,' said Caterina. 'And you were quite right. I should have noticed. After all I am responsible for her – how strange it is. And your Hetta is such a tower of strength that one forgets everyone is not like her. But where are all our men? We seem to have been in purdah for the last couple of days. I wouldn't have thought Greville would neglect his mother so.'

'I expect she's told him to keep away because we are so busy. And Frank is helping Lewis with arrangements at the opera house. There was a little feeling of opposition at first at the idea of an Englishwoman on their sacred stage, but the duke's orders have taken care of that. And of course Greville must be quite busy if he is really intending to give in his notice and escort his mother back to England.'

'What?' Caterina had been trimming a seam with her embroidery scissors and they slipped and pierced her finger.

'You didn't know? I did wonder. Suck it, Cat. Don't let it bleed on the velvet.'

Jenny had indeed told Greville to stay away, but he appeared as commanded on the morning of the performance to escort her to the opera house for her one rehearsal there. 'And don't abandon me,' she told him when they arrived. 'I may need your services as interpreter.'

'But surely one is being provided?'

'Yes, but I haven't met him yet,' she said. 'I mean to keep my explanations to the barest minimum. A long-winded translation would be the kiss of death, and some of these Portuguese gentlemen do seem to like the sound of their own voices.'

They found her little group of accompanists waiting on the stage of the great crimson and gold opera house, which, empty, echoed strangely to their voices. 'It's going to be a depressing rehearsal anyway,' said Jenny with unabated cheerfulness. 'My kind of music needs its audience.' She smiled at the one stranger in the little group. 'You must be Senhor Carmona who is so kindly going to interpret for me.' Holding out a friendly hand. 'I am sorry not to have met you sooner; may we go straight to work now? You shall be our audience, Grev. Find yourself a seat and listen well.'

He soon saw what she meant. She had divided her performance into three groups of songs, each prefaced by a brief introduction. But, where her speech took perhaps three minutes, Senhor Carmona's invariably took twice as long. It was partly the language itself, he thought, but it was also that Carmona liked the sound of his own voice.

'It won't do.' He turned to see that Lewis had settled quietly in the next seat. 'The duke sent me to offer any help,' Lewis went on. 'That fellow's a self-important ass; he's padding it. Our Portonian audience will never stand for it. But what a performance!' They were silent as Jenny sang a Mozart aria. In the little silence that followed Lewis rose and shouted, 'Bravo!' Then, moving forward to climb on to the stage, he bent to kiss Jenny's hand. 'I am here as the duke's messenger,' he told her. 'To make all smooth for you. Can I help in any way?'

'Yes.' She looked from him to Carmona. 'Forgive me, Senhor Carmona.' Then, back to Lewis, 'It was too slow, was it not?'

'I thought so. You know how impatient we Portonians are, Senhor Carmona. I have a suggestion to make, Mrs Forbes, if you will not think me over-bold. I grew up speaking both languages. I think I could draft you a more condensed version if you would let me have your text.'

'But I can't ask you to speak it for me.' She went straight to the point.

'And I won't,' said Carmona, bristling.

'No, alas, I can't.' Lewis ignored him. 'I shall be in attendance on the duke. But your son could do it. His accent is remarkable for an Englishman – forgive me, Greville. And it will make a family affair of it.'

'Impossible!' Greville had followed him onto the stage.

'Nonsense,' said Jenny. 'Evening dress, I think. You had better go and put it on now while Lewis gets to work on my text. I am sure Senhor Carmona will be only too happy to help.' And she set expertly to work to soothe that angrily astonished gentleman.

The recital was to be early because of the difficulties of transport. Jenny stayed at the opera house for the light luncheon that was all she ever ate before a performance. A very reluctant Greville joined her for it, duly clad now in impeccable evening dress.

'You look just the thing,' she told him approvingly. 'And don't so much as open your mouth to protest, because I shan't listen to a word of it. Just bear in mind that no one is going to take the slightest notice of you while I am on stage. You've not seen me in costume yet.' She was still in her morning dress. 'I can tell you I am going to be stunning. That Caterina of yours is an amazing designer. I wish I could hire her permanently.'

'Not mine, alas. And who is to escort them to the theatre?'

'Frank Ware, for one. What a delightful boy that is, and growing up by the minute as one watches him. I am enjoying myself, Grev, don't spoil it for me by being difficult.'

*

Lewis was discussing the problem of an escort for the ladies with Frank Ware. 'We do take Greville for granted, don't we?' he said. 'I wonder what my mother is going to do when he leaves. But I met Mr Craddock in the street and suggested he call at the house and offer his services.'

'Oh, did you?' said Frank.

If Caterina was surprised to find Jeremy and Frank escorting them instead of Greville she concealed it well. The Gomez and Sanchez boxes at the opera were next door to each other and she normally used only one of them, but today she was glad of both. All her little party would have admirable views of the stage. She was in the Gomez box with Harriet; Hetta and Ruth were next door. As always, gentlemen were coming and going among the boxes, but her party had arrived almost at the last moment and the duke's appearance in the Carrancas box soon stilled the house.

'I do hope Greville manages,' Caterina whispered to Harriet.

'Of course he will. And so will she.'

Manage was not the word. From the moment Jenny came on stage, wearing the scarlet gipsy dress Caterina had created from the habit of a long-dead Sanchez cardinal, she held the house in the hollow of her hand. She explained, in her English and Greville's Portuguese, that she would begin with a mixture of Portuguese and English folk songs, and soon had her audience laughing and stamping its feet with her. Their applause lasted through the few minutes during which she left the stage for a lightning change of costume.

She had flown in the face of precedent by declaring against an interval. The longest, central part of the entertainment consisted of more serious songs, ranging from Handel to Rossini, as Greville had predicted, and was received with still more enthusiasm. Another quick change and she appeared in dark-blue satin to make a brief speech, with Greville following her again. 'He has stage presence too,' Harriet whispered as the audience settled to listen, and Caterina nodded, swallowing tears. Her old friend looked suddenly a stranger, miles away in his mother's world.

At last, Jenny raised a hand for silence. 'My last song is one I have composed myself for the occasion,' she told her spellbound audience. 'With the help of my musician friends here. It tells of Sebastian, the lost king, and how he will come again to place a crown on the head of Maria da Gloria, God bless her.' She, and Greville after her, spoke this straight to the royal box and Dom Pedro rose to acknowledge the wave of applause.

A ballad with a haunting refrain, this last song brought the house to its feet. There were tears in Caterina's eyes, and she started when Frank touched her shoulder. 'The duke has arranged for you to leave first,' he told her. 'Come now.' They were out of the theatre while the applause was still raging, and missed the tide of scandal that washed through the house when it finally died down.

Jenny's last dress was designed to do for the party too, but just the same she and Greville were inevitably among the last arrivals. Lewis was there to greet them and lead them into the saloon where Dom Pedro was installed in state with the newly arrived Marshal Solignac at his side.

'No, no.' The duke would not let her curtsy, but kissed her enthusiastically on both cheeks before introducing Marshal Solignac: 'Who is to put an end to all our difficulties.'

'Believe that, you'll believe anything,' Jenny told Greville as they moved away. 'A Peninsular veteran who has learned nothing and forgotten nothing.' She took a glass from a tray proffered by an anxious-looking Carlotta. 'What's wrong with this party, Grev? Something is going on.'

'What do you mean?' He looked around the crowded room.

'I wish I knew. But I can feel it. Ah, there's Frank, he'll know.' An imperious gesture brought Frank across the room to join them. 'No time for that.' She cut short his speech of congratulation. 'What's going on, Frank?'

'I'm glad you're here,' he said. 'Both of you. I've just heard it. There's a foul story going round among the English here. Something about Caterina and her upstairs room. Hints ... innuendoes ... I don't know what to do ... I was looking for my mother.'

'Lewis?' suggested Greville.

'He might do more harm than good,' said Frank.

'Who started it, do you know?'

'Josiah Bankes, I'm afraid.'

'Then Rachel Emerson is behind it,' Greville told him. 'I saw them talking at Foz, the day she left. I did wonder. Where is Bankes, Frank?'

'In the small drawing-room. Talking to Jeremy Craddock.'

'Let's go.' Jenny led the way with a determination that made people fall back to let her pass.

But when they reached Caterina's small private drawing-room it was to find Lewis confronting Bankes and Craddock, his voice crackling with rage. 'You will say to me, now, what you have been saying about my mother.'

'It's only what everyone is saying.' Bankes looked as if he wished the earth would open and swallow him.

'What is everyone saying?' Caterina had just joined them. 'Mr Bankes—?'

But he was literally speechless. 'I am glad you are here, Madame Fonsa.' Jeremy Craddock was oddly formal. 'To explode it once and for all. It's a shabby enough story going round, picked up, I am sorry to say, by Mr Bankes here from Mrs Emerson as she was leaving. She told him a nasty tale of some horror hidden in your attic, here in the palace. A Bluebeard's chamber where no one is admitted. Where you go secretly, early every morning, taking food.'

'Taking food!' Now he really had surprised her.

'To your monstrous, hidden child, madam.' Josiah Bankes had found his voice.

'Well!' Greville, watching in helpless agony, saw the emotions chase each other across Caterina's face, saw amusement prevail. 'Very well,' she said. 'You had better come and meet my monstrous child, Mr Craddock. I think we can do without Mr Bankes. Lewis, you will come?' Her eyes swept the little group: 'Jenny, Frank, Greville,' and then raising her voice. 'Carlotta, candles please. I am taking a party upstairs.'

'*Minha senhora!*'

'Upstairs to the attic,' she repeated with steel in her voice.

'Caterina, are you sure—' The protest came from Frank Ware.

'Yes, Frank, quite sure.' But they had reached the saloon where the duke had detached himself from Solignac and was looming over Harriet. 'Your Grace,' she moved very stately across the room to him. 'Will you do me a great favour? There is a story going round, here in my . . . in my son's house . . . put about, I am sorry to say, by some of those whom I thought my English friends. They say I have something unspeakable hidden away upstairs. I am taking them up to see just what I have there. Will you do me the great honour of coming too and acting as a witness?'

'Gladly, *senhora*.' He came forward and would have taken her arm, but Carlotta was there to equip them all with candles.

'It will have to be single file on these stairs, I am afraid,' said Caterina when they reached the upper flight. And then, as they arranged themselves in the hall that ran from front to back of the top floor, she reached into a pocket of her dress and pulled out a key. 'Now for my monster. Be careful with your candles, please,' as they followed her into the room.

It took a moment or two, as the flickering candles steadied in the still air of the room for the little group to understand what they were seeing. The duke spoke first, gazing at the bold black and white cartoon that stood on its easel, facing the door. 'Charles Forsyte!'

Frank, standing close to the door, candle raised to give a better light, took in the broad charcoal outlines and turned to Greville. 'Thank God,' he said.

This cartoon was entirely flattering to the duke. Caterina had dressed him in the warrior outfit normally associated with Sebastian, the lost crusader king of Portugal, and given him just a hint of a halo. He had his daughter by the hand, and together they were trampling underfoot a dragon with Miguel's face.

'You knew?' Harriet whispered to Jenny.

'Grev told me. Look!'

The duke had bowed low to take Caterina's hand and kiss it. 'I owe you more than I can ever repay, Mr Forsyte. Will you allow me the pleasure of telling your guests downstairs?'

'Of course.' She smiled at him. 'The masquerade is over, sir.'

'But may I hope that the good work will continue.'

'Yes, but I think, not here.' And with that she turned and led the way downstairs.

Chapter 18

Hetta and Ruth were in the state dining-room making sure that everything was ready for the buffet supper Caterina had planned, and so missed the move upstairs. They returned to the saloon just in time to see the duke come in from the far doorway, handing in Caterina as if she were a queen.

'Ladies and gentlemen.' His voice stilled the babble of talk. 'May I introduce to you one of my most valued supporters, Mr Charles Forsyte.'

'What?' Ruth turned to Hetta, amazed.

'Oh, yes.' Hetta did not pretend surprise.

'Look at poor Lewis,' said Ruth, her heart going out to her half-brother as he stood there, visibly dumbstruck. 'He didn't know!'

'No, I'm afraid he didn't, Ruth. I think he is going to need us both.' Hetta started working a quiet, purposeful way towards Lewis through the astonished crowd. Frank was already with him, talking earnestly.

As the two girls approached, Jeremy Craddock also came up to Lewis. 'Such a relief,' he said. 'You must be a proud man, Lewis. I never believed a word of it, of course.'

'I'm sure you didn't.' Frank intervened, his voice a challenge. 'Knowing Mrs Emerson, the source of the story, so well as you do. I am a little surprised you thought fit to repeat it. Mr Bankes has left, I see.' Hetta watched with interest as the two men's gaze locked and held, then Jeremy muttered something and turned away. Turning from him, Frank saw the two girls for the first time and flushed crimson.

'Miss Emerson – Ruth – forgive me!'

Ruth was very white, but her voice was steady. 'Nothing to forgive, Mr Ware. If my mother was really the source of that unspeakable story, it is I who should be asking forgiveness.'

'Nonsense,' said Hetta, her arm in her friend's. 'And see what good has come of it. The truth is out at last and nobody the worse. Just look at the duke explaining to that fat French marshal what a wonderful woman Charles Forsyte is.'

'You mean you knew?' Lewis spoke at last, his voice an outraged accusation. 'My mother told *you*?'

'She most certainly did not. I guessed. I know her so well, love her so much, watched her do that brilliant portrait of the duke. I was living in the house, remember. Oh, do look! Isn't the duke taking it splendidly!' There was a little silence as they all watched him take an arm each of Jenny and Caterina and sweep them in a kind of triumphal procession into the supper room. 'We had best be moving too.' It was as near as she dared come to reminding Lewis of his duties as host, and as she spoke, she saw Jenny Forbes turn back in the doorway and beckon to him. He was off at once and she found herself alone, as Frank drew Ruth firmly away in the other direction.

It began to seem as if the double celebration would never end. Jenny and Caterina, surrounded by voluble admirers, passed them cheerfully to and fro between them. When Jenny pointed out that Caterina had designed the dress she was wearing, Caterina responded that the idea for the cartoon of the duke as Sebastian had come from Jenny, who had had the story from one of her Portuguese accompanists. 'And what a crowning mercy *that* was.' A quick look assured her that the duke was well away on the other side of the room doing his duty by Marshal Solignac.

'The monster in your attic.' Jenny could laugh at it now. 'But it's quite true, there are some he can't have liked so well.'

'He'll remember them in the morning. That's another reason why I think it is time for me to leave.' And she turned away for another complimentary speech.

When the duke left at last, he gave Lewis what he laughingly called a royal command to spend next day with his mother. 'You must persuade her that she is not to think of leaving us.'

'I'll do my best, sir.' But it was Jenny Forbes he sought out when he returned from seeing the duke off at the palace gates. The crowd was thinning now and he used his privilege as host to get her into a quiet corner of the room. 'Mrs Forbes – may I call you Jenny? I think of you as Jenny. You must let me tell you what you've done for me. You've changed my life; given it a purpose, made me think quite differently about women.'

'Better, I hope.'

'Oh, *yes!* To see you holding that audience in the palm of your hand! Holding me too. I'm your slave, Jenny. When you sang "Greensleeves" I cried. I'd do anything for you.'

'Dear boy.' She must get this just right. 'I'm more touched than I can say. But my salad days are over. I cried all my tears away when Greville's father was killed at Trafalgar.'

'At Trafalgar?' It was a date he was bound to know. Almost thirty years ago.

'Yes, dear Lewis. Think me as wonderful as you please, but pray don't forget how old I am, under the greasepaint. And now we should be helping your wonderful mother with her farewells.'

'Wonderful! My mother? She has made a public fool of me. Letting me stand there mumchance while she revealed herself as Charles Forsyte! As if I have not had enough to bear from her already!'

'Perhaps you should think a little of what she has had to bear from you. And *for* you. Anyway, Lewis, she is all the mother you have got. Here is something you can do for me. And for yourself. I do urge you to sleep on it before you say anything to her that you may later regret.'

'Dorothy Procter kissed me,' said Caterina, when the last guest had left. 'There's a surprise. Let's all have one more glass of wine and congratulate ourselves. I'm so glad you and Frank are staying the night, Harriet. And, Lewis, can you?'

There was a little silence. Jenny looked at Lewis. 'Yes,' he said at last. 'I am given leave by the duke, and charged to persuade you not to think of leaving us. You cannot surely mean it, Mother? Where in the world would you go?'

'That's the surprising thing, Lewis.' She spoke straight to him, as if they were alone together. 'You won't believe it, I hardly do myself, but I had a letter from old Lady Trellgarten this morning. An invitation. Almost an appeal. The post seems to have escaped the customs house fire.'

'Yes, it did. But – that old besom? You can't be seriously thinking of accepting?'

'I am, you know. She says she's an old lady now, needs her family. We're all she's got, Lewis. You and I and Jeremy Craddock, and I don't count him. And you are committed to the duke and his cause. I'm not. In fact, I am a little tired of them both.' She looked away from Lewis at last and her eyes met Greville's. Lewis must never learn of that scene with the duke. 'I think I shall pack up my paints and pencils and go to Wales.'

'But Mother. . . .' Lewis paused, aghast, suddenly aware of what it would mean to lose her. A strange little silence fell. Outside, the rain teemed down and a log collapsed in the hearth.

'Cat, you can't,' Harriet spoke at last. 'You've lived here all your life.'

'Not all of it, Harry. You should remember that. It's a strange thing, but when I was in England, I was always homesick for here, but now I am here – have been here – I'm tired of the gossip and the quarrelling. It lost you your husband, Harry. In some ways it has lost me my son.' Her glance, resting on Lewis, silenced his protest. 'We all know there's not going to be peace here for years, and I want some peace in my life. I've been thinking for a while that it was time to go home to my mother's country. What has happened here tonight seems to have settled it for me.'

'And Charles Forsyte?' asked Harriet.

'Don't you think he might have a freer hand in England? You may tell the duke from me, Lewis, that I shall do my best to serve his cause there. You will all have to keep me posted.'

'Mother, you can't leave me!'

'Can't I, Lewis? Do you know I think you might go on rather better without me.' She looked at him for a long moment, then rose. 'Forgive me, Jenny, I am forgetting what a long day you have had. Time for bed, I think. You'll stay, please, Greville? There are things I shall need to discuss with you in the morning.'

'But—'

'No more "buts" tonight. Please. Sleep well, all of you. A splendid party. As it turned out.'

For once, Caterina did not go up to her studio next morning. She wanted to be the first at the breakfast-table, but Jenny was close behind her. 'You've not been upstairs?' she asked.

'No. I'm taking the day off, like the girls.'

'And Lewis,' said Jenny. 'He'll need it, I'm afraid, poor lamb. It's hit him hard, you know.'

'All my fault. I should have told him sooner. But how was I to know it would come out like that? It's all been such a muddle. Is it cowardly of me to want to cut and run?'

'No, I think it may be very sensible. I long to hear more about this Lady Trellgarten, but here are the girls.'

Harriet was close behind them, with apologies from Frank and Greville. 'They have gone to see Bankes,' she explained. 'He seems to have been in a very strange state when he left last night. They were actually afraid he might do himself or that poor silly wife of his a mischief. And that's my fault,' she said. 'I should have done something about Bankes long ago, despite my poor Frank's Will. I've let him live in a fool's paradise, I'm afraid.'

'I'm sure that Frank will cope,' said Ruth, and coloured, while Caterina thought that Greville had been glad of the excuse to get away. She was busy trying to convince Harriet that there was nothing she could have done about her husband's Will, when Lewis joined them, looking as if he had not slept at all.

'Mother, I owe you an apology.' It began as a formal speech, well rehearsed, then he broke out of it. 'But why didn't you tell me?'

'I'm sorry. You're quite right, I should have. I was saying so to Jenny just now. Shall we forgive each other, Lewis? Please?'

'So long as you agree to stay.' It was ungracious, and he knew it. 'The duke needs you.'

'And your loyalty lies with him,' she said. 'And quite right too. But, no, Lewis, I'm sorry, but I find this morning that my mind is quite made up. I'm tired of conspiracies and feuds—'

'You can't seriously mean to go and dance attendance on that old tartar Lady Trellgarten, Mother. You don't know her.'

'You seem to forget that I am a tartar, too. And something else: I'll not be dancing attendance. You're forgetting Charles Forsyte, Lewis. It's vulgar to say so, but he is beginning to earn a nice little competence with his drawings. I'll not be dependent on Lady Trellgarten, or anybody else. Yes, Carlotta?'

'The duke has called, *senhora*. He wishes to see you and the Senhora Forbes.'

'Goodness,' she said. 'More persuasions? Stand by me, Jenny. Harry, come too and see fair play.'

Left alone with them, Lewis looked from Ruth to Hetta. 'What in the world am I going to do?'

'Sit down and have some breakfast,' said Hetta. 'You look worn out with worrying.' She poured a cup of coffee and passed it to him. 'Food will make you feel better.'

'She really means it,' he said. 'My mother. I didn't believe it last night.'

'Oh yes, I think she does. She's been talking about England for a while. I have wondered—'

'But it was the English who started those foul stories—'

'Maybe she thinks the ones at home will be better.'

'I know what she means, if she does,' said Ruth, surprising them. 'There's something so ingrown about the English colony here. They don't learn Portuguese for a start; it's disgusting.'

'Well, have you?' asked Lewis.

'I'm trying.'

'That's like you.' She had his full attention now. 'Why hadn't I thought? You're the answer, Ruth! If my mother goes, and I still don't believe she will, but if she insists, you must come here to the palace, stay here, I mean, and housekeep for me. You're my sister, after all; it will be perfectly respectable. We'll comfort each other, you and I, brother and sister. What's the matter?'

She looked at him, between laughter and tears. 'Oh, dear Lewis, I am so sorry. Frank Ware asked me to marry him last night, and I said yes. I'm so happy—' She reached out to clutch Hetta's hand. 'I didn't mean to tell you like this.'

'You didn't need to tell me,' said Hetta, embracing her. 'I knew last night, and I can't begin to tell you how happy I am.'

'How did you know?' asked Lewis furiously.

'By using my eyes, of course, something you so signally fail to do, Lewis. The same way that I knew your mother was Charles Forsyte. If you were to try thinking a little more about other people and a little less about yourself I think you would be a happier man, Lewis da Gomez y Fonsa.' She turned to Ruth. 'Be an angel, Ruth dear, and go away. I am going to feed Lewis his breakfast, and quarrel with him.'

And Ruth, with an alarmed glance at both of them, fled.

'No breakfast, thank you,' said Lewis coldly. 'And as you well know, I am not Lewis da Gomez y Fonsa. I'm a nameless bastard.'

'If you say so. But you seem to be the duke's right-hand man just the same, and if you ask me, Lewis, he is going to need you. That Marshal Solignac looks like being just as much of a disaster as his predecessors. Have you heard that Jenny Forbes knows both Saldanha and a friend of his, one of those remarkable Napiers, a sea captain who seems to take an interest in the Pedroist cause? If I know anything about Jenny, she will have the duke changing his mind about Saldanha before she leaves, and then perhaps there will be some hope for us all. And if you say something about interfering women I shall hit you, Lewis, and so I warn you.'

'How did you know I was going to say that?' She had stopped him in mid-sentence.

'Because I know you so well.' She took a deep breath. 'Because I love you, Lewis, always have, always will, God help me. And, please, don't say that bit about the nameless bastard again either.'

'Hetta!' He was gazing at her with surprised delight. 'You know me better than I know myself. Can you still love me doing that? Has it been you all this time? Oh God, what a fool I have been! How could I not understand?'

'The fool I love, Lewis.' They were silent, looking at each other for a long moment, then slowly, irrevocably, they drew together.

Carlotta, coming to see why breakfast was going on so long, took one look and withdrew to her own rooms, where she sat for a long time, silent with happiness.

★

'Well, I don't think we did too badly.' Jenny turned to Caterina after
the duke had left. 'You resisted his pleading without actually
affronting him, and I really think I have got him seriously thinking about Saldanha and his friend Admiral Charles Napier. Not a
bad morning's work. And here comes Harriet, full of good news.
You're looking very pleased with yourself, Harriet, if I may make
bold to say so. And I think I know why, too, but I don't believe
Caterina noticed Ruth's glowing face at breakfast.'

'Ruth?' asked Caterina, puzzled.

'You had other things to think about, Cat dear,' said Harriet.
'Frank told me last night. He's in a blaze of happiness, bless him.
He's loved her for ever, you know. I didn't like it at first, and
anyway I didn't think he had a chance.' They were all silent, thinking of Rachel Emerson's revelation. 'But she accepted him last
night, and do you know, she told him it had always been him. Some
instinct must have told her that her feeling for Lewis was a blood
one. I'm so relieved.'

'Oh, poor Lewis,' said Caterina.

'Nonsense,' said Jenny.

'What do you mean?' Caterina was suddenly furious. 'How dare
you?'

'Look!' said Jenny.

The door had opened to reveal Lewis and Hetta, hand in hand.
'You're all here,' Lewis said. 'I'm glad. I want to tell the whole
world. Hetta has made me the happiest of men.'

'Hetta?' Amazement in Caterina's voice shaded into delight. 'Oh,
Hetta, I am so pleased!' She opened her arms and Hetta went
straight into them for a long, silent embrace. 'But when? How?'
Caterina asked at last.

'Just this minute over the breakfast he wouldn't eat,' said Hetta
cheerfully. 'I pushed him into it, Caterina. I decided it was time he
had happiness thrust upon him, and now look at him.' She turned
to Lewis. 'Here is your last chance, Lewis, to say it is all a mistake.
Speak now or forever after—' But her smile was radiant.

'Mistake!' he said. 'No, the mistake has been all mine, these last idiotic months, and Hetta, God bless her, has opened my eyes at last to what was always there. Mrs Ware,' formally to Harriet, 'it's more than I deserve, but may I have your daughter's hand in marriage?'

'With all my heart,' said Harriet. She held out a hand to Caterina. 'Oh, Cat, I am so happy!'

'And so am I.' But she felt, all at once, infinitely alone. 'Yes, Carlotta?'

But Carlotta, in the doorway, had eyes only for Lewis and Hetta, still holding hands. 'May I offer the congratulations of the servants' hall, *minho senhor, minha senhora?* And may we prepare the Fonsa festive bowl?'

'Prepare anything you like, Carlotta,' said Lewis. And then, belatedly, 'Mother?'

'Of course.' Why did she feel so remote from their celebrations?

'Carlotta is probably the only person who knows what it is.'

'It's entirely too long since we had an engagement here in the palace,' said Carlotta happily, 'but indeed I remember how it is done.'

'Then do it,' said Lewis. 'And here's Frank.' He held out his hand to his friend. 'I have news for you, Frank. I am to be a brother to you. I hope you don't mind?'

'Mind! I've never been so pleased in my life. Dear Hetta, shall I congratulate you?'

'I don't see why not.' Hetta hugged him. 'But what of Mr Bankes?'

'Gone clean off his head, poor fellow. Greville is with him. He asks you to go to them, Jenny. Mrs Bankes is in a bad way, too, as you can imagine.'

'Indeed I'll go,' said Jenny, 'though I am sad to leave such a scene of rejoicing.' She was the only one to see how isolated Caterina was feeling, and thought that her own going might make it worse, and do no harm.

She arrived at the Bankes's house as the doctor was leaving. 'A sad case,' he said when he had finished congratulating her on her performance the day before. 'A very sad case. Death would be the kindest thing for poor Mr Bankes. A complete derangement, and the poor lady in not much better case. But I have administered

powerful opiates to them both and things are quieter now. You son
has been a tower of strength, madam, as was to be expected. But it
is a case, really for a woman friend. I have taken the liberty of sending for Mrs Procter, always a help in times of trouble.'

'Oh, bless you, Doctor,' said Jenny.

She found Greville sitting in the Bankes's gloomy little parlour
drinking a glass of white port. 'I do thank you for coming.' He rose
to receive her. 'You'd better have some too. Pilfered from Ware and
Company, I have no doubt. It's a sad story. I thought it better not
to leave Frank alone with them in case of some more foul Portonian
talk. Lord, I'll be glad to get out of this place, Jenny.'

'No port, thanks. You're needed at the palace, Greville. The
doctor tells me he has sent for that nice woman Dorothy Procter,
and I will stay till she gets here, but you must go to Caterina.'

'Me? Why?'

'Because she needs you. It's now or never, Grev. Frank is engaged
to Ruth, as you must know, but what you don't know is that Lewis
and Hetta are also engaged.'

'Lewis and Hetta? I don't believe it!'

'It's true, though, and a very good thing too. I like that girl. And
so does Carlotta, I'll have you know. She is preparing the fatted calf
– there seems to be some traditional Fonsa celebration for engage-
ments and all the wheels are moving towards it. Caterina finds
herself a stranger in her own house today. Go to her, Grev and good
luck to you.'

'But—'

'No time for argument. I'll join you as soon as Mrs Procter gets
here.'

Smiling her determined way through the rejoicings, Caterina was
almost glad to be summoned to receive Jeremy Craddock. 'I have
put him in your parlour,' Carlotta explained.

'Thank you.'

'Caterina, I came to explain, if I may.' He greeted her almost
abruptly.

'If you wish.'

'When I heard the scandalous tales Bankes was spreading, I

thought the only thing to stop him was a confrontation. Of course, I did not believe them for a minute.'

'Of course not.' Her tone was neutral.

'And how right I was! And now I find a house full of rejoicing, Caterina, which leaves you strangely alone. And gives me the courage to approach you once more.'

'With the old story? Then I must give you the old answer, Mr Craddock: no.'

'Think again, Caterina. We need each other, you and I. You are going to be ousted from your place in this house by a young bride, and I have had enough of this scandal-mongering life in Oporto. And now I know you for what you are, Charles Forsyte, how proud I will be to introduce you in London society as my wife, how happy to collect ideas for your brilliant cartoons. Perhaps a change of theme to London politics? Imagine the sensation there is going to be, the pleasure of sharing it!'

'I said no, Mr Craddock. Please believe me.'

'You cannot possibly be hankering after Greville Faulkes, Caterina. A dull devoted dog who threw away a promising career to dangle hopelessly after you.'

'What in the world do you mean?'

'You really didn't know? Back in '25 when Stuart was sent to Rio he invited Faulkes to go too, on my advice. It would have been the first step in the political career he had always wanted. He had the chance and all the qualifications. He turned it down, poor lovelorn fool, and look where it didn't get him!'

'Thank you for telling me, Mr Craddock. No, I didn't know. And thank you, too, for your flattering offer, which I decline, once and for all. Good day.'

He left her with her whole world upside down. How could she have taken Greville so much for granted? Jeremy had told her all those years ago, when he first introduced Greville to her, about the quarrel with his grandfather that had ended his hopes of a seat in Parliament, but as he made himself quietly indispensable to her, she had forgotten all about it. And now to learn that he had had another chance of a career, seven years ago, and turned it down. For her sake? Seven years ago. Lewis had been sixteen, coming home with dubious reports from Stonyhurst and she had just been finding her vocation as a cartoonist. It was that spring, she remembered with a pang of guilt, that she had learned that the great Goya was in exile at Bordeaux and had gone to study with him for an immensely useful few months, leaving Greville in charge of everything at home. The offer must have come then and been declined for her sake. And she had never known.

'Yes?' To Carlotta at the door.

'The *senhor* told me to ask you when we should serve the Fonsa bowl.' For her, there was only one *senhor*.

'Not quite yet, Carlotta.' She could not face all that happiness yet. 'Half an hour perhaps? There is something I have to do upstairs first.' How strange that after all these years she could now legitimately plead her work as an excuse.

But in the attic she found she could not work. The cartoon of Dom Pedro struck her as a bit of sentimental trash. It's time I left, she thought. I need a change of subject. A change of everything? Well, that old tartar Lady Trellgarten should provide that. The more she looked at Pedro/Sebastian the less she liked him. And as for the romanticized figure of young Maria da Gloria! She was moving forwards to snatch it off the easel and tear it across when a voice from the doorway stopped her.

'Don't do it, Caterina,' said Greville.

'Why not?' she asked. And then, 'How did you know?'

'Because I know how you feel. It's not one of your best, but it is most certainly your luckiest. Don't spoil that luck by destroying it now. That really might start the duke thinking about the others, and that would never do until you are safely out of the country. Besides, there is Lewis to consider.'

'You're right as usual.' How blessedly familiar it was to be discussing her work with him again. 'Greville, I've missed you so.' Oddly, she found herself thinking about Hetta pushing Lewis into happiness. 'Everyone says you are planning to go back to England,' she challenged him.

'You're not the only one with a problem grandparent in Wales, Caterina. I am sure it will surprise you as much as it did me, but I have had a letter by the packet too. From my grandfather. He seems to want me now, poor old curmudgeon. He offers as a bribe his support if I stand in the next election. How am I going to break it to him that I am a Whig, do you think? And the beauty of it is, Faulkes Abbey is only fifty or so miles of dreadful roads from Trellgarten. I shall be able to come and see how Charles Forsyte gets on in the new climate. I've missed you too,' he said with obvious effort. 'These last few weeks.'

'But why? Why have you stayed away?'

'I have some pride, Caterina. When Sanchez came back into your life, I knew I was beaten.'

'What?' She could not believe her ears. 'You cannot think—'

'How could I help it? When he saved Lewis's life for you—'

'I thought you did that. Oh, dear Greville, what fools we have been. Have you really let the shadow of what I once felt for Sanchez stand between us?'

'Well, you did refuse me twice!'

'Because I thought you were asking me out of pity. You have never said you loved me, Greville Faulkes.'

'What?' And then, 'Do you know, you are absolutely right. So I am the fool, but how could I for a minute imagine that you might care for me?'

'You've still not said it.' But she was smiling at him now.

'Of course I love you, Caterina. I've loved you from the very first time I saw you, when you hardly even noticed I was there because I had brought your son to you. All I have wanted to do was to serve you.'

'I know it now,' she told him. 'Jeremy Craddock has just told me about Stuart's offer, back in '25, and how you turned it down.'

'Well, of course I turned it down, you were away studying with Goya. And very profitable it was too. Caterina, can this really be true?'

'Well, I rather think so,' she told him. 'What we have to decide, Grev, is whether we live with my grandmother and visit your grandfather, or vice versa. And in the meanwhile don't you think perhaps it is time that you kissed me?'

'You called me Grev! I like it.' He held out his arms and she went into them, and stayed there.

*

Having prepared the Fonsa loving cup, Carlotta rang the great bell in the main hall to summon the family for the celebration. Lewis, standing by the huge silver bowl on its ebony base raised the ladle and looked about him. 'But where is my mother?' he asked.

'And my son?' said Jenny.

'Here we are.' At the sound of Caterina's voice they all turned to see her standing in the doorway, Greville close beside her. She was wearing her painter's smock and he had a great smear of charcoal on the end of his nose. 'We have come to join the celebrations,' she said. 'And add to them, I hope.'

'You most certainly are.' Jenny kissed her. 'I never dared do that before,' she said.

'Good God,' said Caterina. 'Are you really going to be my mother-in-law?'

'And you my son?' Still holding Caterina's hand, Greville turned to Lewis.

'Let's drink to that,' said Lewis.